Wood Riddance
Lovewell Lumberjacks
Book 4

Daphne Elliot

Melody Publishing, LLC

Copyright © 2023 Daphne Elliot. All Rights Reserved

No part of this book may be reproduced in any form or by any electronic or mechanical means, including information storage and retrieval systems, without prior written permission from the publisher.

This book is a work of fiction. The names, characters, places, and events in this book are the product of the author's imagination, and any resemblance to actual events or places or persons, living or dead, is entirely coincidental.

Published by Melody Publishing, LLC

Editing by Beth Lawton at VB Edits

Cover design by Erica Connors

Photography by Jeanne Woodfin Photography

Cover Models: Ryan Stacks and Anna Stacks

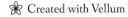 Created with Vellum

*To all the angry women. We ride at dawn.
The patriarchy isn't going to smash itself.*

Prologue
Adele

2 years ago

This could not be happening.

I sat up straight and tried to control my breathing. It was a technique I'd learned in therapy after my dad died. There weren't many things I could control in life, so I focused on box breathing. In for four, out for four.

Because the rage that was usually set to a low simmer inside me was threatening to boil up again.

"I think there's a mismatch here," he said, sitting back in his seat with the kind of unearned confidence that made me homicidal.

I clenched my fists. How was this happening *again*? I'd date someone for six months or so, and then they'd dump me. For any number of lame and questionable reasons.

I just wasn't worth hanging on to.

As he explained, ad nauseam, why his work was so important and why he was so special, I zoned out, studying his face for clues as to how things had gone so wrong.

Weak chin, patchy stubble, and beady eyes. Long ago, I had learned to never go for the hot ones. They were always full of themselves and thought they could do better. I had liked Blake. He was quirky, and I enjoyed his dry sense of humor.

"I think we have different values, goals," he said expectantly.

Licking my lips, I racked my brain for an appropriate response and came up empty. "Sorry?"

"I'm ambitious, and academia isn't for the faint of heart," he said slowly, like I was a child.

I snorted. I wasn't sure what academia was for most of the time.

"And I'm in my thirties now. I need a partner who will be an asset when it comes to my career."

God, I was such an idiot. I'd left work early and curled my hair, excited for a night out. We had made plans for him to spend the weekend, so I had deep cleaned my house and stocked the fridge in preparation.

In all these months, we hadn't gone out much. Only to the annoying pub near campus where he and the other junior professors would drink cheap beer and one-up each other, each trying to establish themselves as the smartest of the bunch.

We had been dating for six months. Sure, we'd kept it casual. I met him a few months after losing my dad in a truck accident, so I wasn't in a place for serious. But we'd been exclusive and having fun. I'd also spent those six months driving to Orono to see him because, apparently, coming to Lovewell was "inconvenient."

I owned my own gorgeous home, while he lived in a dingy apartment with the other junior faculty. But according to him, staying close to home was important because he needed to ensure he was rested and focused. You know, because his job was so important. Talking to bored, hungover freshman about the fucking Crusades.

And I was "just a mechanic." Novel, sure, but ultimately unimportant to fancy fuckers with PhDs like him. I was less important, despite my higher income, my position leading a large team, or the level the responsibility I was tasked with. The entire point of my professional life was to ensure the safety of dozens of employees at Gagnon Lumber.

I could sense it, the anger and rage bubbling up inside me. It had taken thirty-plus years to learn to control. But right now, I wasn't sure I could stop it, and I wanted to preserve my dignity.

"Just so I understand," I said, sarcasm dripping from my voice. "You're dumping me?"

He nodded, looking way too calm for someone who might be swallowing his teeth in the next few minutes.

"Then why are we here?" I hissed. "Why did you drive to my house and pick me up and take me to one of the nicest restaurants in the state?"

He shrank back. "I planned to do it when I arrived, but you looked pretty, you know, like you made an effort. I felt bad, so I figured we could have a nice meal."

My eye twitched and bile rose in my throat. "Are you kidding me?"

"I don't want to make this messy, Adele. It's one of the things I really liked about you. How no-nonsense you are. Not like other women. I assumed you'd understand."

And now I was ready to explode. It was how I operated. Once wronged, I'd hate you forever. So despite how excited I'd been to spend the weekend with him, the switch had flipped. I now despised him and wanted to throw him into the ocean.

"Understand what? That you think I'm not good enough for you?" I snarled.

He paled, leaning forward. "Keep your voice down."

I smiled, enjoying how nervous he looked. "Get. The. Fuck. Out," I said slowly, swirling the wine in my glass.

"Don't be hostile."

"This is me playing nice. Leave. Now."

I looked at him coolly, determined to retain my composure. Castrating him with a butter knife was oh so tempting, but I wouldn't make a scene. He wasn't worth it. There was no salvaging this. He didn't see me as worthy, and I had learned a long time ago not to beg people to accept me or love me.

Sipping my wine and staring out the window, I ignored him as he walked out. I refused to give him any indication that I cared about his flat, pompous ass.

The waitress appeared, looking nervous. "You can take his beer," I said, picking up my menu and giving her a quick smile. "I'll be ready to order in a minute."

She nodded and scampered off.

Another day, another insecure, unworthy man. Story of my goddam life.

It wasn't like I hadn't put myself out there. I'd joined the apps, and I went out of my way to leave my small town and head to where there were more options. I wore makeup and made small talk and attempted to be less scary.

But at five-eleven and with a traditionally masculine job, as well as a complete inability to suffer fools, most of the male population was scared off on sight.

I was beginning to lose faith. My mom and dad had adored each other, and they'd loved each other fiercely for almost forty years. I'd grown up witnessing the love they had for one another every day of my life.

Wood Riddance

So I knew it was possible. Companionship, love. Granted, my two older brothers were also chronically single, and my youngest brother, Remy, had an awful fiancée we barely tolerated. So maybe the soulmate kind of love was skipping this generation.

I wanted to hold on to my hope that someone would see the real me. But so far, every guy I'd met had decided I wasn't worth it.

As soon as I was certain he had left the parking lot, I took a look around. I'd order dinner and then cross my fingers I could get a ride share to take me all the way back to Lovewell. If not, I'd swallow my pride and call one of my brothers.

The bar area was bustling with people chatting and drinking as the sun began to set outside. It was one of those industrial style places, with exposed duct work and water served in mason jars. Not really my style, but I was hungry, and I'd be damned if I let shithead Blake ruin my evening.

And then I looked up and met a familiar set of dark brown eyes.

Fuck me sideways.

Finn Hebert. At the bar. Staring at me. I reflexively reached for the butter knife on the table. Of all the cocky asshole shitheads to witness me getting dumped. Why did it have to be him? Was Mr. Canton, my sadistic eighth grade math teacher, unavailable? Did Ritchie LaVoie, who'd taken my virginity and then joked about it with the whole school after, have a previous engagement?

Because while tonight had been humiliating as it was, knowing a Hebert, and *that* Hebert, of all people, had witnessed it, only made it worse.

All while looking especially handsome. His long hair was pulled back into a man bun. He was wearing a plaid shirt with the sleeves rolled up to expose the tats on his forearms, and his dark jeans were molded to his legs. The man wore clothes really well. *Bastard.*

Finding clothes that fit my tall frame was always a challenge. But this asshole was NBA-player tall and looked like he'd stepped out of a hot Viking lumberjack magazine.

He picked up his beer and sauntered over far too gracefully for someone who was the size of a baby giraffe.

"Everything okay?" he asked, looking down at me.

"Yes." I glared at him. "My date had an emergency. I'm trying to enjoy my glass of wine."

"Great. I'll join you."

Before I could protest, he had taken Blake's chair and was leaning over to clink my glass with the lip of his bottle. I held my middle finger up against my wineglass.

He ignored my rude gesture, instead looking around the space. "I've never been here," he said, bringing his beer to his lips.

I watched the muscles of his throat contract and raised one eyebrow. Why was he being so nice? Had he used all his dad's money to buy a better personality? I was in no mood for chitchat, especially with this overgrown frat boy.

Briefly, I fantasized about whipping off one of my heels and throwing it across the table so it lodged in the middle of his smooth, tan forehead. My aim was impeccable. There was a reason I had won so many axe-throwing tournaments. And I knew I could do serious damage.

But then I dipped my chin, taking in my flats. Blake was self-conscious about his height, so I'd stopped wearing heels—though I had quite a collection—in order to appease him.

I smiled to myself. He was such a dickweasel. I wanted to go back to my shop, invent a time machine, and travel back six months so I could decline his offer to buy me that first drink. Because what had I been thinking?

Looked like I had hit the desperation stage. Perhaps I should call it a day and adopt some cats.

"Are you laughing *at* me or *with* me?" Finn said, interrupting my thoughts.

I pinned him with a sharp glare. "Obviously *at* you. I was planning my upcoming cat adoption. I'm prepared to fully embrace my spinster identity."

"Seems a bit premature." He dropped his forearms to the table so his hands rested not far from mine. "I'm single, in case you were wondering." With that admission, he gave me a wink. His posture was relaxed, and despite my better judgment, I was curious. What had led this big, intimidating guy with all the tattoos, a young daughter, and a cocky smirk back to Lovewell?

"I'm not," I snapped a little too eagerly, "interested."

He shook his head and leaned in. "You single? I suspect you may be after that Poindexter stormed out of here."

I shrugged, not willing to give him the satisfaction of being right.

"Good. He's not good enough for you."

I snorted. "He thinks otherwise."

He took another sip of his beer. "Guys like him always do. Not a great loss. Someone better will come along."

I tipped my wineglass back, desperate for a refill. "Not likely," I said, catching the server's eye.

"You're a strong, blond goddess. On what planet are you not good enough for him? You're basically a superhero." He scratched his chin. "I get a strong She-Ra vibe from you."

I laughed, secretly flattered. Most of the time, I felt tall and unwieldy. I was far from one of those tiny, delicate women.

Nope, I was more like the large monster lurching through the city as bodies fell in my wake.

"Definitely. Can you keep a secret? I'm a bit of a comic book nerd. And trust me, you are definitely She-Ra."

Shit, he was good-looking. And he had the good sense to compare me to a beautiful, powerful, feminist superhero. I had to be careful, though. Because beneath the serious Viking facade, Finn Hebert was a charmer.

And in my just-dumped, vulnerable state, I could not afford to be charmed.

"Let me drive you. I'm heading there anyway."

I shook my head, signing the credit card receipt. He had fought me on paying for dinner, but I'd insisted we split it. The last thing I needed was to be indebted to a Hebert. It was bad enough that I'd eaten dinner with him. I'd pay for my own rainbow trout.

"I'm good," I said primly, digging my phone out of my bag. "I'll call a rideshare."

"You will not. It'll take forever to find someone willing to take you out to the sticks. Plus, carpooling is better for the environment."

I gave him a dramatic eye roll.

"Come on. My mother would never forgive me if I left you here. She raised us right." He cocked a brow. "Or at least she tried to."

"She wouldn't know."

He laughed. "My mother knows everything. As does yours, by the way. They probably know we're arguing instead of driving to Lovewell right now."

Wood Riddance

It was late, and my weekend had gone to shit. I'd probably spend tomorrow working. After I hit the gym, of course. Maybe, just maybe, I should lower my weapons and accept a little help.

"Fine," I said, standing up and pushing my chair in.

His answering smile made my stomach drop. And when he put his hand on the small of my back and gently led me through the restaurant, something inside my chest fluttered. There weren't many people who could make me feel small, but his size and his presence were comforting. And *that* was unnerving.

He opened the door to his truck, and I climbed inside. It was immaculate.

I didn't know what I had expected. Maybe empty protein shakes and condom wrappers? Regardless, the person I'd eaten dinner with tonight was shockingly different from what I assumed all Heberts were like. They owned a rival timber company, and our grandfathers had had a falling out sometime in the 1950s, so I'd spent my life hating them. They were rich and entitled and thought they were better than the rest of us. While our family and others struggled to survive, the Heberts were flaunting their wealth, all while actively trying to buy out the other local timber companies.

Riding beside Finn down the lonely rural roads made me itchy and self-conscious. Maybe it was his confidence. Or maybe it was the way he carried himself. The straight military posture mixed with the bad boy tattoos and long hair.

"I've had a shit day myself," he said as I sat perfectly still, keeping my focus locked on the road ahead. "Had to drive all the way to Bangor to sign legal paperwork. My ex, Alicia, is a lawyer."

I nodded, not sure how to respond. We had grown up in the

same tiny town. I knew Alicia Walker, his ex-girlfriend and the mother of his child. Her grandmother had lived down the street from my parents. They had hooked up when he enlisted in the Navy but had never married. There was all kinds of local gossip and speculation as to why. I'd always assumed it was because she realized he was a Neanderthal. She was a smart and motivated person. No wonder she'd become a successful lawyer and had left him in the dust. These days, the rumor was that she was engaged to another lawyer. Apparently, some people could find their happily ever afters. Just not me.

"You could try to make polite conversation," he said, sounding annoyed. "Your manners leave much to be desired."

"Newsflash. I don't give a shit what you think of my manners. And being polite is overrated. Why is that the gold standard for womanly behavior? I have no interest in pretending to care about what you think of me."

He whistled. "I guess it's not a shock you got dumped, then."

"Fuck off. Your commentary about my love life is unwelcome."

"Only calling it like I see it, She-Ra."

I rolled my eyes and went back to ignoring him, studying the lane markers on the road instead. His monster of a truck was beginning to get a little too small. Finn wasn't just physically large. His booming voice and deep chuckle made his presence almost all-consuming.

I hated it. Or, more accurately, I hated how I felt around him. Off my game, on the defense, and out of my depth. No thank you.

Thankfully, he got the message, and once again, we rode in silence. Once we hit Lovewell, I busied myself directing him to my house.

Wood Riddance

He put the truck in park out front. "You live here?"

I nodded. My house was my sanctuary. A craftsman cottage on a neat acre, it had a white picket fence, a porch with rocking chairs, and my gardens in the back. It had taken years to save for and even longer to fix up, but it was mine.

I unbuckled my seat belt and reached for the door.

"We should do this again."

I shot him a look. "Good one."

"Why not? Because our families hate each other?" He cocked a challenging brow. "Who cares? We're adults."

I turned and studied his face. *In for four, out for four.* Finn Hebert already knocked me off balance. And his casual assertion that we should hang out only made me more nervous.

I leaned forward, watching as he bit down on his bottom lip.

"Because I dislike you. And, more importantly, because you couldn't handle me."

He stared at me for a long moment, the heat of his gaze making my body shiver. And then he slid his hand into my hair and gripped it tight before pulling my lips to his.

His lips were full and soft, in complete juxtaposition to his rough, strong hands. Both of which were in my hair.

He was hungry and intense yet gentle at the same time. A dizzying combination that kept me coming back for more.

A slight moan escaped my throat, and I angled closer, fisting his flannel shirt. What was hiding under this shirt was no secret. I saw this guy at the gym every day. His chest was broad and strong. Though the one mystery was whether he had chest hair, and suddenly, I was desperate to find out.

Fuck, this is bad. I hated Finn Hebert. I hated his family and everything he represented. But my body didn't care.

Instead, it ignored my brain's plea to jump out of the truck and never look back.

I pulled away long enough to breathe before diving back in, reveling in the taste and feel of him. He groaned, letting one hand slide down my neck, his rough fingers teasing my skin.

My heart nearly jumped out of my chest at the sensation. I should have stopped. This couldn't happen. I knew that, but I was already mentally figuring out how to get him into my house without my neighbors seeing. The last thing I needed was the town rumor mill kicking up.

But before I could form cogent thoughts, he pulled back and gave my hair a gentle tug, then released the strands. The glow of the dashboard illuminated his symmetrical face as I attempted to catch my breath. My heart was pounding like I'd run a marathon, and I swore my nipples had poked holes through my very expensive bra.

I looked up to find him grinning. Fucking grinning. Clearly pleased with himself that he'd almost made me orgasm on first base. As if kissing the shit out of me was somehow amusing to him. What a smug prick. I should have known he'd be like the rest of them. A taller, hotter, military version, sure. But he was no different from every other asshole I'd kissed in my life.

And then I snapped.

"What the shit?" I said, pushing against his chest so he fell back against his seat, trying to muster all the indignation I could. "Did I say you could kiss me? Or is consent optional for you?"

He continued to smirk. It was an infuriatingly sexy one at that. "Are you forgetting the part where you grabbed me and stuck your tongue down my throat? Let's not pretend you weren't kissing me back, She-Ra."

I said nothing. There was no point in denying my participation. Best to ignore it and move on.

He folded his arms over his expansive chest. The move was so distracting it took me a moment to remember why I was mad.

Damn hormones. It was my own fault. I always dated guys who were lousy lays and couldn't keep up with my libido.

Not that Finn would have a problem. No, that kiss alone proved he'd be thorough, attentive, and just wild enough to satisfy me.

I squeezed my eyes shut. I was supposed to be mad. No, furious. This cocky Viking thought he could do whatever he wanted.

I sat up straight, grabbed my purse, and reached for the door handle.

"Thanks for the ride home," I said primly.

"Anytime." He was still grinning at me.

"Maybe next time, keep your mouth to yourself."

I opened the door, ready to step out, but before I could, he leaned over the console, his broad shoulders crowding me.

He lowered his gaze to my chest, where my nipples were likely acting like traitorous whores desperate for attention. "Maybe next time I'll use it on other parts of your delicious body."

And then he winked. *Winked*. The audacity.

I opened the door, jumped out, and strode to my front door without looking back.

On the way, I rummaged around in my giant purse, praying I'd find my keys quickly.

Of course he remained idling in the driveway, waiting for me to go inside.

With shaky hands, I finally got the door open, and I

slammed it shut the second I was safely inside, then slid down to the tile on the other side.

I tilted my head back, taking deep breaths to calm my racing heart.

Finn Motherfucking Asshole Viking Degenerate Hebert had kissed me. And I liked it.

I touched my swollen lips. This would obviously never happen again. I hated the guy. I hated his family. And I wanted nothing to do with any of them.

But on the bright side? Since he'd sat down, I hadn't thought about getting dumped once.

Chapter 1
Finn
Present day

"I am not working with him. Fuck him and fuck his criminal family," she spat, her eyes fiery.

Beside me, Henri Gagnon had crossed his arms over his chest. He looked as exhausted as I felt.

This was the last place I wanted to be. In a million years, I never thought I'd show up, hat in hand, to Gagnon Lumber looking for work. But my entire world had imploded over the last year, and right now, my options were limited.

Thanks to my criminal father, the Hebert name was mud in the timber world. Murder charges, as well as drug trafficking and kidnapping and a laundry list of other felonies, would do that to a reputation.

It left me with few options. I was a pilot, and that was where my job experience started and ended. The US Navy had seen to that. I'd moved home two years ago after being promised steady employment with the family business, top-of-the-line equipment, and the potential to develop and launch my own business.

Henri was a good guy. Like his dad, he commanded respect

and was known to be honest and fair. Our dealings since my return had been nothing but professional, and he had given me no indication that he was holding my father's crimes against me.

His sister was a different story.

It was no secret that she hated my family, and by extension, me. There was a time when a truce had been a slight possibility, but that ship had sailed when we'd all learned the truth: my father had murdered her father to protect his drug-smuggling operation.

She hadn't gouged my eyes out yet, though. That was a feat in itself and a testament to the type of people the Gagnons were. Good, honest, upstanding. Worlds apart from the elder generation of Heberts.

Their father, Frank Gagnon, had been a beloved member of the community. Charitable and loyal, he adored his wife and four kids and went out of his way to help anyone who needed it.

My father, by comparison, was obsessed with money. He'd cheated on my mom, neglected and emotionally abused his six sons, and alienated almost everyone in this town. And that was before all the crime. Oh so much crime.

But work was work. And I wasn't qualified for much else.

I refused to not be involved in my daughter's life, so I'd do whatever it took to make a living. And my dad, from his prison cell, was in no position to help finance the flight tourism business I dreamed of and had been working toward. So I'd have to start from scratch.

And the Gagnons needed a pilot.

"There are plenty of other qualified people in the area," she groused, refusing to even look in my direction. Adele was probably the most terrifying woman I'd ever met. And, in my book, that was a compliment of the highest order.

Right now, she was wearing coveralls that were unbuttoned and tied at the waist, leaving her in a black tank top that showed off her muscular shoulders and small, round breasts.

She had a long, graceful neck and always wore colorful jewelry. Today she was sporting dangly rainbow earrings. Her dirty blond hair was piled on top of her head in a messy knot, with pieces escaping in every direction.

She was arresting and so damn distracting. I could almost imagine what it would feel like to tuck a piece of that hair behind her ear. Or caress her soft cheek while she looked up at me with those dark blue eyes.

Years ago, I had jokingly called her She-Ra, and I stood by that comparison today. She was a princess of power. Sadly, she was directing that power at me, as if I were her enemy. I'd be lucky if I left this building with my balls intact.

Henri pinched the bridge of his nose and huffed. I didn't envy his position. The lumber industry was tough, and working with family came with its own set of challenges. "He owns a plane, Adele. We need a plane."

She snorted. "His daddy bought it for him."

Henri ignored her. "Now that we've purchased the new acreage, we've got major work to do. Planning and surveying and road repairs. We need a pilot. Finn needs work and is more than qualified."

"I've got drones too," I added.

"No one asked you," she snapped, her irises twin blue flames of hatred.

Henri gave me a tense smile. "Yes. Top-of-the-line survey drones. And he's trained to use them."

"Are you fucking kidding me?" Adele planted her hands on

her hips and glared at her brother. "You're hiring him because he's got cool toys? What is this? Grade school?"

Gritting my teeth, I dropped my chin and let out a slow breath. I knew there would be hostility. Hell, I faced hostility everywhere I went these days. But I wasn't interested in taking continuous verbal abuse from this woman.

Despite her obvious physical charms, Adele Gagnon was far from my favorite person. And while we had once shared a brief connection, it was clear she'd prefer if I stayed as far away from her and her family business as possible.

I stood and stuffed my hands into my pockets. "I can give you a minute."

"Sit," Henri barked at me, though he never took his eyes off his sister.

"I don't take orders from you," Adele said in a petulant tone reminiscent of my ten-year-old daughter's when she was displeased with me.

Across the room, her shoulder muscles flexed as she crossed her arms over her chest. Adele and I went to the same gym, and I'd be lying if I said she didn't fascinate me and impress me every time I saw her. I secretly looked forward to bumping into her there, both because I enjoyed pissing her off and because I liked looking at her.

Adele had the kind of traffic-stopping beauty that, when combined with her surly, go-fuck-yourself attitude, shriveled the balls of most men in her vicinity.

But I was not most men. She intrigued the hell out of me. There was a time, in fact, when I had been so taken with her that I planned to get to know her better.

Obviously, that ship had sailed. But I couldn't help how drawn to her I was or how often I hoped I'd bump into her, at the gym as well as anywhere else in our little town.

Chapter 2
Adele

Blood still boiling, I waited for the door to close. Thankfully, Henri had finally sent Finn down to wait at reception. I closed my eyes and breathed in for four and out for four before facing down my eldest brother.

"What the fuck are you thinking?"

We were building this business *together*. Yes, Henri was CEO, but we were a team. Henri, Paz, and me. The pillars of this company. Remy helped when we needed him to, but these days, he was mostly focused on his athletic career and endorsements.

But the three of us? We consulted each other. We commiserated when things were bad. And most of all, we led with respect. For one another and for our employees.

So this?

This was too much, too soon.

"Why him?"

Henri might have been surly, but he kept his tone even. "Because he owns a plane."

I squeezed my hands into fists and gritted my teeth. "Hebert Timber owns the plane."

"Nope." Henri shook his head. "It's in his name. His daddy bought it for him."

I rolled my eyes.

"Didn't buy it outright, though. Only made the down payment. Now his son is stuck making them." Henri took a step closer, still far too casual about all of this. "He'll consult for us, help with planning prep and research. And he'll fly when we need him to. In return, he won't lose his plane."

That set me back a bit. As much as I knew about our machinery, bush planes were a completely different animal. I did, however, know that they cost as much as a house, if not more, and that they were a bitch to maintain. That was a pretty big debt to be saddled with.

I stared at my brother, squeezing my fists and releasing, over and over, desperate to punch something. The rage was pooling inside me, scalding every organ it touched, and no number of breathing exercises would relieve the emotions consuming me. I felt overwhelmed and powerless and scared.

"I know you've had a really... a really hard time." Henri's voice was tentative, low. "And I know this has probably thrown you for a loop, but it'll benefit our business. He's a qualified pilot who is trained in drone surveying. Skills like that don't exist anywhere else around Lovewell. Hell, we'd be hard pressed to find someone with training as extensive as his in the whole state of Maine."

My eye twitched and fury still burned in my chest. Dammit, why did Henri have to be so rational? Sometimes I missed the grumpy bear who used to tear through this place in a huff. Alice and the kids had softened him, and while I was thrilled that he'd found so much happiness with them, the old Henri would have kicked Finn's ass into the goddamn forest.

He took off his hat and ran a hand through his hair. "We're expanding; we're growing. We've got all this new land to plan and survey. The forestry consultants will be here in a few weeks. We need photos and maps and a plan before then. And the fastest way to get where we need to be is by air. You know that."

Though I was loath to admit it, that was true. The terrain up here was unforgiving and treacherous at times. It was little more than limited roads, wild weather, and over twelve hundred square miles of wilderness. A properly outfitted bush plane could be a huge asset to us.

Especially since we'd purchased another one hundred square miles of land from the Heberts and expanded our territory. We were looking at more crews and more roads to maintain. Not to mention building camps, workshops, and other necessary infrastructure to support the expansion. These were good problems to have, especially after the way we'd struggled after Dad died.

It made sense to have a pilot at our disposal. And if he could legitimately do survey work with his drones, then having him on our payroll would save us a ton of time and money in the long run. But this decision didn't sit right in my stomach.

I hated Finn. And honestly, he'd be a damn distraction. The guy couldn't blend in to save his life. He was like seven feet tall and looked like an extra from one of those hot Viking shows on Netflix. His shoulders could barely fit through a standard-size doorway.

He'd be in my space, in my way. And the thought made my skin crawl.

"We owe him," Henri said, raising one brow in challenge.

And there it was. The reason I wouldn't punch Finn Hebert on sight, despite his last name.

Because when shit had hit the fan and my family had been in danger, he'd jumped right in to help. Even though it meant defying his father.

I had some respect for the man. I couldn't deny that. But that didn't mean I wanted to spend time with him.

"But Dad..." I said weakly. I was grasping at straws and spinning out. My eight-year-old niece, Goldie, would probably be a better negotiator than I was right now.

"Listen," Henri said, situating his hat on his head again. "Mitch Hebert killed Dad. Finn had nothing to do with it. He was serving overseas when Dad died, for God's sake. Cut the man some slack."

I squeezed my eyes shut and willed the ache in my chest to recede. There was no way I was winning this argument.

"Fine."

"Great. Because you'll be his supervisor."

My stomach dropped and I scoffed. "You must be joking."

My oldest brother shook his head and shrugged a shoulder. "Paz is wrapped up in the financials and dealing with the lawyers. I'm supervising the largest crew we've ever had while also overseeing the planting, road repairs, and expansion. And Remy's on the competition circuit all summer."

I glared at him, my blood running hot once more. But before I could drum up an argument against the arrangement, my brother continued.

"Plus, you have that empty office down in the shop. Set him up in there. I'll have Ellen get him a computer, and he can get to work on the surveying project."

I said nothing. I was too far gone. If I opened my mouth

now, I'd probably breathe fire and singe my brother's bushy beard.

"You can shoot all the daggers you want. We both know this is a good call, so share your fucking sandbox and play nice."

I stomped out of Henri's office and slammed the door behind me for good measure. Just because he had logic on his side didn't mean I'd let him off the hook anytime soon.

And as I whipped around to stomp down the hall, I barely avoided smacking full-on into Lucifer himself.

Side-stepping him, I grunted in annoyance and strode toward the stairs that led down to my office.

"Hurry up," I said.

He followed me silently. Down the stairs from the office area to the open bullpen, past the desks, the massive job boards, and the administrative staff, out the side door, and into my shop. My kingdom.

More than anything, I wanted to create a world different from the one I'd grown up in. Where Goldie and the women who come after me would be respected and treated like equals, regardless of the profession. That was why I'd gone to such great lengths to recruit, train, and hire women in my shop.

At U Maine, I was one of only a handful of women in the engineering program. That, coupled with my height and resting bitch face, made college a less than amazing experience. Everyone always wanted to know why I did what I did. Why I didn't go for my PhD after my master's and why I didn't pursue mechanical engineering, instead going to work for my family business.

The short answer? I'd always loved the work. I'd wanted to be part of this world since I was a little kid. My whole life, I'd worshipped my dad and my grandpa. I'd been intrigued and entranced by the stories they told about the family business and life in the woods.

But from a very early age, I knew that all those stories were about men. The women were at home or in the kitchens at camp, cooking for the men who worked hard cutting down trees every day.

And it made me want more. A seat at the table. Not that my dad or any of my brothers had ever stood in my way. From the moment I expressed interest, they made room for me.

But there were not nearly enough women in this business. Or most businesses in general.

So, in my little corner of the universe, I did my best to keep the door open for the women and girls who would come after me.

From childhood, I set my sights high. I didn't want to be anyone's secretary or assistant. I wanted to rise above the place where I would have to prove that I was as smart and capable, if not more so, than my male coworkers every single day.

I'd done that already, in college and grad school, and it was exhausting.

Here, I was queen of this kingdom. And although the hours could be long, and I'd certainly never get rich, I could be myself.

I ran my team the way I wanted. I swore like a sailor and wore grease-stained coveralls with jewelry. My team was loyal and supportive, and I went out of my way to recruit and mentor women for this line of work. Together, we'd built something special. We kept hundreds of people safe and kept this business running by collaborating with one another as well as the other teams at Gagnon Lumber. By staying organized and playing all the girlie pop music we wanted. And I was damn proud of that.

Finn followed me as I entered the building. As we passed,

Jenna, Charlie, and Estrella popped up, wide-eyed. I shot them all looks, and that's all it took for them to get back to work.

This was our sanctuary, and very few people ventured in here. Paz braved it once a quarter to talk about budgets, but most people avoided this place. Mainly because I scared them.

It was a tactic I employed because I couldn't have people messing around with my machines and tools. Especially clueless men who couldn't tell a torque wrench from a hex key. And I only hired people I trusted.

Estrella made her way across the open area and scanned the steel shelves that held screws. It only took her a moment to find what she needed, because each size was stored in a carefully labeled plastic box. Efficiency and precision were essential here. If we made mistakes, people could die. That was a reality I was all too aware of.

I led Finn to the far end of the shop, across from the massive garage doors where we loaded equipment, to a small, windowless office. Inside was an old steel desk and a chair that had seen better days.

"This is you," I said. "Ellen will get you a computer and any of the tech you need to play with your toys."

He laughed.

"Something funny?" I shifted, putting my hands on my hips. I didn't care that he towered over me. I would not be disrespected in my shop.

"I'm not here to offend you," he said with a shake of his head.

My eye twitched, and the anger that had slowed to a simmer in my gut heated a fraction. I did not have time for this shit.

"Take a look around," I said, holding one arm out. "This is my shop, my team, my equipment. Touch anything, move anything, or even look at any of it the wrong way, and I will break all of your fingers. Understood?"

He nodded, pressing his lips together. "What a warm welcome."

I was in no mood for sarcasm from the hot guy who no doubt hadn't had to work for much in his life because of his good looks and his rich criminal daddy.

"I don't want you here. I don't trust you or your shit-for-brains corrupt family. But this is business. So in the spirit of business, get in my way and you're done. I don't care what my softie brother says. Do your thing and then get out."

"Yes, your majesty." The asshole actually bowed his head.

"I'm watching you, Hebert."

I turned on my heel and left him in the dingy room, then headed across the open area to the boards. On the far wall, six whiteboards tracked what was coming in and out and who was assigned to which jobs.

He-Man trotted over to me and brushed up against my leg. I bent down to pick him up, my heart calming the moment he brought his nose to the crook of my neck and gave me a good sniff. I'd found him, skinny, matted, and terrified, hidden under a truck last year, and I'd fell in love instantly. Scratching behind his ear, I hugged him close, feeling his body relax in my arms. His proximity calmed me as effectively, and right now I needed to be calm. I needed to be in control.

Estrella, my number two, sauntered up beside me. She had come to me from the regional tech school after being harassed by a bunch of sexist pricks during the final internship needed to complete her program. The men were threatened by her skills and her lack of a Y chromosome and took it out on her.

She was tiny and tough and was driven to learn all she

could. So I'd offered her a job after graduation, and she'd been here for five years.

"We're a day ahead on feller four," she said, peering over at the office where I had left Finn and raised a brow.

"I'm not talking about it," I said.

She nodded. "Understood. How much do we hate him, boss?"

I smiled at her, grateful for her loyalty. "I despise that motherfucker."

She rubbed her hands together and shot me a menacing smile. "Then we'll haze the shit out of him."

With a laugh, I gave He-Man's chin a good scratch and headed back to my office. God, I loved my job.

Chapter 3
Finn

I pulled up to the school sick to my stomach. I'd known the Gagnons wouldn't welcome me with open arms, but I may have underestimated how much Adele despised me.

Couldn't blame her. She had her reasons. But it hurt, nonetheless.

Being associated with him. The assumption that I'd behave the way he had because I was unfortunate enough to be his son. I hated it.

And the pain in her eyes hit me in the gut. There was a time I thought we might be friends. Even more than friends, if I was being honest.

Now? It was obvious there was no chance. I'd be lucky if I could keep my job for more than a week. Hell, I'd be lucky to survive that long in her presence. That glare would stop a weaker man's heart. And I wasn't sure how long my own could tolerate it.

I jumped out of the truck and headed up to the gym,

waving at Alice Gagnon, the school principal. She was herding small kids to the carpool area for camp pickup.

Merry was near the swings with a couple other kids, but before I could get to her, a hand landed on my arm, halting me in my tracks. *Fuck.*

"Finn."

The petite woman who still had a hold of me wore elbow-length false eyelashes and sky-high heels.

"So good to see you."

I gave her a tight nod. "Veronica."

"Oh. Call me Ronnie," she trilled, her talons still locked around my forearm. This was the thing I hated most about being a single dad. The moms.

Since Alicia worked long hours, I did most of the pickups and drop-offs. I soaked in every extra minute with Merry I could get before leaving her with her mom for the night. Our custody arrangement was flexible, mostly because we got along so well, and so far, it suited all of us. I had dinner at Alicia and Mike's frequently, and we spent holidays together.

But being a present parent made me a prime target for every single woman within a hundred-mile radius. There had been a time, right after Alicia and I split, when I enjoyed the attention. Anymore, it was exhausting. Single moms came out of the woodwork to chat me up at every event I attended with my daughter. They all had cutesy nicknames like Ronnie, Sherri, and Lainey, and they fawned all over me with their cloying perfume and too-tight tops. Their efforts took from the time I had with my daughter, from the moments where I was happy to stand back and observe my little girl with her friends. The worst part, though? Was that while most of them were trying to get into my pants, they were also talking shit about my family behind my back.

Wood Riddance

The whispers, the gossip, the pity. It was unbearable most days, though not wholly unsurprising. My dad *had* gone from small-town rich guy to murderer-slash-drug dealer in the blink of an eye.

I gave her a tight smile. "Sorry, in a bit of a rush today."

"You never texted me back about a playdate," she said, giving me an exaggerated pout.

"Oh, right. Sorry," I threw over my shoulder as I picked up my pace. My legs were easily twice the length of hers and she was wearing stilettos, but somehow, Ronnie kept up. "We really need to get together."

Merry caught sight of me and snatched her backpack off the ground quickly. Eyes locked on mine, she gave me a slight nod. "Dad!" she screamed, running straight for me. "You're late." She mimed looking at an imaginary watch, then she gave me the kind of disappointed look I was used to seeing from her mother.

"Sorry, baby," I said, kissing the top of her head.

"Let's go." She grabbed my arm and yanked, heading for the parking lot. I gave Ronnie a nod and jogged after my little girl.

When we were safely in the truck, Merry turned and raised one brow.

"Nice save," I said. Damn, my daughter was as sharp as a goddamn tack.

"Why can't you tell Miss Landry that you don't want to go on a date with her?" She folded down the mirror and adjusted her ponytail. She had her mom's dark hair and dark eyes, but the rest of her was pure Hebert, from the height down to the attitude.

"Nice try. Get in back." I thumbed over my shoulder. Her distraction techniques were good, but not *that* good.

She sighed and dropped her head back, but without argument, she climbed into the back seat. "Mom says you should always be honest and up-front with people."

"Your mom's correct, as always. It's awkward."

"Speak for yourself. It's more awkward to see all the moms drooling over you. Can't you wear dad clothes and get a dad bod and act like a lame dad or something?"

I laughed. "I am a lame dad."

"*I* know that. But the world doesn't get it."

I shook my head. "Sorry, kid."

She slumped against the back seat, but not before leaning forward and adjusting the radio station.

As we drove and joked, the stress of the day melted away. I would make this work. I would succeed. There was no other option.

Because I was stuck. Pure and simple. And I'd do what I had to in order to get through this. To get myself and Merry to a better place.

Michael "call me Mike" was a good guy. He adored Alicia and Merry. But he was corporate to the bone. Drove a fucking Volvo, always wore a collared shirt, and listed one of his hobbies as "grilling."

He was the antithesis of me. Though I chose not to read too much into that. Alicia was still my best friend and my co-parent, and she deserved happiness. She'd followed my ass around for years, taking care of Merry and putting her own dreams on hold.

And if this was what she wanted, practicing family law in Bangor and a life with a guy like Mike, then I would not stand in her way.

But it meant I was stuck here.

Wood Riddance

I hadn't planned to leave the Navy so early. I'd always seen myself as a lifer, despite how hard the last deployment had been. But Alicia was set on coming back to Lovewell. She wanted Merry to grow up near her grandparents and cousins. And I appreciated that.

Even if it meant I had to come back too. Because my baby girl was the most important thing in my life, and I would never, ever pass up a minute with her.

I had missed so much time with her while I was in the Navy. My service took me away from her too often, and I promised I'd never let that happen again.

So, like the good sailor I was, I showed up here, ready to settle in and give it my all. Even if it meant working for my father.

It helped that he wanted nothing more than to have his war hero son home. He wanted to brag about me to all his cronies and flaunt me and Merry around.

So he bought a plane. That's how he lured me back into the family business. With the title to the bush plane and a promise to invest in my air tourism company.

Didn't take long for that to go to shit. And my brothers and I were stuck trying to save the family business and our own asses.

Alicia and Mike were both successful lawyers. They could provide Merry with everything she needed. And it stung. Because I was her dad, and I would be damned if I slacked on the most important job I'd ever have.

So I would work. Even if it was for the Gagnons. I would keep my plane and start my business. And along the way, I'd never miss a birthday or a parent teacher conference or a soccer game.

"You know you don't have to feed me," I said with a groan. Though I couldn't be sure if it was a groan of exasperation or of satisfaction. Despite my belief that grilling did not qualify as a hobby, Mike could cook the hell out of a rack of ribs.

He laughed, picking up his plate, then Alicia's. "I always make too much. You know that." He dropped a quick kiss on Alicia's head before carrying the dishes back to the kitchen. "And you're family."

I wanted to hate him so much, but I couldn't—especially when he made ribs that good—and that was unsettling.

Alicia met Mike shortly after we moved back to Lovewell. It was clear from day one that they were destined to be together. And it burned me. Deeply. Not because I was jealous of him or because I wanted Alicia for myself, but because she'd found it. The real thing. After wasting her twenties with my dumb ass, she went out and found a successful, ambitious guy. The kind of guy who could give her and Merry a wonderful life.

Me? Until today, I'd been unemployed. I had a convict for a father, a trashed reputation, and a family business circling the drain.

"Merry. Get the rest of these."

My daughter sighed loudly but grabbed my plate and hers, leaving Alicia and me in the sunroom. The house was new construction. It was enormous and had state-of-the-art everything. It made my sad apartment that much more pathetic.

Merry had her own room and bathroom and a huge yard, and they were talking about putting in a pool next year. They'd probably get her a dog, the thing she wanted more than anything—aside from a sibling.

Wood Riddance

Me? I had spent most of my life rejecting material wealth. My dad was ostentatious and snobby, and I'd worked hard to ensure that I was nothing like him.

No one joins the military for money, and I wanted a greater purpose.

I rarely had regrets, but right at this moment, taking in my surroundings, I was kicking myself for not settling for some kind of corporate job. Because Merry deserved everything she ever wanted.

"You're not okay." It wasn't a question.

I shrugged.

"The new job?"

"It's a go," I said. "Not ideal circumstances. But—"

"It's flying." Alicia finished my sentence. She knew me. Probably better than anyone. She knew how deep my love of flying went. There were times she had resented it. That I didn't have the same kind of passion for her. But we were long past those days.

"Henri Gagnon has been decent. But his sister, Adele? Let's just say if anything happens to me, you know who did it."

"Are you seriously making a murder joke right now?" Alicia asked.

I shrugged. Okay, maybe it was too soon. "At this point, I've got to laugh about this shit."

"Didn't you have a crush on her once upon a time?" Alicia played with the stem of her wineglass and shot me a sly smile.

"No," I practically barked, protesting way too much.

"Bullshit." That smile turned into a full-on grin. "And you still do, apparently."

She knew me too well. Trying to hide things from her was pointless anymore. After all these years, she could read me like a book.

"You should ask her out. I'd rather you date her than a member of the trashy MILF brigade who chases you in the school parking lot."

My stomach dropped. How did she know about that?

"I have friends in this town," she continued. "Not to mention our daughter complains about it endlessly."

With a smirk, I shrugged. "I can't help it. All this pure masculinity cannot be contained."

She snorted and rolled her eyes. "Let's take a walk. I want to talk to you about something."

With a nod, I pushed back and stood to my full height. Once I'd tucked my chair in, I picked up the few remaining dishes. My mother raised me right, and I would always do my fair share.

In the kitchen, Mike and Merry were singing along to Taylor Swift. There were moments where I was envious of how close the two of them had become, but when those feelings struck, I reminded myself that he was one more adult in my daughter's corner, and I couldn't be upset about that.

Once the dishwasher was loaded and they were wiping down counters, Alicia and I slipped out.

The air was still a bit cool. It was June, and this was Maine, after all. But the humidity was already seeping in. It wouldn't be long before the dog days of summer were here.

The street they lived on was lined with cookie cutter McMansions with impeccable landscaping. It was so out of place in a working-class town like Lovewell. But the area had changed, and it was changing still right before my eyes.

"Merry is having a hard time," she said softly, keeping her focus fixed on the sidewalk in front of us.

I nodded, making sure to shorten my strides so Alicia didn't have to fight to keep up. It hadn't escaped my notice. Merry was becoming more withdrawn by the day.

"The last year has been so hard."

Guilt sank like a stone in my stomach. My fucking family legacy—nothing but violence and crime and shame—haunted my little girl too.

"Did she mention anything specific?" I ran my hands through my hair. Shit. The last person I wanted suffering was Merry.

"Only that kids were being cruel. Making comments, not wanting to play with her, that sort of thing."

"We met with Principal Gagnon in the spring," I said lamely. Alicia and I had thought we could stanch some of the rumors if we faced things head-on.

"She was great." Alicia peeked over at me. "But she can't control everything kids hear or say."

Dammit. The initial fervor had been deafening, but I was under the impression that things had died down.

"I think the anticipation of the trial starting this fall is making it worse."

My heart lurched at the thought. "You said it will probably be delayed."

"Yes. But that doesn't mean public interest isn't picking up. People are curious and gossipy. This is a small town, and until recently, the Heberts were the resident untouchable rich people."

"Hey." My tone lacked any kind of force. Her statement was true. We had grown up privileged. Even with what had happened between my parents, we were provided for. We'd always had so much more than many of our classmates and neighbors.

"It's true. But you know me. I want to cut anyone who hurts our girl."

I put my arm around Alicia's shoulders. "I know that, mama bear. I'll talk to her."

Dammit, I'd been so naïve. I'd thought I was the one getting the heat, facing the whispers and the dirty looks. And I could handle that. But my child? That was too much.

Just like when I was a kid, I wanted out of this place. The moment I graduated from high school, I was gone. As far away from my shithead father as I could get. Now, at thirty-five, all I wanted to do was flee. And my reason hadn't changed a bit.

This was killing me. We'd made the move back home to give Merry safety and stability and a carefree childhood. The poor kid had gotten anything but.

Military life had been hard on Alicia and Merry. They'd suffered through it for my benefit. Now I'd do anything to give them what they wanted. But coming back here had felt like a mistake from day one.

And now we had a miserable, anxious ten-year-old who needed all our support.

"She's got to keep her chin up and ignore them," Alicia continued. "There isn't much else we can do."

I winced. Of course she'd advocate for taking the high road. She was a good person like that.

My mind wandered to Adele and her fiery personality. If she were on this side of the scandal, she'd probably torch the school down and make every one of those kids wish they had never even looked at Merry. I laughed to myself. I admired her fire. Except, of course, when it was aimed in my direction.

Alicia was right, though. Handling things maturely was usually the best option. But it was one thing to deal with this bullshit as an adult. It was something completely different when a child—my child—was the one being hurt. I couldn't be rational about this.

I could handle the shame and hurt and the confusion over what my father had done.

But the impact on my baby girl? Unacceptable. I was going to fix this.

Chapter 4
Adele

I wrapped up the day's project a little earlier than I'd planned to, but once I'd gotten my workstation cleaned up and the tools put back where they belong, I walked straight out the door that led to the small staff parking lot. We had a massive fenced area out back for parking machinery and storing parts and large tools, but this side lot was only for our cars.

Jumping into my Jeep, I forced myself to take in a deep breath, then another. My stomach was in knots, my shoulders were so tense they were bunched practically to my ears, and I was sweating through my tank top. To say this day had knocked me flat on my ass was an understatement.

Thoughts and feelings battled in my brain, making my head spin as I tried to make sense of all of this.

I wanted him dead. All of them. I wanted all of those fuckers in the ground.

They had taken my father away.

They'd tried to kill all three of my brothers.

I closed my eyes and put my head on the steering wheel.

He hadn't been behind any of the attempts, as far as I knew, but that didn't make him any better than the rest of them. There were reasons our families had despised each other for generations.

And Henri had allowed him in the building? Surely there were other dumbasses out there with pilot's licenses looking for work. I'd watch a YouTube video and take my chances in the air before trusting a Hebert.

My heart raced as I pulled my phone out of my pocket and shot off a quick text to Parker.

I hadn't even left the parking lot when she called. Damn, she was a great friend.

"What's the emergency?"

"Hebert shit."

"Gym?" The woman didn't miss a beat.

"Yup." I turned onto Route 45 and headed toward Forest Fitness, the grungy, no-frills warehouse where Parker and I trained together.

Not only was she my brother Paz's girlfriend, but in the last several months, she'd become my best friend. She had come to Lovewell last year to help investigate Dad's death. Somewhere along the way, between stakeouts and undercover information gathering and being kidnapped, she'd fallen in love with my brother. Paz was the last person I expected to settle down, but here he was, smitten and constantly begging Parker to marry him.

It only fueled my belief that there really was a person for everyone. My brother was a grouch with a giant stick shoved up his ass, yet Parker could handle him. It helped that she was former state police with several black belts and could drop him on his ass when he got out of line.

Yet another reason I adored her. In the beginning, I'd

resisted the connection. I didn't have much time for friends, beyond my staff at work, but she refused to take no for an answer. So, slowly, we'd become friends and workout buddies.

Now, I was thankful she hadn't given up on me. Parker got me. And she didn't let me pull away. Didn't let me hide behind my snark and my resting bitch face. She also wasn't afraid to call me out when I was being stubborn, judgmental, or downright bitchy. The ability was annoying more often than not, but once in a while, she helped me see another perspective or rein in my fury.

When I pulled into a parking spot near the building, she was already waiting by the door, her dark hair in a ponytail and two sets of boxing gloves dangling over her arm.

I grabbed my gym bag from the back seat and hustled to the doors.

"Ready to punch shit?" she asked, stepping back so I could enter first.

I was so fucking ready.

"Are you gonna give me the details?" Parker asked, holding the heavy bag while I let a flurry of jabs and hooks fly.

"Henri hired a Hebert," I grunted. The name alone inspired me to pick up my pace and intensity, and I threw in an uppercut.

She nodded, adjusting her gloves.

"What did Paz tell you?"

"I texted him. Told him that you were upset and it better not be his fault or I'd withhold blow jobs for the next year. He swore he had nothing to do with it."

Stepping back from the bag, I held back the bile that rose at the mental image she'd created. As much as I appreciated Parker going to bat for me, I could have lived without the other details.

"According to Henri," I said, "we need a pilot. And the Heberts have a plane. And state-of-the-art drones."

"Of course they do," she said, side-stepping the bag so we could see one another.

"Finn Hebert apparently needs work. Since, you know, his murderer of a father destroyed their family business."

Parker nodded, giving me a knowing look. She knew every detail inside and out. She was the one who'd connected Mitch Hebert to the opioid trafficking and linked him to a shell business run out of the local trailer park. And for all her trouble, she'd been kidnapped. She and my brother had only narrowly escaped, and Paz had taken a bullet to the ass as a souvenir.

It was only a graze, and he'd recovered fully, but so far, he'd made sure we all remembered his heroics. I doubted he'd ever let us forget. But the thought of how much worse things could have been haunted me.

"Keep punching," she said, bracing herself behind the bag again. "This is next-level fuckery."

"Henri has him working in *my* shop! He told me that I'm supposed to keep an eye on him."

"Let's go kick Henri's ass," she said, wiping her brow. "Or we should tell Alice. She will definitely withhold blow jobs."

I held my hands up as the bile made a reappearance. "Please stop mentioning blow jobs and my brothers in the same sentences."

"Regardless, I think Henri feels bad for him. He's such an annoyingly good person."

That was the problem with my brother. He was too nice. Sure, he had this grumpy exterior, but it was all a front. My dad had been the same way. Trusting to a fault. After we discovered that Richard's nephew Norman had been the one to tamper with my dad's brakes, causing his death, Remy and I wanted Richard out. Sure, he'd been with Gagnon Lumber for decades, but he'd allowed his criminal nephew at camp several times, giving him access to kill my dad.

But Henri and Paz had overruled us, reasoning that he was Dad's best friend. They assured us that Richard felt horrible that his actions had played a part in our father's death. Since he wasn't implicated in any of the criminal activity, they saw no reason to let him go. Still didn't trust that crusty old fucker, though.

And now Finn? What kind of business philosophy involved hiring the mortal enemies of one's family?

"His situation is awful. I'm sure even you can muster up some sympathy for him," Parker said.

I stopped and turned to my friend, pinning her with a glare. "I do not. He's complicit much like the rest of them. Any genetic link to the man who killed my father is unacceptable."

"Mitch didn't technically commit the murder."

That was Parker—always a cop. Always assessing the technicalities.

"Yeah, yeah. His henchman did it." I waved one gloved hand. "But when my dad found his stash house, he ordered the accident. And that's enough for me."

Parker took her gloves off and held my water bottle out to me.

"I'm on your team, and I'm outraged for you. But let's establish the facts here. There is no evidence—truly none, whatsoever—linking *any* of the six Hebert sons to *any* of their father's crimes. In fact, it appears he went to great lengths to keep them out of the bad stuff."

Tearing off one glove, then the other, all I could do is blink at her. She'd been kidnapped by this man and almost killed, yet she didn't have a problem with his sons? Even the men who worked alongside him at Hebert Timber day in and day out?

She put up her hands defensively. "I'm only stating the facts. You can hate them, but calling them complicit isn't accurate or fair. From what I've heard, they're devastated."

Dropping to the floor and leaning against the cool cinderblock wall, I gulped my water. Usually, physically exhausting myself helped. Punching and sweating and lifting heavy things was how I coped with all the sadness and uncertainty. For the last few years, from one shitty problem to the next, it had kept me focused and sane.

Parker slid down the wall next to me, bumping my shoulder gently.

"You suffered a huge loss. The trauma of your dad's death, as well as all that followed, will take a long time to heal."

"I don't think it'll ever heal. Not entirely," I said.

I had lost so much. And I'd almost lost even more.

And seeing Mitch Hebert and his associates in jail? It did nothing for me.

For years, I dreamed of discovering the truth surrounding my dad's death. Obsessing over every detail, meticulously going through the wreckage of his truck to look for clues.

Back then, I thought it would help. I thought knowing would help the pain, the loss, the emptiness inside me.

But the emptiness remained even after we discovered the cause of his death. Then I told myself that seeing those responsible brought to justice would ease the pain. But as much as I wanted to show up to every preliminary hearing and read every submission on the court docket, I couldn't do it.

Dad was still gone, and nothing would bring him back. So I

kept going. Slogging along, knowing that nothing would stop the loss that gnawed away inside me.

"I'm not healing. I'm not moving past this. I'm going to stay angry," I said.

"Wow that sounds healthy," Parker sneered.

"Fuck off." I pushed against her with my shoulder. "Why can't I be a rage monster forever?"

"You can't." Her voice was softer than I'd ever heard it. "You are capable of so much more. This plan, to stay mad and never work through it all, is dumb as shit, and you know it."

I looked over at my friend and cocked a brow.

She mimicked the gesture. "You don't keep me around for my makeup tips, bitch. I'm not going to lie to you."

I put my arm around her. "Thank you."

"Who knew you were such a good cook?" I said, carrying my dish to the kitchen.

Paz shrugged. "I'm only trying to prevent Parker from cooking. Keeps me from having to clean up the giant mess she'll inevitably make in the kitchen."

Parker flipped him the bird while snagging the bottle of wine to refill both our glasses. Prior to Parker's arrival in Lovewell, I had seen the inside of my brother's house maybe once, but now we had dinner here regularly. They even kept dog bowls for He-Man, who was currently lounging on the couch.

At first, I felt like a third wheel. Early on, I tried to beg off or cancel on their dinner plans, but Parker eventually wore me down. After homemade jambalaya and some really excellent white wine, my heart rate was finally slowing.

Wineglasses in hand, we headed to the back deck and sprawled out on the beautiful lounge chairs that faced the mountains. Parker set the wine bottle on the table between us and tipped her head back to look at the stars. He-Man zoomed around the yard a couple of times before tiring out and falling asleep in my lap.

She chatted about the cases she was working on, filling me in on what she'd discovered since the last time we'd hung out. After solving my dad's murder and singlehandedly bringing down an international drug trafficking organization, she was in demand, but she was trying to take things easy.

She'd hired a part time assistant to help her manage the workload, which she desperately needed since, as a key witness in the case against Mitch Hebert, she was still spoon-feeding the FBI the necessary evidence.

"Maybe it's my investigative instincts, or maybe it's the wine talking, but I think there is more to the Finn Hebert story."

I shifted, bringing my glass to my lips, and He-Man yipped in protest.

"I've watched him make eyes at you at the gym for a year now. You might as well come clean."

"Come clean about what?" Paz stepped through the French doors carrying plates of blueberry pie with ice cream. Sometimes I still didn't recognize this man. This was my grumpy, asshole brother, yet he was delivering pie with a smile and dropping a kiss to his girlfriend's head like some sweet, doting book boyfriend.

He sat on the edge of her lounge chair and handed me a plate.

"Courtesy of Bernice."

Parker beamed at him. "You did not pick this up after work."

He winked at her. "You said you were craving pie this morning. You know, after." He shot her a look that stole my appetite instantly.

Parker shoved a forkful of pie into her mouth and turned back to me with her brows raised and her eyes bright.

In response, I dropped my chin and shook my head.

She got me. Without needing any explanation from me, she shooed Paz away. "Girl talk only, stud muffin. Get lost."

He leaned down and kissed her for far too long before retreating into the house.

"Start talking," she said. The bright expression was gone. All that remained was her deadly serious investigator face.

"Two years ago, I was dating this guy named Blake." I tilted my head back, studying the stars. "In retrospect, he was terrible. But Dad had recently died, and I was so lonely." A sigh escaped me before I could catch it. "He dumped me, publicly, at a really nice restaurant in Bangor. And lucky me, Finn happened to be there to witness it."

Parker shook her fork at me. "Aw. Shit. Yes. Did he fight him?"

"No. He insisted on joining me for dinner and then gave me a ride home."

"That Blake asswipe left you thirty minutes away without a car? How did you not break his nose?"

I cringed. Constantly donning the identity of big, bad killer woman got old sometimes. And the assumptions that I was a breath away from violence at any given moment was both untrue and unfair.

Yes. I was serious and assertive, and yes, maybe I had a bit of an anger problem, but I wasn't a lunatic. People assumed I had no feelings, that I punched and kicked my way through life. But really, it was the opposite. On the inside, I felt so breakable. So fragile at times.

During undergrad, the guys in my engineering program called me "nut crusher" for no other reason than I was tall and competitive. But having my feelings and emotions written off because I presented myself as strong and independent stung more than anyone knew. Including my siblings and their significant others.

"I was upset," I explained. "And I was at a really low point for many reasons." Chasing something I thought would fix me. But it didn't. "Finn drove me home, which was really nice of him."

"And?"

"And we kissed."

Parker sat straight up, her plate of pie falling onto the deck. He-Man, who seconds before had been deep in slumber, pounced, licking up every speck of blueberry. As if even he knew Bernice's pie was not to be wasted.

"So the hot Viking kissed you."

"Yes. And it was intense. He suggested we hang out again, but I shut him down."

She nodded. "I admire your willpower."

With a huff, I stuck my tongue out. "I saw him around town a lot. With his daughter, at the gym or the diner. There was always this tension."

Parker rubbed her hands together. "Ooh, now this is getting good."

I dipped my chin, snuggling farther into my hoodie, as a familiar sense of trepidation grew in the pit of my stomach.

"And then last summer, when Remy and Hazel were in trouble, I needed help." Even mentioning it brought me back to the cold dread that had overtaken me when I learned my brother was in danger.

"So you called him," Parker said, interrupting my thoughts.

I nodded. "I didn't know what else to do. All I knew was that he had a plane."

Paz had called Mitch Hebert and explained the situation. When he asked for help, Mitch had refused, saying his plane was undergoing maintenance and was unavailable.

So I acted. I called Finn, told him Remy and Hazel were in danger, and thirty minutes later, we were taking off from Lake Millinocket. I never bothered asking how he got the pontoons on or gassed it up that quickly. He didn't hesitate to do the right thing.

"Then the two of you flew to the rescue, and the rest is town legend."

I shrugged. "Something like that. It was such a surreal experience, and I was coming down from an adrenaline high. I thought he was so heroic and humble. He defied his father to help my family. And in the immediate aftermath, it felt like something had shifted between us. That something might happen."

"But it didn't."

I shook my head. "It's for the best. Because a couple of months later, we learned the truth about his dad."

"It doesn't change what he did, how he dropped everything to help," Parker said softly.

I closed my eyes and took a deep breath, focusing on the feeling of the cool summer air in my lungs. "It doesn't. But it does change how I feel about him. He went from a man I could tolerate, felt gratitude toward, to a man I can't stomach being near. Now Henri and Paz want me to 'get over it,' but it's not that easy."

"I know, babe. You've been through a lot."

"Not as much as all of you," I snapped, my eyes welling with tears and my heart aching so badly I felt as though my chest might cave in. My entire family had paid the price for Mitch Hebert's criminal actions. Parker herself had been kidnapped. Paz too. Henri had almost died after the truck he was driving had been tampered with, and Remy and Hazel had been hunted by drug traffickers. Me? I hadn't been shot or kidnapped or chased by bad guys with guns, yet I was the one who couldn't get over it. Couldn't process all the needless violence and suffering and pain.

The emotional tidal wave was threatening to consume me, and that was my cue to leave. I refused to ruin Paz and Parker's happiness with my needy bullshit. The poor woman had already spent the evening picking up the pieces of my mini breakdown.

So I made my goodbyes and carried He-Man, who refused to walk to the damn car, then headed home. As I drove, I ran through my interactions with Finn today.

I couldn't get how he'd looked out of my head.

Still enormous. Still intimidating. His arms wrapped in ink. His long hair pulled back.

But something was missing.

He had always possessed this swagger. He was massive and intimidating at first glance, but he laughed and joked a lot. He had the kind of confidence that kept him from taking himself too seriously.

The man I saw today? He was different. It was like the light had gone out of him.

The energy, the hunger for experiences I had admired for so long, was gone.

His eyes were dark and stormy, without a hint of their usual playfulness.

For fuck's sake, he didn't even bother to flirt with me. Never, in the two years since we'd bumped into each other at that restaurant, had he passed up an opportunity like that.

Shame washed over me as I navigated the dark roads. For the way I had acted. Not with Henri—he deserved my wrath for not consulting me. But with Finn.

I hated him and his family and everything they had done. That sentiment hadn't changed. His father was still alive, albeit awaiting a trial that would certainly land him in federal prison, while mine had been gone for almost three years. He should have been here, playing with his grandkids and sneaking kisses with my mom when they thought we weren't watching.

But I had been unprofessional today. I'd lost my cool. Something about that guy made me twitchy, and the thought of having to work with him had me struggling to keep my dinner down.

The nausea was made worse by the sorrow that had been my companion for three years. Everyone around me was moving on. Yet I was still trapped in my grief.

My throat closed up, and tears pricked the back of my eyes. I was never getting my dad back. He was gone. And somehow, I was the only one struggling to accept this. My mother, after being buried in crushing grief for more than a year, had found herself again. Found a purpose working at the school and doting on her grandkids.

And my three brothers had all fallen in love. Hell, Henri was in the process of adopting two kids. They were building families and homes and careers, and I was being left behind.

Good old Adele, doing the same thing every day. Stuck in her anger and unable to push through. Story of my goddamn life.

Chapter 5
Finn

The only way to salvage this weekend was by heading out for a long run. So I grabbed my weight vest and set off to figure my shit out. It was humid, and the mosquitoes were already the size of bloated sparrows. I'd regret not bathing in Deet, but the urge to get out and move was too powerful. I had a lot going on, and the only remedy I'd find would be through sweat.

I'd learned that back in second grade, when it was impossible for me to sit still. When I couldn't finish math worksheets or stay in my seat for an entire movie.

My dad's solution was to scream at me and insist I was stupid. For a long time, that stuck. It wasn't until much later, when Mom took me for testing, that I learned that this was a part of who I was.

In order to focus, I needed to be challenged. And that usually involved exhausting my body first. I couldn't think when I was itchy and distracted.

And right now, I had a lot on my mind.

Making my way through town, I doled out kind smiles to

everyone I saw and winced when most looked away. I knew what they all said behind our backs. I'd heard the whispers, and I saw the pity in their expressions.

Our family name was mud in this town. Four generations of Heberts in Lovewell and almost a hundred years of providing jobs to the community. In an instant, all the respect our family had earned, all the friendships and goodwill, were gone. Because of my criminal father.

My brothers and I, of course, were tainted by association. Not that anyone would say it to my face. My height, the tattoos, and my time in the military took care of that. People had been intimidated by me since I surpassed the six-foot mark in middle school. I was used to it. Which was why I always worked to speak softly, always did my best to wear a smile, and always kept my movements slow and subtle.

But now, what was the point? The people of Lovewell, even those I'd known my whole life, only saw the son of a murderer when they looked at me.

I followed the river toward the mountains, leaving the neat rows of houses behind. The homes were more spread out here. Fewer cars passed, and I didn't pass a single person. Here and there, I'd encounter a barking dog behind a fence, but otherwise, my only company were the squirrels that scurried past and up trees and the mosquitoes.

I could deal with this.

The worst part about being in the military was all the running. When I separated from the Navy, I swore up and down I'd never run again. I said a lot of stupid shit back then. Yet here I was. Because running did what no medication could. It slowed my brain and body down. Plus, it was virtually impossible for a guy my size to be fast, so it was always a humbling experience. Especially during PT, when 160-pound guys would fly by me, making me feel like a Clydesdale.

Some days, I needed the ego check. Today wasn't one of those days. On no. Adele Gagnon was the best ego check on the planet. The United States government should hire her, pronto. She'd play the perfect bad cop in any diplomatic negotiation. I could only imagine how quickly peace treaties would be signed if she were berating the world leaders involved.

I laughed to myself. In this daydream, she'd wear a skirt suit. You know, the sort of skirt that's knee length and conservative but still tight as fuck? Yeah.

Shit. I should not have been thinking about her body.

With a shake of my head, I hoofed it up the hill, set on running until I got Adele out of my head.

She was so intense and beautiful, and she was just mean enough to make me ache for her. There was something wrong with me, because I loved it.

Life was hard, and I had little time for weak people. I respected those who pushed up and through.

And Adele was next level.

On a creeper, her top half hidden under an engine, wearing coveralls that barely hid that round, juicy ass—

Shit, I was thinking about her body again.

Instead of being put off by her prickly personality, I found myself drawn to her.

Sure, she had sharp claws, but buried beneath that was a well of passion, a personality so intense she could probably keep up with me. Nothing she said to me wasn't deserved. At least she, unlike the cowards who made up the rest of this town, had the stones to be honest with me.

Plus, I had no doubt she was a hellcat in bed. Probably loud and bossy. The kind of woman who would claw the shit out of my back and leave teeth marks all over my body.

Shit, now I was hard. Running in flimsy gym shorts and a weighted vest through town at dusk. *Way to be a predator, Finn.*

I needed a reality check. And a swift kick in the ass. Right now, I had to focus on making ends meet, providing for my child, and building the business I'd been dreaming of. My plans had been derailed, but I'd be a shit sailor if I wasn't still pushing forward. The goals I'd set had been delayed, but that meant I had more time to find investors and study the way the local tourism industry was growing.

Flying for the Gagnons would get me more hours in the air and a chance to become even more familiar with the terrain. Avgas wasn't cheap, and this way, my flight hours and the cost would be on the lumber company's dime. I'd take every chance I could to fly, prickly bosses or not.

I'd get there. I'd build my business and make Merry proud.

Cresting the hill, I banked around the south side of the river. Jude would be home, so I headed in his direction. He was painfully predictable. It drove me crazy, but it suited him perfectly. He was the quiet, creative one. Always playing his damn guitar or out hiking in the woods with his dog. He was the complete opposite of Noah, his twin, who was an adrenaline junky. That kid was always climbing mountains, surfing big waves, or jumping out of planes. Since birth, he'd been scaring the shit out of my mother almost daily. He was currently in California, working as a woodland firefighter and ignoring all the family drama back east.

The twins were only four years younger than me, and yet we'd never been close. Despite their differences, they had always had one another and still texted every day. We were lucky if Noah called on Christmas, but Jude always knew what he was up to.

I knocked on the door, and in response, Ripley barked. The mutt was his best friend and protector. Jude had found her in the woods while working at camp last year and had brought her home.

She followed him around endlessly. She'd even tried to climb into the crane with him once. When the door swung open, the first thing I did was give her ears a good rub. She was sociable and affectionate, the exact opposite of Jude.

If a Bernese mountain dog had a baby with a feral wolf, Ripley would be it. But she was a good girl and took care of my brother, so I couldn't complain when she jumped on my chest and put her paws on my shoulders. I didn't mind that she was the size of a small horse. Honestly, she was the perfect Hebert-sized dog.

"Running?" Jude asked dryly. His sandy brown hair was cropped short and his round glasses were perched on his nose. Today's funny T-shirt read: *Middle Earth's Annual Mordor Fun Run* and featured a giant eyeball. I wasn't totally sure what it meant, but it was probably something highbrow and nerdy.

"Yes. You gonna let your big brother in? Maybe offer me a glass of water?"

In response, he shrugged and stepped away.

"Wow. Mom really lowered her standards with you," I teased, stepping over the threshold.

He punched my shoulder and turned toward the kitchen. Ripley was on his heels the whole way there and sat, watching him with so much love and affection, as he pulled a glass down from the cabinet.

His house was a tiny cape up past the river. He had bought it a couple of years ago, before everything went to shit. It was neat as a pin, as always, displaying his meticulously organized collections of guitars, records, and comic books. It was Jude in every way.

I was proud of all he'd done at such a young age, but it stung a little that my younger brother had become a homeowner before I had. Back in my Navy days, it had barely crossed my mind. Moving every couple of years and leaving Alicia and Merry at home while I deployed made renting ideal. Now, though, I was hitting my mid-thirties and I had a kid. It was time to plant those roots. And I'd wanted to, but that was yet another plan that had been derailed by my father.

After chugging the glass of water, I refilled it and set it on the counter while I unhooked my weighted vest and hung it on the back of one of the wooden kitchen chairs.

"Gus is headed over with dinner," Jude said, taking a small stack of white plates out of a neatly organized cabinet. "You should stay."

Pursing my lips, I waffled. I'd told myself recently that I should spend more time with my brothers. But my day had already been long and unpleasant. The last thing I needed was more arguing.

Things between us all had been strained lately. There were six of us Hebert boys. Gus was the oldest, and he'd worked side by side with Dad for years. He'd done everything my father asked of him. Worked every grunt job and bent over backward to please him in the hopes of someday taking over the company. Dad, of course, sidelined Gus in favor of his own brother, Paul. Even so, Gus had remained loyal and dedicated to the business.

Owen was the next oldest, and like me, he'd hightailed it out of Lovewell the day he turned eighteen. He hadn't so much as spoken to my father in years, and he rarely came home to visit, despite my mother's frequent requests. He'd made a name for himself as an accountant-turned-corporate CFO in Boston.

Then there was me, the middle child. The ADHD nightmare. The Navy had mostly straightened me out, but clearly, I was still a work in progress.

The twins came next, and they had never been particularly close to dad. Probably because they were so young when our parents divorced. They'd spent most of their time with Mom, and Dad had always overlooked them, instead giving the majority of his attention and money and love to Cole. Not that they minded, they did their own thing, which usually involved getting lost in the woods and Noah coming home with some kind of terrifying injury.

And the youngest, my half brother Cole, was off playing hockey.

Not pro. Semi-pro.

Despite the loads of talent he possessed and all the lessons and coaches and expensive equipment my dad had provided over the years, my brother had not been called up to the pros. After college, he had been drafted by the Boston Blaze in the third round, but he'd spent the last seven years languishing in the minor leagues with a few stints in Europe.

Cole was more likely to be found partying than training, which explained his career stagnation. He wasn't too far away—Rhode Island, maybe?—but he didn't take much interest in our family or the business, and I hadn't seen him in years.

Gus and Jude were close, despite their seven-year age difference. They both worked for Dad and lived for the timber business. Both were still struggling to accept what Dad had done. I was the outsider here, the interloper.

"No thanks." I shook my head. "Wanted to hydrate before I headed home."

Daphne Elliot

"Don't do that," he said. His eyes were full of sympathy behind the lenses of his glasses. "Stay and talk to us. We live in the same tiny town, yet I never see you. This place isn't much, but it's better than your sad apartment. Eat pizza, drink a beer. We can start a fire out back later. Come on, stay."

By the time he'd finished talking, my chest was tight with emotion. Jude was a man of few words, so those few sentences were akin to an epic monologue for him. And it tugged at me. Things had been so strained and awkward. Especially given how differently we all felt about Dad.

"Things have changed so much. We're not some big happy family..." I said.

Jude put the plates down on the counter with a heavy clank and stared at me. "But why can't we be? Why can't we do things on our terms?"

I shrugged, searching for the words to formulate a response, but he wasn't finished.

"For so many years, we lived in Dad's shadow and under his control. You're not the only one spinning right now, Finn. We're all fucked up over this."

He was right, of course. I was struck with a bolt of white-hot shame at his call-out. I had been so in my head, so obsessed with the impact of Dad's actions on Merry and on myself, that I'd failed to check in with my brothers. Their careers—hell, their entire lives—had been built around Dad and Hebert Timber. They had even more to lose than I did.

Jude shuffled to the back door to let Ripley out. "Think about it. For so many years, he controlled us. Tried to mold us into what he wanted us to be. Lashed out when we didn't meet expectations." He shook his head. "Now, though? We're free of him."

I regarded him, and he watched me just as intently as we

Wood Riddance

let those words hang in the air between us. Somewhere within me, the scared eleven-year-old who'd gotten yet another bad report card was letting out a sigh of relief. The eighteen-year-old who'd been screamed at for enrolling in ROTC let his shoulders relax a little. Those versions of me and so many more had borne so much anger and disappointment from him. Maybe Jude was right. Maybe we were free.

But freedom came at a cost. It always did.

And I had a feeling we'd be paying for a long time.

Chapter 6
Adele

By the time Monday rolled around, I was calm and ready to face what lay ahead. The weekend had been quiet, as they usually were during the summer. Gagnon Lumber did the majority of its cutting during the winter when the ground was frozen. It made transport easier and minimized damage to the forest floor.

It was one of the advantages of logging in Maine. The ground stayed frozen longer in northern areas like ours, and it froze so thoroughly that we could use heavier equipment. That, of course, meant we could get the jobs done faster. Other regions, where the ground didn't freeze completely, required lighter equipment and more hours, which cut into profits and efficiency.

We had summer and fall cut sites, too, but the majority of our land was winter cut.

In Maine, spring lingered, even in late June. That meant thaw and water and mud, which was not ideal for cutting or transport or road maintenance. The crews typically spent

August and September repairing and upgrading the roads in preparation for the beginning of the season in October.

Our summers were short and, therefore, extremely busy. Along with the summer cutting, we spent the season working on our equipment so that it was all in tip-top shape when the ground froze.

Today, though, had been one of the slower days. Slow days made me even more itchy.

I would be a professional. This was my goddamn shop and my company. His presence may have been unwelcome, but I'd get through it. I always did.

Thankfully when He-Man and I had arrived at the office, he was nowhere to be seen. There was a tan, military-style backpack on the chair in the office/closet I had assigned to him, but there was no other trace of the man.

Good. I could focus.

I updated the board, checked in with Estrella, who was taking apart a front-end loader, and placed an order for a few parts with my supplier. All in all, the day wasn't a bad one.

But I should have known it wouldn't last.

I sensed him before I saw him. Mainly because He-Man got out of his memory-foam dog bed and growled. It took a lot to make my sweet baby growl like that, but the spawn of Satan would do it, for sure.

Near the end of the day, the door to the shop slammed, and heavy footsteps sounded on the cement floor. When Finn turned into my office, He-Man pounced, barking and lunging at his legs.

"What the shit?" Finn shouted, jumping back as He-Man reared up and caught his pant leg in his teeth. "What is this thing?"

"He-Man," I said firmly. "Stop. Come."

Wood Riddance

The dog froze and looked over at me, as if to ask why he couldn't bite the bad man. When I eyed him and pointed to the floor in front of me, he reluctantly backed away, then trotted over and jumped into my lap.

"Good boy," I said, burying my face in his fur and scratching his ears.

"Um. What the hell was that?"

I looked up. "You're still here?"

"Yes. What is that thing?" He frowned, looking nonplussed.

I cradled He-Man close. "This is my sweet baby, He-Man. He's very protective of me. I guess he could sense your evil."

Finn raised one brow. "That yippy little shit tried to bite my ankles."

"You seem to have survived." Shrugging, I looked him up and down mockingly. "And don't underestimate him. He's an eighteen-pound killer. Aren't you, baby?"

I scratched his ears again, always proud of my boy.

"Why are you here?" I asked when the giant of a man continued hovering.

"I work here. Henri and I worked out a plan for drone surveillance, and he wanted me to run it by you. Equipment and software are being set up now so I can get it all done quickly. While I've been waiting for that to be completed, I figured I'd get to know the other employees."

I blanched. "Why? Your position here is temporary. We'll hire a real pilot at some point."

"I am a real pilot," he said, the corner of his mouth quirking. "Ask the US Navy."

Shooting him a withering look, I huffed. "Not one I can tolerate. I'd much prefer one who isn't the spawn of a murderer."

Finn pulled up the chair directly across from my desk and sat in it. He-Man lunged at him, but I held him back, tucking him against my chest.

Placing those massive inked forearms on the surface, he leaned forward. "How many times do I have to tell you that I'm not him? I barely had a relationship with my father. I don't want trouble. I want to work."

His dark eyes met mine, and he held my gaze for a moment longer than necessary to make his point.

Heart thumping in my chest, I sat still, deliberately not responding. Because what I wanted to do was scream and throw torque wrenches at his handsome head. Instead, I held He-Man close and focused on breathing through the rage. It was late, I was tired, and I had a date with a new episode of *Succession* later.

I was gathering up the courage to kick him out of my office when my phone buzzed on the desk, right next to his giant paw.

Before I could react, he snagged it and held it up in front of him.

"Hey." I dove forward, upsetting He-Man, who hopped off my lap in the process. But he pushed his chair back and stood, examining the screen.

"Hold up," he said, his attention still fixed on the device. "These are LuvStruck alerts."

My stomach dropped and my face flamed. As if every part of me didn't already hate this guy enough, now he was going to mock me for using dating apps? Not today, Satan.

I stood and crossed my arms, going for authoritative. "Give me my fucking phone, Stretch, or I'll take it from you, and I will not be gentle."

He smirked. "That is not the threat you think it is, but here."

He held it out, but he was still halfway across the room, so I was forced to round my desk to get it back.

"Go forth and date," he said when I tore the device from his hand.

Annoyance flashing through me like a storm, I narrowed my eyes. "Is it so strange for a person to be on dating apps? Let me guess, I'm so terrible and ugly and mean that I have no business dating. Is that it?"

I was fuming, yet he only raised a brow and dropped back into the chair he'd been occupying. "Project much, She-Ra?" he teased, leaning back and spreading his legs wide. "I was only curious. Figured some lucky guy with balls of steel and a really good life insurance policy had locked you down already."

I clutched the phone with both hands. "Nope. Still looking for Mr. Right."

He chuckled. "Fascinating."

"Fuck off with your smug judgment."

He held up his hands in surrender. "No judgment here. It's rough out there. And you're talking to someone who hasn't been on a date in years. It's not like women are lining up these days, what with my father being a murderer and all."

I grinned. Finally some good news. "It warms my heart to know the women of Penobscot county have such high standards. Maybe there is hope after all."

Before I could bask in the glory of putting him down, he pushed back, the legs of his chair scraping against the floor, and stood. We were close, maybe six inches away from one another. His body took up every spare inch of space in my office, a physical reminder of how big he was.

He tilted forward a little so we were eye to eye while maintaining the distance between us and dropped his voice. "Or maybe you've been waiting for me all these years. Since that hot make-out session in my truck."

His warm breath coasted over my skin, the scent of cedar sending a shiver rippling down my spine. He was so damn tall he had to lean down to talk to me. Most men were at eye level, if not shorter. I didn't like feeling small and powerless, especially around someone like Finn, who exuded power and confidence.

All the rage I had spent the weekend tamping down reared up inside me. "Do *not* bring that up." I took a step back and relished the cool air that filled the space between us. He-Man was at my feet, sensing danger. "If you value your life, don't say another word about that night."

He scratched his beard, still not understanding the gravity of this situation. "Your face right now? It looks like you've been possessed."

Clearly, this man had a death wish.

"You joke, but I'd love to access some dark magic right now. Do you have any idea how satisfying it would be to curse you?"

He crossed his arms over his expansive chest as a slow smile spread across his face. "Don't worry, your presence enough of a curse."

"Then get the fuck out of my shop and go back to your lair," I growled, irrationally annoyed by how tight his T-shirt was. "Don't you have somewhere to be? Some kind of villain convention to attend so you can reminisce about the good old days when you could burn mouthy women at the stake?"

He moved so fast I didn't have time to react. Before I knew what was happening, I was backed up against my desk and caged between his arms. "That's where you're wrong." His voice dropped an octave, making goose bumps rise along every inch of my skin.

"I enjoy your mouth. Quite a bit."

He was so close, and he was staring at my lips so intently they tingled. "I want to feel that mouth everywhere."

Was he going to kiss me? I didn't want to find out. So I did the first thing that came to mind. I punched him, as hard as I could, in the shoulder.

He stumbled back, clutching it. "Fuck, She-Ra."

I took the opportunity to step behind my desk again. "You're lucky I didn't break your nose. Don't ever talk to me like that."

Still clutching his shoulder, he glared at me. "Don't tell me you didn't like it. Look how you're squirming. Look at the way your nipples are poking through your bra."

Crossing my arms over my chest, I hid the evidence that backed up his argument.

"Nice one, by the way. No stretchy cotton for you. That's clearly some expensive lace."

The nerve of this asshole!

"If my brothers knew you were looking at my bra, they would kill you."

He laughed again. Why was everything so funny to him?

"Oh, please. Like you'd pass up the opportunity to do the job yourself. You'd probably be angry if they didn't include you in the fun of dismembering me."

He was right. Dick. I couldn't tell my brothers about any of this because they would be furious at Finn *and* at me. Then they'd have lots of questions and get all protective and shit. I had been beating those instincts out of them for decades, and this would be a major barrier to progress. No, Finn was right. I had to handle this myself. As usual.

He took another step back, as if preparing to leave, and a

hint of relief flickered to life in me. Good. Get him out before more damage was done.

But then he paused and tilted his head to one side. Even in the terrible fluorescent lighting, this guy was as gorgeous as a model. Like one of those super-hot guys who posted wood-chopping thirst traps on TikTok.

"Last year," he said, looking down at his hands, "after what happened with Remy..."

A chill ran through me. It was such a scary time.

"I was working up the courage to ask you out." Lifting his head, he regarded me with those dark, intense eyes. "Would you have said yes?" In the blink of an eye, he had transformed from jovial Viking, hell-bent on driving me crazy, to vulnerable.

At the time, I was so filled with gratitude that I probably would have. Because nothing was more important to me than my family. And Finn had defied his own father to help mine. That version of him? I still held on to it, but I knew I had to let that go.

"I can't believe it was only a year ago."

He nodded, focus still locked on me. "So much has changed. So much has happened."

An ache bloomed in my chest as I held his gaze. "I would have said yes," I said softly. "I will always owe you for that. For Remy."

He shook his head. "You don't owe me anything. You can call me any day, any time, and I'll be there." Tucking his chin, he dropped his attention to the desk between us and ran his hands through his hair. "Is there any chance?" His words were barely a whisper.

"No. Not anymore," I said, both relieved and sad to make my intentions clear. "Not after..."

He nodded again. "Yeah. My dad."

And as I stood there, witness to the pain on his earnest face. I felt it.

The thaw.

As much as I wanted to despise the man and everything he represented, I couldn't. After losing my dad and almost losing my brothers, holding my ground on one side of a silly family feud didn't seem worth it. I couldn't forgive, and I'd never forget, but I would tolerate. I would do it for the business and for my dad, who truly believed in giving people second chances.

I had to do better. "Let's get through this. Work together."

Swallowing thickly, he dipped his chin. "Yeah."

"No flirting, no innuendos, no teasing. Okay?"

He winced. "That's gonna be a challenge. Maybe if you agreed to stop wearing those cute outfits…"

I looked down at myself and held out my arms. "Um, I'm covered in axle grease. Trust me. This isn't me trying."

He chuckled and held out a hand. "Truce?"

I slid my palm against his, trying to ignore how big and strong it was and the way my heart jumped a tiny bit when our skin touched.

After holding on for way too long. I dropped his hand. Willing my walls to come back up.

"Now that we've settled that, get the fuck out of my office."

Chapter 7
Finn

"Dad."

I blinked up at the ceiling, confused.

"Dad." The word registered with me this time.

I jumped up to find Merry standing in the doorway, silhouetted by a dim light coming from down the hall.

"Everything okay?" I said, trying to force my eyes to adjust to the dark room.

"I can't go to camp tomorrow."

"Okay, sweets," I said, still waiting for my brain to boot up. "Are you sick? I'll find the thermometer." In four strides, I was standing on the cold tile floor of the bathroom and flipping on the harsh fluorescent light. *Shit, that was blinding.*

"No. I'm not sick."

She followed me, looking so small and scared in her unicorn pajamas with her dark hair a mess.

I ushered her out and toward the kitchen, where I got each of us a glass of water. "Wanna tell me what's up?" I asked, taking our drinks to the living room. I settled on the couch quietly, giving her some time to respond.

Parenting a tween was not for the weak, and I had learned the hard way to give her time and space to put her concerns into words.

She plopped onto the cushion and curled up against me. "I don't want to go. The kids there are so mean. And Bella's family is on vacation, so I have no friends at all."

That statement was punctuated by a dramatic hair toss.

Pulling her closer, I murmured, "Mom mentioned things were tough."

"People are so mean. Kids don't wanna be my friend because of Grandpa Mitch. Some of them laugh at me. They say that I'm gonna be a jailbird too."

My heart lurched, and I had to keep myself from going rigid. She didn't need to see how angry I was at kids her age. While asshole kids had always existed and always would, this was poking at a very raw, very fresh wound for both of us.

"Abby Ward said our whole family is going to hell."

I rolled my eyes and huffed. The Wards were all dicks. I supposed that kind of shit was genetic.

"Things were so different," she said. "Before."

I pulled her closer and dropped a kiss to the crown of her head. "I know, baby. And I'm so sorry. I want to fix this for you so badly."

"Mom says it will blow over."

I closed my eyes, praying that it would. But this town had a long memory. I wasn't certain it ever would.

Stroking her hair, I took a moment to gather my thought so I could give her a dad pep talk. But then she did the thing. The thing I can't handle. She cried.

Seeing any woman cry, no matter her age, made it almost impossible to think rationally. And when the person crying was my little girl? Every instinct in my body screamed "fix this," and I couldn't function rationally.

So that was how I ended up agreeing to let her skip camp.

After finally getting her back to bed in her room, I paced the living room. Not that there was much room for pacing. And I had to be careful. We were on the third floor of an old brick building, so sound traveled. And the guy who lived below me, Dylan, was not my biggest fan.

I had nothing against him, but he was Remy Gagnon's best friend and brother-in-law. Since the day I moved in two years ago, he had kept his distance. I'd never had a beef with him, and for most of our lives, we'd coexisted pleasantly. These days, though, he was one more Lovewell citizen who hated me.

I checked to make sure Merry was truly asleep before killing all the lights. Her bedroom was tiny. Like barely big enough for a twin bed. But I'd let her decorate it herself. That was how we'd ended up with a giant glittering chandelier, yellow ruffled bedding, and framed Taylor Swift posters covering almost every inch of wall space. I couldn't give her the kind of home Alicia and Mike could, but she seemed content when she was here.

Tonight, we had made tacos. Then we'd danced around to our fave T-Swift songs—hers was "Anti-Hero," and mine was "Love Story." What could I say? I was sentimental. Then we fit in a few games of chess before bed.

Working through the restlessness that had reemerged even though it was the middle of the night, I continued my quiet pacing. What would I do with her tomorrow? I was set to start installing the drone mapping software on the computer system and I needed to get the survey plotted out first thing. It would take a week or two, and then I'd get the drones up in the air.

I would have preferred to be in the air myself, but the

drones were cost effective and quick. Once we'd mapped out the new land, I'd get up there and take some photos so we could identify areas that needed repair and others where we could pursue further development.

It wasn't glamorous work, but it was an improvement from what I'd been doing at Hebert Timber. Before Dad was arrested, I'd spent most of my work hours shuttling guys back and forth to the camps. It could be entertaining at times, but it was monotonous. I itched for something new, a chance to push myself, but I feared I'd left all those opportunities behind when I left the Navy.

Could I bring her to Gagnon? She was ten, and she could handle herself. She went to Alicia's office frequently. We could make it work. I had only started, and I didn't want to make a bad impression, but my baby girl was hurting.

I came to a stop and closed my eyes, mostly worried about one person's opinion.

Would Adele be mad? Would Merry like her? And why did I even care?

We rolled into Gagnon Lumber early with donuts. I had confided in Merry that the folks at my new job were not exactly thrilled to have me there. I didn't want her to be caught off guard if we encountered someone who was unkind.

"Dad, bring food. Everyone likes the guy who brings snacks," she'd declared, like it was the most obvious thing in the world.

So we hit the bakery on the way in, grabbing two dozen designer donuts that I hoped would keep my coworkers happy while I staged an impromptu take-your-daughter-to-work day.

Wood Riddance

Did Adele like donuts? Probably not. If that ass was any indication, she ate chicken breasts and barbells for breakfast, not fried dough stuffed with sugar and cream. But it didn't change how excited I was about the prospect of watching her lick icing off her fingers.

Inside the main office, Merry said hello to each and every person she encountered and offered donuts all around before we finally made it to the shop. Charlie and Estrella were already working, and the sound of a popular boy band song from the '90s echoed through the massive garage.

"This place is cool," Merry said. She was wide-eyed as she took in the carefully labeled tools, parts, and bins that lined the walls.

A tractor took up the space in the middle of the work area, the hood open to reveal the engine inside. It was as big as most cars and probably more complicated.

My knowledge of vehicles with wheels was limited, and I did not envy the work this team did. The shop at Hebert Timber was much bigger but far less organized. The walls were plastered with posters of half-naked women, and every surface was covered in cigarette butts and oil stains older than I was.

No wonder Adele was able to get all this work done early *and* under budget with a limited crew. The workspace she'd created here was clean, efficient, and respectful.

It hadn't occurred to me until now how much Merry could benefit from spending a little time here. This was a place where women worked in traditionally masculine positions and did the jobs far better than most men could. She'd seen the inside of Alicia's law firm a million times, so I was grateful for the contrast.

Charlie sauntered up when she caught sight of us. She was in her early forties, with a gray streak in her dark ponytail, and was by far the friendliest of the bunch. "Good to see you, Hebert," she said, offering a hand to Merry.

She was a single mom, and I'd seen her at school functions a few times with her sons, but I didn't know much else about her. Unlike Estrella, who avoided me, Charlie made an effort, and that meant a lot to me. Being here was hard enough without the constant reminder of how unwelcome I was.

Merry wandered around the open space, munching on a donut and studying all the strange parts and tools in the shop. Her eyes widened when she saw an acetylene torch hanging on the wall, and she stopped in front of it, head tilted back so she could assess it.

Before I could steer her into my office with her books and art supplies, Adele came striding through the shop, ponytail bouncing and eyes narrowed.

I stood up a little straighter, not sure how to greet her after our interaction the previous day.

She ignored me. Instead, she zeroed in on Merry. Wearing a pair of bike shorts and a baggy Racine T-shirt knotted at the waist, she looked like she'd come from the gym. Even sweaty, she was insanely gorgeous. Her proximity alone made my heart rate tick up a little. This interaction felt important, somehow, and I couldn't figure out why.

I needed today to go smoothly.

Adele squatted down and held out a hand. "Adele Gagnon."

Merry smiled at her, delighted to be treated like a grown-up. "Meredith LaVoie Hebert," she said in a very formal voice, but then she added, "everyone calls me Merry."

Adele smiled at her.

"I hope it's okay," I said, stumbling over my words. "She wanted to tag along."

"Not a problem. My niece and nephew are always running around here. I can't help it that I'm so much more interesting than Henri." She shrugged, a hint of a smirk tugging on one side of her mouth.

"So you're hanging with us today, huh?" she asked Merry, scratching at her chin. "You look a lot smarter than your dad."

Merry giggled at that, bringing a hand up to cover her mouth.

"Even so," Adele went on, "I'll go over the house rules, just in case."

Straightening up and donning a serious expression, my daughter nodded.

"You can ask anyone any question you want. We'll teach you whatever you want to learn. But do not touch anything, lift anything, or jump off anything. Got it?"

"Yes."

"Welcome to the shop," Adele said, avoiding my grateful smile. "It's Monday, which means Charlie picks the music, and she's all about boy bands."

Merry's face lit up. "Like BTS?"

"Hell yeah," Charlie shouted from across the room. She gave Merry the finger heart signal. "I'm a member of the Army."

Merry was in her element, looking around and studying all the tools, machines, and tables. And apparently Adele. "You're tall," Merry said, openly staring.

I cringed a bit, but Adele seemed entertained.

"Yup."

"That's so cool. I'm tall. Or at least I will be. That's what Dr. Smith says. My dad is super tall, and my mom is short. But I think I take after him." Merry sidled up beside me and stood on her tiptoes, marking her height on my chest.

"What about you? Do you have a tall mom or a tall dad or what?"

Adele laughed. "They are both tall-ish."

"Cool. My dad always makes me watch tall-girl sports. Like basketball and volleyball. I think he wants me to feel good about being the tallest kid in my class, but I really don't mind."

"Good," Adele said firmly, offering her fist for Merry to bump. "Being tall is awesome."

The smile that spread over Merry's face made my stomach clench. She was positively vibrating with excitement. "Do you like donuts?" she asked. "We brought donuts. I want to make sure my dad makes lots of friends at his new job."

"That's so sweet of you," she replied. "And smart. Your dad isn't great at making new friends, is he?"

"Hey." Despite my protestation, Merry and Adele laughed, not even bothering to turn my way. And I liked it. Maybe a bit too much. The tall, gorgeous, badass woman conspiring with my daughter against me. What should be terrifying was actually pretty adorable. Shit. My crush was not going to get any easier after this.

Adele spun, ready to head to her office from the looks of it, but she stopped and peered at Merry over her shoulder. "There's someone else you should meet." She let out a whistle.

That damn dog came running in response. "This is He-Man."

The tiny demon dog trotted over and stopped a few feet away. He looked up at me and let out a small growl, his teeth peeking out from between his gums.

I could barely hear the sound, though, because Merry let out an ear-piercing scream. "Ooh. Oh my God, I love him. He's *so* cute. Can I pet him?"

She was on the floor before I could warn her that Cujo had

fangs. But to my relief, his response to her affection was to lick her face rather than attack like he had when I'd met him.

"I *love* him."

"Good," Adele said. "You can keep him company for me. I have a lot of work to do, and he gets angry when I don't play with him."

I caught her eye, surprised she'd finally allowed herself to look my way, and gave her a head nod, grateful for her kindness to my daughter and her willingness to understand my predicament.

"Can I give him some of my donut? This one has bacon on it."

Adele dipped her chin. "Sure, but only a small piece."

Merry ran happily toward the donuts with He-Man yapping at her heels.

"I'm really sorry," I said, raking a hand through my hair. "She didn't want to go to camp this morning, and I wasn't sure whether this would be okay with you."

She regarded me for a moment, almost as if she'd forgotten I was still here. "It's fine. She's way less annoying than you are."

And then she turned and walked away without another word.

And I couldn't tear my eyes off her.

After a quick meeting with Henri and his forestry consultant, I headed back to the shop. Merry had been given strict instructions to stay inside my closet-sized office. We'd brought along a book, her iPad, and an arsenal of snacks, so I figured she'd be entertained for the thirty minutes I was gone.

Though when I stepped into the tiny space, she was nowhere to be seen.

I did a lap, looking for her behind large equipment. Eventually, I worked up the nerve to check Adele's office, and that's where I found her, curled up on the love seat, asleep. He-Man was in her lap, his head nestled in the crook of her arm.

Adele was sitting at her desk, her hair in a knot on top of her head, typing furiously on her laptop.

My stomach dropped. "I'm sorry," I said, striding toward Merry. "I hope she didn't bother you too much."

Adele shook her head and turned her gaze on me for an instant before going right back to the screen in front of her. "No bother at all. She's cool. Must get it from Alicia."

Dropping into the chair on the other side of her desk, I watched her work. Tiny wisps of blond hair curled at the nape of her graceful neck. She wore a gold pendant that looked like two intertwined gears.

"Done staring?" she asked, directing her attention to me again.

I coughed. "Yeah. Thanks for this." I held out a hand, indicating my sleeping daughter.

She nodded. "You gonna tell me what's wrong?"

I leaned back in the chair and cocked a brow. "Do you care? Or do you derive power from my pain?"

She pressed her lips together and rolled her eyes. "That's exactly it. Tell me all about how miserable and shitty your life is. It'll charge me up for the week."

I didn't want to smile, but the excitement that flashed in her eyes as she insulted me was captivating. Adele was a live current. She practically shot off dangerous sparks any time I came near, but that wasn't much of a deterrent. I wanted to get closer, despite knowing that I would get burned.

I tilted forward, putting my forearms on her desk and lowering my voice. "It's Merry."

Her eyes widened, and she sat a little straighter. "She okay?"

"She's having a hard time." I watched as her expression changed. The fire in her eyes banked and was replaced by true compassion. The rapid switch threw me, but I kept going. "We moved back here to give her stability. So she'd have the love of her extended family. Alicia and I grew up here, and our families are here. It seemed like the best choice. But it's been unbearable since my dad's arrest. For a second this spring, it felt like things were dying down, but now that the trial is coming up, it's all come back with a vengeance."

"Are kids teasing her?"

I nodded. "Living here feels impossible most days. She's being teased a lot. And the comments? These kids can be downright nasty. Then there are the adults who shoot us dirty looks and gossip about my family nonstop."

"That's fucking bullshit," she said. The fury was back, though she kept her voice low to keep from disturbing my little girl, who was still sleeping serenely on the love seat. "She's only ten."

My chest squeezed in response. I appreciated her fury on Merry's behalf. "We can't escape it. If it's not hostility we're confronted with, then it's pity and whispers. Rumors."

She closed her eyes and let out a long breath, like she understood. And she probably did better than most. Because she had been the recipient of plenty of pity. The small-town rumor mill was inescapable and endless.

"People suck," she said quietly.

Usually, my interactions with this woman were nonstop.

Shouting, wild gestures, and the exhilarating feeling of sparring with a worthy adversary.

But in this moment, she was still, quiet. She listened. And there wasn't an ounce of pity in her eyes. Only compassion. So I kept talking. "If it were up to me, we'd leave and never look back. But her mom is settled and happy here. We came back so Merry could have the best possible childhood. But right now, that seems impossible."

"You're brave." For once, she wasn't lobbing an insult at me. No, there was no fire behind her words, no anger in her eyes. And I felt that compliment in my bones.

Unaccustomed to her kindness, I opened my mouth to make some kind of quip. But I clamped my jaw shut. It was just like me to ruin a human moment, to bluster over the vulnerability I had shown.

"I'm trying," I said instead, my heart heavy in my chest. "To fix everything. To make it right for Merry. But I'm just so tired."

"That's why you're here. Working for us." It wasn't a question.

I nodded and held her gaze, hoping she could sense my sincerity. Sense how important this was. "I need the job. And I'm trying to make it work for Merry."

"I respect that."

We sat like that, regarding one another, for an uncomfortably long time. What the hell was happening? Were we becoming friends? My heart pounded as I studied her.

My palms were sweaty, and I could feel the weight of her gaze on my skin. My brain spun with things to say, but I found myself completely tongue tied. So I stood, breaking the spell, and woke Merry gently. The day was coming to an end, and I was due to drop her off at Alicia's tonight, where I was sure to get an earful about letting her come to work with me.

Wood Riddance

Once she'd stretched and yawned and hopped up from the love seat, Merry gave both He-Man and Adele giant hugs and said her goodbyes.

As we were walking out, I turned to close the office door behind me.

"Stretch?" Adele said. "You're doing a great job with her."

With a silent nod, I pulled the door closed.

She may have possessed the personality of a fire-breathing dragon, but Adele's heart was good. And that only made this situation more dangerous for me.

Chapter 8
Finn

The day had been a long one, and Merry's troubles weighed heavily on me. So the last thing I wanted to do was attend a family meeting with my brothers. It would only add to that weight. But when Owen texted, he swore that it was important. He was doing all he could to work out the financial side of things for us, while I was messing around with drones and flirting with my sort-of boss.

So I guess I could hear him out.

Merry was bopping around in the back seat of the truck, energized after her nap with that yappy dog.

"You should ask her on a date," she said, taking her headphones off.

"Who?"

"Miss Gagnon. She's nice and has a dog. And she's tall, like you."

The smile that spread across my face was a genuine one, even if they'd been hard to muster lately. I appreciated her priorities.

"Not gonna do that, kiddo. She's my boss. And it's

complicated."

With a hum, she watched the scenery go by out her window, like she was considering my argument, but after a moment of silence, she ignored it completely. One of her go-to negotiation tactics.

"I mean it, Dad. She's a little bit scary. Which is a good match for you."

"Why do you say that?"

"Because you look scary too. On the outside. You've got all those tattoos, and you're super tall. But on the inside, you are so sweet and awesome. I think Miss Gagnon is like that too."

My heart just about melted. This kid was constantly rocking my world. She did not miss a single detail, and her heart was so big.

I turned down Main Street, trying really hard not to pull over and give her a hug and complain that she was growing up too fast. These days, I was lamenting that constantly. I swore that five minutes ago, she was crawling, or we were worried that she wasn't speaking in full sentences yet.

Now she was doling out wisdom and routinely kicking my ass.

"Mom is really happy with Mike. And they're gonna get married."

"I'm happy for them." My reply was an honest and easy one. Merry had adapted well to Mike and, as far as I could tell, wasn't pining for her mom and me to get back together. "Your mom is my best friend," I said, glancing at her in the rear-view mirror. "I want her to have a wonderful husband and a wonderful life."

"But what about you, Dad? I want you to have a wife. That way you can have a wonderful life too."

Jesus. I almost swerved off the road at the certainty in her tone.

"I don't need a wife."

"Sure you do. I'm already ten. I'm gonna grow up and go to college and become a teacher and a singer and a fashion designer and a veterinarian someday. I'll be busy. You need a wife to keep you company when I'm gone."

I smiled at her in the rear-view mirror. "Sounds like you will be super busy."

"That's why you need a wife. But I think you should start with a girlfriend."

"That sounds wise." I nodded, biting back a smile.

"Yes. Kind of like how I keep asking for a dog and you tell me to start with a goldfish, even though that's boring and not really what I want."

Her logic was impeccable, and every one of her arguments, though unrealistic, made my heart swell a little more. My girl was nothing if not persistent and thoughtful.

"That's why you should go on a date with Miss Gagnon and see if she wants to be your girlfriend."

"Mm-hmm." I hummed noncommittally, desperate for this conversation to end and relieved when the sign outside Alicia's neighborhood came into view ahead.

Merry left it at that as I navigated down the street and pulled into the driveway, praying the conversation was over.

"And," Merry said, grabbing her backpack from the seat beside her, clearly not as ready as I was to leave this topic behind, "if aliens invade, she could fight them off and protect you."

"I can protect myself." Leaning down, I gave her a hug and a kiss on the head.

"I know that, Dad. But wouldn't you want someone to help you fight off the aliens?"

With that final question, she turned and skipped toward the front door, leaving me confused and exhausted.

"We're going to have to sell. There's no way around it." Owen's voice was tinny through the phone's speaker, but that didn't hide the seriousness of his tone. Jude, Gus, and I sat around the table, with Owen on speaker.

Cole had been included on the text chain, but he hadn't bothered responding. And Noah had appointed Jude his proxy, completely checking out of his responsibility. Typical.

Of all my brothers, I was closest to Owen. Probably because we'd had the same goal growing up: get out. And we both had. He was smart and focused, and he'd always known what he wanted.

A stable career, big city life, and plenty of distance from our dad.

He was an accountant by trade and was the CFO of one of the largest construction companies in Boston.

He was tall, but that's where the physical similarities between the two of us ended.

His hair was darker, and he wore Clark Kent–style glasses.

He could chop wood and climb trees like the rest of us, but that wasn't his style.

He was all skyscrapers and trendy restaurants. His condo in Seaport had a wall of windows that looked out over Boston Harbor.

He was also the only one of my brothers who'd visited me from time to time when I was stationed in Virginia. And he loved to spoil his niece. Not that she acted even the slightest bit spoiled.

"We sold off a bunch of land and machinery," Gus protested. "That had to have helped get us out of the red." His normally tan face was pale. He was taking this hard, and I didn't envy him. This was his life. Carrying on the family legacy meant everything to him. He had taken Dad's betrayal the hardest, and he'd struggled to come to terms with what the man had done. He wanted to believe that it was all a giant mistake, that Dad was innocent, but deep down, he understood that it wasn't. Didn't make the pill any easier to swallow, though.

He was the oldest, and he was a quiet, contemplative guy. He lived on several acres in a vintage Airstream he had gutted and renovated a few years ago, enjoying his solitude and the quiet of the forest. If everything fell apart, I truly wasn't sure how he'd cope.

"And Finn's flying for the Gagnons," Jude said. "That'll cover the plane expenses."

"I can do this," Gus said. "We can turn things around. Dad kept me on the outside for so long, but now that I've got more control, I can fix this. I can run the business."

Owen sighed, the sound of it crackling down the line. He hated this. Crushing dreams. Always being the voice of reason.

"I'm not doubting you, brother. But the books are a mess. I can't tell which transactions are legit or which income came from Dad's criminal empire."

Every time I thought about it, my stomach roiled and bile rose in my throat. My dad. A murderer. A drug dealer.

There was no love lost between us. I had kept my distance from a young age.

When I was a kid, our family looked picture perfect from the outside. My mom truly was a superhuman, wrangling five boys, putting home-cooked meals on the table every night, and volunteering at school and with various organizations around town, all while keeping the massive house my dad had built for her spotless.

My dad was my hero, at least in my younger years. He'd taken his grandfather's business and had made it a huge success. During a time when most people around here were suffering, Hebert Timber grew and thrived. We had grown up having everything we ever wanted: trips to Disney World, the best sports equipment, and parents who doted on us.

But that only lasted a short time.

I was seven years old when my world fell apart.

My mom and dad sat us down and told us they were getting a divorce.

Turned out my dad had been having an affair with his twenty-year-old secretary. And she was pregnant with my youngest brother, Cole.

Mom filed for divorce, moved us to a much smaller house, went back to school, and got her nursing degree. She did almost all of the child rearing while my dad went off and married Tammi.

He was in and out of our lives when it was convenient for him, plying us with extravagant gifts rather than the time and attention we craved. Putting up a compelling front so that just about everyone we knew believed he played an active role in raising us, yet only involving himself when it suited him and leaving my mom to do all the hard work.

Mom pushed through it all, building a life for herself and for us. She was more of a parent to Cole than either of people who'd contributed to his DNA, since his own mom wasn't particularly interested in parenting. My saint of a mother put aside her hurt to love him like she loved the rest of us. She raised the five of us, sometimes Cole, and she never complained, always had a hug and a smile for us and a batch of cookies in the oven.

And she taught us to cook, do laundry, mow the lawn, and take care of one another and our neighbors. Still to this day, I cannot imagine how she did it all. But every time I think about it, I'm reminded of just how much I owed her.

On the other hand, I had no delusions that my father was a good guy. We had never been close and he came in and out of our lives when it was convenient to him. After Merry was born, I'd hoped to somehow bridge the gap, if only for her sake. Now? There was nothing to salvage. Except the company that bore our name.

Which we were definitely going to lose.

"You know what that dirty money means?" Owen asked. "It means the feds are gonna swoop in. They're gonna seize the shit out of everything we've got. Most of Dad's assets are frozen. Thankfully, the structure of the timber company gives us some leeway to at least try to keep things going. But the houses, the cars, the investments?"

"We don't need that shit. We need our land and our equipment. We can figure the rest out."

Owen scoffed. "Did you know that Dad had accounts in the Cayman Islands?"

Of course he did. The fucker did everything he could to evade paying taxes.

"They're all frozen right now," Owen explained. "If he's found guilty—and let's face it, that's a certainty at this point—then they'll take it all. It's called forfeiture. And the feds are excellent at it."

Jude threw up his hands. "So we're screwed." He took off his glasses and used his T-shirt—one that read: *Zombies eat brains; don't worry, you're safe*—to clean them for what had to have been the tenth time tonight. He was beyond done with this conversation and was about five minutes away from kicking us out of his house. Ripley, sensing his distress, padded over and put her head on his lap.

"Grandpa's land trust is our only option. It's what allowed us to sell that acreage," Owen explained patiently. "Those funds can keep the business going, fund payroll, and keep a limited number of trucks on the road. For the time being, at least."

"We're also down a large percentage of employees," Jude added.

"They'll come back once things level out. The people here need the work." Gus pounded his fist on the small table. "We've got to at least try. What else will we do? Timber is in our blood. This company was built by our ancestors. We can't just walk away," he shouted, which was rare for my oldest brother. He was mellow by default.

But his anger was only fueling mine. Owen was the number cruncher, and he was doing all he could for our family. He wasn't the one rotting in prison. The man who'd destroyed our family's reputation and had just about destroyed the business too.

Gus was taking his anger out on Owen when he didn't deserve it. "We don't have a choice. Dad did. And he fucked us," I spat.

But of course, Owen had it handled. He dealt with assholes every day. "I wasn't the one who flushed the family legacy down the toilet and contributed to the greatest public health crisis of our time," he explained, his voice surprisingly calm. "I have a job. I have a life. I'm doing this for you guys. Not for Dad. Not for Uncle Paul. For my brothers. Because I love you."

Wood Riddance

Gus got up and paced around the small kitchen, but he kept his mouth shut.

"I've been out a long time and I will not get dragged back in," Owen said.

In my periphery, Jude nodded. We weren't going to pull him back here. My favorite thing about Owen was that he did not bullshit. He was always honest and always up-front, even in his hatred of Lovewell and my father. So as much as his report on the business hurt, as much as it was gutting Gus, I trusted him.

I clapped my hands, the sound loud in the space that had gone silent moments before. "So we sell." It was the inevitable outcome.

Gus glared at me. Jude continued to pet Ripley and ignored the conversation entirely.

"If only it were that easy," Owen said. "This company is in tatters. The books are a shit show. There's a lot of work to be done if we want to attract a serious buyer."

"Jesus Fucking Christ," Jude shouted. With that, he stood abruptly, his chair scraping harshly across the floor, and strode out the back door with Ripley on his heels.

Gus followed suit, clearly unwilling to discuss the next steps.

I leaned back, running my hands through my hair. "Looks like it's just you and me, Owen."

Despite my mom's best efforts to instill in us the love and loyalty of a tight-knit family, we were splintering. And it gutted me to witness the way my father and his fucked-up legacy were coming between us.

But the battle lines had been drawn.

And I knew what side I was on.

Chapter 9
Adele

"**D**o you think maybe you just date terrible guys?" Parker reclined on the chaise lounge, lifting her sunglasses and giving me a pointed look.

We'd congregated on my back patio, which looked out at my garden. Thursday night girls' night had become our tradition. My sisters-in-law had insisted, and I had felt too guilty to decline. Alice usually hosted, and Hazel, Parker, and I joined, with my niece Goldie making occasional appearances.

But tonight, Alice had some important principal business to attend to, so it was Parker, her best friend Liv, Hazel, and me. For the first time, I'd invited all of them over. Parker was here all the time, but I still struggled with having people in my space. Nothing like a night with the girls to force me out of my comfort zone.

At first, I fought it. Even when Alice did all the hosting. It was too much hassle, and I didn't want to be forced into bonding. I was a loner, always had been, and I'd always been good with that. I had my crew. We were all close and worked well together.

But then Parker dragged me into this. And I had to admit, it wasn't terrible.

There was always wine, and Alice was a fantastic cook. Goldie, my eight-year-old niece, often tagged along, and she was hilarious. The four of us were all so different, but it felt good to have girlfriends. Our conversations were random and off the wall at times, but being with them got me out of my own head.

"Probably." My track record was shit. I wouldn't argue with that. "But it's not like there are a lot of single guys in Lovewell, or even the surrounding areas. And I did try for a while."

I handed Parker a glass of chilled rosé from the bottle I'd pulled out of the wine fridge—hey, this was my house. I could have whatever I wanted.

"You did. No one would ever accuse you of not putting yourself out there," Hazel said, raising her glass of sparkling water in my direction. "You have more bad date stamina than any woman I've ever met."

Growing up, I idolized my father. What I failed to notice, though, was that my mother was the glue that held our family together.

And he loved her. Damn. I'd never once doubted that my parents loved each other. And that example, of a love that lasted and grew and evolved, had stuck with me.

That was why I hadn't completely given up on finding a partner. Because I knew what was possible.

But the road to finding that person had been bumpy since the beginning.

Boys hadn't shown much interest in me in high school, and I'd always had to make the first move.

I was "intimidating," according to many. In reality, I

believed it had more to do with not being the ideal type of woman.

Perky and *cute* and *sweet* were words that had never been used to describe me. I had sharp edges and an even sharper tongue. I was taller and stronger than most guys. And while that didn't bother me in the least, I'd found that it narrowed my options in the dating pool dramatically.

I approached dating like I did most things. With unmatched intensity and more than a little insanity. It was no secret that women like me needed to work harder at this than others.

At a young age, I learned that I had to take what I could get. Girls like me—tall, strong, opinionated—were never chosen first unless sports were involved. And while that truth stung even today, this tough reality was a hell of a lot better than changing myself for a guy. I'd accepted long ago that I was an acquired taste, and I dated accordingly. But lately, I had grown tired of putting in all the effort only to be disappointed over and over again. So I'd put myself on an indefinite dating hiatus.

"How long has it been?" Liv asked, twirling a lock of red hair. She was from Portland, and she looked like some kind of forest nymph. Long red hair, massive blue eyes, and that kind of artsy style that no normal woman could ever pull off.

Strangely enough, she wrote grisly crime thrillers for a living, and I'd enjoyed every one of them immensely. Since Parker had moved here permanently, Liv had become a frequent visitor to our town. Most everyone here had read her books by now, and it was not uncommon to sit in the diner and hear them debating theories about the identity of the murderer in each one.

"A while." I reclined in the chair, surveying the flowers in my garden. It was almost July, and things were finally perking up. We were about a month away from full garden glory, but I was feeling pretty proud of myself at the moment. "I needed a break." It had been almost a year. Not that they needed to know that.

"Jake?" Hazel asked.

"Yeah. He got back with his ex." I did not mention that he did so on the day of my brother Henri's wedding, when he was scheduled to be my date and meet my entire family.

"What about the other guy? The dude who was into Latin?"

"He was a Latin professor," I corrected, taking in the oranges and purples of the beginnings of a beautiful sunset. "And don't ask."

"Why not? It was so promising. He was hot, and he was super into you."

I sat up and sighed. "On our second date. He told me that he is a cuckold."

Liv sputtered and choked on her wine. Beside her, Parker patted her back, but she never took her attention off me.

Hazel looked thoroughly confused. "What is that?"

God, she was so innocent sometimes.

I shrugged. "He told me that, in order to be in a relationship with him, I'd have to agree to have sex with another man while he watched."

Hazel's eyes bugged out of her skull. "But why?"

"Apparently that's what he needs to be happy..."

"It's a kink," Liv added. "Nothing wrong with it."

"Not at all," I said. "I consider myself pretty open-minded, but that one in particular isn't for me." And maybe it hurt my pride a little. Maybe it was silly or old-fashioned, but I wanted a possessive kind of love. A man who wanted me and would never even consider sharing. I'd yet to experience that type of devotion or protectiveness. I had always been disposable.

"It's not for me either," Parker said, then she snorted. "Could you imagine your brother letting anyone look at me, never mind do other stuff?"

Hazel threw her head back and laughed. "Girl, I feel that."

With a shudder, I gagged. I loved these girls, but they never stopped bringing up shit like that, no matter how many times I reminded them that they were talking about my brothers.

Thankfully, Liv moved the conversation along. "There's nothing wrong with being single. Do you really want to give up your independence so you can be shackled to some guy who can't be bothered to lift the toilet seat?"

She had a point.

"And this house." She sat up straighter and waved a hand wildly. "Look at this place. Look at what you've accomplished on your own."

Clinking her wineglass with mine, she shot me a smug smile. I did love my house. It was my space, my sanctuary. If I wanted a pink couch, I got a pink couch. And if I wanted to blow a stupid amount of money on a wine fridge, then I could. Because I was free. And although it could get lonely at times, things could certainly be worse.

He-Man jumped into my lap and hit me with a set of stereotypical puppy dog eyes, so I fed him a piece of very expensive Gouda.

"How are things going with He Who Must Not Be Named?" Parker asked.

Her question made my stomach drop. Dammit. I did *not* want to talk about him with the rest of this group. With a scowl, I threw a cracker at her to make sure she understood my annoyance.

Liv looked up from her phone, her eyes wide and curious. "Catch me up."

"It's nothing," I mumbled into my wineglass.

Every eye was still trained on me, and every one of them wore looks of anticipation. Even He-Man wasn't buying it.

"Henri hired Finn Hebert, military hero, pilot, and lumber Viking," Parker explained, garnering another glare from me. "For obvious reasons, this distresses Adele."

"Ooh," Liv crowed, scooting closer. "You had me at lumber Viking. Is he your ex?"

"No," I snapped. "He's a Hebert. His father—" I clamped my mouth shut, trying to rein in my fury.

Silence fell over the group as each of my friends looked from one another to me. The only sounds came from the crickets and the frogs while they waited for me to continue. And dammit if every one of them wasn't wearing an expression full of pity. Finn was right. It was the worst. "Anyway. We've always disliked one another. Now it's even more than that, obviously." I waved my hands. "But according to my brothers, we need a pilot. And for some reason, they've tasked me with babysitting his giant, obnoxious ass."

I gulped my wine, ready to move on from talk of Finn Hebert and his shit family. It was hard enough dealing with him in my space each day. I didn't need the ghost of him hanging around after hours too. Yes, he kept a low profile and he wasn't in the shop full time, but his presence lingered, nonetheless, and it was messing with my head.

"There's more to the story," Hazel added, raising one brow.

"What?" Liv asked.

"Last year, Remy and I were in danger." She clutched the compass pendant around her neck, the one that had belonged to my great-grandmother. "Finn Hebert came to our rescue."

Wood Riddance

Liv was fanning herself. "Holy shit."

"Yeah. Even though his dad forbade it, when Adele asked, he jumped into his plane, no questions asked."

The terror of that day bubbles up inside me, threatening to cut off my airway. I had been in my shop, like always. Paz had come over from the offices to tell me that Hazel had gone missing after the cabin she and Remy had found had been ransacked. Remy took off on one of the ATVs in search of her, and we lost track of him for almost a full day.

It was terrifying. There had clearly been drug traffickers in the area, and for hours, we worried Remy and Hazel had been kidnapped or worse. Eventually, we got the call that they were safe but stranded in a remote part of the forest that was unreachable by the roads.

Paz called Mitch Hebert, looking for assistance. Hebert Timber was the only one of the four logging companies in the area with planes and a pilot. Without an ounce of care, Mitch insisted his equipment was not available to help us.

The second Paz relayed that information, I called Finn. Forty minutes later, we were in the air, headed to find Remy and Hazel, who had hiked to meet us at a remote lake. He didn't hesitate when I called. Didn't ask questions. I told him my family was in danger, and he showed up for us. I don't remember much about the flight, aside from my terror and how comfortable and capable Finn looked piloting the plane.

That night, after Remy and Hazel had returned safely, Finn and I stood outside Henri's cabin. Few words were spoken. Hell, we'd barely spoken that entire day, but something passed between us. Gratitude. Or maybe some kind of deeper understanding. Whatever it was, it hit me hard. My hatred for him melted away and was replaced by respect.

"Let me get this straight," Liv said, sitting a little straighter in her seat. "Your family was in danger, and his father refused to help. So you made a phone call to the lumber Viking with a pilot's license, and he defied his family and took you out in his plane to rescue Remy and Hazel?"

"Yes," Hazel and I said in unison.

"And you have not banged this guy?"

"No." I shook my head and took another gulp of my wine. "There was a time when I considered it, though."

"Of course you did. You watched him pilot a plane into the wilderness. On a rescue mission, no less. If your panties didn't melt off, then you need a doctor."

I laughed. Liv was a fun addition to our little group, but she did not get it. "It's irrelevant."

"Help me out," Liv said, eyeing Parker.

"He's stupidly hot," Parker said with a smirk. "He works out at our gym, and he spends the entire time drooling over Adele. The man is obsessed. And can you blame him? Have you seen her ass? I swear she does extra squats just to punish the poor man."

My face flamed, and my chest squeezed so tight I thought I might suffocate. "Stop. I will always be grateful for his help that day, but it doesn't erase all the horrible things his father has done."

"Hmm." Liv pressed her lips into a line. "So now you're stuck with him?"

"It's temporary." I ducked my head and sighed. "I'll get through it."

"Do you really want to only *get through it*?" Liv asked, her green eyes dancing. "Or do you want to get under him?"

My stomach twisted at the implication. With a low growl, I threw a cube of cheese at her. Naturally, she caught it and popped it into her mouth.

"It's okay to be attracted to him and still hate him. That dynamic could actually make the sex hotter."

I chugged the rest of my wine and snatched the bottle off the table so I could pour myself another glass. It was time to check out of this conversation.

Just the thought of that man made all my insecurities rise to the surface, and I wasn't interested in confronting any of them. Especially after what he had shared about his daughter. As much as I was content to torture him for the rest of our shared existence, his child did not deserve to be treated the way she had been.

For so long, I'd been angry. And I'd felt entitled to that anger. I'd been wronged. My father had been taken away from me. My family had been put in danger. Our world had been rocked, and I'd used that to justify a lot of the rage that clung tight to my very being.

But lately, a niggle of doubt had formed and crept its way into my consciousness. We Gagnons weren't the only ones hurt by the events that had taken place over the last three years. And my pain was no more or less than anyone else's pain.

I wanted to see things in black and white, good and evil. But there was so much more nuance. I just wasn't ready to face it.

Hazel left soon after I changed the subject, eager to tear Remy's clothes off—though I threw a cube of cheese her way too as I gagged at the image she painted by announcing that sentiment to us. Shortly thereafter, Liv fell asleep on my pink couch with He-Man as a pillow. That left Parker and me to clean up.

"I know how much you love a good pity party," she said, loading the dishwasher, "but it may be time to get back out there. Get on the apps. Try again."

My stomach sank, but I kept my attention averted and wiped down the countertops.

"Just saying. It's been a while, and your comments have been feeling more bitter lately. Why not see what's out there?"

"There's nothing out there," I said. "Men don't want women who push them and challenge them and demand equal treatment. They want compliant idiots."

"You sure about that?" She cocked one brow in a smug way that infuriated me.

"Yup. They want a second mother. A woman who will tell them they're amazing no matter how lazy or messy they are. Who'll be up for mediocre sex any time their man feels like it."

Was I being totally overdramatic and bitchy? Yes. But I was tipsy and feeling sorry for myself. Parker was my best friend. That was the only reason I allowed her to see me like this. She loved me and wouldn't hold it against me or gossip about my sulking. Also, she'd kick my ass back in line.

"Hmm. I can't say that every experience I've had with men has gone like that." She tilted her head and gave me a placating smile.

"Shit, please don't bring up my brother right now. The cheese I bought for tonight was far too expensive to vomit up."

Parker was the only close friend I'd had in years. My brothers and I were close, and I got along well with my employees, but I'd never been able to really connect with another woman until I met her.

She got me. She was a badass ex-cop who had somehow managed to domesticate my asshole brother Paz—which was no small feat in itself—while simultaneously solving my father's murder. I was lucky to call a woman this fiery, this gutsy—who also had a heart bigger than most—my friend. However, she had the very annoying habit of calling me out on my self-pity bullshit.

"I'm only suggesting you pull your head out of your ass. It's time to get out there. Loosen up. The business is thriving now, and you're growing. You're allowed to take a breath."

Slinging a dish towel over my shoulder, I flinched. That was all I'd heard these days. That it was over. The bad guys had been caught. It was time to move forward.

The rest of my family was attempting to move on. To find closure and put the horrors of the last few years behind them. Me? I still couldn't accept the violence my family had experienced. My brothers brushed it off, but their lives had been in danger. And our dad had been killed.

All for greed. Greed that was destroying communities with opioids.

I needed to understand how it could come to that. To make it make sense.

"I can't take a breath," I said, my voice unsteady. "Arrests are not convictions. You know that. And we still don't have the full story. Not about Dad."

What we did know was that one of Mitch's henchmen, a dumbass fuckup named Stinger, had done some work for us in the past. He gained access to our trucks at camp and sabotaged the slack adjuster on the brake system of one of them.

My dad, who normally sat behind a desk, had jumped behind the wheel of said truck to deliver a late load of timber to the mill. It wasn't uncommon for him, even though he was the CEO. But it was notable because he was being set up.

"And Henri," I said.

She ground her teeth and ducked her head. This ate at her too. My bestie could pretend all was right in the world again now that Mitch Hebert and his cronies had been apprehended, but she was nearly as hung up on these details as I was.

"Trust me, I've pored through every document over and over. The FBI and state police have taken statements from dozens of people who know the suspects or could have come into contact with them. Paul is singing like a canary in lockup. Still, no one has been able to piece together what happened with Henri."

More than a year after Dad's death, my eldest brother, Henri, had been involved in a similar accident. When he lost control of the truck, he'd jumped out. He'd survived, but not without several significant injuries.

When I did my own investigation of his truck and my father's, which still sat out in the yard behind the shop, I discovered similar scratches on the slack adjusters. The tampering was almost identical.

"Stinger and Grinder have alibis for that date. They weren't anywhere near the camp." This was nagging at Parker too, but like the good friend she was, she always did what she could to keep me from falling down the paranoid, obsessed rabbit hole.

Too late. "It was not a coincidence."

"I know. I believe you."

Her response made my skin itch.

"No. You need to understand. This isn't some far-out conspiracy theory. I saw the damage to the brakes with my own highly trained, extremely experienced eyes. The same type of wrench was used in an almost identical manner to mess with the slack adjuster. That makes it very likely that the saboteur involved in each crime was the same person." My chest tightened so painfully it was hard to breathe. It happened every time I ran through the evidence. It had been almost two years since I'd discovered the tampering done to the brakes on my father's truck, and I'd obsessed over it every day since.

His death had been ruled an accident. Both by the state police and the department of transportation. But I'd known from the day it happened that my father was far too skilled a driver and far too familiar with the roads in the forest and the conditions that day to have lost control of his truck the way the authorities claimed. Henri, though, had forbidden me from hauling Dad's truck into the shop to take it apart.

But a year after his death, crippled by grief, I did it. And that's when I discovered the slack adjuster that had been damaged.

And every minute since, dread had lingered in my gut, warning me that we were all in danger. Sure, a couple of shitheads had been arrested, but that didn't mean the threat had passed.

Parker knew this. She had enough experience and knowhow to understand that there was always another layer, another set of bad guys up the chain. The men awaiting trial were not the only ones involved. The trafficking ring had been far too successful for far too long to not include dozens of players or more.

Regardless, she'd been pushing me to move on. To heal.

"The truth will come out eventually. Attempted murder is kind of a big deal. No one would willingly cop to that and get hit with more charges."

I dropped onto a stool at the island and closed my eyes. She was right. Everyone else had been cleared. The police had interviewed all Gagnon employees, and they'd subpoenaed employment records and security camera footage and every other record imaginable.

She sidled up to me and bumped my shoulder. "Eventually, we will know."

Eventually? Parker was intelligent enough to know that was the least comforting thing she could say to me right now. Eventually, we'd know who'd attempted to murder my brother? Unacceptable.

We'd installed cameras all over camp and headquarters, and we'd hired a security consultant to help secure our facilities and equipment. We'd taken every possible precautionary measure.

But I couldn't shake the feeling that the danger had not passed. This was not the time to get complacent.

"Please think about it," she said, placing her hand on top of mine where it rested on the cool granite top of the island. "We're all worried about you. Why not go on a couple of dates? Maybe they'll help you relax. At the very least, they'll distract you from your new coworker."

I nodded, though I had no intention of following through. Mostly because it would take a lot more than a few dates to distract me from Finn Hebert.

Chapter 10
Finn

The Fourth of July had been the highlight of my summers growing up. This town did it right, with day-long celebrations, a parade, games, and, of course, the obligatory fireworks.

Our small town barely had the budget for it anymore, but somehow, Mayor Lambert always acquired an impressive collection of fireworks. He even hired professionals to set them off from a barge on the river. For a town in dire straits, I thought it was a bit over the top, but I was in the minority.

Nothing got the citizens of Lovewell together like a festival. Everyone would be there, though I very much wanted to skip this particular holiday. The last thing I needed was face time with the entire town.

One more pitying look, one more person who refused to make eye contact, and I'd truly lose it. My sensitivities had heightened further since Merry had confessed to how she was being treated. The knot in my chest tightened every time I looked at her. Especially now. She was glued to my hip as we made our way through the block party on Main Street. We'd come back to our hometown to give her joyful childhood memories, not constant anxiety.

Food vendors and trucks, picnic tables on the green. And music. That was why we had really come by. Jude was playing with Jasper Hawkins, a semi-famous local musician, and his band. They had been asking him for years to join the band officially, but he always refused, choosing instead to play gigs with them here and there.

Merry gave him an enthusiastic wave as he tuned his guitar on stage. He was so talented. Though we all thought he'd make a career with his music, he hadn't finished his degree. Jude was the outlier of the Hebert family. The quiet, sensitive one who kept his cards close to the vest. The rest of us preferred to yell and fight and work out our problems with axes and tree stumps, but not Jude. When things were tough, he'd retreat into his own little world with his comic books and his guitar.

So despite how difficult things had been, I was happy to see him out and about in town.

String lights hung from the trees where the makeshift dance floor had been built, and all around me, people were hugging one another in greeting and chatting, while children ran wild along the green. Picnic tables had been set up in an open area and were bordered by food trucks. The rest of the town common was filled with games.

Volleyball, gaga ball—which Merry was obsessed with—horseshoes, and a dunk tank that raised money for charity. Despite how much the town had changed from my youth, our Independence Day celebrations remained the same.

Though I didn't know whether to be sickened or comforted by that, my complicated feelings for my hometown would have to wait.

Merry and I ordered food from one of the trucks and found

Wood Riddance

Alicia and Mike as the band started up. The four of us shared poutine as we listened to the music and chuckled at the kids running wild in the grass.

"Dad," Merry said, sipping her blueberry soda. "Promise me you won't ask me to dance."

Alicia snorted as my cheeks burned. "Why not?"

"Because you always ask me to dance." She huffed. "But you should be dancing with a lady, not me."

"You are my lady."

She patted my hand, her little eyes full of pity. "Sure, Dad."

"Who would you like Dad to dance with?" Alicia asked, her eyes sparkling with mischief.

I shot her a glower, but in return, she laughed at me and stuck her tongue out.

Merry stood and climbed on top of the picnic bench so she could scan the crowd. It had only grown since we'd arrived. Many people were sitting around tables eating and laughing, and several were already twirling around the dance floor.

"Hmm." She pursed her lips and tapped her chin, then dropped back down to the bench.

"Couldn't find anyone good enough for your dad?" Mike asked, throwing his arm around Alicia.

I made a mental note to punch him later if I had the chance.

"Nah," Merry said. "I was looking for Miss Adele. She's Daddy's boss. And she's so pretty."

Across from me, Alicia's eyes lit up. "Have you met her?" Dammit, the wheels in her head were already turning. If Merry didn't pipe down, I'd be hearing about this for months.

"Yup. When I went to work with Dad. Miss Adele takes apart engines and listens to cool music. *And* she's the boss. She even let me play with her super cute dog."

Daphne Elliot

I shot a look at Alicia, then Mike. Both wore grins and were sitting ramrod straight, hanging on Merry's every word, enjoying this way too much. They'd both been on my case about dating lately. Ever since they'd transformed into a pair of those smug coupled-up people who wanted everyone to be, as Merry says "all heart eyes at each other."

Sadly, I didn't see a future like that for myself. Especially not in Lovewell. Not that they would take no for an answer.

Alicia turned her smile on our daughter and only encouraged her more. "Sounds like you really like her."

Merry bounced on the wooden bench beside me, making the tabletop shake. "Yes, I do! She's so cool. Dad should ask her on a date."

Merry was snuggled up with her mom, ready for the fireworks show to begin, but I needed to move. The warm night had sweat collecting along my hairline and down my spine, and the crowd was making me itchy. I couldn't fake smile at one more person. So I walked up the riverbank toward soldier's hill. The hillside was patched with brambles, but I hiked up through the trees nevertheless, ignoring the way they caught at my jeans, until I found the small clearing that overlooked the town.

The noise from the festival was a dull murmur up here, and the peace that settled in any time I was in nature finally allowed me to take a deep breath. I had always loved town events and enjoyed seeing my friends and neighbors, but tonight, it was almost intolerable. Why did my neck itch? Why was I feeling so hyper-defensive?

Finally letting my shoulders drop, I propped myself up on a

bolder and considered the idea that my hometown may never feel like home again.

"What are you doing here?"

I startled at the interruption and turned toward the voice.

Adele was heading up a well-maintained path that connected another area of town to the clearing. She was wearing shorts that showed off her mile-long legs and a hoodie. She had a flashlight in one hand and kept it pointed at the ground.

"Just came up for some quiet," I said, my face heating. I was not the kind of guy to get flustered around women, but this woman unnerved me. Threw me off my game each and every time I was in her presence. Maybe it was her unabashed dislike of me. Or maybe it was the ache that gnawed at my gut every time I laid eyes on her.

She trekked over but made sure to keep her distance. God forbid she get within ten feet of me. "This is my secret spot." She surveyed the river and the green below us. "I don't really like fireworks, so when I was a kid, I'd climb up here and wait them out. It's the perfect place, really. You can still see them, but the trees muffle the sound."

I nodded, secretly pleased that Adele Gagnon was scared of fireworks. Made her seem almost human.

But then she had to go and ruin it. Tossing a glare in my direction, she reverted to the tone she seemed to reserve only for me. "So get outta here."

"I was here first." I shrugged and went back to my perusal of the landscape. "And maybe I need the quiet too."

She was silent for a moment, and she didn't move. When I finally dragged my attention back to her, she was glaring at me, her eyes pure fire. But in an instant, that fire banked and was replaced by an emotion I'd never seen from her. Remorse.

She put her hand over her mouth. "Shit. I'm sorry. You've been to war. I didn't make the connection."

"It's okay. It's not a PTSD thing. I needed a break from the festivities, but I appreciate your concern."

Her shoulders dropped and she let out a breath. "Thank you," she said with uncharacteristic kindness. "For your service, I mean."

"You don't have to." I kept my response simple, doing everything I could not to revel in the respectful way she was speaking to me for once.

She squinted. "Yes, I do. I may not like you, but I still appreciate and value your service to our country."

I gave her a salute. "Thank you, ma'am."

Her face morphed from kind to enraged in seconds. "Did you just ma'am me? Do you want me to throw you off this rock ledge?"

"There she is." I laughed. "I was worried for a moment."

"You're a dick," she spat.

"That would be Lieutenant Commander Dick to you, ma'am," I said, delighting in riling her up.

Arms crossed over her chest, she turned toward the river, where the fireworks show was beginning.

I heaved myself off the rock and sauntered to her side with my face tipped up as I watched the explosions light up the night sky. She was right. The trees muffled the noise up here. The view was spectacular too—the fireworks lighting up over our tiny town, nestled between majestic mountains and endless forest.

"Do you miss it?" she asked softly, never taking her eyes off the show.

"Yes." I sighed. "Every day, actually."

Her response was a silent nod.

Wood Riddance

"I woke up every day with a purpose. My every action was in service of something bigger than me. It's been a few years, and I still can't wrap my mind around civilian life."

She looked up at me, her eyes full of understanding. Beneath the hard exterior, I suspected she had her own set of regrets and frustrations.

I shuffled closer, hoping I wouldn't spook her, until we were shoulder to shoulder, looking out at our little world.

"My goals and my priorities were clear. Cut and dry. Here? Everything is confusing."

She turned my way and took a small step back. Behind her, colors exploded in the dark sky. It was ridiculous to spill my guts to a woman who despised me like she did. But in this moment, I wanted her to know me.

"There are no rules here." I ran my knuckle along her chin.

She let out a tiny gasp, but she didn't move. Her eyes were steely, but she wasn't backing away.

"Every day, I wake up trying to make sense of the world." Tilting her chin up, I dipped forward. I wasn't sure what I was doing, but I was helpless to stop it.

"I get it," she whispered.

And if I didn't know better, I'd say she leaned in closer.

Our faces were inches apart, the fireworks forgotten as they exploded around us.

This was it. I was going to kiss her. And she wanted me to. A sense of calm washed over me, taking with it the weight on my shoulders and the knot in my stomach. This was right. And I was going for it.

I leaned in, closing my eyes and soaking in her warmth, relishing the euphoria that flooded my veins as her lips ghosted against mine.

Before I could experience the total bliss that was kissing Adele, though, she pulled away.

I opened my eyes and focused on her stricken face. That's when it hit me. Something was wrong.

She pulled me by the arm to the trail I'd come up as screams from below registered.

Shit.

My instincts kicked in, and I took off, bounding down the steep rocks toward the green, my adrenaline pumping. Merry. I had to get to Merry.

Adele was right behind me as I sprinted with my heart in my throat.

Nothing could have prepared me for the mayhem I encountered on the green.

Handfuls of people were screaming. Others were running. And a few were even snapping photos as an absolutely enormous moose did battle with the volleyball net.

I stopped short, scanning the crowd for Merry, and Adele barely avoided crashing into my back.

Heaving, I snapped my attention to her, then back to the moose. "What the fuck is that?"

"Aw, shit. It's Clive."

Across the grass, the moose, with netting literally wrapped around its antlers, slammed into a picnic table, sending it flying.

"Dad."

I spun, finding Merry running toward me, with Mike and Alicia close behind her. I took off for her and grabbed her under the arms, picking her up so I could keep her safe while I assessed the threat.

"I feel so bad for him," she said, squeezing my neck. "He's scared."

"He's destroying the damn town," I yelled, walking backward toward my truck. The crowd had dispersed, but there were still dozens of people watching in fascination as a bull moose tore through our small-town celebration.

Tables were overturned and food was thrown everywhere. And still, the damn net was tangled in his antlers. He bucked and tossed his head wildly.

How did no one realize how dangerous this was?

"Let's go back to the car," I insisted, nudging Mike as I continued moving slowly away from the moose.

"No way. I want a video of this," Merry protested, grabbing my phone out of my hand.

"Are we sure that's Clive?" Alicia asked at my side.

"Yes," Merry insisted, throwing one arm out and pointing. "He has a big scar on his back leg. Wait till he turns around."

Sure enough, a long, jagged scar cut across his hip. I shook my head. All this time, I was worried about my daughter adjusting to life in rural Maine, but if she could ID a moose at fifty yards, so clearly, then she'd be fine.

"Let's get you home," I said, eyeing Alicia and Mike over her head and lifting my chin, signaling for them to follow me to the parking lot.

"Dad, look." Merry pressed a palm to my cheek and forced my face forward again.

Clive was near the pavilion now, and he was galloping straight for a huge display of blueberry pies. There were probably fifty of them, lovingly baked and displayed by Bernice, the official pie queen of Penobscot County.

Bernice herself was screaming as he barreled for her table.

The crowd stilled, letting out a collective gasp. It was one thing to take out a volleyball net and a few old picnic tables. But mess with Bernice's pies? That was how vendettas began.

But the moose was undeterred. He ran full-on at the tent,

bucking his head, sending the net swirling. And then it happened.

Impact.

Pies.

Antlers.

Blueberry carnage the likes of which this town would never forget.

And one tiny old lady screaming obscenities at a fifteen-hundred-pound moose. Clive had a reputation for not giving many fucks, but he'd messed with the wrong woman. I could practically see Bernice plotting his death from across the green. The rest of the townsfolk snapped photos and fell into fits of laughter, and the moose wandered off again.

"This is the best Fourth of July ever!" Merry giggled, squeezing me tighter and kissing my cheek as I loaded her into my truck. I looked up and saw Adele giggling with her family a few yards away. She gave me a nod and my heart clenched. I'd been so close to kissing her again. Figures that damn moose would ruin it.

Chapter 11
Finn

"Pretty, pretty please." Merry begged, tugging on my arm. "I need blueberry pancakes *so* bad."

She had her head tipped back and she was giving me the look she referred to as "sad puppy eyes." The expression that I simply could not say no to, despite the insanity of the attached request.

"Fine. We can walk over to the diner. There may be a wait, though. Saturday mornings are busy."

She pumped her fist in the air and bopped along the sidewalk beside me, happy to have gotten her way. Alicia and Mike were down on the coast looking at wedding venues, so Merry and I planned to hike, then settle in for a movie marathon. We'd start with her all-time favorite, *A League of Their Own*, as we usually did. I had seen the movie more times than I could count. I'd even dressed up as Jimmy Duggan last Halloween. I'd watch it a thousand more times if Merry wanted me to. Nothing made my girl so happy. We'd follow it up with *Bend It Like Beckham*, another one of her favorites.

Dissecting Taylor Swift lyrics to find secret messages had

been one of her suggestions for the night—and something I'd spent a lot of time doing in the last few years—but watching movies I knew every line of was far less taxing on my brain, so I had no interest in complaining. I smiled down at her. She was getting so tall and grown up. My heart clenched. I'd always seen myself raising a whole bunch of kids.

When I was a kid, our home was total chaos, but we loved it. With so many boys running around, we were never short of playmates, and this great wilderness was our playground. Merry was the most amazing thing to ever happen to me, but sometimes I ached for more. For a wife, more kids, barbecues with my brothers on the weekends and joint Christmases, where we wore PJs all day and ate too much.

I had mostly avoided the diner as of late. A fixture of my childhood, it was the epicenter of Lovewell life and, therefore, Lovewell gossip. I'd have to face it sooner or later, and my girl wanted pancakes, so it looked like the time had come. I needed another cup of coffee to keep up with her for the rest of the day anyway.

When I held the diner door open, I was met with the chattering of patrons and the ringing of the bell above us. It was nostalgic. The sounds hadn't changed a bit in decades.

The place was packed, as it always was on weekends. Stepping inside, I scanned the dining room, hoping to find a small table available or two open seats at the counter.

Immediately, a hush fell over the room, and every head turned our way.

Merry stepped back, snaking an arm around my waist and ducking behind me.

I couldn't blame her for wanting to hide. The scrutiny was intense. Dozens of patrons were watching me with either curiosity or pity, and many with a sprinkle of scorn.

And my poor daughter was feeling the judgment.

She tugged on my arm and whispered, "Let's go."

I surveyed the room, standing a little straighter. It was a cross section of our community. Retirees, families, and a big table full of tween girls who couldn't contain their giggles. Adele sat in a corner booth with her mother. Our eyes locked, and her gaze narrowed.

Lowering my head, I looked down at Merry, who'd moved so close to me she was tucked under my arm. Her little mouth was turned down and her eyes were glassy. At the sight of my daughter's dejection, a part of me broke. I had to get her out of here. There was no saving this for us. This place would never forgive or forget, and I didn't know why I thought it would.

I grasped Merry's hand, ready to make a hasty exit, but before we could turn and leave, her voice echoed through the quiet room.

"What is your problem?"

Heart lurching, I turned to her. She wasn't looking at me, though. No, she was pacing through the diner, glaring at every person in her path. Even Bernice, never one to stand down, was frozen, her ever-present coffee pot held aloft.

"This is not how we treat people," Adele said, spinning on her heel to begin her trek back to the other side of the dining room. "You should all be ashamed of yourselves."

A few people murmured in protest, but that only made a fire ignite in her eyes.

"Really, Mrs. Leary?" she said, striding over to where the older woman sat with a group of ladies. They wore twinsets and holier-than-thou expressions. "You're going to throw stones? This town supported you when your son got drunk and drove into the hardware store."

Mrs. Leary's face was purple and full of indignation, and

she was sputtering like she was gathering up a retort. But Adele continued, her hands on her hips like she was only getting started.

"We all chipped in to help with repairs. And didn't we do a bake sale to help pay for him to go to rehab? Yet you and your friends have nothing better to do than gossip, and it hurts good, hard-working families."

She pivoted to another table. "Father Renee, don't you preach about forgiveness on Sundays?"

He nodded, not daring to make eye contact with her.

"Correct," she said, answering her own question. "You, for one, should know better than to jump on this judgment bandwagon. Because if we believe a person is guilty by association, then you and your archdiocese comrades would be in big trouble. Eh, father?"

The priest's face fell as several patrons around the room sniggered.

Merry and I were frozen, watching this unfold. She was still tucked up against me, but she was peeking out under my arm, intent on Adele.

She pointed at the table of young girls. "I'll be sure to text every single one of your parents about your behavior this morning. And don't forget, your school principal is my sister now."

Their little faces went ashen as that threat landed.

Adele was in the middle of the diner now, commanding the attention of everyone there. "No one here is faultless, and we've all been associated with people we wish we could distance ourselves from. Our town has not survived for this long because we turn our backs on one another.

"This is not the Lovewell my great grandparents founded. And it's time you all get your shit together, because if not, you will have me to answer to."

Wood Riddance

The room remained silent, and every jaw in the place was slack as she spun on her heel and headed back to her booth.

Halfway to her table, one person spoke up. "But your father!"

She turned and stalked toward the man who dared to put up a fight. It was Mayor Lambert. He was an affable guy who had coached my peewee baseball team for several years. I'd known him my whole life, and he'd always been involved in the community. Even before he became mayor. He loved his job and this town, and he took his duties seriously. Honestly, he was the last person I thought would join the angry mob.

He was perched at the counter with a fresh slice of blueberry pie with homemade vanilla ice cream on top sitting in front of him.

Adele loomed over him, silently inspecting him for a long moment. I thought she would curse him out. Instead, she grabbed the plate and a fork and took a big bite of his pie.

My jaw hit the ground.

"You don't get pie," she said, her voice low. "Pie is for kind people who don't gossip about or judge others."

The mayor's eyes widened, and his face flushed. He probably wasn't used to having his authority challenged.

Shoveling another bite of pie into her mouth, she scanned the crowd. "Bernice, don't you dare give him more pie. He doesn't get pie until he learns how to be a decent fucking human."

Bernice, the sassy owner of the diner, nodded at Adele, her beehive bobbing as she did. That small interaction was the most shocking part of this entire encounter. Bernice wasn't known for taking anyone's shit.

Still holding the mayor's pie, Adele tilted her chin higher and scrutinized one person after another. "This ends now. You will not punish good people, and you will not damn a child for the actions of one evil man. We're better than this."

With that, she pivoted sharply once again and prowled toward us. Her expression was still set in a severe scowl as she moved closer. I was glued to the spot, baffled and at a loss for words. But when she approached, she didn't speak to me. Instead, she kneeled, softened her expression, and looked straight at Merry. "My mom and I have room in our booth. Do you want to join us?"

Merry studied Adele with stars in her eyes, and finally, a tiny smile lifted one side of her lips. "Okay."

Adele heaved herself back up and led us to the booth, where she gestured for us to slide in before taking a seat next to her mom. She still commanded the attention of every patron in the place. They hadn't stopped watching her since she opened her mouth to defend us. "Now eat your damn breakfasts," she said, giving each and every one of them a pointed look, "and stop being assholes." With that, she lifted her hand, gesturing at Bernice for more coffee.

"Sorry about that," she said to Merry, picking up her menu. "I'm in the mood for pancakes. What about you?"

My daughter gave her a bright smile, then opened her mouth and proceeded to expound on her love of pancakes.

I exhaled, feeling the knot that had tightened the second we stepped into the diner finally loosen. People had gone back to their meals and conversations, and the tension that had thickened the air began to dissipate. Mayor Lambert snuck a few looks in our direction, but otherwise, things cooled down.

My pulse slowly settled, and my breathing returned to normal. In the military, I had learned to assess threats. I'd had to use that skill many times overseas. It was ingrained in me. How could I have underestimated how dangerous it

Wood Riddance

would be to bring Merry into the diner on a Saturday morning?

I was still silently berating myself when a small hand covered mine.

"It's okay," Mrs. Gagnon said softly. "It's not your fault." She was of medium height with dark hair cut in a neat bob. She had all the appearances of a sweet middle-aged woman, but there was a fierceness in her eyes that reminded me of her daughter. If I had to guess, she was also a force to be reckoned with.

I'd seen her plenty over the years, but I hadn't been able to look her in the eye since learning that my father was responsible for her beloved husband's death. That shame washed over me once more as I sat across from her now. Would I be apologizing for his actions forever?

"I'm sorry," I said.

She tilted her head and assessed me for a long moment. Finally, she breathed a quiet "thank you" and patted my hand. The contact was comforting, friendly. She wasn't judging me. She didn't hate me. And with that realization, the wave of shame began to wane.

It was only then that I picked up the sound of Merry's laughter. She and Adele were playing hangman on the paper menu, and Adele had chosen the word *booger*.

Adele sat across from Merry, laughing right along with her. Her blond hair was in a ponytail, and she wasn't wearing a lick of makeup. She had clearly come from the gym, but the sight of her took the breath right out of my lungs.

This woman was exceptional in every way. She was brave and kind and more empathetic than I'd ever realized. There was absolutely no way I wasn't going to spend the rest of my life pining for her.

Daphne Elliot

Two years ago, we had kissed. A moment I still relived almost every day. After that night, I vowed to make her mine. To take my time, get to know her, and lock her down forever. Because she was one of a kind.

Things had changed. She'd never be mine now. But fuck if I didn't wish it were possible.

Chapter 12
Adele

I didn't care. Really. I didn't. He was another asshole in a vast ocean of them who stood in my way every day. But we were the only ones here.

And without a word, he'd jumped in to help me clean the shop.

Our work was complicated and messy, but we worked most efficiently when each and every aspect of the shop was in order and put to rights. So at the end of each day, every tool and piece of equipment was cleaned, checked, and put away.

Like a restaurant kitchen, we started from scratch every morning.

Evening cleanup was a team effort. But the day had been so nice, and the sky was so clear. I wanted my staff to enjoy it, so I'd sent everyone to Richardson's for ice cream. And yeah, maybe part of my motivation to shoo them out was because I wanted to be alone.

My favorite Taylor Swift playlist was blasting and I had just taken off my coveralls when Finn showed up.

And wouldn't you know it. He knew how to catalog and sort wrenches exactly the way I liked it done.

Bastard. I busied myself silently but couldn't resist sneaking looks at him. Because the sight of this man holding tools in his massive hand—especially with a rag thrown over his shoulder—was doing something to me that I didn't want to acknowledge.

Though I'd been itching for time alone, I couldn't deny I was appreciative of his help and his initiative. So the least I could do was attempt to be polite. Which, in my case, meant remaining silent. If I opened my mouth, I feared I'd either hurl insults or attempt to shove my tongue down his throat.

I'd narrowly missed the latter on the Fourth of July. I had almost mauled him in the woods that night. Thank God Clive had the good sense to cause mayhem. Because if I'd besieged him the way my body had demanded in that moment, I never would have recovered.

Merely brushing my lips against his had altered my DNA and sent me into a weeklong lust spiral. Now I was finally getting a hold of myself. There was no way I'd allow myself to tempt fate again.

"You know," he said, locking one of the storage cabinets. "You struck me as more of a *Reputation* girl. *Folklore* is an inspired choice."

My heart tumbled in my chest. "You a Swiftie?" Could it be possible that this man could discuss the divergent tones and themes of each album?

He smiled. "Of course. I have a ten-year-old daughter. Sometimes we have entire conversations using only T-Swift lyrics."

God, why did he continually and unwittingly have to

remind me of what a great dad he was? It only poured gasoline on the simmering fire of attraction I was desperate to extinguish.

"Also—" He pulled the hair tie out of his hair, shook his head, then pulled the strands back up again.

I made a mental note to snap my jaw—which had hit the floor—shut. His hair was thick and shiny but just wild enough to be sexy.

"I wanted to thank you. For what you did at the diner."

Dropping my chin, I busied myself with wiping down one of the worktables. "It's no problem."

"Adele." The tone he used was sharper than I'd ever heard from him.

I stopped my assault on the stainless-steel surface and looked up.

His blue eyes were dark, penetrating. "I'm serious. You stood up for Merry and me when no one else would."

Forcing a grin, I brushed off his praise. "Most people in town are bigger assholes than I am."

He stalked toward me and splayed his hands on the table, edging in close to me so I was forced to meet his gaze. "You are not an asshole."

"Right." I huffed and lifted one shoulder. "I'm a bitch."

He slammed a hand down on the table, making it vibrate beneath my fingers. The sound echoed through the cavernous space. "You're not a bitch. You're fierce and brave, and you don't owe me anything. But you went out of your way to protect my kid, and that's a big deal to me."

I nodded, feeling like I was going to swallow my tongue. He didn't walk away or even break eye contact. When I'd jumped up and berated the townspeople in the diner, it hadn't felt like a big deal. It was something that needed to be done. But now, the weight of it sat firmly on my chest. The daughter of Frank Gagnon publicly defending the son of Mitch Hebert.

The town was no doubt still gossiping about it.

Still standing too close for comfort, he nodded toward the main door to the shop. "I like the sign."

Following his line of sight, I turned to the sign hanging directly across from the door to the shop. It read: *Do what you can, with what you have, where you are.* I had made it myself years ago. When I'd taken over here and was trying to get my footing.

He held out his left arm and twisted it until his palm was turned up. I leaned in and studied the intricate knot tattooed on the inside of his forearm. *When you're at the end of your rope, tie a knot and hold on* was inked around it in script.

"You're a TR fan," he said softly.

His words did something funny to my heart. It almost felt like it was floating in my chest. Very few people knew the origin of the quote on the sign.

I took a step back, needing to put more space between us so I could pull in a lungful of air that didn't smell like him. There was something intimate about examining a person's ink, and his thick, ropey forearms were, like the rest of him, frustratingly masculine and sexy.

"I am," I said, snatching my rag off the table. "Big fan. America's most badass president."

He stood perfectly still, grinning at me as I busied myself. "I'm also a big national parks lover."

My traitorous stomach flipped then. Why couldn't he be awful? Why couldn't he be obsessed with video games or something equally off-putting?

Wood Riddance

If he really was a national parks nerd, then I'd officially lose my shit. Between the forearms and the compliments and the Teddy Roosevelt deep cuts, I was already dangerously close to reenacting that kiss. Throwing in a love for our country's parks would be a total disaster.

But the shop was clean, and every tool was in its place. It was time to lock up and get as far away from Finn Hebert as I could.

He had other ideas. "Acadia was my first. What was yours?"

"U Maine offered these freshman orientation trips. There were a bunch of options, but I had never been out west, so I chose a backpacking trip through Rocky Mountain National Park."

It was an expensive endeavor, but I begged my parents. My dad was easier to convince, and, thankfully, he'd helped me convince my mom. He always had my back, especially with Mom, who had always been overprotective of me. But he'd done it, and then he'd driven me to Bangor to pick up a hiking pack and supplies, making me promise to take lots of photos of the trees out there.

The memory never failed to bring a smile to my face. God, I missed him so much.

"The park is spectacular. I was only eighteen, but I was totally obsessed with all of it. The history, the geology, even the rangers. I wanted to soak up every single detail. It's not only about the vast untamed wilderness, you know? It's about the planning and preparation and infrastructure that go into protecting the place and making it accessible to people."

"America's best idea," he mused, crossing his arms. "My ultimate destination is Denali."

I gasped. "Me too. But in the lower forty-eight, I'd say Glacier is at the top of my list."

"I've never been, but the glaciers are melting, so you should go soon."

My heart lodged in my throat at the thought. But I shrugged, ready to move on. Before Dad passed, I'd take two weeks off every summer and travel. The summer before we lost him, I hiked and camped in Yosemite while obsessing over the redwoods. But for the past few years, I hadn't felt like I could take time off. Even in the slow season. Things at Gagnon Lumber were so hectic, and even now, while the financial side had improved, things had still been rough.

"Sure thing. I'll gas up my jeep," I snarked.

"I mean it. Take it from me. It's so easy to get wrapped up in your life and develop tunnel vision. Work, sleep, eat, laundry, taxes. On an endless loop."

I scrutinized him where he stood on the other side of the table. The man who had given up his dreams for his family. Who was hanging on to a life he didn't want because he was putting his child's needs ahead of his own. A man who was living in the shadow of his father and facing the consequences head-on.

"When you're standing in the wilderness, it's easier to remember that the world is so much bigger than you. It allows you to appreciate all the things you miss when your world is reduced to the monotony of daily life."

My throat was thick, and words had escaped me. I had always categorized Finn as a meathead. Never, until this moment, had I realized how deep and thoughtful he was under the Viking warrior exterior.

So, to calm my racing heart and force the emotions

Wood Riddance

bubbling up inside me to recede, I settled for grabbing my bag and getting the lights.

Silently, he followed me out and escorted me to my car.

Once I'd found my keys, I climbed into the driver's seat. Twisting at the waist, I reached for the door, but he leaned in, resting his hand on the frame of the jeep above my head.

"We're not as different as you think, She-Ra."

Chapter 13
Finn

I leaned back in the chair, desperate to get out of this room and move. But Gary, our lawyer, droned on. Though it was a Friday evening, we had assembled at the Hebert Timber offices because Gary had information about the case against Dad and its impact on the business.

Owen was on speakerphone again. He'd phoned in from his office in Boston. Cole hadn't bothered to even acknowledge the text chain. Neither had Noah. So only Gus and Jude and I were stationed around the table in the massive conference room.

When we were kids, headquarters was located in an old warehouse. It was a good size but full of scuffed desks and those printers that required continuous form paper—the kind that fed in one long chain, where each page was separated by perforations, as well as the edges.

About a decade ago, Dad and uncle Paul had built this place. Dad called it a "campus," which the rest of us thought screamed *pretentious*. The office building looked like the set of one of those lawyer dramas my mom loved to watch. This conference room was bigger than my apartment, and the shiny mahogany table could easily seat twenty.

I ran my hand along the surface. It was of highest quality. At least we'd get a good price when we eventually had to liquidate the furniture and equipment. The massive projector and the artwork were probably worth something too. And given how much Gary charged per hour, we'd be listing this shit on Craigslist sooner rather than later.

Gary was a corporate guy out of Portland. Owen had found him, and we'd hired him to represent the company in the criminal proceedings and any civil suits that came out of them. Owen had urged us to hire representation, since so much of the case was wrapped up in the business. Since the six of us were now responsible for Hebert Timber, that meant he sort of represented us. And while he wasn't my dad's lawyer, he worked with Dad's and Uncle Paul's attorneys and was our best source of information.

He and Owen jumped into a debate regarding taxes that I neither understood nor was interested in, so I tuned them out. Immediately, my mind wandered to Adele. Was she still at work? Did she have plans tonight?

The thought of her on a date made my stomach ache. I wanted to see her. Talk to her, spar with her, find any excuse to touch her.

I hadn't seen her in two days, and already, I missed her. Not that I could tell her that. She'd tell me to go fuck myself and probably punch me in the nuts for my trouble.

But it didn't change the fact that her glares and her annoyed sighs made the hard days worth it. Once in a while, when her guard was down, I'd even catch her checking me out. The way she traced her fingertip over my knot tattoo had haunted me for almost forty-eight hours. The lightest touch had made my heart race and my vision tunnel.

Moments like that were what gave me an inkling of hope that I might have a chance someday. She could deny it all day long, but she felt what I did. The energy that flowed between us.

"He still won't plea," Gary said.

That got my attention. I shook myself from my Adele-induced haze and sat a little straighter. My dad was a stubborn bastard, but he couldn't possibly think he'd be found not guilty, could he? For Christ's sake, Parker Harding had recorded him confessing to almost every crime he was being tried for.

"We've got to convince him," Owen insisted, his tone an angry rasp. He resented every minute he had to spend cleaning up Dad's mess. "This can't go to trial."

I winced, and the pit of dread that had taken up residence in my stomach the day my father was arrested grew. The legal fees he'd rack up if he didn't plea would be astronomical. "He's not cooperating," Gary explained, his expression soft, patient. "These are the feds; your dad is small change to them. They're after the big fish, and your dad is in a great position to help them. In turn, he'd surely receive reduced sentences."

My dad generally had no problem snitching to help himself. There was no code of honor by which he lived, and he had no morals to speak of, so we were shocked that he wasn't already singing like a canary.

"We can talk to him," Gus said. "Convince him to give them the information they want."

"It's not that simple. Your father's enterprise was sizable, but it was only one arm of a much larger cross-border drug trafficking operation. Without actionable intel for the feds, he's not likely to get a favorable deal. We don't know who else he was working with, how he was brought into this, or how deep it goes."

"What can we do?" This question came from Gus.

"Nothing right now. Discovery will take quite a while, and a case of this size will take years to work through the system. There's no rush."

"Untrue," Owen said. "We're hanging on by a thread here. We need resolution so we can sell while this company still has a shred of value left."

I pinched the bridge of my nose while Owen and Gus debated selling and subdividing and all sorts of other possible solutions. They would never see eye to eye.

They were wired differently. Gus was a romantic. He loved the woods, and he loved the family legacy. He'd spent his life preparing to lead this company. No matter how much Dad sidelined him, he persisted.

He'd refused to go to college after high school, but eventually, about a decade later, he earned a business degree while still working full time. He wanted to prove to Dad that he could run the company someday.

When he wasn't working, he was building furniture, reading poetry and entering timbersports competitions.

Owen was eighteen months younger, but worlds different. I swore the man wore suits even on the weekends. He attended charity events and Red Sox games, and his idea of hard labor was an early morning session on his Peloton. He was ruthless and practical and precise.

Naturally, the two of them were constantly at odds. They were night and day. It was inevitable.

This argument only emphasized how little being involved in the family business interested me. If it wasn't clear already, it was blatantly obvious now that it was time to get serious about finding investors, doing my research, and making plans.

Maybe it was because I was working for the enemy. Or maybe it was the time I'd spent with Adele. Either way, I was finding my fight again. I had spent the last six months wallowing in self-pity, but I wasn't the type of man who gave up easily. I needed to get creative and get off my ass. File paperwork, research insurance, and plan routes to take with potential investors.

The plane, as long as I could make the payments, was mine. Other than Merry, that was all that mattered.

That and maybe figuring out why the hell, of all the people in my life, I was most desperate to talk to Adele about this. She'd be a wealth of great ideas. She'd test all my assumptions and catch details I hadn't even thought of yet. And yes, she'd probably insult me in the process, but I'd enjoy every minute of it.

As my brothers continued to snipe at one another, I became more and more convinced that I needed to see her. Not because I was wildly attracted to her—though I was—but because I had this energy bubbling up inside me, and I knew she would get it. She was a doer too. She couldn't sit still if her life depended on it, and I had no doubt that she could kick my ass right into gear.

According to my watch, it was already after eight. I was itching to get out of here and swing by Gagnon. If I was lucky, she'd still be working.

For now, I wouldn't dissect why I needed to see her so badly. I didn't have the mental energy to question it. But when I got in my truck, I knew exactly where I was headed.

Chapter 14
Adele

Friday. Thank Jesus. An entire week of Finn Goddamn Hebert up in my space. My shop was my sanctuary. The place ran efficiently, and I loved my team. We had our routines and our checklists and our traditions.

But now we had a surly Viking in our midst, and everything was being destroyed. He barely spoke, and he spent all his time either playing with his drone outside or talking to Henri. But I couldn't shake the feel of his gaze on my skin, and I couldn't concentrate on anything but him.

I had started wearing mascara to work. It wasn't a conscious decision. Not at all. More like a subconscious compulsion. And I hated myself for it.

I was not that woman. I did not wear makeup at work.

This was my safe space. In this building, I was the boss. I was capable and powerful. I could escape the bullshit that tainted the rest of my life. The depressing dates, my ticking biological clock, and that crushing feeling of loneliness that sometimes crept in when things got tough.

Mascara was a betrayal. Like an admission that he was

here. And there was a part of me, deep down, that felt like a coat of shit on my eyelashes would help me face him day in and day out.

Shit, I should go back to therapy. Clearly, I was cracking up.

I'd cut the crew loose at four. It was a beautiful mid-July night, and we were, as usual, ahead of schedule. Plus, I desperately needed some time alone.

I left He-Man sleeping on his bed in my office and headed out back, past the puppy play area, to one of the shipping containers.

A few years ago, I'd converted it. I'd run lights and I'd set up a makeshift gym here. But recently, I'd added something new.

My axes.

Once in a while, Henri came out and threw with me. He was good. Not as good as me, but he put up a fight. He was the one who'd convinced me to replace the old particle board with proper wooden targets, complete with regulation-size bull's-eyes.

A rack with the throwing axes, a stone for sharpening, and a whiteboard for keeping score were mounted along one wall.

Phone in hand, I flipped on my "Angry Feminist" playlist on Spotify, then set it on the floor near the wall and warmed up.

Some people did yoga, others took baths, but me? Throwing bladed instruments was what calmed me. This was my Zen time.

Focus and precision were paramount. Controlled breathing was an absolute must as I prepared for each throw. It forced my body into a state of calm clarity, thus easing my mind and all the tumultuous thoughts swirling inside it.

Tonight, I needed it more than usual.

"You're really good at that."

Turning, axe still raised, I came face to face with Finn Fucking Hebert. As if my day hadn't been shitty enough.

He took a step back and threw his hands up to shield himself. "Easy, She-Ra. I come in peace."

Lowering my axe, I scowled at him. Dammit. There went the sense of peace I'd just harnessed. "Do you need something?"

He shoved his hands into the pockets of his jeans. "No. I forgot my phone charger, so I came back. Found He-Man, but not She-Ra. Then I heard a noise back here and figured I should investigate."

I *hmph*ed, annoyed. Maybe more with myself than I was with him. My brain was sending signals reminding my body that he was intruding on a sacred moment for me and that I should want nothing more than for him to skedaddle his way out of here, but my heart was a little bruised. Because he wasn't here for me. He'd only returned because he'd left his phone charger behind.

"It's me. You can go away now."

"Can I watch?"

"No." I flipped my axe in my hand, refusing to look at him and willing my body not to react to his desire to be near me.

"Why not?" he asked, taking a step forward and crowding the entire space.

As a woman, I was constantly being reminded that the world believed I should take up as little space as possible. Finn Hebert clearly believed he'd been given the opposite instruction. The container was only eight feet wide, and his massive frame practically filled every inch, leaving me surrounded by his maleness. It was annoying, and it totally ruining my planned meditation.

And he had the absolute audacity to show up wearing jeans. Old jeans, all worn and smooth and clinging to his thick and powerful thighs. Asshole. The way he hovered, arms crossed and grinning at me, made my body light up in ways it definitely shouldn't have been. I hated this man. And even though it was a bit of a relief to see shades of the cocky bastard I used to know—before his father's arrest, and before the town had turned on him—these interactions had to stop.

Because being stuck in a steel box with him, at night, with an axe in my hand, spelled disaster.

"Leave." It was a demand. Without waiting for him to acquiesce, I walked up to the line and took aim. Slowly, I pulled my elbow back and threw. Holding my breath, I watched the axe make one perfect rotation before hitting the target.

Behind me, a low whistle rent the air.

"You're still here?" I huffed, whipping around again.

He walked closer, ignoring my comments. "You're pretty good at this." Without stopping, he skirted past me and yanked the axe out of the wooden target. "Mind if I give it a try?"

"Yes." Planting my hands on my hips, I shot him a glare. "I do mind."

Turning the axe in his hand, he studied the handle and hefted it, getting a sense of its weight. Completely ignoring my dirty looks, he stepped up to the line.

As he brought his arms up, I shuffled back, giving him space, and watched as the axe spun wildly, bounced off the target, and fell to the floor.

"Not as easy as it looks, eh?" I said, smugness building in my chest.

He turned, wearing a grin. "Still fun to try."

I took another axe from the small rack and elbowed past him. Once I'd lined myself up, I breathed deeply, focusing on the weight of the blade in my hand and looking directly at the bull's-eye. Then I let it fly.

"Fuck," he said when it hit the red bull's-eye.

"What? You surprised a woman could throw an axe like that?"

"No, ma'am," he said, shoving his hands into the pockets of his jeans. "That's some deadly aim."

I picked up another axe and turned toward him. "Thank you. And if you ever *ma'am* me again, I'll slice your balls off and feed them to Clive."

He ducked his head and chuckled, as if my threats of bodily harm were amusing. "What's the deal with that moose? Why hasn't anyone shot him yet?"

I gasped and pulled my shoulders back. "How dare you malign Clive? He is a valued member of this community."

Finn mirrored my movement, taking a step closer. "He's a semi-domesticated moose who loves to fuck shit up and cause property damage. He should be made into jerky."

"Do not ever repeat those words," I warned. "You think the town hates you now? Mess with Clive, and they'll run you out of here with torches and pitchforks."

He frowned and shook his head. "I don't get it. He's a menace."

"We keep you around, don't we? It's obvious our standards are set pretty low."

Ignoring me, he sauntered to the other end of the container, giving me a wide berth on his way past. He studied the target, then picked up the spray bottle I kept on the floor and sprayed it down thoroughly.

My heart lurched in my chest again. Dammit. It might be time to get that checked out. How would he know to do that? Keeping the wood moist made it softer, in turn encouraging axes to remain lodged where they hit. But what was he doing?

He wiped his hands on those damn jeans and raised one brow. "Let's play a game."

Heart thumping against my ribs and suspicion rising, I regarded him. "Do you want me to explain the rules? The scoring?"

He shook his head, picking up an axe. "Nah, I'll learn as we go."

Narrowing my eyes, I studied him, searching for any sign that he was messing with me, but his expression remained passive, innocent. *Must be an idiot.* So sure, why not make things interesting? "Bull's-eye is six points. The next ring is four, and then three, two, and one. You get ten throws. Best score wins."

"Like I said, I'll figure it out." He shrugged.

"How about a friendly wager?" I asked, my voice dripping with honey.

He nodded and took a step closer. "Great idea. If I win, you let me take you out."

The embers still heating my belly caught fire, and the heat rose up my chest and into my cheeks.

I could not let that happen. But I couldn't deny a teeny, tiny frisson of excitement coursed through me at the thought that he wanted to take me out. Clearly, I was in dire emotional straits if the interest of this miscreant was making me feel good.

I had to extinguish this.

"When I win," I replied, "you will never ask me out again. You'll refrain from all flirting, and never, *ever* mention *that* night."

His grin almost split his face in half. "You mean the night I kissed the shit out of you in my truck?"

His cocky expression made me want to throat punch him.

"Do not speak of that."

"Why not? It was amazing," he said, his blue eyes sparkling.

It was moments like this that I wished I had actual superpowers. What I wouldn't have given to shoot lasers at him.

"Amazing?" I giggled. "It was fine."

In an instant, all the cocky arrogance drained from his face. "Fine?"

"Yeah." I shrugged, picking up an axe. "Like five out of ten."

He coughed, as if the thought of being average had made the air evacuate his lungs. I was enjoying this. Maybe a little too much.

I thought he'd retreat with his tail between his legs, but clearly, I underestimated Finn Hebert. "Let's do this," he said, picking up his own axe. "Now I'm definitely going to win. I will not accept five out of ten. I'm earning my second chance."

"You have no chance. I'm going to embarrass you, and then you'll be forced to leave me alone, do your job, and stop being a pain in my ass."

He tossed the axe in the air. It made one perfect rotation before he caught the handle cleanly.

"Sure thing, She-Ra. Ladies first." He gestured for me to step up to the line but didn't back away.

Not one to be intimidated, I stepped right up and lined up my shot.

"You know what?" he said, crowding me in a way that made me want to bury this axe in his head. "We should really make things fun. How about for every bull's-eye I hit, you remove one item of clothing?"

Daphne Elliot

My stomach dropped, and all logical thought left me. I didn't dare turn and look at him. He still hovered, and if our faces were too close, there was no way I could control my reaction. I would punch him, or worse, kiss him again.

"Whatever," I said, keeping my focus set on the target while I willed my heart to stop racing. "If you want to strip naked, I don't care."

I stepped forward and let the axe fly. Immediately, I knew I'd released it too early. It landed high, in the three-point ring. I cursed myself for allowing him to get to me. I was good at this. I had won competitions, for fuck's sake. And I'd let Finn get in my head. There was no way in hell I was losing.

"My turn." He stepped forward and gripped the axe properly, like he knew what he was doing.

And then he hit the bull's-eye.

His smile could have lit up Times Square. And damn did it make the bastard look even more handsome.

He scratched his beard, unable to contain his glee at besting me, before grabbing the dry erase marker from the tray below the whiteboard I'd mounted on the wall opposite of the rack of axes.

On one side, he wrote *She-Ra*. On the other, *Stretch*. Then he gave me three points and himself six.

Eyes on me, he capped the marker and set it down. "Now," he said. "Lose the shirt."

I tucked my chin and took in my black tank. "I didn't agree to these terms."

"Yes, you did. You said, and I quote, if you want to get naked, I don't care. Thereby assenting to the suggestion. Take it off."

"Shoes first," I protested.

"Nah. That's dangerous with axes. Shoes stay on." He jutted his chin at me. "Shirt."

I was not dressed for strip anything. All I had on was a pair of running shorts and a tank top. I had come out here to blow off steam. Had I known how this night would progress, I would have put on every piece of clothing I owned.

I was fuming. The anger stoked those embers still burning low in my stomach. *How dare he?*

Except...

I had the power here. And by power, I meant boobs. Because there was no way his beginner's luck would last if my boobs joined the party.

They weren't anything particularly special, but he was a man and, therefore, dumb and easily distracted.

"Fine," I pouted. Then, slowly, and I mean glacially, I pulled up my tank and tossed it over my head. With a smug smirk, I strutted over to the rack of axes.

His gaze seared my skin as I pulled in a deep breath and let it out slowly. My bra was black and relatively simple, but it was sheer. It should have made me feel self-conscious, but I was determined to brazen this out. I would not lose, no matter what it took.

And my plan was working. He had gone silent. Good. Now I could focus on kicking his ass and reminding him that he should know better than to mess with Adele Gagnon.

I turned in his direction, making sure he got the full effect of my Target lingerie before leaning over to carefully choose an axe. They were almost identical. There were variations in each handle, but for the most part, they were unremarkable. He didn't need to know that, though.

In my periphery, his eyes bulged and he scratched the back

of his neck—one of his tells. This smug bastard was going down.

Stepping up to the line, I drew on every ounce of willpower in my body to focus on the target rather than the way his attention traced along my bare skin like a caress. I was going to bury this shit in the bull's-eye and never look back.

Taking one more breath, I threw and released the axe at the perfect moment, sinking it.

I turned back, wearing a smile laced with malice. "Shirt, Stretch," I teased. I sauntered to the whiteboard and recorded my six points. But my celebration was short-lived when he started to pull his T-shirt up.

Dammit. I should have said jeans.

He knew I was watching, so he pulled it up slowly, so damn slowly, revealing his muscular, tan, inked torso one inch at a time.

Jesus, Mary, and Joseph. If the beard and the height and the overall Viking warrior thing hadn't tipped me off already, his physique would have given it away. He was *all* man. Thick and strong, with massive shoulders and pecs dusted with dark-blond hair. And the abs? *Fuck,* those abs. They were split by a happy trail that led to the waistband of those damn jeans.

"Done checking me out?" he asked, chuckling.

At the call-out, I practically choked on my tongue, and another round of heat engulfed me. This time it was so stifling a bead of sweat dripped down my spine. Whipping around, I busied myself tallying the score, even though we'd only begun the second round.

He threw again, missing the center.

"Four points," he said. "Since you're so concerned with scorekeeping."

We went back and forth for our next few throws. Despite

what I'd assumed about his ability, he had clearly thrown before. His technique and strategy were too honed. I'd have to up my game.

On my sixth throw, I hit another bull's-eye and jumped up and down in celebration.

"Eat shit, Hebert."

I spun, still bouncing, only to find him hypnotized by my breasts. His jaw was slack, and his eyes were hazy.

I crossed my arms over my chest. "Pants."

Without a word, he stripped off those criminally sexy jeans, leaving him in only the work boots he slipped back on and a pair of boxers. They were blue with yellow rubber duckies on them. Silly and fun and not at all what I had expected.

I diverted my gaze quickly and took in slow, even breaths, not wanting to get distracted. The score was close, but I was ahead. And I still had my shorts on, thank God.

Normally, I bested my opponents without difficulty. It *had* been a while since I'd competed, but regardless, this was not my A game. Despite that, I *would* pull out a win. I had to. My pride depended on it.

My next throw was shit, though, and he followed that with another bull's-eye.

So I lost my shorts.

Thankfully, I had on spandex briefs. Full coverage, stretchy, and breathable. The demands of a physical job meant anything too dainty would be uncomfortable, and lucky for me, none of my downstairs was on display. He didn't seem to mind the granny panties, though, if the way his breath hitched as my shorts hit the ground was anything to go by.

But then he hit another bull's-eye. Motherfucker.

He turned and stroked his chin. "Ooh, She-Ra. This is such a hard decision."

I closed my eyes as my heart dropped into my stomach. This was not happening. I wasn't the kind of woman who went around flashing my bits.

"Bra," he said after a long deliberation.

He was enjoying this far too much. Not only was I going to get him out of those ridiculous boxers and laugh at his tiny dick, but I would win too. Then I'd make sure he honored the deal and left me alone.

I had to think long term. Showing him my boobs was a small price to pay.

I made a big show of unhooking the back of my bra and letting it fall to the floor.

His jaw went rigid, but he maintained eye contact.

In turn, my thighs attempted to clench, but I willed the muscles to relax. I would not give him the satisfaction of seeing what his attention did to me.

"Shit, She-Ra," he said, his voice low and growly. Another thing I enjoyed way too much.

"Don't feel special," I said as I snagged another axe. *Damn, shirtless axe-throwing was probably a major safety hazard.* "You're just another in a long line of undeserving men who've seen my tits."

"How long a line?"

"None of your fucking business." I stepped up, and with no preparation, no thought, only the desperate desire to end this game and get away from this magnetic, infuriating mountain of a man, I threw the axe. "*Fuck yes*. Lose the boxers, asshole."

He was slack-jawed as I pulled the axe out from where it was deeply embedded in the red. Good. I needed the points.

Despite my burning curiosity, I kept my eyes on the scoreboard. The last thing I needed was to be distracted by his dick. But I couldn't resist sneaking a look at his ass while he threw.

Wood Riddance

Just like the rest of him, it was muscular and perfect. Two tiny dimples right above his tailbone. That bastard didn't have a single flaw. It was maddening.

Being fully naked must have gotten to him, because he hit the second ring, only scoring three points. One of his worst throws of the night.

I tallied up the scores. My next throw had to be good. The score was close, but I could pull this out if I did things right.

As he walked to the other side of the container, I crossed my arms over my chest and averted my eyes. In my periphery, he had his hands cupped over his junk. Clearly, we were both rethinking this whole strip axe-throwing idea, because this metal box was shrinking by the minute and the air was growing thicker.

The doors on the far end were open, letting in the cool night air, but the heat between us was suffocating. I considered grabbing my clothes and making a run for it, but my pride got in the way. This was my private space, and I had to show this cocky asshole that he couldn't waltz around eyeing me like a piece of meat.

I faced the target, thanking God I still had my panties on, took a deep breath, and closed my eyes. *You are Adele Motherfucking Gagnon. You will bury this axe in the bull's-eye and never look back. Because you are a goddamn apex predator who does not lose, especially to a man. A man who makes you feel simultaneously aroused and enraged at that.*

I opened my eyes, wound up, and sank my shot. *Yes.* I was up by seven points, making it impossible for him to beat me with his one remaining throw. The game was over, and now I had to get out of here as fast as I could to avoid more bad decisions.

"Good game, She-Ra."

Pulling my tank top over my head as fast as I could, I ignored him. Covering myself immediately was paramount because the feel of his attention on my naked body was making my stomach clench in ways I had been repeatedly telling it were not okay.

He turned his back and slid on his boxers quickly. But then, cocky grin firmly in place, he marched right up to me and crowded me against the rack of axes.

"I'm glad you won," he rasped, tilting so close our breath mingled, causing my heart to clench. "Because when you finally give me a chance, it will be because you can't take the tension anymore. Because you want me as much as I want you. Not because of some stupid bet."

I said nothing as my pulse raced and the heat of his body soaked into mine.

But then he grasped my hand and brought it to his lips. "Oh, Adele," he said, scanning my half-clothed body with a look of pure, hot lust.

And then he pressed his lips to my knuckles, never breaking eye contact. I stood, frozen, confused, and turned on, while he gathered up his clothes and confidently strode out, leaving me to wonder who the true winner was tonight.

Chapter 15
Finn

"What do you want?" Adele growled, flopping into an armchair in Henri's office. Her hair was pulled back in intricate braids, and she was wearing her coveralls unbuttoned to her waist. Beneath it, her tiny tank showed more than a little cleavage. "I'm busy."

"Take a seat." Henri grunted. "Thanks for blessing us with your presence, my queen."

"Better," Adele said, sitting up straight. "Talk."

"Finn is planning to fly out to Site 211 this week."

I had been grounded for more than two weeks and was itching to get into the air. Even if it meant flying over former Hebert land. We had sold a little more than a hundred square miles to the Gagnons a few months back. It was on the northern edge of our holdings and hadn't been touched in years. The cutting was excellent up there. My father would have known that if he had been doing his job instead of trafficking opioids, but at least we'd sold it at a great price.

I swallowed thickly, hoping to clear the lump that formed in my throat each time I was around Adele. We hadn't spoken since our game of strip axe-throwing, and I was finding it difficult to form coherent thoughts, let alone sentences. "Probably Thursday. I'm waiting to see what the weather looks like."

"There are a few structures out there, decent roads, and some equipment," Henri said. "I think it may be helpful for you to join Finn when he goes."

Adele shot her brother a withering look. "Why? I have a lot of work to do here."

"Don't lie to me. You're months ahead of schedule on maintenance and you let your crew cut out early all the time." He hid his smirk.

It was no secret that Adele treated her employees incredibly well. I'd witnessed it myself. They were loyal to her, and she mentored them, championed them, and fought for them when necessary. It was one of the many things I admired about her.

"Sorry I'm so good at my job. Should I be less competent to make you feel better about yourself?" she hissed. Henri and Paz may have been known for being grumpy, but Adele had them beat. Her scowl could scare away a moose at fifty yards.

"This land hasn't been touched in a decade. The drone data is fantastic, so we're making plans to add it to our cutting operations for the winter." He took his hat off and ran his hand through his dark hair.

By the wary expression he wore when he put the hat back on—one I'd never seen on his face unless his sister was involved—I'd bet he'd be popping some antacids after this meeting.

"But I need to see what we're working with on site. Can we store machinery? Can we house people? Since it's so far from the main camp, what are the options? Roads are shit, but we can get a crew out there for repairs if it's got the kind of resources we need to house and support the operation."

"If this is so mission critical, then why don't you go with him? Or send Richard. Isn't he in charge of roads?"

"Can't. Also, no one is more particular than you are. You can't tell me you'd allow a single piece of equipment up there if it wasn't up to your standards."

She crossed her arms. The move would probably scare the literal pants off an average man, but her brother didn't back down.

"You keep telling us you want to be a full partner in this business."

"I am a full partner," she retorted. "You and Paz collude to cut me out of the big decisions."

"And here we are, making an effort to bring you in. This is your opportunity to oversee our expansion. Paz is up to his eyeballs with contracts and lawyers, and you and I both know you wouldn't want him assessing road quality for your trucks anyway."

Her eyes were narrowed to slits and her back was ramrod straight. Damn, she was furious. "No, I do not. Paz doesn't even know how to change brake fluid."

"Exactly my point." Nodding, Henri dropped his elbows to the desk, clasped his hands, and pressed them to his mouth. From my vantage point, it looked like he was hiding a smug smile.

I hadn't been here long, but I'd already discovered that Henri was shrewd and strategic. To run a multigenerational family business with his siblings, he'd have to be. All the Gagnon siblings, while smart and good at what they did, had vastly different personalities. Having witnessed a few meetings, I could only imagine what Thanksgiving dinner was like.

"Fine. I'll spare a few hours."

"Finn is going to teach you how to use some of the camera

equipment so you can collect as much information as possible. This expansion is going to make us the largest and most productive timber company in the state." He winced the moment the last word left his mouth and shot me a sheepish look. "Sorry, man."

I shook my head. Damn if I didn't hate the pity. I couldn't escape it, even here. "I have no attachment to the land. It's just trees to me."

It was a means to an end. Selling off acres in hopes of bailing out the business was no skin off my back.

Owen had handled the sale from Boston. That was his specialty. Contracts and accounting and debt ratios. He was great at it.

I wanted nothing to do with Hebert Timber. Like my brothers, I hoped the doors could remain open. It would be horrific for our employees and subcontractors if we had to sell the business. But I trusted Owen. If he thought this deal would help us continue operating, albeit at lower capacity, then I did too. But my future had nothing to do with logging. I had my eyes set on starting my business and taking care of Merry. If I had to work for the Gagnons to do it, then I would.

Unsurprisingly, Adele left the office still fuming. I found her at her desk that afternoon, where she was pounding the keys of her laptop into submission.

"I've been tracking the weather and the GPS coordinates. Looks like the best time to leave will be Thursday around noon," I said.

I kept my tone light and approached her slowly. If I startled her too much, she might throw a wrench at my head. And given her aim with an axe, I had zero doubts that she'd hit be dead between the eyes.

"The rules still stand." She didn't even look up from her screen. "And no mentioning the other night."

I held my hands up in surrender. There was nothing in this life that could make me forget the sight of her mostly naked body. I'd balance an apple on my head and let her knock it off with an axe if it meant I could see her tits again. Not that I would say that out loud, of course.

"We've seen each other naked," I said, raising one eyebrow. "We can move on now. It'll be a quick trip. We'll be back before sundown."

She grasped the top of her laptop screen and slammed it shut, pinning me with one of her signature glares.

"She-Ra," I soothed. "I know that look usually shrivels every set of testicles in a five-mile radius, but it won't work on me."

"Shut up," she growled. "And forget about the other night."

"As if I could. Seeing you naked might have been the highlight of my year. I gotta tell ya; I can't get you out of my head."

"I won." She grunted. "No more flirting. No more staring at me like you want to devour me."

That was a blow. Not only because the urge to do just that was unrelenting, but because she could read me so damn well. Though I supposed I'd never really hidden my attraction.

"I'm not Red Riding Hood, and you're not the Big Bad Wolf."

I smirked. She was partly correct. She was no Little Red Riding Hood. She was a wolf, just like me. That right there was what made her the most fascinating woman I'd ever met. She wasn't sweet, and she wasn't innocent. She was powerful and dirty and all my fantasies come to life.

"Got it. No flirting. No talk about nakedness. Any other rules?"

"The most important one." She cocked a brow at me. "Don't piss me off."

Ha. As if that were even possible. "My breathing pisses you off, She-Ra," I said, taking a single step closer.

"True." She pushed her chair back a few inches and regarded me. "But when you're flying a plane with me as a passenger, I want you to keep breathing, so I'll grant you a stay of execution."

I bowed my head in mock gratitude. "You are a benevolent queen."

"You can go now."

She swiveled in her seat, averting her attention from me, and put her booted feet up. Settling back, she picked up her phone from where it sat face down on the desk. Without another word, she swiped at the screen, effectively dismissing me.

My eyes were drawn to her purple nails as she gripped the device tightly. It took a moment to realize she was watching me with both brows lifted. Right. I was making this weird.

I turned to leave. But then my curiosity got the better of me. And maybe my yearning to be in her proximity. The pull between us was strengthening every day, and I wanted to be near her for another moment. Then I'd leave. So what if I was a masochist? Her insults excited me, and when she was angry, it lit up all my nerve endings. Yeah, there was something wrong with me.

Sauntering back over, a glutton for punishment, I caught sight of her phone screen and stepped up behind her, bending low so my beard tickled her ear.

"Are those dating profiles, She-Ra?"

She immediately clutched the phone to her chest. "So what if they are?"

"Lemme see," I said, holding out a hand.

"Fuck off and get out of my office."

"Come on," I teased. "We both know you have a bad picker. Let me see what's out there."

She hesitated for a second, which gave me an opening to grab her phone. I was a big guy, but my reflexes were still quick.

"Asshole," she cursed, but she was smiling. Sometimes I thought she liked this game of cat and mouse as much as I did.

It was only a matter of time before she threw something at me or kicked my ass, so I'd enjoy it while it lasted. I studied the app on her phone. One I'd never heard of—LuvStruck. I clicked on her matches.

"Okay, Brad," I said, perusing the photo of a boring-looking dude in a polo shirt.

"Likes dogs? Lame."

"Dogs are great," Adele protested, sitting up in her chair.

"I agree with you," I said, looking up from the device. "But is that really worth putting on a profile? It's like saying you like sunlight or pizza. Duh. Boring."

I kept scrolling. It was like slowing down to pass by a car wreck. It was gross and voyeuristic, but I couldn't contain my compulsion to know exactly who Adele was talking to. If I had any sense, I'd delete the apps off her phone, but instead, I dug deeper.

"And this joker?" I held the phone up so she could see the photo. "Who does he think he's fooling with that comb-over?"

She tried to snatch it from my hand, but I lifted it above my head and out of her reach. It was one of the many advantages of my height. "Don't be a dick. Not everyone has great hair like you do."

Daphne Elliot

"True, but if a dude's bald, he should be proud of it. Rock that shit. This"—I wiggled the phone in the air—"screams insecure. And he says he's *searching for his soulmate?*" I stuck out my tongue and pretended to gag. "Probably a coercive narcissist. I bet he love-bombs women and then discards them when he gets bored."

I had met too many guys like this. Who manipulated women's emotions to get what they wanted. They craved adoration, and they'd cross any boundary to get it.

Was I perhaps reading too far into Adele's potential dates? Abso-fucking-lutely. But I was running with it full steam ahead, and there was no way I was putting on the brakes. I'd disqualify every single jerk who had ever even considered signing up for LuvStruck. There was no way she was going out with any of these guys. Or any guy, for that matter.

"How do you even know this stuff?" she asked, wearing a thoughtful expression that held just a hint of confusion.

I gave her a wink. "You're not the only one who's been to therapy, She-Ra. And no, you're not getting the phone back." I kept scrolling, hitting the thumbs-down icon for every single match. I wanted them all gone. If she opened the app and found she had no matches, maybe she'd notice the guy sitting in front of her damn face.

"No way for this guy," I said, looking at an average-looking guy wearing medical scrubs.

"Why?"

"He's a veterinarian."

"What's wrong with vets?"

I dipped my chin and gave her a look. "He murders animals for a living. Sweet. No. Probably a sociopath."

"You are not well."

"Not denying it."

I scanned the profiles of every bland, boring dude in a hundred-mile radius, feeling both overwhelmingly jealous and a bit cocky. Because this was the competition. Sure, there was the whole *my dad is a murderer* thing. And my stagnant career, I supposed. But I could compete. I'd just have to convince her to consider me.

"Wait." I held up a finger. "What's this icon? Have you been messaging with any of these guys?" I clicked on the mailbox icon, and sure enough, some dumbass was shooting his shot with Adele.

I clicked on the profile option. "Dane," I said, almost gagging on the name. What the fuck kind of name was that? "Looks like he owns an insurance company and enjoys skiing in his spare time."

Her eyes turned murderous, and she locked her jaw tight. *Oh shit*. Now I'd hit a nerve. "He seems nice," she said, crossing her arms over her chest in a clear attempt to convince herself that this guy was even close to good enough.

"So that's what you're into? The corporate type." Saying it made my stomach clench. Why was I doing this to myself? It was time for me to give this woman her phone back and exit the room. This was not going to help my unhealthy obsession with her.

She shrugged, schooling her expression into something that only remotely resembled nonchalance. "Look around. It's northern Maine. There aren't many choices up here. And he's been really nice so far."

I scrolled through the messages. They had been chatting for a couple of days. Dammit. My vision was starting to turn red. Had she been messaging him the day we threw axes and she was eyeballing my dick? Because if so, the joke was on him.

"Insurance is boring." I huffed a laugh. "How could someone like you even tolerate this guy?"

She continued to shoot daggers at me, but I kept going. This was crossing the line. Still, I couldn't stop myself. "Ah. He wants to meet you for coffee? What a shithead. You know that's code, right? He wants to make sure you look like your picture. Coffee is such a cop-out. Commit to the date, man."

"There is nothing wrong with meeting for coffee." Adele's words were placid, but her tone was anything but.

"Twenty minutes is not a date. You wanna go out, then go out and get to know each other. You deserve a hell of a lot more than coffee."

"Enough!" She stood and plucked the phone out of my hands so quickly I didn't have a chance to pull it away again. "Go away. I know you enjoy torturing me, but this is cruel. There is nothing wrong with online dating. I deserve to find my person, so kindly fuck off." Her voice shook slightly, which was an enormous departure from her normal confidence.

Shit. I had let my jealousy and alpha caveman instincts take over, and I had hurt her feelings in the process.

"You misunderstand me," I soothed, lowering my voice and lightening my tone. "I'm mocking these shitty dudes. Not you. Never you. You deserve so much better."

"You are the last person who gets to determine what I deserve." Those words had the temperature in her office dropping ten degrees. Her defenses were back up.

"Fair. But at least let me help you. Here." I held out a hand and gestured for her to return the phone. "Let me see your profile."

She gripped the device tighter, like she was worried I'd snatch it from her again. "No."

"I could help," I urged with a shrug. "Give a guy's perspective."

She scoffed. "Are you an online dating expert?"

"No. I hate this shit. But I'm a guy, and I'm the best help you've got right now."

With a sigh and a slump of her shoulders, she handed it over. Damn, I didn't think I'd ever seen her so defeated. There was no way I would have pegged this gorgeous, competent, intelligent woman as self-conscious. What had she been through that had her convinced these mediocre dudes were even worth her time? On what planet were men not lining up for a chance to talk to this goddess?

I took a minute to study her profile and flip through the photos.

"Here's the problem," I said. "Look at these profile pics."

"What's wrong with them?"

"They don't even look like you."

"Hey."

"Not in a bad way. But seriously. What is this?" I held up the phone and showed her the photo of her wearing a dark purple dress that hit at the knee. Her hair was straightened, and her face was covered in more makeup than I'd ever seen her wear.

"That was taken at Henri's wedding last year. I thought I looked pretty." Her face was red now, and I sensed I had waded into dangerous territory. She'd obviously become a pro at hiding her insecurities since I hadn't noticed a single one until today, but the confident façade she clung to was beginning to crack.

"You do look pretty in this picture. And that's the problem. You're *not* pretty."

"Hey," she growled, clenching her hands into fists at her sides. "That's cruel."

"No. I'm not explaining this correctly. You're not pretty; you're beautiful. Gorgeous. You're powerful and you're breathtakingly hot."

She sucked in a breath, and a blush crept up her neck and into her cheeks.

I tossed the phone onto the desk and stepped back. "Like right now. You're dirty from working all day, but if I took a photo of you, with your coveralls tied around your waist and your bra strap peeking out and the grease streaked across your cheek, your inbox would blow up."

"You're delusional," she retorted, but her tone had no bite.

I splayed my hands on the surface of her desk and angled close so I was in her space. "The woman sitting in front of me is sexy. She's the kind of woman a man takes out on a proper date. The kind of woman he only hopes will give him the time of day. You are not some generic, polite, pretty-enough girl a guy sizes up over tepid coffee."

Her breath caught, and she searched my face. "What kind of girl am I?"

My heart hammered in my chest. I wanted to pick up the desk and throw it out a window. Anything to take away the barrier between us.

I held eye contact, letting the crackle of tension build between us. God, I wanted to grab her face and kiss her. But she was vulnerable, and I had promised to stop.

So I dropped my head.

"You're not a girl, Adele. You're a fucking goddess."

With that, I forced myself to spin on my heel and leave her office. If I stayed for a moment longer, I'd do something I'd regret. And she didn't deserve that.

Wood Riddance

As I stepped over the threshold, I turned back. She had dropped back into her chair, and she was watching me with wide eyes and her mouth agape.

"Thursday," I said. "Meet me at the runway. I'll be the tall, handsome pilot ready to show you the time of your life."

Chapter 16
Adele

I should not have been so nervous. Finn was a competent pilot, and I'd flown with him before. But the dread swirled in my stomach before I had even put my car in park. This was not how I wanted to spend my Thursday.

Taking a sip from my travel coffee mug, I steeled myself for this day. I was a professional. This was my family's business. We were headed to check out the new land and the viability of a potential second camp for our team. That was it. Easy peasy.

I would take photos, make notes, and consider what kind of equipment could be stored and maintained out there. Then we'd fly home. Alice had already texted to say she was making lasagna for girls' night, and Parker had sent a photo of three bottles of rosé she had picked up. Somewhat surprisingly, I was looking forward to spending time with my girls. Keeping the whole strip axe-throwing thing to myself had been killing me. They were trustworthy and would keep the information from my brothers if I asked. And I would ask. Because I needed other perspectives in order to fully process that interaction.

It had been one of the sexiest experiences of my entire life, and yet we had never so much as touched. Was that why my brain was going haywire? Because I'd gotten a look at Finn's naked ass and would never be the same?

Or was it because I hated him a little less every day? Because, try as I might, I couldn't muster up the anger I used to hold on to so tightly. The blinding rage had subsided and transformed into more of a strong dislike.

The cooling of my rage, combined with the endless reminders of how beautiful he was, was confusing me. And the prospect of hours in a confined space with the man was enough to make me consider running into the woods and taking my chances with Clive.

"She-Ra. You made it." I heard his voice before I saw those long, thick legs striding toward me.

Fuck. Fuck. Fuckety fuckers. He was wearing sunglasses. Aviators. His hair was tied back. Damn, he looked hotter than usual, and that was a feat, because the man was gorgeous on a bad day.

Did he do this on purpose? Jackass.

"Ready to fly? We're all gassed up."

He held an arm out, pointing at the small runway that fit precisely between buildings and a storage yard that was far larger than anything we had at Gagnon. I'd always wanted to snoop around and see what sort of equipment they housed here. Hebert Timber had been much larger and far more successful than my family's business. They had a flashy office building and all sorts of toys, including a runway on the property. These days, we all realized the luxuries were products of crime instead of old-fashioned hard work, but that didn't make me want to scope out their tools any less.

"Let me guess. You wanna see the shop?" He tilted those

sunglasses down a few inches to eye me, and I swear I broke out in goose bumps.

I shook my head, hefting my backpack over my shoulder. "No. Let's get this over with."

With a nod, he turned and led me to the plane. It was white, with dark-blue stripes that flowed from the nose to the tail.

He ran his large hand along the body of it in reverence. "She's a Cessna 206."

It was a decent-sized plane. It had six seats and some cargo space, and I could hear the pride in his voice when he talked about it.

"I've already completed the run-up checklist. I'll get the door for you."

I watched with fascination as he removed the chocks from the wheels and helped me inside. In the cargo area he loaded his camera equipment and some surveying tools.

He handed me a headset as he turned on the engine, flipping lots of switches and adjusting instruments and looking completely at ease.

"So we've got a nice long runway here," he explained. "And we taxi for a bit while I adjust and gain speed. We need sixty miles per hour to rotate and eighty-five to climb out."

I sat in awe as the plane accelerated and he gently eased the nose up. We gain speed, and Finn gracefully took off. My heart was in my throat as we soared through the air and the town below us got smaller and smaller, but Finn seemed more relaxed than he had on the ground.

"This is my favorite thing in the world," he said, staring out at the horizon.

In this moment, he was more like the Finn Hebert I had kissed two years ago, the man who oozed confidence and swagger and wore his big heart on his sleeve. There was no hint of the cynical, withdrawn person he'd recently become.

"I feel nauseous."

"Don't worry. You're in good hands."

I didn't doubt that. He had complete command over this machine. I couldn't help but be a bit awed by it all. I understood and appreciated what it took to handle big machines on the ground, so I could only imagine the degree of skill he possessed in order to fly.

His movements were so steady and confident. Each adjustment, look, and flip of a switch was precise and deliberate. Despite my best efforts to ignore the way each movement affected me, they called to my inner perfectionist.

Being in the hands of someone who knew what they were doing was the sort of thing that would help a normal person relax.

Me? Nah. This got me going. My hands were clammy and my pulse raced as I watched him. My curiosity, and dare I say a hint of desire, grew with each passing minute.

"You gonna stare at me or look at the mountains?" Finn asked, one side of his mouth quirked up.

Embarrassed, I turned to look out the passenger window.

It was breathtaking. The rugged terrain stretched out in front of us, the endless forest giving way to majestic peaks.

"We can land at the site. In the '90s, back before my dad idiotically abandoned efforts up here, his pilot would fly guys up here to work. It may be a bit overgrown and bumpy, but the drone footage indicated that it's clear enough for a landing. If I can't, we circle around and come home."

Turning back to him, I willed my stomach to settle and my heart rate to stay steady. "Sorry. Do you mean that there is no runway?"

"It's a bush plane." He shrugged. "We'll be fine. I'm trained in STOL."

"What does that even mean?" So much for staying calm. My stomach rolled at the idea of crash-landing.

"Short takeoff and landing. It's standard procedure in the bush. Runways are a luxury, so the plane is built to function in remote areas."

"Last time we took off from the lake."

"Yup. Those were pontoons. There's no body of water near where we're headed, so I've got the standard landing gear on." He patted the instrument panel and smiled. "Marge is one tough broad. She doesn't need much space and loves a bumpy ride. Don't you, girl?"

"Marge? Your plane has a name?"

"Of course she does. My great grandpa Jack? He was my mom's grandfather. He flew bombers during World War II. His B-26 Marauder was named Marge, so I used the name to honor him. He lived to be ninety-five. So many of my favorite childhood memories involve him and the stories he'd tell about his flying days."

Damn. This man chipped away at the ice around my heart a little more each time we interacted. "That's very sweet."

He shrugged. "My family is a lot bigger than my shithead father."

My roiling stomach had settled, but now it was twisting into knots. All this time, I'd been judging him for his father's actions. Yet he had five brothers and a mother and any number of family members who were not horrible monsters.

"This plane. I'll do anything to keep her. Hell, I'm working for the enemy, so I suppose I already am."

We soared over Lake Millinocket and hit a few bumps. I yelped, but he quickly steadied us.

"You're going to kill me," I snapped, not quite ready to let go of all my ire. Without it, how could I ensure I kept my distance?

He chuckled, adjusting his instruments. "Really? I was sure you were immortal. You know, since you sold your soul to Satan and all."

"Just fly the fucking plane." I made sure there was plenty of bite in my bark, though I had to school my expression to keep from smiling at his quip.

"With pleasure, She-Ra. Enjoy the views."

Competent men didn't intimidate me. Parker had once referred to competence as my kink. Now I was beginning to wonder if she was right. The more I watched Finn fly this plane, the more hot and bothered I got.

The expert way he manipulated the flight controls and his relaxed posture in the cockpit were so goddamn sexy.

He was clearly good at what he did. And that was a problem for me.

Maybe it was because my job required total precision. Attention to detail and perfect calculations. My sister-in-law Alice called it my Virgo energy, but it was more than that.

I had spent so many years of my life learning and developing my skills. I knew what it took to be an expert at something: dedication, focus, and self-control.

So I valued those traits in others. And right now, Finn's capability was setting off alarm bells in my brain. My lady parts were sure to follow.

"You love this," I said after several minutes of unabashedly studying him and his every move.

He nodded. "Since I was a kid. Even then, there was nothing I wanted more than to fly. Still gets me every single time I'm up here."

"I'm glad you found it. Your purpose. So many people never do."

"I'm lucky, I guess. And that's why I'm willing to fight so hard for my dreams. The thought of losing the one thing outside my daughter that gives me meaning and purpose terrifies me."

I regarded him. The way his T-shirt hugged his broad shoulders, the sexy aviator sunglasses that hid his eyes, the veins in his forearms each time he moved. *Damn.*

We flew in relative quiet. The hum of the engine was the only sound as we soared over trees and rivers.

"Look down there." He pointed at a small pond in a clearing.

A dozen moose were gathered near the water. From up here, they looked like ants.

"I wonder if Clive is there," I joked.

"What is the obsession with that moose? He's a goddamn menace, and you all treat him like some kind of cuddly town mascot."

My breath caught in my lungs. *How dare he?* "Watch yourself Hebert. Clive is beloved."

"He does nothing but cause property damage and mayhem. I'm shocked no one has turned him into jerky yet."

I gasped. "You are on very thin ice in this town already. I can't protect you if you disrespect Clive. And you better believe the pitchfork wielding mob *will* come for you."

He laughed. "Does that mean you *want* to protect me?"

"Of course not." I shook my head and grinned. "I'll be leading the angry mob. I'm giving you fair warning."

He chuckled. "Thanks for the heads-up," he said, checking his instruments and adjusting our altitude. "The Navy sent me all over the world. But one of the coolest places I've ever been is

Alaska. It's a lot like Maine, really, except bigger, colder, and way more wild. Lovewell may as well be Chicago compared to most towns up there."

With a hum, I nodded. It was my dream to someday visit Alaska. I'd read dozens of books and watched every documentary about Denali National Park I could get my hands on.

"But other parts aren't so different. They don't have many roads, and the ones they do have are often destroyed by the weather. The best way to travel to those unreachable places is by air. I met several pilots while I was there. A lot of former military guys, but some who grew up in the bush too."

He adjusted our course slightly, and the plane banked to the left.

"I saw how they made their livings. Some flew for oil companies, some delivered goods to remote villages, and others took tourists out to explore the wilderness. That's when I realized that if I had to be stuck in Maine, that's what I'd do. Share this place. The unreachable spots that only a plane can show you."

His words were earnest and passionate. It was obvious he'd put a lot of thought into his plans and that they meant a great deal to him.

"Like Big Eagle Lake."

"Exactly. Think of all the beauty in this area that isn't accessible by roads. And think about all the people who visit Maine each year."

"Lovewell isn't really a tourist town."

He lifted one shoulder, his attention still trained on the sky ahead of us. "But it could be. This region is growing and changing. Our town could too. Imagine if the inn was open again. And imagine if we brought back some of the town festivals. Our area has incredible camping, hiking, and fishing already.

I'm not saying I could do it all myself, but there is major potential here."

He wasn't wrong. There were a handful of vacation rentals in the Lovewell area—some of which my brother Henri owned—and they were always in demand.

"Your dad supported this?" I asked tentatively, watching his face to see how he'd react to the subject of his father.

"Yes. If I agreed to come back and work for him, he said he would invest." His mouth turned down and his shoulders slumped just a fraction. "Obviously, that's not happening anymore."

I nodded, ignoring the way his reaction to the mention of his dad and his derailed plans tugged at my heartstrings. "Where does this leave your dream now?"

"It's dead. Mostly." He pressed his lips together and sat a little straighter. "But I've still got Marge. She's the best gal a guy could ask for. As long as I can keep her, I won't give up on the dream completely."

"I admire your passion," I said, hoping the whirring of the engine muffled my offhanded compliment. "And I think you should still go for it. You know, 'dare mighty things.'"

His head snapped toward me, and a grin spread across his face. "And win glorious triumphs?" he asked, completing the quote. "Are you okay? Altitude sickness setting in?"

I looked out the window and ignored him as heat crept into my cheeks. Damn Finn Hebert and those damn sunglasses and forearms and flying skills. "It's a good idea. I can at least admit that. This is clearly your passion. Don't give up because things haven't worked out the way you planned."

I kept my eyes on the horizon, worried I'd crossed some invisible line. Up here, without the weight of all the problems I'd left behind on the ground, I was struggling to hate him.

"Okay, She-Ra, enough daydreaming about me. Get the camera."

Silently, I snagged the camera bag from behind my seat and attached the massive lens, as he had shown me, while he decreased our altitude. Once we were where he wanted us to be, I snapped photo after photo.

"Atta girl. For a newbie, you're handling this well."

Still holding the camera aloft, I cocked one brow and turned to him. "Trust me, I have plenty of experience with big equipment."

Chapter 17
Finn

Site 211 was full of surprises. From the air, it looked like a small clearing, with a few buildings and dirt roads. But once we'd set foot on land? It was a completely different story.

The windows of the bunkhouse were broken, and there were several cases of beer from the '90s stacked up neatly inside.

The cookhouse had clearly been home to several bears over the years. Most of the appliances had been pulled out of the walls and overturned, and there was debris scattered everywhere.

"I can't believe this place," Adele said when we stepped into the shop located at the edge of the bumpy, unpaved road.

It was nothing more than an enormous pole barn filled with junk. Naturally, the lights were out. We had located the massive diesel generators in a shed behind the cookhouse, but they were long out of fuel. Luckily, there was enough sunlight that, with the aid of a flashlight and the camera flash, we could get a sense of the place and what it contained.

Adele was in heaven, inspecting every inch of the large building while I took measurements and photos elsewhere.

After an hour, I found her still poking around, shining her flashlight and headlamp at each and every tool and gear in the place, mentally cataloging all the equipment. I spent a moment admiring the view of her bent over, ass in the air, looking at the engine of an old car she had discovered under a tarp.

I was so busy smiling like an idiot that I missed the first crack of thunder.

"What was that?" She stood ramrod straight and pushed her hair out of her face.

Side by side, we shuffled along the dirt floor to the front of the building, where we'd left the old garage door open.

Dark clouds had settled along the horizon.

I scrambled for the sat phone I'd clipped to my belt and pulled up my weather app. "Shit," I said, rubbing my beard as a massive storm formed on the doppler.

"What's going on?" she asked as we stepped out of the building.

"This storm was supposed to head north to Canada. Should have missed us entirely," I explained, tilting the screen, where a large blob of orange and red and green was moving almost directly over our location.

"You said you checked."

"I did. I've checked every day this week, including this morning, and everything looked good."

Adele planted her hands on her hips and shot me her signature glare. "What the hell?"

"I'm not Thor. I just look like him. I can't control the weather, no matter what you might think."

Her glare only deepened into a scowl. She did not enjoy my joke. "You wish you looked like Thor. You're like Thor's dollar store second cousin. The one everyone dreads having to invite to Thanksgiving."

"Doesn't matter." I shrugged, zooming in on the doppler radar for a better look. "What matters is that a big storm is coming."

"Do not tell me we're gonna fly that tin can in a lightning storm."

I shook my head, my heart picking up speed only a fraction. "I could do it, but I'd rather not. Looks like it'll last a few hours. We can wait it out."

She eyed me from head to toe, that mouth still turned down, until an earsplitting crack made both of us jump. Not fifty yards from where we stood, a tree split, and branches and splinters were falling to the ground.

"Shit." Adele shuffled back until she was sheltered by the roof of the building. "Lightning."

Still a bit shaken, I assessed her. Her eyes were wide, and her skin had gone ghostly. Dammit, she was scared.

"We'll be okay. We've got plenty of shelter."

"I'm not afraid of lightning, dumbass," she said, closing her eyes like she truly couldn't handle my idiocy. "I'm afraid of being stuck in the woods with your useless ass."

"C'mon. Let's grab supplies from the plane," I said, turning on my heel and taking off toward the makeshift runway where I had landed. She followed, keeping pace as I jogged.

I climbed onto the wing to access the rear of the fuselage and threw down a large duffel and a heavy waterproof trunk.

When I hopped back down, she was already holding the duffel, so I grabbed the trunk and nodded toward the building, signaling that I'd follow her lead.

Once we crossed the threshold, I dropped the trunk and grasped the bottom edge of the industrial garage door. It resisted at first, but I gave it a strong tug, using all my weight, and finally, it budged, letting out a screech on its way down.

She flicked on her headlamp as I unzipped the duffel and pulled out a pink lantern that belonged to Merry.

"What is this stuff?" Adele asked from behind me.

"All bush pilots are legally required to carry certain survival supplies," I explained, peering over my shoulder at her. "This trunk is equipped with a medic kit, a raft, an axe, some MREs, a water purifier, and a sleeping bag." I punched in the code to unlock it and threw open the lid. "The duffel has snacks, batteries, more flashlights and a blanket."

I flipped on my headlamp and sifted through the contents of the duffel next. Once I'd found a granola bar for each of us, I pulled an old wooden bench over to sit on.

She took the granola bar I held out to her and studied the wrapper like it held the secrets to the universe.

"Why are you so relaxed?" Her hair was bunched up around the strap of her headlamp. It was adorable. "We're stranded in the woods in the middle of a fucking lightning storm. A tree could fall and crush us."

I took a bite of my granola bar and studied her for a long moment before responding. "We're in a building."

"An old, shitty building with a metal roof. There are probably more mice in residence here than there are people in the state of Maine."

I couldn't help the chuckle that escaped. "Didn't figure you for the high-maintenance type."

Beside me, her eyes narrowed. God, I loved to rile her up. "I'm not high maintenance. I'm concerned. You flew us to the middle of nowhere in the middle of a biblical fucking storm. Why wouldn't I be a little worried?"

I leaned forward, resting my forearms on my thighs, and

dropped my head between my shoulders. Damn, all of a sudden, I was tired. It had already been a long day, and now I had to contend with two equally terrifying adversaries: Mother Nature and Adele Gagnon. Given the choice, I'd take my chances with the former, but I had no such luck today.

"I'm not happy about this either. Do you think I want to be here? Hell no. You act like I planned this."

"You said you were tracking the weather," she snapped.

I shook my head with a huff. Dammit. If she was crazy enough to think I did this on purpose, then there was no reasoning with her.

"Are you shitting me? That plane is all I have in this world, and I'm terrified it'll be damaged out there." I threw an arm out in the direction of the runway. "This is the last place I want to be. But I've had training, and I know it's better to stay cool and assess the situation than it is to freak out and shriek like a banshee."

She had yet to sit on the bench. She stood a couple of yards from me with her arms crossed over her chest and her feet planted wide. Our headlamps were pointing directly at one another, and the light illuminated the way her chest rose and fell with each angry breath.

Sure, this situation wasn't ideal, but we had shelter and a satellite phone and snacks. It could be so much worse. Hell, I'd lived through a lot worse.

"You can shit-talk me and yell all you want. Won't change the fact that we're stuck here until this passes."

Her face was stony and her body was rigid, sending me a clear message to go away. But I was a stubborn bastard and couldn't stop myself.

"Sit down and eat your snack. Let's make the best of this."

"We don't have to speak" was her response.

"True," I said with a dip of my chin. "But it will make this more pleasant. Let's get to know each other."

She scoffed and took a step back. "I already know everything I need to know about you."

Rolling my shoulders, I worked out the tightness in my neck. If I was going to go ten rounds with She-Ra, I needed to loosen up.

"Former military, so you've got good posture and crave discipline. But you've got some lingering authority issues, hence the long hair and tats."

She wasn't wrong on that front.

"Daddy issues, clearly. And you're an adrenaline junky. You hate standing still and get itchy when you feel stuck. You're always looking for the next adventure, the next challenge." She cocked a knowing brow and took a step closer. "I'll bet you don't read or watch TV to relax. That probably makes you feel twitchy. I'd wager that you physically exhaust yourself for fun."

My heart tripped, and my chest went tight. Damn. Was I that easy to read? Or could she see me in a way that no one ever had? I felt more exposed and raw listening to her than I had in years.

"You're a devoted father. But when it comes to women, you're a commitment-phobe. Probably the casual hookup type. You get bored easily, and you're always ready to move on to the next shiny object that catches your attention."

"That's where you're wrong." I sat up straight, holding back the well of indignation rising up in me. "I never date and I never hook up. I'm looking for something real and special," I confessed, averting my focus to the floor between us. "And since that's impossible to find, I'm good with being alone."

Wood Riddance

My admission was met with silence, so I mustered my resolve and dragged my gaze back to her face.

For a moment, just a fraction of a second, I swore understanding swam in her eyes, but in an instant, the look had morphed back into one of hatred. In that tiny window, though, when her guard was down, it almost looked like there was a little bit of relief mingled with the understanding. Like she'd realized her assumption was wrong. And maybe she was happy about it.

I saw her too. I saw the tough, angry facade she showed the world. And I saw the thoughtful, loving woman underneath. The one who went out of her way to care for every member of her crew. Who doted on that feral dog. Who'd defended Merry and me when no one else would.

I stood, and the dusty old air shifted around us. "But by all means, continue to believe what you want. You're clearly great at that."

She crossed her arms, one of her tells. Her vulnerability was peeking through.

"Let me say this first, though. I see you too, She-Ra. And I'll never be able to express my true appreciation for what you did at the diner. Not only did you stand up for Merry and me, but you gave my little girl some much-needed hope. You reminded her that there are people on our side." Blowing out a breath, I stuck my hands in my pockets and rocked back on my heels. "And you did something I haven't been able to do. You showed her what it means to stand up and do the right thing. Even when it's hard or inconvenient. Even when you're alone." Keeping my attention fixed on her, I paused, hoping the gravity behind my words would really sink in.

"As her father, I am so grateful to you."

Adele huffed dismissively. "It was nothing."

"It wasn't," I urged. "It was so much. I know you did it for her, not for me."

She nodded.

"But I'm still blown away by you. Because, as much as you want to hide it, you've got a big, squishy heart and a protective streak a mile wide."

I took a step closer, and her eyes widened in response. Every cell in my body was screaming at me to touch her, but I restrained myself. I kept my hands stuffed in my pockets and gritted my teeth to ignore the impulse.

"I can't fight it," I murmured, ducking my head and watching her. "My attraction to you. I know you hate my guts. I know you'd love nothing more than to disembowel me, but I can't help it."

She gasped, but I didn't stop there.

"I clearly need a lot more therapy. And possibly some kind of electroshock treatment. But I look forward to seeing you. Hearing your laughter. Usually you're laughing at my expense, but I'll take it, because the sound lights me up inside."

My mouth was dry and my heart was pounding, but it needed to be said. Maybe it was the storm that gave me courage, or maybe I'd finally lost my mind. Either way, I didn't care. I took another step closer.

"Don't," she said, holding up one hand. "I can't handle games right now."

Damn. All I wanted to do was close the distance and show her how serious I was. "I'm a grown man. I don't play games. I go after what I want. Have you not noticed the way I've salivated over you for the past few years?"

Slowly, so as not to spook her, I moved another foot closer. Close enough that I could reach out and cup her cheek. And that's exactly what I did. "I know what my father did. I know that I'm a marginally employed single dad with little to boast about. But never, ever doubt my attraction to you. It could power a fucking rocket to the moon."

Feeling bold, I looped a hand around her middle and pulled her in until our chests were flush. "I dream about you," I rasped, looking down at her beautiful face, at the freckles that dotted the bridge of her nose. "I lie in bed in my tiny, shitty apartment, and I think about what would have happened if I'd taken a shot last year. That day, when we found Remy and Hazel, I looked at you, and for the first time, I saw something other than disdain in your eyes when you turned your attention on me. I saw respect and admiration."

She bit her bottom lip in response. That slight movement alone made all the blood in my body rush south. This woman would probably kill me if she felt my reaction to her. Yet I was desperate for it.

"I could feel the connection building between us. But I was too scared to take the risk. I've been kicking myself every single day since. You are my dream girl. Now that we're stuck here together, I'll be damned if I don't shoot my shot."

Slowly, I tilted forward, brushing my lips against hers. In turn, she pushed up on her tiptoes and dove in. Damn. She wanted this as badly as I did.

Her lips were soft and lush and sent me reeling. Any hope of control was lost in the next instant, when she threw her arms around my neck and gently bit my lower lip. Our lips tangled as my hands pulled her closer until our bodies were flush.

But before I could deepen the connection, she flattened her palms on my chest and pushed me away.

"What the hell?" she yelled, her eyes blazing with anger.

I held my hands up in surrender, but she disregarded my attempt to defuse the situation. She charged me and pushed me again, even harder this time. So hard that I stumbled back and hit the rickety wall behind me.

"I don't want this," she shouted, her voice echoing through the building. "I don't want to want you."

Damn if I could suppress the smile spreading across my face. "But you *do* want me."

Covering her face with her hands, unable to even look at me in the dark building, she groaned. "Of course I do. But I hate it. I hate that even the slightest touch makes me light up inside. And I really hate seeing how great you are with Merry. It guts me."

I wanted to throw my arms around her and kiss the shit out of her again, but I refrained. She needed to get this off her chest. "Why?"

"Because it's so much easier to despise you if you're an evil Hebert. But you're not. You are weirdly sensitive. Stupidly hot. And you actually care about people. It's awful." Her chest heaved, and every line on her face was etched in distress.

I wanted nothing more than to wrap her in my arms and kiss away all her worries.

Inching closer, I ran my fingers down her arm. "Sounds terrible."

"I hold grudges for life. Ask Sarah Murray or Luke Pierre. You're supposed to be an asshole. Not funny and sexy and really good at axe-throwing."

Biting my lip, I held back a smile, lest she decide to murder me for making light of her tribulations.

"I truly don't know whether to strangle you or rip off your pants right now."

Throwing my head back, I guffawed. "It's early. We've got time for both."

Her responding laugh unlocked another well of desire

inside me. I had never felt a need this great, and I needed her to understand. But before I could voice my thoughts, she was pushing me up against the wall, her strength evident in the force of the impact.

And then she was kissing me again, leading the charge with her lips and her tongue and her hands. It was wild and frenzied and everything I'd ever dreamed of. A loud crack of thunder boomed in the distance, but nothing would stop me now. Without hesitation, I explored her body, stroking and grasping at every inch of her perfect skin.

Angling my head, I dove in deeper, pulling her ponytail to give me more access to her luscious mouth. The need to pull back and take a breath was becoming urgent, but I never wanted to stop. Finally, I couldn't fight the sensation any longer. I pulled away slightly, though I kept my hand tangled in her hair.

Her breaths were as ragged as mine as the storm raged outside. The old building did nothing to soften the sounds of breaking tree limbs and the rain lashing against the roof. "This doesn't mean I like you."

"Then what does it mean?"

Her words were harsh, but her tone only sent bolts of electricity coursing through me. "Absolutely nothing."

Standing straight again, I held her face in my hands and regarded her expression. "I don't accept that. I can't accept that." I dipped down again and trailed kisses along her neck, biting her earlobe and savoring the gasp it elicited while I worked the button of her shorts.

I was on fire for this woman, my body ablaze and my heart melting. All good sense and logic had gone out the window.

I needed her and she needed me and we were hashing this out now.

Lightning wouldn't strike twice. That was the saying, right? And I would never have this shot again.

"I hate what you represent." She gasped, tangling her hands in my hair, pulling it from the elastic I had it tied back with.

"I am not my father," I growled, running my fingers along the edge of her panties. "You want to hate me? Hate me because I can bench press more than you or because I tell a lot of dad jokes. But not because of my last name or the horrific things my father has done. Let me show you who I am. Let me prove it."

"Okay," she gasped against my lips. "Show me who you are."

I growled, releasing years of pent-up frustration and finally letting the desire I felt for her course through my veins. "With pleasure, She-Ra."

Chapter 18
Adele

This thing between us had taken on a life of its own. Despite kissing my sworn enemy—whose kisses were nothing short of hungry—my body was flying high. All thoughts of thunderstorms and old warehouses evaporated. I lost myself to the warmth of his strong hands on my body and the caress of his tongue.

He kissed me like a desperate man. Like he had crash-landed in the wilderness and finally found water. He was relentless, kissing me as if he could not get enough of my lips.

Despite his intensity and the building storm outside, he didn't rush. Instead, he savored every taste of my skin.

"Enjoy it, Stretch," I breathed as he worked his way back up my neck, his nose brushing the sensitive spot behind my ear, sending a round of tingles through my extremities. "You won't get another chance."

"Sure, She-Ra," he growled, like he was placating me.

I should have stopped it. It was a terrible idea. But in that moment, it felt inevitable. We'd been building to this since our moment in his truck two years ago. The attraction had been there, and it had only amplified. Anymore, I couldn't remember a time when he didn't intrigue and excite me.

We were stuck together miles from civilization, forced to take cover from the impending storm. I was a human woman, after all. And this bearded lumberjack was saying all kinds of swoony things and kissing me like I was his oxygen.

He'd unbuttoned my shorts, and now he was working them over my hips. Through it all, he didn't pull his mouth from mine. For someone with such massive hands, his touch as he worked the denim down my legs was gentle and light.

In return, I pushed his T-shirt up, desperate to get my hands on his skin.

He chuckled, his breath hot on my skin, as he pulled it up. "In a hurry, huh?"

Ignoring his teasing, I flattened my hands against him and moved them up his sculpted chest. Shit, it felt even better than it looked. All hard muscle and ink and a few interesting scars. His teeth found my earlobe as I pulled on his belt. Damn, it was impossible to miss the hard length of him straining against his jeans. His erection, so long and strong, peeked out of the waistband of his underwear when I unbuttoned his pants. Escaping his demanding mouth for a moment, I squatted and gently kissed the tip before popping back up again.

"Jesus Christ, She-Ra," he growled, wrapping a hand around my ponytail. "Warn a guy. I'm already too close."

I smirked as he pulled me closer. The second our lips brushed, though, he was the one to pull back.

"This shirt needs to go."

Obediently, I stepped back and let him pull it off. Before I could even bring my arms down, he was unsnapping my bra. For such a large man, he had alarmingly fast reflexes.

I hadn't even pushed his pants down his hips before he had

one nipple in his mouth. The wet heat sent goose bumps rippling across my skin. I arched my back to give him more access. As much as I usually detested the man's mouth and the words he spoke, I really enjoyed when he used it on my body. His hands joined the party, immediately creating a throbbing ache in my clit. Nipple stimulation had never been my jam, but he was manhandling my breasts in a way I couldn't get enough of.

"I've been dreaming about these amazing tits. They're so perfect. I've wanted to get my hands on them for so long. So I could lick them and suck them and come all over them."

My core clenched in response to his words. Shit, why was this so good? "What makes you think I'd let you?" I quipped.

He stopped and grinned against my skin, so cocky and self-assured. "Because I bet no man has ever been brave enough to try. You'd love the power trip."

Jesus. He knew me too well. Reducing this man to rubble had basically become my life's goal in recent months. Yet the visual of him losing control all over me, worshipping me? It was impossibly sexy. And damn if I wasn't tempted to let him do exactly what he'd been dreaming of.

To make matters worse, the bastard dropped to his knees and threw one of my legs over his shoulder. He was ruining me little by little. Each step he made only solidified my desire for him. The desire I'd pushed down and swore I'd locked tightly in a box. It wasn't often that guys went down on me. It was even more rare for it to happen the first time we were together. The act was so intimate and required a great deal of trust. It was something my previous partners and I had warmed up to after a while.

But not Finn. He was diving in with gusto, biting and kissing my inner thighs. The sensations made my head spin and the leg I was balancing on shake. Finn supported most of my weight, but I grasped the metal table beside us to keep from pitching to one side.

"It's too dark for me to properly appreciate this," he said, reaching behind his back.

His grip on me loosened, and I slapped the hand I'd had buried in his hair against the wall to steady myself. The next thing I knew, he was strapping on a headlamp and flicking it on. Then, with a quick grin, he dove back in. This was certainly the only time a guy had used an external light source to find my clit.

But he did. Easily. And repeatedly. With his tongue and his fingers.

"Seriously? You need a headlamp to get the job done?" I said, gritting my teeth as he gently eased one finger inside of me.

"You said I had one chance. I'll be damned if I don't do my best work."

I threw my head back, my snippy comeback fleeing when he alternated between quick nips and rhythmic flicks, ramping up the pressure in my core. The motion made my toes curl and my ears ring and all the blood rush from my head. A few more seconds, and I'd be screaming my way through an orgasm. But I wanted to feel him. All of him.

"I want." I gasped. "You. Inside me." I squeezed my eyes shut as he added another finger. It wasn't nearly enough. I knew what he was packing, and if this was my one shot, I wanted to sample the goods.

"Gotta get you ready for me," he said without slowing. "I can't wait to feel you come on my cock."

I was already dangerously close, and the pressure was only building. He was so in tune with my body. Without a single direction, he'd found the right rhythm and pressure. I could get used to this. *Shit.* No I certainly would not get used to anything related to Finn Hebert.

"I'm good," I said, banishing that thought from my head. *One time.* That was it. I'd repeat it to myself until it sank in.

He stood and dragged a hand over his face, tilting his chin so his headlamp didn't blind me.

God, the sight of him made my knees weak all over again. Reaching out, I palmed his shaft over his maple leaf boxers. They had to go. I needed to see what I was working with here. So I eased them down to his knees. Then I cupped his balls with one hand and stroked him from root to tip with the other. Yup. Long and thick and straight. He could be a dildo model.

Ripping the headlamp from his head, he tossed it to the ground, where it illuminated the space enough for me to really make out his facial features. He squeezed his eyes shut and braced himself against the wall. "Jesus. Your hands feel so good. But I don't have a condom."

Without stopping, I whispered, "I thought sailors were always prepared."

His eyes snapped open. "I have MREs and a fire starter and emergency blankets." He groaned when I squeezed his shaft a little tighter. "I can even do some light field surgery with the medic kit. But I didn't think condoms would be necessary for wilderness survival."

I smirked and licked my lips. "Then you've never experienced the wilderness with me."

"Noted. Next time I'll pack dozens."

"As we discussed, this is a one-time thing, Stretch." I gave his balls a gentle tug.

The sound that left him in response turned the heat

building in my core molten. "You'll be back for more. I promise." He growled.

My body was a live wire, primed and ready. Despite the storm and our dingy accommodations, I had never been so turned on in my life. I wanted him. I *needed* him. After the longest dry spell in history—which had come after several years of lukewarm sex—I was owed this. One night of passion and intensity and a whole lot of insults.

"I'm on the pill. And I've been tested."

"Same. Tested." He grunted, his jaw rigid and his entire body taut. "No issues. And it's um... been a while. Couple of years."

Interesting. Though the cravings getting the better of me overshadowed my curiosity over the length of and reasoning behind his dry spell. I needed to get this monster inside me.

Heart pounding, I swallowed and went for it. "I'm good if you are."

His eyes snapped to mine and he heaved out two jagged breaths. "I'm good."

He leaned in for a long, angry kiss before shaking out the sleeping bag he'd pulled from the trunk and laying me back on it.

"Fuck me like you mean it." I moaned, lifting up my hips to give him better access.

"No, I'm going to fuck you like you deserve," he said, dropping his hips to my pelvis so his dick brushed against my sensitive clit. "Thoroughly, and with no mercy. And when you're coming on my cock for the third time, I promise you this: you'll be ready to admit that you don't hate me. You'll know then that I'm the only man who could ever do this to you."

What was with all the talking? I could be orgasming right now. "Third time? Cocky much?"

Granted, I'd previewed the goods during our strip axe-throwing tournament. He certainly had a reason to be cocky, but there was no way I'd stroke his ego by saying as much. Expert head excluded, I still couldn't rule out the possibility that he was terrible in bed. Guys with big dicks always were. They thought that their size meant they didn't have to put in effort.

But then he pushed inside me, and a gasp escaped me before I could clamp my mouth shut. His self-satisfied smirk made me wish I could take it back, but then I was too busy trying to get control of my limbs to care. Finn was filling me so completely and expertly that I was already pulsing around him.

And then he moved, his arms bracketing my head and his large body ranging over mine. The sight of his tense shoulder muscles was enough to make me clench around him. He was so hot and so in control. Each stroke was strong and even. Not wild. Not erratic. Deliberate. With purpose. As if he was carefully priming me for something spectacular.

He trailed his lips along my neck, biting and kissing all my secret spots, murmuring curses and praises as he went. And I could feel it. The early flutters as I gripped him with my inner muscles and let the first waves of pleasure wash over me.

"Harder," I cried, bucking my hips to meet him.

And then I was lost. Soaring and flying and screaming his name as everything faded into the background. All of the reasons this was such a bad idea melted away as my body convulsed beneath him, shaking with pleasure. He was still going, making me feel things in places I wasn't sure existed in my body.

"Good," he breathed, looming over me. "That was your warmup round."

"Excuse me?" I squawked, though there wasn't much heat

behind it. As annoyed as his comment made me, I hadn't properly recovered yet. "You do not get to render an opinion about my orgasms."

"Yes. I certainly do. That was insulting. Barely a tremor. I can do better." He dropped back down and thrust harder.

I bit my lip to hold in another moan. It did feel so damn good.

"Hey," I said, annoyed at how good he was at this. "It was nice." Figured I'd bring him down a peg or two.

He stopped and looked me dead in the eyes. "Nice? Oh, She-Ra, now I'm going to have to fuck all the nice right out of you. I want you grunting and shrieking incoherently. I want you so gone that the only word you can utter is my name."

Before I could protest, he was pulling me up to my feet. He spun me around and slapped my hands on the table. "Use this for leverage," he whispered in my ear, sending a shiver up my spine.

I was naked and blissed out but also on edge. Maybe he was right. Maybe I had another in me.

He pressed his hand to my back between my shoulder blades and pushed until my body gave in and I bent forward. I didn't argue, and I stayed where I was, but I peered over my shoulder when he didn't immediately enter me again. Behind me, he lightly trailed his fingers down my spine. The other hand was wrapped tight around his cock. His eyes were drinking me in from head to toe.

Though my legs trembled in anticipation, I forced a sneer. "Are you going to use that monster dick, or should I put my clothes back on?"

He responded with a hard smack to my ass cheek that lit up every one of my nerve endings. I dropped my head between my shoulders and shuddered. I stayed like that as he lined himself up, and I let out a long, low moan as his hand landed on my other cheek and the crack echoed through the building.

"You have the perfect pussy," he said, grabbing my hips and roughly pushing inside me. "It's wet and warm and so delicious. And you look incredible taking my cock. So beautiful."

He slammed into me then, and I gripped the table hard to keep from losing my balance. Every throbbing, rock-hard inch of him was buried inside me, causing my pussy to clench and my core to ignite. The flames of desire instantly caught and burned hot. It was inevitable. I was on the brink, ready to come again. I wanted to hold back, just to spite him, but it felt too good.

"Is this the best you can do?" I taunted weakly, barely able to get the words out. My pulse was racing and my entire body was aching for release.

"*Shh*," he said, trailing his fingers down my spine again. The gentle caress was at odds with the violent way he fucked into me. "Take it. Take every inch. You're clinging to me, and I love it. I'm not stopping until you come so hard you can't stand up."

His fingers trailed past my tailbone, down the cleft of my ass, and came to rest gently on my back door. He stroked me, then applied firm pressure.

That was all it took to incite full-body tremors. My orgasm detonated like an atomic bomb, and I lost all control. I screamed his name, bucking up against him and clawing at the table. Every cell in my body was on fire as the pleasure washed through me in waves. He didn't let up. Relentlessly, he filled me with every thrust, dragging my orgasm out. This was one for the record books, both in duration and intensity.

"That's a good girl," he said, spanking me again. "Keep

squeezing me. Keep going. God, this feels so good. I don't know how much longer I can last."

"Let go." I moaned, my face pressed against the cool metal table. "I want you to lose control. Please."

He gripped my hips so hard I knew I'd have bruises. But it only made me more desperate. He was in control. He was manhandling me and fucking me senseless. And I loved it.

Within seconds, his thrusts became erratic. Then he went rigid, letting loose inside me. It was strangely thrilling. He continued to thrust, jerky and uneven, and I reveled in it, feeling every single tremor.

"You are spectacular," he gasped. Still inside me, he collapsed against my back, kissing my neck and shoulders.

In that moment, I felt the most unexpected feeling bloom in my chest.

Affection.

Chapter 19
Finn

W e had created a bunker in the old shop. Tarps from my plane and the emergency blanket and sleeping bag gave us a nice, clean cocoon. Outside, the storm raged on, the rain creating a symphony of sounds on the metal roof.

I found Merry's small pink lantern and brought that in as well. In our little shelter, we sat side by side on the blanket, munching on granola bars and Goldfish.

"I can't believe you had bags of Goldfish in your survival gear."

I threw a handful into my mouth and chewed. "I've got a kid," I said once I'd swallowed. "I have goldfish everywhere."

Her hair was all messy, and all she had on was a thin cotton tank top that did nothing to hide her peaked nipples. Damn, I wanted nothing more than to push her back and nip at them.

"Now," she hedged, her tone suddenly serious and her face flat, "I will skin you alive if you even think about telling anyone about what happened today."

"No need to get defensive, She-Ra," I teased, hiding the

punch to the solar plexus her words had landed. This had been unexpected, sure, but it wasn't meaningless. At least not for me. "You don't have to push me away, you know," I said, softly and a little more resolutely. "I don't want you to regret this. I won't."

"You say that now. But you don't mean it."

"Don't tell me what I do and don't mean. If you have something to say, then say it."

By her posture and the tone of her voice, it was clear her walls were coming back up. I'd fought so hard to bring them down, though, and I wasn't giving her an out now. I wouldn't back down so easily.

She shifted and crossed her arms. "This is nice." She waved a hand between the two of us in our little fort.

"Nice?" I snapped, sitting straighter. "Nice? Wow, you really know how to compliment a guy."

"I mean hanging out," she said, her face softening a fraction. "Being silly, eating granola bars in the woods half-naked. Being stranded out here is not ideal, but this is nice."

"And the naked fun?" I asked, raising one eyebrow.

She looked away, and a flush crept up her chest. "Also nice."

I rose up onto my knees, closing the distance between us. "Okay, clothes off. You need a reminder of what I'm capable of." Looming over her, I grasped her chin and forced her to look at me. "I refuse to accept being labeled as *nice*. I will, however, settle for mind-blowing, the best you've ever had, or life-changing."

Dipping low, I took her mouth roughly, and, thank God, she responded by wrapping her arms around my neck and pulling me closer. The storm outside was raging, but the real lightning was inside, arcing between us.

"Let's leave this here," she said against my lips as she

worked the button on my jeans. "A nice experience. A shared adventure."

Pulling back, I scrutinized her. Though she hid it well from others, the vulnerability rolling off her was palpable. This woman had been burned before. She'd been cast aside by dumbasses who didn't understand just how fucking spectacular she was.

I kissed down the column of her neck, secretly rejoicing when she shivered in response. I'd already tugged one strap off her shoulder, and I'd be damned if I didn't spend the proper amount of time worshipping her body. Round one had been fast and intense, but this time, I'd go slow. Make sure the word *nice* was expunged from her vocabulary forever.

"I'll give you an adventure. But trust me, when I'm done, you're gonna want even more."

She gasped as I took her nipple into my mouth. "Okay, Stretch," she sighed. "Give me an adventure."

Like me, Adele was the type who required a vigorous workout before she could think straight. It explained her constant presence in the gym, and also why, after another three orgasms, she was finally ready to relax and talk to me.

If that was what it took, making her come dozens of times so she'd open up to me, it was a tax I'd happily pay.

"You smell good," she said, nuzzling against my bare chest. We probably should have put clothes on, but since we were likely sleeping here, it didn't seem pressing.

"Can I ask you some questions?" Her voice was softer than I'd ever heard it.

I pulled her closer, tucking her head under my chin. "I'm an open book, She-Ra. You can ask me anything."

She pulled in a deep breath, her chest pressing against my side, and dragged one finger along the lines of the tattoo on my left pec for several long seconds before she finally spoke. "I want to know what happened with Alicia."

The tightness in my chest loosened, and I hummed. This was an easy one. "Alicia and I were both going through shit when we got together. I was stationed in Virginia, alone and settling into life in the Navy, and she was going to law school and struggling to keep up. We'd always been friends. And then we were more."

I stopped for a moment, letting the sounds of the rain fill the air. Talking to the woman I was obsessed with about the mother of my child was tricky, but this version of Adele, thoughtful and vulnerable and honest, was easy to open up to.

"Those years were really important to me. They always will be. She and I grew up together. Figured out how to be parents, and eventually functioning adults, together too."

She chuckled.

"And we got Merry out of the deal. But our relationship was never quite right. Neither of us was happy, so we decided to be co-parents and best friends instead."

"You make it sound so easy. So mature."

It was not easy. Especially during the first few years after we separated. But I'd gotten lucky with Alicia. Together, we figured our shit out and worked to be the best parents we could be for Merry.

"Eh, we've had our moments. But she's really something. She adores Mike, and he's perfect for her. They take trips and learn about art and wine and all kinds of stuff that's never interested me. He's great with Merry, too, but he's never overstepped or tried to take my place. He doesn't try to be her dad."

"It must be hard to see her moving on."

"I'm happy for her." I shrugged. "She deserves the best." Sometimes, in my lonely moments, I felt guilty for not making it work for Merry's sake. But the older I got, the more I'd made peace with the way things had played out. Alicia and I weren't in love. That was okay, and Merry would still have a wonderful childhood with loving parents. Not only that, but now she had another adult in her corner. Three people who loved her unconditionally and always had her back rather than two.

Adele shifted and pulled away. The loss of her hit me immediately. I sat up, trying to pull her back. I needed this. The feel of her in my arms, the smell of her shampoo as I snuggled closer.

But she resisted. Instead, she sat cross-legged, facing me head-on. "Do you still love her?" Her voice was firm, but there was a hint of hesitation there.

"Of course I do," I said, without missing a beat. "I love her as a friend, as the mother of my child. She's been by my side through all the good and the bad, the highs and the lows. We support each other and root for each other. I can't imagine my life without her."

Her eyes were soft, but the set of her jaw was hard. Damn. She was uncomfortable.

"So yes," I continued, desperate for her to understand but also adamant about being honest. "I love Alicia deeply. But not in a romantic way. Not in that passionate, can't-live-without-you way. No, I've never experienced that."

She put her hand on my chest and regarded me. "You're a good man. I'm sure it will happen someday."

Ignoring the pit that formed in my stomach, I shrugged.

"Maybe not. I had a messed-up childhood, and going to war didn't exactly help. Now? I'm stuck up in Lovewell, and I have no idea what the future holds."

She leaned in closer, tucking a strand of hair behind my ear. "You undersell yourself. There's a lot of potential in here." She tapped my chest.

The movement made my stomach flip. "If I ever find that special someone, not only will she have to love Merry, but she'll have to understand that Alicia will always be a part of my life. Forever and ever. We are a family. Me and Merry and Alicia and even Mike. This person has to want to join our weird little family."

"Anyone would be lucky to join your weird little family."

I pulled her close and kissed the top of her head. The gesture was probably way too familiar and intimate, given that we had been shouting at each other a few hours ago, but it felt right.

When day broke, the storm had passed. The tarp and sleeping bag had made the conditions bearable, but a musty old warehouse during a lightning storm was not exactly luxurious. Still, we'd made it work.

The awkwardness set in the moment we were both awake.

Spending the night wrapped around one another probably had something to do with it. When I'd opened my eyes, her face was on my bare chest, and the tiniest bit of drool had pooled at the corner of her mouth.

Waking up with Adele in my arms was a dream come true. Drool and all. It made sense. It worked. And it felt perfectly natural.

"Before we head out, we should talk about this," I said gently.

The open and thoughtful Adele was gone. In her place was

the surly woman I'd come to know well over the last couple of years. Her response to my suggestion was to cross her arms and turn away. This was not a good start.

She kicked at the dirt floor, avoiding eye contact, and then busied herself folding up the sleeping bag.

"I'm gonna go check the plane," I said when it was obvious that she wouldn't engage in conversation.

The way her body sagged in relief hit me like a roundhouse to the gut.

I clenched my fists, searching for the words that would make her understand how much she meant to me. I couldn't turn my back and pretend none of this had happened.

When we were together, for that one brief moment, I'd felt alive again.

But her cold regard after all we'd shared last night ate at my confidence and my resolve. So without another word, I turned on my heel and headed out to my plane.

Chapter 20
Finn

The flight home was silent and uneventful. When we landed, I taxied into the small building my dad had designated for me to use as a hangar. It was probably only a matter of time before it was sold off too.

And then I had to deal with the plane. I needed to keep Marge in fighting shape and couldn't afford costly repairs.

After making sure everything was secure, Adele thanked me and ran straight to her car.

I could practically smell the burning rubber as she peeled out of the parking lot at top speed. As her car crested the hill, I dropped my chin and sighed. I should have worked harder to talk to her. To break down the barriers she had put up this morning.

I'd finally had my chance with her. And yet, somehow, I'd ruined it.

The restless energy and racing thoughts continued into the day. A workout didn't help. Ice cream didn't either. All that was left was to get it off my chest. So I went to the one person who would get it.

Daphne Elliot

"You did what?"

Alicia was leaning over the massive kitchen island, her brown eyes wide. She worked from home on Fridays and was wearing her casual work clothes, which were still nicer than anything I owned.

I buried my head in my hands. She never took it easy on me. Which was why, after everything, we were still best friends. I needed an ass-kicking right now, and my ex was the best person for the job.

"I'm in over my head."

"No shit. You need to back up. Start at the beginning and don't leave anything out."

She put a pod in the coffee maker. She knew me well enough to know I'd need the hit of caffeine to get through this and that I didn't need any more prodding to open up.

So I told her everything. Recent events, past events. Our kiss a few years ago. The crush I'd had on Adele in high school, even though she never once spoke to me. All of it.

And she listened. She'd grown up right along with us. She knew the Gagnons and was well-versed in all the drama between our families. Of all the people in my life, Alicia was my safe space. I could tell her the truth, and I did.

We had been friends our whole lives, and when she moved down to Virginia to attend law school, we reconnected. I was stationed down there, and though I didn't miss Lovewell, I missed my brothers and my mother. Alicia was the closest I could get to being with family. She was lonely, too, and working her ass off. Damn, she was smart.

So we hung out, keeping each other company. Right before my first deployment, we became more. I was terrified and overwhelmed and headed into war, and I was desperate to cling to something comfortable and safe. She was my rock. She supported me through three deployments. When she got pregnant, it all seemed inevitable. She and Merry and I would be a happy family.

But eventually, she wanted more. Though it wasn't until she told me that she wasn't in love with me that I even registered how unhappy she was. How complacent I had been.

She wanted to move back to Maine. Raise Merry near her parents. She was offered a position at a family law firm in Bangor, and by then, she was tired of military life. Tired of being left home to raise our child while I was overseas.

I assumed I'd fly until the Navy told me I was too old for it. That was my dream. But my daughter was more important. A happy, healthy child was my dream now. So I finished out my contract and came back.

And we'd been making it work ever since. As co-parents and as best friends. But by the way she was looking at me now, I knew I'd messed up.

When I'd finished, I fell silent, anxious for her feedback. Except all she did was sit back and drink her coffee while she considered me, probably running through every detail. Finally, after what seemed like hours, she spoke.

"You have feelings for her?"

I nodded.

"And it seems they are reciprocated. Or they were."

Past tense.

"So why are you making this complicated? Talk to her."

"I did. I tried," I argued.

She rolled her eyes. *This* was where Merry got her sass. "She's been through some serious trauma. As have you, by the way."

I waved her off with a huff.

"A hot hookup in the woods is fun and all, but give her time to process and think. Then talk to her like an adult. Doesn't have to be complicated."

My stomach sank. Dammit. Sure sounded like she was taking Adele's side here. "You're supposed to be my best friend."

"I am your best friend. I know you better than anyone on this earth. And I know that you go full speed all the time. You act before you think. You take risks with your body and your heart." She pressed her lips together and gave me a sympathetic smile. "Not everyone is like that."

She wasn't wrong.

"And Adele Gagnon? Really?"

I hung my head as a wave of sorrow washed over me. "I know. She's out of my league."

She shuffled over and shoved me. "I'm not saying that at all. You are one of the greatest men I've ever met. Honorable and kind and true. She'd be lucky to have you. But she's carrying around a lot of pain. She's always been angry and distrustful. Even before her dad died."

It was true. Adele was complicated and prickly on her best days. And she'd been hurt before. Hell, she'd been dumped on the night we kissed two years ago.

"Take a minute. Think about what you want. Then find a way to let her know you're in this for as long as it takes. Show her you care without pressuring her."

Alicia was beautiful, always had been, but since she'd gotten her dream job and found Mike, she was glowing. Her natural confidence shone through. She was living on her terms, and that was what I had always wanted for her.

"I'm really proud of you," I said.

She tilted her head and frowned in response.

Wood Riddance

"Mean it. You're crushing it. After wasting your twenties with me, you course corrected. And look at you now."

She laughed and patted my cheek. "First of all, no time spent with you could ever be a waste. Yes, we weren't soulmates, but we grew up together. You helped me learn to adult and encouraged me through so much. If not for you, I wouldn't have grown into the woman I am today."

"Sure." My heart squeezed a little at that, but it was hard to believe that the self-centered idiot I was in my twenties could have helped anyone grow.

"Remember when I was ready to drop out of law school and you pushed me to keep going?"

I shrugged.

"And you were there, cheering for me, holding my hand, and taking all of my insults while I pushed out a nine-pound baby."

I smiled, and my heart buoyed at the memory. "Best day of my life."

She squeezed my hand. "Mine too."

Merry decided to join us three weeks early. Like her dad, she couldn't sit still, so she chose to make a grand entrance. Alicia was in the parking lot of the grocery store when her water broke. She called me and told me far too calmly that she was in labor. I, on the other hand, panicked and rushed to her, worried our baby would be delivered outside a grocery store by strangers. Little did I know that we wouldn't meet our daughter for another twenty-seven hours.

"I love that little pain in the ass," I said.

"Me too. And you deserve all the love." She put a hand on my arm and squeezed. "There are so many different kinds. Now that I've found Mike, I know how special it can be. I want that for you."

God, I was lucky. This woman very easily could have chosen to hate me and make my life miserable, but instead, she only wanted the best for me. I had a lot of work to do to be worthy of her and Merry, but she made it all seem within reach.

"I feel like such a fuckup. My family name is mud. And for so long, my identity was tied to the Navy, but now that part of my life is over. And to top it all off, I can't provide for Merry the way you and Mike do. Look at this house." I held out an arm and scanned the open-concept space. "Look at the life you're giving her."

It only took about two heartbeats to wish I could go back in time and keep my mouth shut. Because I'd laid out every one of my insecurities, and I wasn't sure I was ready for any more hard truths from my ex-girlfriend.

"Don't you dare talk to my best friend slash baby daddy that way." Alicia said, her serious mom voice coming out. "Our daughter is surrounded by loving adults who work their asses off to make her childhood magical. She wants for nothing. You are an amazing dad. Big houses and fancy gifts don't change that. You, of all people, should know that."

I nodded. Damn. There it was. The call-out. Growing up, all I got from my dad was material shit. A car, sports camps, random dinners out when he felt like it. He wasn't there for the hard stuff. He didn't listen when I needed advice or help with homework.

If I did something special, he'd show up and somehow be sure he took credit for it. He loved when we made him look good, but other than that, he either ignored me or belittled me.

He didn't speak to me for a full year after I joined the Navy. Told me I was throwing my life away. Little did he know that the Navy was what breathed life into me. My time in the service helped me understand my purpose. I learned how to be a good man because I was surrounded by them there. He sure as shit didn't teach me about values and honor and selflessness.

"We are a family. A damn good one. We may not be like the rest of town, but who even wants that? You have always been fearless. Going after what you want regardless of what others think about you. It's one of your best qualities. Being confident in who you are. And I hate to see you like this. Riddled with self-doubt and anxieties. This isn't you. So if you like this girl, then go after her."

"I have been." Since the moment I started at Gagnon Lumber, I'd been going out of my way to spend time with her, watch her, get to know all her quirks. Hell, I'd been doing half of that before her brother hired me. Watching her like a creep at the gym, at the diner, anywhere we'd run into each other.

"Good. So you're not a total mess. Keep going. Don't give up."

"But my dad..."

Her nose flared as she threw up her hands. "You are your own man, Finn Hebert. And you're the best kind. If she can't see past your dad, then fuck her.

Chapter 21
Adele

I was in desperate need of a way to blow off steam. Conflicting emotions were battling within me, pummeling my heart and picking apart my brain. I fought, though, and I fought hard, even knowing that I'd lose this war.

Because my feelings for Finn were big and scary and overwhelming.

And my attempts to shut them down and pack these away neatly, like they were wrenches lined up on precisely labeled shelves, had all been futile.

Sadly, feelings were not tools. They couldn't be put away and taken out when the job required it. Nope, they floated around all day, disrupting lives and making simple things difficult.

Like sleeping. Hadn't been doing much of that lately, since I couldn't stop replaying Finn's words in my mind. Both the romantic ones and the dirty ones.

That feeling I had always yearned for? Being wanted and

desired and craved? I had read about it in books, but I'd thought it a work of fiction.

Turned out it was possible. And it was intoxicating. It could turn an unsuspecting person into a walking sex zombie who couldn't function in society. I certainly didn't need the aggravation.

So instead of going to work, which had been my plan, I texted Parker and headed to the gym. She'd kindly picked up He-Man yesterday when I called her from the sat phone, and I owed her big time. I also needed a sanity check. Because not only had I slept with Finn Hebert, but I was finding myself desperate to do it again.

While waiting for her to arrive—she was probably snuggled up with my brother—my phone dinged.

> Stretch: Can we talk?

I covered my face with my hands. I could not handle this right now. But apparently, he wasn't done.

Stretch: I realize that's a sketchy thing to text. I suck at communicating. What I meant was, I'd like to have an adult conversation about what happened between us.

Stretch: Preferably in person. But no pressure.

I laughed. Now he was being polite? After all the dirty things he'd whispered in my ear last night? After the way he'd manhandled me and doled out more orgasms in one night than I'd had in my previous six-month relationship, I didn't trust myself to respond.

"What do you mean you slept with him?" Parker hissed between sets of deadlifts.

She scanned the gym, using the floor-to-ceiling mirror to

make sure no one was listening. The walls had ears in Lovewell. But I was too distraught to worry about discretion.

"Is this a thing? Is it gonna happen again?" Her face said it all. Telling her had been a terrible idea. But not as terrible as what I'd given in to when we were stranded in the forest.

"No," I lied. "One time only."

"Okay, good. Not that I'm judging you. How could I? I have eyes and ovaries. I've seen that man. And you weren't of sound mind. It's not your fault."

My heart sank. Dammit. I didn't want to want him, but I'd thought Parker would be slightly giddy when I broke the news. She'd been encouraging me to get out there again, after all.

"Sweetie, I don't mean it like that," she soothed. "You deserve all the orgasms. But I know your brothers *and* this town."

The reminder made my stomach lurch. Because she *was* right, but I hated the reality of how this would play out if my family caught wind.

Sure, I had gotten swept up, but not entirely. The connection between us was undeniable. Inevitable, even. As if we'd been building to this conclusion for a long time.

"There's more to the story."

"How much more?"

I grabbed a plate and slid it onto the bar. "We've been flirting for a long time. And I've kissed him before. Just once. It was two years ago."

"How am I only learning about this now?" She secured the weight with a collar and put her hands on her hips. "I thought we had become official best friends."

"It was years ago." I waved her off. "Before I met you. It never seemed relevant."

"Sticking your tongue down the local Viking hottie's throat is *always* relevant, Adele." She crossed her arms and tapped her foot on the foam flooring, signaling that she wanted all the details.

"You know how Henri gave him an office space in my shop? It means that I see him almost every day now. Turns out he's not the terrible monster I thought he was. He's sensitive and funny, and he's an amazing dad."

As much as it pained me to get the words out, it was the truth. It'd be easy to reduce the whole family to evil, murderous felons—hell, that's what I had been doing until recently—but Finn was a good person. He treated everyone he met with respect and had been nothing but an asset to the company.

He was also annoyingly handsome, and he refused to stop flirting with me.

Parker was watching me, her eyes wide and her mouth ajar. "What?"

She leaned forward and whispered, "You. Like. Him."

"I do not," I protested, rearing back in disgust. "I can't like him. But if things were different, I would definitely like him."

"Do you hear yourself right now? *Can't like him* isn't the same as *don't like him*. I'm not going to judge you for who you sleep with. That's your business, and I'm here to support you..."

"But...?"

She let out a heavy sigh. "Can you imagine what would happen if your family found out? The fallout would be nuclear. Paz would self-destruct. There'd be a mushroom cloud over our house. And Remy and Henri and Alice and your mom..."

I shot her a look. There was nothing more tiresome than machismo. I was more than capable of taking care of myself. My brothers knew that. They also knew they'd lose body parts if they tried to interfere in my dating life. "They know to stay out of my private life."

Wood Riddance

"Yes, but what about if your private life involved a Hebert? I don't have an issue with Finn. In my experience, all families have shitheads, and he is not his dad. I can separate how I feel about him from how I feel about his father. But I'm afraid your family might not be able to. I'm only looking to protect your beautiful heart."

I squeezed my eyes shut. Damn, I wished my engineering skills extended to time travel so I could go back and not get on that plane. Life would be so much easier if I hadn't slept with him. If I hadn't experienced how protective and tender he was. I had always hated thunderstorms, and he'd made me feel so safe.

That feeling was almost impossible to shake.

"He's not a bad guy," I said weakly.

Parker racked her weights and raised one brow at me. "Didn't you used to call him Satan's Asshole?"

"Yes. Among other things. But he's annoyingly decent."

She continued to watch me without speaking. Shit, was this what she was like in an interrogation room? Did she play the silent type who waited out the perpetrator, made them sweat before they caved and confessed?

"And tender," I said, giving in and opening up. "And dammit, he's really good in bed."

"I knew it." She pumped her fist. "Now we're getting to the good shit. Please tell me it's proportional to the rest of him. 'Cause that guy is, like, almost seven feet tall."

There was no doubt my face was bright red. If the heat didn't give it away, my reflection in the mirror sure did.

"Okay, okay. So the Viking lumberjack is hung and has layers. Shit, this is getting complicated."

"Tell me about it."

She adjusted her ponytail and frowned.

"Now that I'm a mature woman in a serious relationship," she said, holding that concerned expression despite how ridiculous that statement was, "I'm going to give you some advice. Stop and think. It's easy to get swept up in the forbidden. It's easy to forget about reality when he's got a big dick." She gave me an exaggerated wink. "Give yourself some time. You've been through a lot. There's no need to rush things. If you want to pursue this, I've got your back. I will handcuff Paz if I need to."

"Gag. You probably already do that."

"Only once in a while." She giggled. "But I mean it. If this is real, I'm on it. I'll wrestle every hater into submission. Just be sure before you take the plunge."

Her advice was solid. I couldn't even begin to deal with this until the dust settled. I was still on an adrenaline high from our flight and the storm and all the orgasms. Was this worth blowing up my life for? Hurting my family? I hadn't even thought about my mom. She'd be devastated if I brought a Hebert to family dinner.

"Go home and try to relax," she urged me gently. "Because you're coming out tonight."

"No way." The last thing I wanted was to deal with people. My only plans for the evening involved snuggling up with He-man and watching reality TV until my brain rotted. That would take care of the pesky memories of Finn.

"Nice try. Shower and put on something cute. We're getting drinks. The whole gang is coming. Alice is even dragging Henri out. They got a babysitter for the evening."

Henri. That pulled a chuckle from me. My oldest brother's idea of a great night was reading a book in front of the fireplace with his dogs and Alice beside him. But he was growing and changing.

Wood Riddance

As much as it killed me to admit it, I should probably spend some time with my brothers outside of work. Now that they were all locked down, we didn't hang out nearly enough.

"You can smoke everyone in darts and collect free chicken fingers."

That sounded like the world's worst idea. "Eh, no thanks."

"You need to work through all this shit. Leave your house. Your dog and your book boyfriend will still be there when you get home. Flirt, dance, have a beer."

"Who the hell am I going to flirt with in this town?"

"Please. It's summer in Maine. There are men everywhere. The local boys and the tourists and the random weirdos."

"Wow. You make it sound so appealing. You and I both know what's going to happen. I'll come out, and we'll hang for a bit, but then you losers will all cuddle up with your significant others, and I'll be stuck hanging out with Dylan."

"He's a sweetheart," Parker crooned.

Dylan Markey had been Remy's best friend all his life. He was an unofficial Gagnon and one of the best people I knew. But, as the only single people in our little group, we always ended up hanging out and shooting pool when the rest of the crowd got all lovey-dovey.

"Of course he is. But I don't hear you denying that you'll get two drinks deep and then be too busy sticking your tongue down my brother's throat to hang out with me."

"At the moment, I'm unable to predict the outcome of the evening. Have you seen your brother? I can't keep my hands off my lumbersuit." She waggled her brows.

"Please stop." I gagged. "You're making it worse."

"I'll stop if you promise to come out for a bit."

I grumbled through the end of our workout, still actively trying to keep my brain from drifting to Finn. It took every ounce of self-control I had not to respond to his texts. But I needed a minute. I needed space from his face and his body and his constant flirting.

"Does he smell like plaid?" Parker asked while foam rolling her hamstrings.

"Plaid is not a smell."

"Disagree. You know what I'm talking about. Solid, capable, manly with a hint of spice?"

Shit, he did smell like plaid.

Duck, Duck, Moose was a dive bar in spirit and the official hangout spot for Lovewell locals. The space was huge, with pool tables, booth seating, and a dance floor. On Saturday nights during the summer, the place was packed, both inside and out on the tiny deck off the back. Hazel was bartending tonight. She had recently finished her PhD and was working on a big research project with the National Institute of Health about the opioid crisis in Maine, but she still bartended when Jim needed her. He hated pretty much everyone on earth, but he had a soft spot for Hazel.

Remy was parked at the bar, where he could be found any night she was working, drinking water and gazing longingly at his wife. All my brothers had fallen hard. But while Henri and Paz leaned more toward stoic, Remy wore his heart on his sleeve. The way he worshipped his wife was both adorable and cringe inducing. Not that he cared what any of us thought.

Dylan sat next to him. He was thoughtful and sweet, and he was handsome too. He was around my height, and with his dark hair, glasses, and broad shoulders that filled out his flannel shirt perfectly, he walked the line between nerdy science teacher and grizzled lumberjack perfectly.

If I had half a brain, I'd be interested in him. It was common knowledge that he'd had a crush on me back in high school. He was exactly the sort of stable, dependable, sweet guy a smart girl would marry.

Because a girl doesn't marry the best sex of her life.

Or the dangerous Viking.

Or the man who makes her think and feel things she can't quite control.

Nope. Definitely not husband material. But Dylan would be perfect.

If only I were into him.

And there was also the pesky detail that he was head over heels in love with Lydia Huron. That crush he had on me in high school stayed in high school. Lydia, though, taught at the school, too, and she was seemingly oblivious to his blatant pining.

But he was a good friend, and we'd gotten closer since my brothers and friends had fallen madly in love. When it came to darts, he was a worthy opponent, and that was usually how we spent these nights out. Loser bought the chicken fingers, which we ate while trash talking and playing another game.

His face fell as Lydia walked in arm in arm with some random dude.

"Who's that?"

He shrugged. "Guy from Bangor. Guess she's dating him."

A little uncomfortable, I decided he needed a distraction. I looped my arm around his and tugged. "Let's play darts."

"I'm off my game tonight. You'll kick my ass," he teased.

"I'll go easy on you," I promised. "Give you some pointers."

He took another look across the room at Lydia and her date,

who were cozied up in a booth on the back wall. My heart ached for him. I didn't know her well, but I had the overwhelming desire to stomp across the bar and kick her ass.

She was petite, with long red hair and a perfect smattering of freckles across her cute nose. I had no reason to hate her, but my loyalty to Dylan overtook logic.

"Can I accidentally hit him with a dart?" I asked sweetly. I had zero doubt that I could nail that fucker between the eyes from across the room.

He rolled his eyes at me and pulled me toward our usual spot, gesturing to Hazel for another round.

We were a few games in when I turned and spotted the one person I was hoping to avoid. Finn. He was striding into the bar. His long legs were eating up the distance quick, and his hair was down. Damn, he looked stupidly good.

I should have looked away. But I froze in place, entranced by him. For someone so tall, he moved with an exceptional amount of grace and confidence.

Finn Hebert made me lose all sense of control.

A flash of a memory hit me right then and there. The feel of his breath on my skin. The way his fingers gripped my hips.

The thrill that shot through me when he pinned me to the ground.

The dirty things he'd whispered in my ear.

Fuck. How could any guy ever compete with that?

And he knew it too. Asshole. He probably took pride in the knowledge that he'd ruined me for other men.

Did he have to look so delicious, too? He had no business looking this good in his blue plaid shirt and jeans at a bar in rural Maine.

Because mine wasn't the only head turning.

Oh no. Every set of eyes bulged when he walked in. It

helped that he was with two of his brothers. I always mixed their names up. The older one, with the thick beard and the younger, quieter one. Together, the three of them looked like they had arrived from a photoshoot for *Lumberjack Monthly*.

They were all beards and attitude, with a side of icy blue eyes.

So tall and broad they made my giant brothers look puny.

A group of older ladies, including Bernice from the diner and Mrs. Martin, my sixth-grade math teacher, actually whistled as they walked by. Though no one was surprised by their outburst. They were known to get rowdy during their girls' nights. Hazel occasionally had to cut them off and call their husbands to drive them home.

It had been a long time since the Heberts had shown their faces at the Moose. I was proud of Finn. This was difficult for him, but he had to show this place that he was here to stay. For Merry.

But I was also pissed off. Because now any chance I had of having a good time had flown straight out the window.

Bastard.

Dylan nudged me, holding out my glass of wine. "Fine," I said, my heart pounding in my ears. I tipped it back, chugging half of it in one go, and turned to the dartboard. I was determined to ignore every impulse in my body, which, inconveniently, was screaming to go over to Finn and stake my claim.

"You sure?" He raised one brow at me. I was usually good at playing it cool, but that man flustered me like no other. I swore he was giving off pheromones so powerful they had turned me into a fourteen-year-old again.

I nodded and returned to the dartboard, desperate to ignore the Viking elephant in the room. Of course, the moment I found my resolve, Parker ran over and nudged me.

"*Damn*," she said, clinking her glass against mine.

I glared at her, but all she did was grin right back at me. Dammit. She was immune to my looks.

"Please tell me you're not going over there. Not with your whole family here."

"Obviously." I huffed. Okay, it was official. I was fourteen again—the huff proved it. "It would cause an international incident."

"Good. I really don't want to have to throw punches tonight. I just got my nails done." She wiggled her blood red manicure at me.

"Don't worry," I assured her with a flippant wave. "I can control myself. I'm not going to scandalize anyone."

Finn and I needed to talk at some point. Soon. He had been shockingly up-front and honest. And as paranoid as I was, I believed him when he said he wasn't the type to play games.

Yesterday, I had run away and ignored his texts. Soon, though, I'd need to face the music and try to move on from this. Behaving like a bratty child was not the answer here, but I couldn't seem to make myself confront the situation. Retreating into myself and ignoring all the lust and like and curiosity swirling around in my head was a whole lot easier.

Despite my inclination to bury my head in the sand, I *did* want to talk to him. I wanted to flirt with him and yell at him. Tell him that what had happened between us had meant something. But I was a coward. And there was no way I could do it in public, especially with all three of my brothers here. They would hit the roof and the town would be talking about it for years. I'd be a mature adult tomorrow. Tonight, I'd stay the course and avoid it all.

Though his presence made that so damn hard.

No matter where I went, I could feel his eyes on me. He

had no idea what that gaze did to my insides. My stomach was twisted up in knots, and my heart fluttered so frequently I thought I might need to schedule an appointment with a cardiologist.

He watched my every move, studying every inch of my body. Had I known he'd be here tonight, I would have put on more makeup. Maybe even worn a skirt to torture him.

I'd donned a worn pair of cutoffs and my favorite pair of Converses instead, but that didn't stop him from ogling me every chance he got.

Finn, the confident charmer, lurked in the corner, staring at me like he was some kind of savage animal biding his time until he could tear my clothes off.

I should have been offended—pissed off, even—at the brashness of his assessment. Instead, I was dizzy with lust and tamping down the urge to walk over there and stick my tongue down his throat.

Finn had always seemed like a good time. Energetic, funny, and self-deprecating.

But beneath that exterior was pure fire.

It blazed so hot it singed my skin from across the crowded bar.

I wanted to be annoyed.

I wanted to be furious.

But dammit, I was only turned on.

Chapter 22
Finn

A licia's words swirled around in my head as I ambled up to the bar. I wanted more. I deserved more. But I feared I'd never get it.

Adele hadn't responded to my texts, and I refused to become that desperate guy who sat around waiting for the crumbs she'd drop for me. She was skittish, I got that, but Jesus.

After our night in the woods, I expected more. I expected better.

We had connected. And not just physically. The sex had been phenomenal, yes, but the connection between us had been so much more than that.

We were adults. Not children. So this avoidance tactic of hers was pissing me off.

I didn't, for even an instant, regret sleeping with her. Even in my maddest state, that would be impossible. Chastened was more like it. I should have known she'd ghost me.

So instead of spending time with my brothers, which had been the purpose of coming out tonight, I was watching Adele's every move like a creep and sulking into my lukewarm beer.

Gus and Jude, though they'd never be mistaken for social butterflies, were at least playing pool and acting like humans. I leaned against the wall and tortured myself with thoughts of her.

At first, she was clustered near the bar with Parker Harding and Hazel and a couple of her brothers.

So I sat and watched her pathetically. She laughed, she smiled, she sipped what looked like rosé.

Her hair was down in a way I'd rarely seen it, and I itched to run my fingers through the silky strands. It hung down her back in a curtain with the slightest wave.

"What do you think?" Gus asked, elbowing me in the ribs.

I blinked at him, tearing myself from my Adele-induced stupor. "About what?"

"The proposal for the land."

"He's not even listening," Jude said, checking his phone. "Cole's on his way."

"He's in town?"

With a sigh, he shrugged, "I guess so. You know how he is. Goes where he wants when he wants, with no regard for the rest of us."

I lost track of the conversation again when Adele wandered over to the dartboards with Dylan Markey.

Truly, I didn't have any issues with the guy. As a neighbor, he was polite enough. He kept to himself, and he taught at Merry's school. He was also Remy Gagnon's best friend, so we'd never traveled in the same circles.

He was leaning in close to Adele, smiling as he chatted her up.

At one point, she put her hand on his arm and threw her head back in laughter. The sight combined with the sound made my eye twitch and my chest hurt. It was irrational, but the thought of her sharing those rare, beautiful smiles with any man but me made me see red.

"Tone it down, brother," Gus warned, lining up his next shot.

I shot him a glare, willing the rage simmering beneath my skin to settle, but it was no use.

"You're like a bull moose ready to fight over a mate. Let it go," Jude added.

I clenched my fists. The anger I'd kept a lid on was beginning to boil over. I couldn't let it go.

She was mine.

At least I wanted her to be. Desperately. I was a caveman, but I wasn't delusional.

Obviously, with her consent, she'd be mine.

And Dylan fucking Markey was whispering in her ear and making her laugh.

I had several inches and at least thirty pounds on the guy, but he was strong in his own right. He could probably hold his own. And if he had the backing of an army of Gagnons behind him? Shit. Things could get ugly fast.

More than anything, though, I wanted to throw Adele over my shoulder and make sure everyone in town knew who she belonged to before I took her home to my bed.

Then I'd spend all night fucking her like she deserved. I wouldn't stop until she begged me for forever.

Yes. That was my fantasy. I was clearly deranged.

It was late, the bar had mostly cleared out, and my mind was buzzing.

Not from the beer. I hadn't even finished my first one, which had long ago been discarded. But from Adele. Her presence.

She was wearing her standard cotton tank and jean shorts.

The edges of those shorts were frayed, and the tiny threads brushed against her strong thighs.

Shit, I wanted to drop to the dirty floor right here, regardless of the people still here, and kiss my way up those legs.

That impulse meant it was time to call it a night. I needed to get out of here, clear my head, and talk myself out of knocking on Dylan's door first thing in the morning and punching him in the face.

I was headed to the bar to close out our tab when Dylan shrugged off his flannel shirt and draped it around Adele's shoulders.

Instantly, my vision went red.

Nope. Not wearing his shirt.

My spine snapped straight and my vision tunneled on her, my brain on high alert. Like I was flying a combat mission and I had one objective. Get that punk away from my girl.

Without a moment of hesitation, I was striding across the bar at top speed. I dodged groups of people and a table of my mom's friends who attempted to say hello.

Nothing registered except the rage pumping through my veins.

The thought of his clothing touching her precious skin sent me into a tailspin, and before I could come to my senses and consider the consequences, I was standing next to her, pulling myself up to my full height, and growling in Dylan's direction.

Unbuttoning my own shirt to reveal the white tank underneath, I shrugged it off, even as several sets of wide eyes landed on my bare arms.

I stepped between them, boxing Dylan out entirely.

"You cold, She-Ra? Here," I growled at Adele and jutted my chin. "Take that shit off."

She looked up at me slowly, her eyes narrowed and her gorgeous mouth set in a firm line of disapproval.

"Go away, Stretch," she said. "I don't want your shirt."

"Wear this." I pushed the shirt into her chest.

Her glower only intensified. I was out of line and I knew it, but there was no stopping me now.

"Is everything okay?" Dylan asked, coming around to stand beside her, reminding me of his presence.

Before I could answer—words weren't exactly flowing from me fluidly in my state of agitation—angry voices piped up around me.

The three Gagnon brothers had assembled on either side of me.

"You got a problem?" Remy said, stepping between me and his sister.

"Fuck off, Remy," Adele said, pushing him back. "Worry about yourself."

"Is there an issue here?" Henri asked, cocking a suspicious brow at me. This guy signed my paychecks, but in this moment, I didn't care.

"I was offering her my shirt," I said through gritted teeth. "The lady is cold."

"She's fine," Remy spat, weaseling his way up beside Adele again.

"Don't speak for her," I growled.

"Why do you care?" he taunted, getting in my face. "Why are you even speaking to my sister in the first place? Go away."

He had always been the family hothead. For a moment, I contemplated if Adele would hate me for punching him in his pretty face. He had recently appeared on the cover of a Racine catalog, and he could probably stand to be taken down a few pegs.

We stared at each other for a moment, both fuming, fists clenched at our sides and eyes narrowed. But then Gus stepped in, putting a hand on my chest and pushing me back.

"We don't want any trouble," he said, guiding me away from Remy.

Adele's little brother stood his ground. He hadn't once flinched in my presence. Next to him, Dylan crossed his arms. Damn. Maybe I had underestimated the mild-mannered science teacher.

"You are all out of your minds," Adele shouted in my periphery. "Everyone back off and take your toxic masculinity with you."

Remy ignored his sister in exchange for puffing out his chest and doubling down on his glare. Behind him, his brothers stood silently. "Do we need to take this outside?" he asked, his voice low.

Over my right shoulder, Jude laughed. "What are you gonna do, Gagnon? Climb a fucking tree?"

"I do hold a world record," Remy replied, lifting his chin a little higher.

I took another step toward him. If a fight was what he was looking for, then I'd be happy to oblige.

But Henri stuck his arm out in front of his brother. "We're done here. Come on, Remy, Adele." The look he shot me wasn't one of rage like his brothers', but one of utter disappointment. And damn if it didn't have its intended effect. Instantly, I felt like shit. But I couldn't roll over now without looking like a coward.

The three Gagnon brothers and Dylan, all standing with their arms crossed, were an intimidating sight. I was man enough to admit it. But I had my brothers with me, and my insane obsession with Adele was apparently rendering me both stupid and impossibly brave.

"I'll handle this," Adele said, grabbing me by the arm. "Outside, Stretch."

"Adele, don't go anywhere with him," Remy protested.

She whipped around and almost bit his head clean off. "Walk away, or you'll get the next ass kicking."

That's all it took for him to stand down. Clearly, he knew she was serious.

As she pulled me through the bar, we passed a table of older ladies who were hooting and hollering.

"You should settle this like men," one of my former teachers shouted. "Wood-chopping competition."

Her friends, which looked to be the majority of my mother's quilting group, giggled.

Mrs. Franklin, the librarian, added, "With shirts off."

They were clearly sauced, but the remarks only added to the rage pumping through my veins. Half the town had seen my little spectacle. And although I should be ashamed and embarrassed, I was more concerned with the feel of Adele's fingers where they gripped my wrist so hard they would probably leave bruises.

She didn't let go, even as we hit the parking lot. The crowd inside gawked and held up their phones, recording us in hopes of catching some of the drama on film to share with their friends. I could only imagine what kind of rumors would be flying through the diner tomorrow.

She marched over to the far side of the parking lot, where we'd have a modicum of privacy, dragging me along behind her. The gawkers were probably hovering close enough to keep their recordings going, but my sole focus was on Adele.

"What the hell is going on?" She looked even more beautiful in the glow of the moonlight.

I itched to pull her into my arms and kiss the hell out of her.

"What the hell, Finn?" she hollered, pulling me from my trance.

I crossed my arms over my chest and stood a little straighter. "Why didn't you text me back?"

"Seriously," she huffed. "You almost started a brawl in a bar because I didn't respond to a text? Toxic much?"

"No. That was because I didn't like seeing you with Dylan."

Throwing her arms into the air, she let out a sardonic laugh. "You are insane. I'm not with Dylan." She took a step closer, planting her hands on her hips. "He's one of my oldest friends and a really nice guy."

"Didn't look that way."

"What has gotten into you? Are you drunk?"

"No. I only had half a beer. I only want to talk to you. I can't stop thinking about you."

Pulling in a deep breath, I ran my hands through my hair, fighting the overwhelming urge to pull it out of my scalp. Lust and anger and hurt coursed through my veins. Dammit, I was butchering this whole situation.

This was not what Alicia meant when she advised me to be cool and take things slow with Adele. "Every minute of every day, I think about you and want you and crave you."

Her head on a swivel, she scanned the parking lot to make sure no one was within earshot and took a step closer. Once the shouting had died down, it looked as though our audience had dispersed.

"We said it was one time. It was a mistake." She avoided eye contact. A sure tell.

"Really?" I said, taking one big step and closing the distance between us.

Her breath hitched at my proximity, and I had to suppress a smile.

"Because it wasn't a mistake for me," I murmured. "I want more."

She looked up at me, her eyes glassy. "You can't have more."

Slowly, I tilted her chin up and regarded her. "We'll see about that."

And then I leaned in and kissed her, taking her mouth gently but firmly. I intended this to be a brief kiss, nothing more than a chaste press of my lips against hers, but once our mouths touched, I couldn't control myself.

I dove in, tunneling into her hair with one hand to get better access and grasping her ass with the other. Nothing made sense. I was acting on instinct. Alarm bells rang in my head, screaming *mine* over and over again, making it impossible to think rationally.

Because she was the opposite of passive, Adele fisted my shirt, pulling me closer and giving as good as she got.

God, this woman was made for me.

When my lungs were so deprived of oxygen I worried I would black out, I pulled back to take a breath. She was in my arms, panting, her entire body aware and awake.

I wanted her so badly.

"Come home with me," she said, her hand resting on my belt buckle.

Yes, my dick cheered.

"No" is what came out of my mouth. Despite how I'd behaved tonight, a scrap of my dignity remained. So I took a step back to put some distance between us. "I'm not your secret fuck buddy."

She gasped, her face a mask of bewilderment. If I had to guess, she was not in the habit of being turned down.

"If we do this again," I rasped, "we do it for real. I don't want second thoughts. I don't want regrets."

Her gaze cooled quickly, and her shoulders rose. Her defense mechanisms were kicking in. "Fine," she spat, turning on her heel.

I grasped her wrist and spun her so she faced me again. "I want you to be mine. I know you've been burned. I know you've been with assholes who strung you along and didn't want to commit."

She rolled her eyes, but the immediate slump of her shoulders told me I was hitting her insecurities square in the jaw.

"But I'm not that kind of man," I assured her. "I know what I want, and I go after it." Releasing her wrist, I took a step back. "So call me when you're ready to stop playing around."

Without waiting for a response, I turned and walked away, leaving her there, in the parking lot, holding my shirt. I had parked down the hill, and it took every ounce of self-control I had not to look back as I made the trek. But I held strong. I wouldn't settle for less than I deserved. No matter how much I craved her.

Slowly, I continued to my truck, breathing in the cool night air and willing my heart to settle.

At the edge of the parking area, I caught sight of my truck, along with something wholly unexpected.

I froze in place, and my heart rate immediately skyrocketed again. *What the shit?*

A huge moose was directly behind my tailgate, and it looked to be digging. It was pawing at the ground with its front

Wood Riddance

hoof, sending dirt flying in every direction. Did moose dig? And why was this one digging a hole behind my truck?

The last thing I needed tonight was a flat tire or a sprained ankle, so I crouched behind a car, keeping a safe distance while I watched.

When he was satisfied with the hole he had dug, he leaned forward and pissed in it. Gross.

I had never seen a moose pee before, but it was horrifying. There wasn't an area to pull around it, so I'd have to back up through it.

My stomach turned. After what had to have been five solid minutes of peeing, I was resigned to sacrificing my poor tires to get the hell out of here.

But no, he wasn't finished.

Instead of walking away. The asshole stepped into the hole and kicked one back leg, then the other. Urine flew in all directions, splashing into the bed of my truck.

I fumbled for my phone, and when I wrestled it from my pocket, I turned on the flashlight. Maybe I could scare it away.

But he was undeterred, kicking it everywhere, all over himself and the surrounding cars. But my poor truck took the majority of the abuse.

Finally, he turned and ambled toward the forest. Holding up my phone, I shined the light on the beast. Sure enough, now that his other side was visible, it was obvious. He had a huge scar across his flank. Fucking Clive.

Why hadn't someone shot this asshole yet? Why did the town continue to put up with him? This stunt alone had me itching to mount his head above my fireplace. Granted, my shitty apartment didn't have a fireplace, but I'd find one for the occasion.

Eventually, I made my way to my truck, avoiding piss lake

as best as I could and gagging at the smell of moose pee that coated the bed. Great. If I could afford a new truck, I'd trade this in tomorrow. Alas, I'd spend tomorrow scrubbing it obsessively.

Wasn't this just par for the course? A moose outside the Moose. Where, only a few minutes ago, I'd had my heart stomped on in the parking lot. Where I'd pissed off her brothers and almost started an all-out brawl.

I couldn't win.

Chapter 23
Adele

Damn, I was a shitty person. After Finn stormed off, I ducked back inside for my purse. Then, without a word to any of my brothers, I headed home. But I couldn't bring myself to go inside. Instead, I sat in the driver's seat with my head in my hands and flipped through the events of the last few hours.

I was the problem. That wasn't typically the case with me, and it burned me to even admit it. From the beginning, Finn had been honest and up-front about what he wanted and how he felt.

I was the one who'd pushed him. Then I was the one who brushed him off and ignored his wishes.

My heart sank, and a rush of shame washed over me.

He deserved more. But could I be the person to give it to him?

Inside the house, He-Man was barking, so I let myself in, picked him up and peppered him with kisses, then took him to the backyard to do his business.

As I stood in my garden, surveying the blooms that had

finally burst to life, the full weight of what I had done settled in.

I was a thirty-three-year-old woman, not a bratty teen. And yet I had acted like one. I had ignored him and frozen him out rather than communicating.

Exactly like so many of the assholes I had dated in the past had done to me. God, it made me sick.

Before I could stop myself, I was filling He-Man's food and water bowls, grabbing my keys, and heading for the door.

Finn lived downtown in a narrow brick building. His apartment was above the bank, right above Dylan's.

I parked out back, next to his truck. When I hopped out, I was assaulted by a strong, foul odor that hung in the air. I spun in a circle, searching for an animal carcass or some kind of toxic waste dump, but I found nothing.

When I righted myself and steeled my spine, ready to face my fate, I caught sight of the blazing lights in Dylan's second-floor apartment. So I texted him with a request to be buzzed in.

A minute later, I was running up the stairs to the third floor and banging on Finn's door.

Several minutes later, just as I was beginning to think that maybe he wasn't home, despite his truck's presence in the lot, he grumbled on the other side of the door. When he cracked it open, he blinked several times, adjusting to the hallway lights.

"Adele?"

"Can I come in?"

He took a step back and opened the door wider. He was wearing nothing but a pair of sweats. His entire body was a work of art. Thick muscle and beautiful tattoos. His hair was pulled back, and I had the overwhelming urge to throw my arms around him and sniff his neck.

I held out the shirt he'd offered up at the bar. "I wanted to return this."

Had I smelled it on the drive over? Yes. Was I proud of that? No. But his scent was as intoxicating as the sight of his body.

He crossed his arms, making things bulge and flex, and my mind went fuzzy. "You didn't have to return it tonight. It's almost midnight."

I nodded, gathering my courage. "I'm sorry."

He said nothing, though his eyes swam with hurt.

"I don't trust a lot of people, especially men. And I haven't been fair to you. I've been undervalued and tossed aside by so many guys over the years, yet that's exactly what I've been doing to you." I took a deep breath. Shit, this was hard. "So I'm here to apologize." I licked my lips and held his gaze. "You're a good person. You deserve better."

He said nothing, his gaze stony. So, having said my piece, I turned to leave.

"I don't want better." His words were a whisper of a plea. "I want you."

I stopped, still facing the door, willing my heart to remain in my chest. I wanted to walk out and not look back. But I couldn't. Deep down, I wanted to be here. With him.

So I turned around, still hovering by the door, and surveyed him. I didn't know what I was doing by staying. Was this what I wanted? Would it even work? Did I even care when he was looking at me like I was the most precious thing in the world?

"You're important to me," he said, dropping his arms to his sides.

Mouth agape, I blinked at him, desperate to sort through my jumbled thoughts and figure out how the hell to handle this situation.

He came closer and cupped my cheek. "When I'm around you, I feel alive again. That feeling I told you about, when I'm in the cockpit? I've been chasing it every single day since I was a kid." He tucked a strand of hair behind my ear. "And it's exactly what I feel when I'm with you."

My heart stuttered in my chest. That had to have been the most romantic thing anyone had ever said to me.

My brain was still struggling to compute his words, and all coherent thought left me. Since I couldn't form the words I wanted him to hear, I threw my arms around his neck and kissed him.

Then those strong hands were on my hips, his beard against my skin.

I needed this.

I'd missed him too.

Avoiding him at work and at the gym had been awful. I missed his smile, his cocky attitude, and the sweet way he looked at me when he thought I wasn't paying attention.

Hell, the way he'd been staring at me at the bar had basically incinerated my panties.

And now I had left my insecurities and doubts at the door. I was his. It was as inevitable as the sunrise.

"Damn, Adele. It's been two days, and I'm dying without you."

He worked his way down the column of my neck, dragging his lips over my skin. Then he picked me up and carried me toward his room, and once again, all reasonable thought left me.

Chapter 24
Finn

I was a man on a mission. Somehow, after a night filled with jealousy and embarrassment and that damn moose peeing on my truck, the tide had turned. I had been given another chance. And I would not waste it.

My apartment wasn't large. My bedroom was only a handful of steps from the door, but I wouldn't pass up the opportunity to carry Adele to my bed. The whole way there, I kissed her and touched her and relished the feel of her body in my arms. I intended to lay her down and worship her. I had already used my words, now I'd follow through with my actions to make sure she'd be mine.

I set her down on my bed and pushed her back, pinning her arms gently and kissing her neck. During our night in the forest, I had discovered a secret spot beneath her ear, and I'd use that knowledge to my advantage.

Adele's body was the perfect combination of soft and strong, and she felt perfect pinned beneath me. Not that she wasn't fighting me for control. Oh no, my girl was kissing me back, and she already had her hands in my hair, loosening it from its tie.

More than anything, I wanted to undress her slowly and carefully. Our first time had been rushed and dark, but now, with all the time and space we needed, every inch of her was begging for my hands and lips. She didn't seem to agree with my plans, though, as she shoved her shorts down and went directly for the waistband of my pants.

"Slow down, She-Ra," I pleaded, cupping her face. "There's no rush."

She pouted, with her bottom lip stuck out and everything. "I can't stand down when your equipment is poking me in the stomach," she said, palming my erection over my sweats. "Get naked."

With a shake of my head, I dipped low, demanding a languid kiss from her. We were alone in my apartment, in a comfy bed. There was no way I wouldn't savor every second of this.

Before I could start my carefully constructed plan, though, she pushed up and rolled me onto my back.

With her hands on my shoulders, she straddled me and rubbed her core against my aching erection. As if this moment couldn't get any hotter, she lifted her arms and whipped her shirt off, then tossed it to the floor. In record time, she'd unclasped her bra and had sent it soaring.

I put my hands behind my head and smirked, soaking in the way she wiggled out of her panties like they were on fire. Once she'd freed herself of them, she settled on top of me again, completely naked.

This angle only highlighted how gorgeous she was. She was athletic, with strong shoulders and legs, but still feminine. Her tits, perfect and round, with dark pink nipples, were just the right size for my hands. I hadn't even touched her, but as I let myself take in every inch, she threw her head back like she could feel my perusal. And just like that, I changed my plans.

Needing something to anchor myself as she kissed, licked, and teased her way down my body, I gripped her hips.

As she went, stroking me over my sweats, she traced some of my tattoos with her tongue.

"You are beautiful," she said, her fingertips teasing along my waistband.

I grabbed her hand and sat up. "And yours," I whispered. "I'm yours, Adele. For whatever you want for however long you want. Any day, any time, I'm yours."

Her face flushed pink, and she grasped the waistband of my pants and boxers. "Then I guess I better enjoy myself."

She kissed down my abs, pulling at both layers until my cock sprang free.

Her eyes widened as she licked her lips.

I almost passed out at the sight. How on earth was this happening right now?

In true Adele fashion, she wasted no time diving in, licking and kissing her way down my shaft, rendering me incapable of speech or rational thought.

My brain went to battle with itself. On the one hand, this might have been the greatest experience of my life. But on the other, she was thwarting my plan. I was going to make love to her. Do all the things so well she'd never leave.

But her mouth... it was so good.

"I have condoms," I blurted out awkwardly as she kissed the crown and swirled her tongue around it gently. She didn't stop, though. She continued her exploration without even a pause. While this was the real-life embodiment of several of my favorite fantasies, I needed to stop her before it was too late.

Threading my fingers through her hair, I tugged gently to garner her attention.

She popped off my dick and smiled up at me. "I'm okay going without. Again."

I nodded so vigorously my head spun as she crawled up the length of my body. I ached to feel the exhilaration of being inside her.

Straddling me on her hands and knees, she pressed her lips to mine and immediately demanded entrance.

"I want to feel you," I said when I pulled away to catch my breath. "I can't stop thinking about what it felt like to be inside you."

I must have said something right, because a blush crept up her neck and into her cheeks. Then she was lining herself up with my aching cock.

She moaned as she sank down onto my length. It was a good thing I was on my back, because I was dizzy with lust and elation and relief. She was here. With me. Never before had I experienced the feeling of being exactly where I needed to be with exactly the right person.

With her back arched and her eyes shut, she looked like a goddess. My heart nearly leapt out of my chest at the sight of her. She was beautiful and powerful, and when she began to rock her hips, I saw stars.

"Look at me," I commanded, gritting my teeth to avoid embarrassing myself and ending things early. Damn, the heat of her wrapped around me as she rode my cock was enough to send me over the edge if I wasn't careful.

Opening her eyes, she grabbed the headboard and ducked low, ghosting her lips over mine. "You like this?" she asked, twisting her hips in some magical way that made my vision blurry.

Palming her ass, I spread her wider, forcing her to take every inch of me. "I don't like it," I said, pressing my head back into the pillow and groaning. "I love it."

A slow, wide smile spread across her face.

"This is perfect. You and me," I panted, desperate to fill my lungs and control the racing of my heart. "You feel it too. I know it."

"I'm feeling a lot of good things right now, Stretch." Her muscles tensed, squeezing me so tight stars were dancing in my vision again. Her rhythm was steady as she skated her hands up her torso to her breasts, but then she was pinching her nipples and upping her pace.

I traced my fingers down her chest and stomach and pressed my thumb on her clit. She gasped and tightened around me further as I rubbed gentle circles.

"God, you look so perfect riding my cock," I growled. It took every ounce of willpower I possessed to hold back. I wanted to flip her over and fuck her through the mattress. But instead, I focused on her face. On the rapture that took over as she chased her orgasm. Fuck, I hoped I could last long enough to see it.

My self-control was rewarded when she writhed above me and her inner muscles clenched. Calling out my name, she shuddered and shook, breasts bouncing, hair swaying, head thrown back in ecstasy. This moment was worth every single second of longing and waiting. Because this was it for me.

"Good girl," I said, tucking an arm around her waist and rolling to pin her to the bed. Caging her in, I thrust inside her, reveling in the aftershocks, letting them fuel my need.

"Tell me, She-Ra. Admit I'm the best you've ever had. That I've ruined you for other men."

She was blissed out and orgasm drunk, but still, she managed to roll her eyes. "You are so cocky."

I shifted, pressing in deeper. "Only because I've got the goods to back it up. Now I'm going to fuck you hard, the way you like, and you're going to come again. Got it?"

She was pinned to the bed beneath me, sated from one orgasm and ready for the next. Her nipples grazed my chest with every one of my thrusts, driving me even crazier. Every part of this woman was made for me.

She moaned and writhed beneath me, blatant evidence that I'd found the angle she liked. So I thrust harder, and in response, she squeezed me tight. Establishing a rhythm once again, I got to work kissing and sucking her peaked nipples.

Her screams of *yes* and *harder* and *right there* kept me focused as my vision began to blur.

Mine, mine, mine. The words echoed in my mind like a chant or a prayer as I tried to stave off what felt like it would be the most intense orgasm of my life. Before I gave in, Adele had to know that I possessed her, body and soul. I'd be damned if she didn't understand before the night was over. That the connection between us wasn't purely sexual. It was spiritual.

Slowly, I cupped her chin. Her eyes were glassy and her cheeks were flushed. I needed her to see me, to get it. When she was focused on me, I slid my hand from her chin down to her neck and cuffed it loosely.

"Is this okay?" I asked, my attention locked on her so I wouldn't miss any hint of trepidation or desire.

Her pupils blew out, and she arched her back and let out a low moan. That was all the encouragement I needed.

Fucking her so hard I was using the bed frame for leverage, I loosened the leash I'd had on my control. Beneath my fingers, her pulse raced. I couldn't control it anymore. My thrusts became wild. And then she clamped down so hard my vision really did go dark.

There was nothing between us. Nothing to shield me from the intensity of her orgasm. And I relished it.

I let loose inside her. Unleashing myself and giving her everything I had.

There was nothing I wouldn't give this woman. Nothing I wouldn't do to prove to her that she belonged to me.

Chapter 25
Adele

"This place is not what I expected," I said, rolling over and nuzzling against Finn's chest. His thick, hairy, inked chest. If I hadn't spent the night getting fucked six ways to Sunday, I'd be freaking out. But I was too tired and far too relaxed after all those orgasms to work myself into a proper panic. Instead, I settled for mild irritation and moderate curiosity. This man had now been inside me several times. Thus, I probably needed to know more about him.

"Mind if a grab a T-shirt?" I asked.

"Second drawer."

Completely naked, I climbed out of bed and ran one hand along the dark wood of the dresser. A few framed photos sat on top, along with a small, ornate box.

After I'd plucked a clean T-shirt from his drawer, I turned and took in the room from this vantage point. As I assessed the space, I caught the way his eyes were locked on me.

"Wow, that's hot," he said, sitting up and pushing his hair out of his face.

I could say the same thing about him. Though I'd already

determined he was the most gorgeous man I'd ever seen, in the light of day, he was even sexier. Yet he was humble, almost to a fault. He was an enigma, looking the way he did and feeling so deeply. At first, I thought the orgasms had scrambled my brain, but it turned out it was the man dispensing them.

"What's this?" I asked, looking at the beautiful box displayed alongside a photo of him in uniform. In it, he was holding a baby I could only assume was Merry and was flanked by Alicia and his mom.

"Nothing." His response was short, almost curt, and so unlike him.

"Can I open it?"

He shrugged and dropped his gaze to the sheet covering his lap. Now *that* piqued my curiosity.

The box fit in the palm of my hand and was made of thick, lacquered wood. When I pried open the heavy top, I found the inside lined with plush velvet. And nestled right in the middle was a medal in the shape of a cross hanging on a blue and white ribbon with a red stripe down the middle.

A lump formed in my throat. This was some kind of precious military medal. "Finn, what is this?" I asked, turning back to him.

He was reclined in the bed, one hand behind his head and all the muscles of his delicious torso on display. "It's the Distinguished Flying Cross," he said in a tone far too nonchalant for the implications I assumed came along with this medal.

"And it's yours?"

"Yup."

"Seems like a pretty big deal. Is this the kind of thing the Navy hands out to everybody? A participation award?"

He cocked a brow and huffed. "No, but it's not a big deal."

"Hmm..." I tapped my chin and set the box down on the

dresser gently. Then I crawled toward him on the bed until we were face to face and I was straddling him on my hands and knees. "If I were to ask your mom about this," I said, dropping a kiss to his lips, "what would she say?"

He laughed, making the ink on his chest and arms ripple. "She would tell you she flew down to DC for the ceremony and that it's awarded to aviators who have participated in acts of heroism or extraordinary achievement during aerial flight." One side of his mouth kicked up in a half grin. "Then she'd show you the photos on her phone for an hour while she bragged about me."

I sat back on my knees, my heart in my throat. "I thought so. So you're a war hero?"

He shrugged again, the infuriating man. "I can be your hero," he teased with a wink.

"Stop goofing. I mean it. You're amazing. Heroism in flight? Most guys who *look* badass are usually the least badass of all. But you, Finn Hebert, are the real deal."

His face and neck flushed. Holy shit. This giant Viking lumberjack war hero was *blushing*.

"What, no snappy comeback?" I asked.

He shook his head. "Nah. It feels good to hear you say that."

All this time, I believed he was cocky and overconfident. But I couldn't have been more wrong.

Taking his face in my hands, I leaned down and kissed him again. "I'll say it every day. You made huge sacrifices. You risked your life for your country and its ideals. That makes you a fucking hero. This town should be throwing an annual parade in your honor."

"Stop." There went that flush again, and his eyes were downcast once more.

"I mean it." I put a hand under his chin and forced him to look at me. "Now that I know this? Watch out, Lovewell. Because you best believe I'll be shoving it down Mayor Lambert's throat after his shitty lack of loyalty at the diner the other day. And Mrs. Leary. She wishes her deadbeat kids had half the bravery you do. I'll be your one-woman hype squad."

He sat up and pulled me closer. The thin white T-shirt I'd chosen offered very little protection from his heat and the way he manhandled me. In fact, I was ready to Hulk out and rip it off myself.

"Does that mean you want to be my girlfriend?" He pressed his lips to my neck at that spot behind my ear and dragged them lower, one inch at a time, erasing all rational thought from my mind. Slipping his hands under the T-shirt, he dragged one up to my breast and kept the other firm on my hip. God, this man and his goddamn hands. As a mechanic, I appreciated hands. His were not only large and strong, but strangely graceful. And he could use them. Capability like he possessed was the ultimate turn-on.

Especially the way he was using them now. Dipping two fingers inside me while simultaneously circling my clit with the pad of one thumb and rolling my nipple with the fingers of his other hand. I arched back, already desperate for more.

"Girlfriend?" I asked, already breathless as he bit gently on my other nipple and tugged. "I'll be president of your fan club."

He shifted me so I was straddling him and lined himself up. Then, with his eyes locked on mine, he entered me, pulling me down as he lifted his hips. So slow, so exquisite. I couldn't stop the moan that escaped me when he was buried to the hilt. This feeling, I couldn't get enough of it. He filled me up and possessed me completely. Leaving no room for doubt that what we had was special.

"I don't want a fan club." He grunted as I circled my hips. "I want everything. I want it all, Adele."

I threw my head back as his thumb found my clit again. I was already on edge, ready to detonate.

"But I know you're not ready. So I'll be patient. But you should know, I always get what I want."

His bedhead was impressive. It had to be after nine, but I didn't care. Usually, I was up early, accomplishing as much as I could on weekends. But I was beginning to see the appeal of lazy Sunday mornings.

"I'll make some coffee," he said, rubbing his eyes. He swung his legs over the side of the bed and stood, giving me an eyeful of his round, muscular ass and tree trunk thighs.

After I relieved myself, I wandered around his place, still a bit orgasm drunk and not ready to join the real world.

The apartment was small, and the building old. But it was spotless. And not in the barren bachelor pad way. He had made an effort. The worn leather couch had throw pillows. Framed photos decorated the walls.

"This is the kitchen slash dining room slash living room slash homework lab," he said, lifting one shoulder without meeting my gaze.

Two mismatched stools were tucked under the L-shaped bar. One fit perfectly in its place, but the other was much shorter.

"We found that one for me." He nodded at the tiny stool and chuckled. "That way, Merry and I can comfortably eat together."

"You're pretty evolved."

"I'm a thirty-five-year-old man. And I'm the father of a smart-as-hell ten-year-old. You think she'd let me get away with eating off paper plates or not decorating?"

"So I should thank Merry for civilizing you?"

"Nah. That would be my mother. I think you'd get along. She raised five boys. That woman takes no shit."

I didn't know Debbie Hebert. Obviously, I knew *of* her. Tireless single mom to five giant boys and ex wife of Mitch Hebert, who had publicly humiliated her back in the day by impregnating his barely legal secretary. I knew everything about everyone in Lovewell, but I had never really interacted with her. "From what I've heard over the years, she's a sweetheart. A beloved nurse who always brings homemade chicken soup to sick friends."

"That chicken soup is pretty spectacular." He laughed.

"Good to know."

"I'll have her make some for you."

"Ha-ha, please," I scoffed. "She'll probably poison it."

"No, she won't. She's got no skin in the game. She divorced my dad when I was eight. Trust me, she holds no loyalty to him whatsoever."

That was a relief. For reasons I did not want to unpack at the moment, I already yearned for Mrs. Hebert to like me. To think I was good enough for her son. But I pushed that line of thinking aside, determined not to overthink what was going on between us, and focused on the kitchen.

The cabinets were light wood, and there were small splashes of blue everywhere. A blue towel, a spatula, even a fancy stand mixer.

The image of Finn and Merry together here in this cozy space made my heart melt in a way I didn't think I'd ever experienced. "Can you show me more?" I asked, accepting the steaming mug he held out to me.

I followed him into a tiny room that housed an ornate day bed and a small dresser.

"This is Merry's room."

"I figured."

"It's not much," he said, his tone suddenly defensive.

Bringing my coffee to my lips, I took in the lovely space. A large glittery chandelier hung over the bed, and the walls were covered in photos and kids' artwork and Taylor Swift posters.

I stepped up to the bed and leaned forward, admiring a large photo collage. Finn was behind me, his presence warm and comforting.

"That's us at Niagara Falls last year," he said, his back pressed to me and his arm stretched out around me. In the photo, they were wearing bright yellow ponchos and mugging for the camera. It still amazed me that this giant warrior of a man had such a goofy side.

"And that's her with Alicia and Mike in Paris."

Alicia was petite and had a chin-length auburn bob. Merry was almost as tall as her already, but she had her hair and eyes.

"Ah. The famous Mike," I said, studying the dark-haired man in the photo. He was thin and had kind eyes. From what I could tell by the picture, he looked to be in his late thirties.

"Yup." Finn let out a deep sigh. "I like the guy. I have to say it out loud at least once a day to remind myself, though. We have nothing in common, but he's kind and trustworthy. That's all I can ask for, so I tolerate him."

"He's probably terrified of you," I said, trying to lighten the mood.

"I made sure of that right off the bat. But I know he'd never hurt either of my girls, so we're good."

My girls. My stomach clenched as those words reverberated in my mind. That night in the woods, he'd told me he wasn't in love with Alicia, but calling her one of his girls sure had me questioning that statement.

He set his coffee cup on the dresser, then took mine and did the same. Then he ran his hands down my arms, gently squeezing every few inches until he found my hands.

"It's not like that," he murmured. "I can see your wheels turning, She-Ra."

I swallowed past the lump in my throat and searched his face. Was I that obvious?

"Don't get jealous. My beef with Mike has nothing to do with my feelings for Alicia. She's the mother of my child and she's my best friend. Nothing more. I want her to be happy and well taken care of forever. My hang-up, as embarrassing as it is, has more to do with Mike being a corporate type with money. He can give Merry so much more than I can, and sometimes that knowledge gets to me."

Popping up on my toes, I threaded my fingers into his hair. "You have nothing to worry about. You're a wonderful father. Look at this princess room." I held one hand out to my side. "Look at all you do for her. I'm glad Mike is worthy of Alicia and Merry, but money has nothing to do with that."

He nodded and pressed his lips to my forehead. "Thank you for saying that. Now let me feed you."

I sat on Merry's stool while he worked in the tiny galley kitchen. For such a large man, he navigated the space like a pro, scrambling eggs and filling the toaster with slices of bread, all while topping off my coffee.

Naturally, he wouldn't let me help. He insisted I sit here and relax, so I took advantage and spent the time admiring him.

"So we've talked about my shit," he said. "Time to talk about yours."

I gripped my coffee mug and held it to my chest. "No thanks."

He leaned over the counter, kissing me gently on the lips. "Yes. We're doing this, She-Ra. Relationship, exclusivity, intimacy of the physical *and* emotional variety." He winked and pulled back to plate the eggs. "So tell me what makes you hesitant about agreeing to be my girlfriend. Is it the term? Too juvenile? I'd suggest wife, but you'd run out of here in my shirt." He licked his bottom lip and grinned. "I'm open to whatever label makes you happy."

I pinched the bridge of my nose. It was so like him not to let me get away with anything. Our physical intimacy was phenomenal, but I wasn't so good at the emotional kind. The only person I was really vulnerable with was Parker, and that was still relatively new and took a concerted effort.

But watching him now, so open and interested in me, and after the ways he'd let me in already—about Merry and his insecurities when comparing himself with Mike, not to mention the toll his dad's crimes had taken on him—I had to try. He'd earned my trust and deserved the reciprocation.

"I'm not ready to be in a relationship," I said.

He didn't respond, but maintained eye contact and gently squeezed my hand.

Blowing out a breath, I tightened my ponytail. Why was this so hard? "I'm still not okay. I haven't been since my dad died. According to my therapist, I haven't processed my grief. My brothers all seem to be moving forward with their lives, but I'm stuck."

Finn tilted his head and gave me a small smile. "These things take time—"

"No." I interrupted him. He didn't get it. This wasn't run-of-the-mill grief. This was bigger and darker and impossible to shake. "It was my fault," I confessed. "Those were my trucks. Henri and my dad. Every single day, visions of those moments take shape in my mind. When I close my eyes to fall asleep, I see it, over and over again."

"It wasn't your fault."

I shook my head, tears stinging the backs of my eyes. "My trucks. My responsibility. I keep hundreds of people alive every day. It's my only job. I'm just the mechanic."

"Adele," he urged, coming around the counter. With an arm banded around me, he spun me until we were face to face. "You are so much more than a mechanic. You're the goddamn conductor of an orchestra. I've never seen anyone as capable and as smart as you are, and I was a member of an elite military unit. Terrible things happened, yes, but you are not responsible."

I ducked my head because the tears were flowing now. Great. We'd had mind-blowing sex, and now I was weeping over eggs and coffee. Any second now, he'd rescind that offer of girlfriend status.

"We know who did it, and they're going to jail. It won't bring him back, and that sucks, but you've got to let go of this. Forgive yourself."

"No," I said, straightening my spine and tipping my chin up. Fuck hiding my tears. "I can't. Not until I know who tampered with Henri's truck. I can't let my guard down. The past few years have been terrifying. My world has been crumbling around me. I'm constantly waiting and watching for the next disaster."

He squeezed my shoulder and brought his forehead to mine. "Hyper-vigilance is a common trauma response."

With a snort, I backed up and wiped at my tears. "Tell that to Paz. If you saw his basement, you wouldn't think I'm the vigilant one in the family."

He didn't laugh. He didn't say a word. Instead, he picked me up and carried me to the soft leather couch and nestled me on his lap. I buried my head in his chest and gave in to my tears once again.

"I'm here," he said softly, stroking my hair. "And you can tell me anything."

How was it possible to feel so safe with him? My enemy. A man I hated, distrusted.

But that wasn't even true. In hindsight, it was obvious that I had been projecting all my shit onto him. And the noble asshole had taken all of it. Now, he was holding me, protecting me from the world and my own guilt.

"How can I go on living my life, searching for happiness and continuing to be productive, when danger still exists?" I hiccuped.

He hummed, the sound vibrating through his chest. "It's not exactly the same, but a lot of soldiers experience this too. Combat mentality. You're so used to being in the shit, to having to watch your back twenty-four seven, that life outside the war zone feels unreal."

He wasn't wrong. Most days, I forced myself to go through the motions. But I kept my guard up while the people around me lived their lives. It was only with Finn that I could lower those defenses and allow myself to exist.

He tucked a strand of hair behind my ear. "I've got your back. These feelings are real and valid. And if you need to know what happened to Henri in order to move on, then we'll figure it out together."

I pulled back and searched his face, feeling truly seen for the first time in my life.

He wasn't calling me paranoid or crazy or questioning my assessment of the brakes like everyone else I had expressed my concerns to. No, without question, Finn was accepting me and supporting me.

For a little while longer, I let him hold me, taking solace in his strong arms. All the while, though, I tried to ignore the very real possibility that I was deeply in danger of falling in love with this man.

Chapter 26
Adele

I had a secret hookup. Or was he a fuck buddy? No. He was so much more than that. A secret lover? Ha, this wasn't a bodice-ripper. Secret boyfriend, maybe? Other than nixing the term *girlfriend*, we hadn't defined our relationship, and I wasn't very clear on the details. Regardless, it was surprisingly fun.

A torrid, secret affair sounded exhausting, but what we had going on was hot. Sneaking around with Finn wasn't just sexy; it was the most fun I'd had in a long time.

So much fun, in fact, that I was strategizing a way to escape family dinner as soon as possible so I could meet up with him. I had skipped last week, and my mom tended to get nosy and ask questions when one of us missed too many, so my best defense tonight was to show up.

In my pocket, my phone vibrated. Discreetly, I tilted forward and slid it out, but I kept it in my lap.

> Stretch: I have a surprise for you.

Daphne Elliot

> Adele: ??? Better be good. Hoping to get out of here soon.

> Stretch: You want me waiting for you? Naked?

> Adele: Not waiting. Vacuuming or doing something useful. But naked. You know how much cleaning turns me on.

> Stretch: Yes, my Virgo queen.

"Would that be nice?" my mom said, her voice so pinched my head snapped up in response.

I knew that tone. I knew it well. Shit. My entire family was staring at me. Heat bloomed in my cheeks, which meant they were probably bright red. Had they caught on to my little dalliance? Why was I suddenly the center of attention?

My mother eyed me while plating a third slice of pie for Tucker. "Adele, what do you think?"

Shit. She was calling me out. There was nothing to do but smile and wait for one of my siblings to fill in the blanks. They weren't great at staying quiet, so I had no doubt I'd be out of the hot seat in a minute.

"We were talking about Thanksgiving," my mother hinted, with a fake smile plastered across her face. Oh no. We could not be doing this again. "Alice offered to host."

Across the table, my sister-in-law was smiling serenely. Since joining the family two years ago, Alice routinely offered to host holidays, and my mother always politely declined. Did Alice *still* not understand that Loraine Gagnon lived for holidays? And that if she insisted on taking over, my mother would probably lose both her mind and her will to live?

Sitting beside his wife, Henri was oblivious. He had already turned away and was deep in conversation with Remy, clearly not keeping his wife in line. I adored Alice, and so did my mother, who worked with her at the school every day. But she did not know the kind of strife she was creating.

"Thanksgiving is so far away," I said lamely. Not sure how to deflect. Being caught off guard meant I was off my game. I shot a glare at Hazel, who looked like a deer in the headlights, and then my gaze settled on Parker.

She gave me a subtle nod, silently signaling that she'd help. The woman routinely took down criminals. She could deescalate the monthly holiday hosting dispute.

"Actually," Parker said, grabbing Paz's. "We have big news."

Paz leaned over and gave her a kiss on the temple. It was a gesture I thought my brother incapable of before he met Parker. "Brace yourself, Mom."

The crickets chirping outside the screen door only emphasized the anticipation growing as we all waited with bated breath for what they had to share.

"We're pregnant!" Parker said after an unfairly long pause.

The entire table erupted into chaos. Squealing (my mom and Goldie), questions (Henri and Tucker), and hugs (Hazel and Remy and Alice).

"Guys, please," Paz said, holding out his arms and gesturing for everyone to sit.

My heart stuttered and my stomach did a weird flip. My best friend and my brother were having a baby. I'd have a new niece or nephew soon. Damn. It took a minute to register the emotion that had washed over me, but when I did, I couldn't help the smile that split my face.

My mom immediately pulled out her phone and snapped photos. Tucker was already concocting a plan to place bets on whether it was a girl or a boy. Everyone was talking all at once, and across from me, my friend was truly glowing. I was surrounded by so much joy and happiness that my chest ached. Though a twinge of sadness hit, too, because Finn wasn't here with me. What would it be like if he were sitting at the table with my family? Would he fit in with the crowd seamlessly like Alice and Hazel and Parker had? We had the room—my parents had purchased this table long ago with our future families in mind—and I wanted to believe my family had room in their hearts for him too.

But what if they didn't?

My family was my whole world. These people right here were everything to me. And being with Finn could tear us apart. Right now, what we had was light and fun and sexy, but he'd been clear about wanting more. Only, what if more simply wasn't possible?

After dinner and several rounds of hugs and congratulations, I headed home, still wrestling with my feelings. For so many years, I'd been searching for love. For companionship and friendship and respect and passion. And there was a small voice in my head that kept telling me I'd found it. I'd found him.

Finn was at my house when I arrived, already making use of the key I'd given him. He was in the backyard with He-Man, who was barking at him like he was an intruder.

He was bent over a five-gallon bucket in the grass. His hair was down and covering his face. I itched to touch him to ground myself.

When my shoes hit the deck, he stood up straight and hit me with a giant grin. "God, you're gorgeous. Get over here."

Obediently, I sashayed my way to him, and when I was within arm's reach, he pulled me in for a long, languid kiss.

"Ready for your surprise?" He waved to the bucket.

"What are those?" I asked, peering over the lip of it.

"Those, my sexy, beautiful woman, are eco-friendly water balloons. They have magnets and can be refilled."

I laughed, my heart floating in my chest. "Water balloons, seriously?"

"It's August in Maine, so it's ninety degrees with one hundred and ten percent humidity. Trust me, water balloons are necessary. Plus." He smacked my ass. "I think you could use the stress relief."

I bit my lip and shivered at the pleasure and pain that rippled through me at the contact.

There had to be at least one hundred water-filled orbs in there in a rainbow of colors. After a moment of contemplation, I had to admit he wasn't wrong. Smacking him square in the chest with a water balloon would probably be really freaking fun.

"Okay. I'm in."

"Good girl. Now go inside and put on a skimpy bikini. 'Cause I'm gonna get you all wet and dirty, and then I'm gonna lay you out in the wildflowers and eat your pussy."

My thighs clenched in response to his dirty words. I secretly liked it when he bossed me around, though I'd never tell him that. At this point, I should be used to the dirty talk and the bossy attitude and the demands, but every single time, it got me so worked up. Not for the first time, I wondered how I'd resisted him for as long as I did.

I was working on a sassy comeback when he peeled off his T-shirt and tossed it onto the back of a lounge chair. *Fuck me.* No matter how many times I saw Finn shirtless, the novelty didn't wear off. His chest activated some kind of evolutionary instinct in me, and the moment his skin was exposed, I lost the ability for rational thought. Instead, my brain defaulted to commands that involved clubbing him over the head and dragging him back to my cave so I could make giant Viking babies with him.

I'd like to think I was a bit more evolved than my cavewoman ancestors, but the broad shoulders, thick muscles, and the dusting of chest hair made me go full Neanderthal every single time.

He bit his lip and gave me a cocky smile as he tied his hair back. "Oh, She-Ra. I love the feel of your eyes on me. But I can't wait another minute to get you all wet."

He shooed me away, and I practically ran to my bedroom to change.

I emerged a few minutes later and found him filling a second bucket. He carefully opened each balloon and filled it to capacity before closing it again. Thankfully, my yard was fenced and flanked by mature trees, so it was unlikely that we'd be seen by any of the neighbors.

He nodded at the bucket he'd filled first, signaling that it was mine, so I grabbed it and stashed it behind a tree. Then I loaded my arms with half a dozen balloons, ready for battle.

Any thoughts I had about him taking it easy on me vanished as soon as the first water balloon hit me in the ass. My spine snapped straight as the cold water splattered, and I whipped around, only to catch a glimpse of him diving behind an azalea bush.

"This means war!" I shouted.

On the deck, He-Man barked wildly in agreement and ran in circles. I got Finn a few times before he darted across the open lawn. I took that as my opportunity and chased him down. He had me in both speed and strength, but this was my territory, and I'd use it to my advantage.

"Do your worst, She-Ra," he shouted, lobbing another balloon with ridiculous accuracy. "Because when we're done, you're all mine."

We ran and dove and shouted as we threw balloons and came up with increasingly dramatic ways to fall when we got hit. At one point, I slipped on wet grass and landed flat on my back. I lay there and laughed for a full minute. Then all my anxiety faded away as I cornered him behind the hostas, two balloons in each hand.

"Surrender," I said, arms in the air. This was the most fun I'd had in years.

He looked at me, his face completely serious, and said, "I already have."

Chapter 27
Finn

The secret keeping was getting harder every day. Especially when Adele and I were spending every possible minute together. On the nights I didn't have Merry, I stayed at her house, and we hung out as often as we could.

I loved snuggling with her on the couch and watching *Ted Lasso* together, cooking together, and waking up with her in my arms. I couldn't help but dream of the days we could go out to the Moose or walk down the street together or finally tell our families.

Because every day I was more certain that she was it for me.

And I wasn't the only one in love. My daughter was completely and totally attached too.

Summer camp had ended, so Merry was hanging out at the shop, where she'd become a junior member of the team.

Today, I'd come down after a meeting and found her elbow deep in an engine while Adele coached her through replacing springs. Girlie pop blared from the speakers and my daughter's face shone with pride.

"Dad," she shouted. "I learned how to rotate tires! I even got to use the fancy drill thingy to take off the lug nuts."

Beside my daughter, Adele shrugged. "The kid's smart and has a steady hand."

Merry beamed at her. And I struggled not to do the same.

It was such a small gesture, but by including Merry, making her feel capable and valued, she was building her up and inspiring her and showing her she cared. This kid had bounced around so much in her life and was struggling to find her place at the moment.

Their interactions made my heart grow each and every time I witnessed them. And every day, it was more obvious to me—this was who Adele was. Beneath the glares and the attitude, she was generous and affectionate.

She taught Merry something new each and every day. She included her, and without fail, she made her feel like a member of the team.

Merry wiped her hands on a rag she'd begun to keep slung across her shoulder just like Adele did. "Why does my dad call you She-Ra?" she asked.

"He gave me that nickname a while ago. She-Ra was a superhero back when we were kids."

"Oh, I know all about She-Ra. She's super cool and has these feminist princess friends. There's a show on Netflix. Wanna come watch it at our house tonight? Dad's getting pizza."

Adele looked between us, biting her lips to keep from smirking.

"That sounds awesome," she said to Merry, "but I made plans with my friends tonight. Every Thursday, we get together. Maybe another time?"

Merry nodded. "How about Saturday? I'm at my mom's

this weekend, but you can hang with my dad." Her blue eyes sparkled as she looked between Adele and me.

Adele gave her a kind smile. "That's a great idea. I'll have to check my schedule."

"Dad," Merry said as we headed to pick up pizza for dinner.

I turned the volume down so "Maroon" by Taylor Swift was barely audible over the speakers and looked at my girl in the rear-view mirror. She was still so small but growing every day. It was moments like this that I treasured. I had missed so much during my deployments.

"I need to talk to you."

I nodded, knowing better than to interrupt when she had something to get off her chest.

"I think you should ask Miss Gagnon on a date."

I gripped the steering wheel and tried to school my features into something resembling placid. We'd had this conversation a while back, and now that things had changed between Adele and me, I was desperate to avoid revisiting it.

"Why do you say that?" I asked, trying to sound surprised.

"She has a crush on you." She was smirking when I darted a glance at her again. "I can tell these things. Madison J. had a crush on Jackson last year, and it was so obvious. She was always looking at him and touching him."

I didn't want to think about kids Merry's age having crushes. That was a nightmare for a different day.

"And Miss Gagnon? She looks at you funny. Like she likes you and wants to go on a date with you. But she's not weird about it, like some of the school moms."

I nodded, at a loss for how to respond.

"I really like her. She's tall and has a dog and is the boss at her job."

"That's true. She is a very cool person." My cheeks were growing warmer by the second, but I kept my focus on the road. Damn. Hearing Merry say that she liked Adele and wanted me to date her was hitting me square in the chest.

"And that day in the diner. She stood up for us, when people were being judgy and mean. She's like a superhero, but in real life, and she fixes machines."

"So that's why you were trying to convince her to have dinner with us?"

"Yup. I figure if you're not gonna find a girlfriend on your own, then I'll have to help you. She's perfect for you."

God, this kid. She did not miss a beat. "Sweetie, I love that you want me to be happy. But I can get my own dates, okay?"

"I want to help you. Mom says men can be intimidated by strong women. Which is why I'm not going to date until my thirties."

I chuckled. Alicia for the win.

"And Miss Adele is pretty *and* strong, so I thought I'd help out. Give you a date idea. She's pretty special, and I wouldn't want some other guy to ask her out before you."

I couldn't argue with that logic. "Thanks," I said softly. "I'll work on it."

Chapter 28
Finn

"What do you mean?" I asked, stopping on the shoulder to catch my breath. It was late August in Maine, which meant 100 percent humidity. I should have left the weight vest at home, but since I now had a woman to please, I was motivated to step up my fitness game.

Plus, I was headed to her place tonight. We were going to spend the entire weekend together, and I was almost giddy. Having Adele all to myself for forty-eight hours was a literal dream come true. So here I was, ensuring that my stamina was up to the task.

"It means that we can't sell unless we get this shit figured out."

I mopped the sweat off my face with my T-shirt and sucked in a deep breath, hoping the hit of oxygen would allow me to focus on what Owen was saying.

"Who is this buyer?" I asked.

"A private equity group. They have a lot of experience in

timber, mainly in the Pacific Northwest. It's the best lead we've had so far."

Private equity and all that entailed was in Owen's wheelhouse, not mine. If I had to guess, though, these dudes in suits could make a hell of an excel spreadsheet but knew shit about lumber.

"Is that the direction we want to go?" I asked.

"Did Gus get to you too?"

"No," I snapped. "I haven't spoken to him in the last couple of days. I'm only asking questions to ensure I understand. To you, the rest of us may seem like we're idiots, but we really do want to understand so we can make the most informed decisions." I forced another deep breath into my lungs, this time to calm the anger bubbling up. "Hebert Timber is not what it once was, but a lot of people here count on us for jobs. I want what's best for Gus and Jude too. They're still operating at a lower capacity, trying to hang on to the legacy and the tradition."

"I thought you didn't give a shit about legacy and tradition."

"I don't. I'm only asking questions, and you're being defensive."

Selling was the best option. I agreed with him there. But in an ideal world, we'd sell to another family-owned business. The kind of people who would take care of our employees and our land and do it right. Not soulless suits looking to extract every cent of potential profit.

"You know I have a career, right? And a life? I got out of Lovewell for a reason. I'm only wasting my precious time on this shit because of the love I have for my brothers and our family legacy."

Kicking at stones on the shoulder of the road, I let him rant. Owen had always been the one who was easy to anger. Like

Dad, he was smart and ambitious, but there was nothing he hated more than being compared to our father.

Regardless, we needed him. Gus and Jude and I had no idea how to assess the books and determine how to move forward. Cole would be even less help. So we needed Owen.

"I get it. I'm sorry you've been dragged back in."

"It's fine. We need more detailed information. I've contacted Mrs. Garner, and she's been helpful, but she's been gone for five years now."

Figured. My dad's longtime comptroller was well into her retirement, but back in the day, she knew everything going on at Hebert. I had no doubt that things didn't go to shit until after she took off for sunny Florida.

"What are you suggesting?"

"Go see Dad in prison."

My gut roiled at the thought, and my chest constricted so tight I was worried I wouldn't be able to walk my ass home without passing out. "Fuck no."

"Gus and Jude have been once before. They're coordinating another trip. Go with them."

"You're out of your mind if you think I'm going to the state pen to see my murderer father."

"That's *our* murderer father," he said, back up on his high horse. "And yes, you are. You'll take a list of questions with you. I'll have my assistant send them to you in the next couple of days. Get answers for me," he urged, this time sounding the slightest bit desperate. "Take notes. You don't even have to look him in the eye if you don't want to, but please go."

I focused on breathing steadily to be sure I wouldn't keel over right here. The thought of seeing him made me sick. But Owen had a point. We couldn't sell without cleaning things up first.

And we needed to sell. I needed my cut so I could start my business, and then we could all move on.

Not to mention, there was a teeny, tiny part of me that felt guilty. Like I had some atoning to do. After all, I'd worked for the business for more than a year and had never noticed my father's shady dealings. Maybe if I helped my brothers get this all squared away, the constant weight on my shoulders would lift.

When I moved back to Lovewell, my father had offered me work. He was practically begging me to join the family business. After years of successfully avoiding it, I gave in, especially when he offered me a brand-new plane.

Flying for Hebert timber was a cushy gig, and it had given me the time I needed to plan my next move while I socked away as much money as I could.

Part of me had hated having to eat crow. Giving in to my father's nepotism. Especially after he had treated my mother and my brothers so poorly. But it meant I could give my baby girl a good life.

But timber had been losing value for years. I should have questioned how he could afford all the state-of-the-art machinery and the cars and the houses. We shared access to the logging roads with three other families, all with timber claims almost as large as ours. Despite also being some of the biggest logging outfits in Maine, they were struggling and making cuts. Yet Hebert had expanded?

I had been ignorant. Willfully. I'd taken the plane and the job, and I'd put on my blinders. I'd let him bribe me into working for him.

So I had a part to play to get things sorted out, as much as I didn't want it. Because like it or not, I had to make things work here in Lovewell, the town that despised my family. I had to figure out how to thrive while surrounded by the people who knew all my dad's dirty secrets.

My daughter was here, and my family was here. They needed me. So I'd do whatever it took.

"Fuck it. I'll go."

There was a fresh blueberry pie, a bouquet of daisies, and a package of frighteningly expensive gourmet dog treats on the seat beside me. I'd win that dog over if it killed me. It didn't matter that he was tiny. He didn't seem to notice how I towered over him. And I had no doubt he'd rip a hole in my arm if I even looked at Adele wrong.

I was upping my game. We'd been sneaking around and hooking up and flirting when no one was watching. But like I'd told her the night she showed up at my apartment, I was all in. What we had was real, and while we were focused on having fun at the moment, we were building toward a future.

The more time I spent with her, the more I adored her. This was so much more than lust and sex. She was hilarious, and she was sweet when she thought no one was looking. And pushing her buttons was my new favorite hobby.

Tonight, I was riding the kind of high I'd only ever felt when flying missions. But right now, there was no danger, no adrenaline. Only lust and affection for this singularly spectacular woman.

Not even the phone call from Owen or the sinking realization that I'd have to face my father soon could bring me down. Damn, I was a goner.

I had turned off route 901 when the phone rang.

"She-Ra," I said when the call connected through Bluetooth. "I know you can't wait to get my clothes off, but I'll be there in five."

"No. It's not that," she whispered. "Mrs. Dupont just walked by and paused on the sidewalk in front of my house. I swear she was looking in the windows."

"Okay..."

"She walks that yappy Pomeranian. You know which one I'm talking about? That dog is pure asshole. He-Man hates it." In the background, there was a quick metal-against-metal sound, like she was pulling her curtains closed. "She's the biggest gossip in town. I think she's onto us."

"I doubt that." I didn't give two shits if Mrs. Dupont knew anyway. Sure, I had promised her we could take things slow and keep things quiet, but I was beginning to feel like a dirty little secret.

"I'm going to leave the garage open. Park in there, and I'll shut the door as soon as you pull in. If you see her, circle the block a few times."

"This seems a bit extreme—"

She hung up before I could call her out on how batshit crazy this was.

Our situation wasn't ideal. This was a tiny town that had recently been rocked by an epic criminal scandal involving both of our families. It stood to reason that people would talk. Certain shitty people, of course, would judge. That was inevitable.

But the world would keep spinning on its axis if she and I were publicly dating.

And we *were* dating—as juvenile as the word was. This was a full-blown relationship.

The world was a dumpster fire. Shitty things happened every day. Why expend so much energy hiding something that was ultimately good and made us happy? That was my take on things.

But Adele had more to lose than I did. My family was already splintered. Even the relationships I had with my brothers were strained. And the less said about my father, the better. No one I truly cared about would turn their back on me, and my dating her wouldn't be seen as a betrayal.

After ensuring the street was empty, I pulled into the open garage. I hadn't even turned off the ignition when the door closed and Adele stepped out of the house.

She pulled me close and gave me the kind of kiss that promised this was going to be a *very* fun sleepover.

"I missed you," I said, handing her the daisies.

She held them to her nose and inhaled. "These are so beautiful."

Inside her cozy cottage, I kicked off my shoes and dropped the duffel I'd stashed in my back seat. The kitchen was all white, with butcher block countertops and checkerboard floors, and the dining nook housed a simple pine table and matching chairs.

"Did you cook?" I said, putting my arms around her and kissing her neck while she put the flowers in a mint green vase at the sink.

She nodded. "Nothing fancy. I'm not Alice. Just roasted chicken and fresh sweet corn I picked up at the farmers' market."

"Smells delicious. But I think I need an appetizer first." My hand was already up under her tank top and headed straight for her bra clasp. "Didn't you get my memo?" I asked, biting her earlobe. "No bra is the best bra."

She arched back into me as I unhooked the offending

undergarment. "I can't live life braless just because it makes your life easier."

"Yes you can. I think it would benefit us both."

She turned around and pushed me back against the island, peeling off my shirt as she went. She tossed it on the counter and popped up on her toes for another kiss.

Her perfect tits and the way she rubbed against my chest made my cock ache. Shit. I couldn't resist ducking low and taking one pink nipple into my mouth.

She gripped my hair. "Stop," she begged. "That feels way too good."

"Wait until I get my mouth on that delicious pussy." I smacked her ass and pushed the waistband of her shorts down. "I'm starving for it."

With a throaty laugh, she palmed my cock through my shorts. "Oh, really? I better put you out of your misery, then."

I picked her up and placed her on the kitchen counter. Then I stepped between her legs and spread them wide.

"Yes. That's a good girl. Spread for me."

Trailing my fingers up her thighs, I took in every inch of her, teasing and tormenting and stopping right before I reached her soaking pussy. This woman might kill me.

One-handed, I pushed my own shorts down, then kicked off my boxers. Stroking my cock, I took a step back and surveyed her. She was laid out in front of me, panting and writhing. Her hair was down and her head was thrown back, her naked body ready for the taking.

More than anything, I wanted to push into her and fuck her hard until she came, screaming my name.

But I was promised a meal. And I'd be enjoying one.

I bent down and dragged my tongue lazily through her folds, pinning her thighs open with a palm splayed on each one.

She gasped and bowed off the island in response.

"You like that?"

She nodded, her face and neck already flushed pink.

"Look at you, so sexy and laid out for me. You want more of my tongue, don't you?"

I tasted her again, eliciting a moan, then flicked her clit and slid a finger inside her. My intention was to tease her. To make her beg. But I loved the taste of her and the feel of her so much I couldn't control myself. Instead of drawing things out, I dove in, licking and sucking with fervor and reveling in her response.

Within a minute, I had two fingers inside her and she was riding my face with abandon, chasing her orgasm while pulling on my hair. What a way to start the weekend.

She was clamped tight on my fingers, seconds away from crashing over the edge, when the dog went apeshit.

Asshole.

Instantly, Adele released me, but I didn't slow.

"Finn," she said, her voice shaking. "Stop."

That one word was all it took. I stood up and wiped my face, scanning her in search of what had upset her. Then I heard it. The doorbell.

"Shit," she said, jumping off the counter so quickly she almost face-planted.

"I can't stand up straight," she said, looking at me with wide, glassy eyes while I steadied her. "Fuck. Fuck. I gotta get that."

She whipped her head from side to side in a panic, then dove for her phone, which was sitting next to the sink, before scrambling for our clothing.

"Shit! Take these." She pushed my clothes into my chest, but she didn't look up from the screen of her phone. "And go somewhere."

"Adele," I said, going for soothing. She had the doorbell app pulled up, but she was flailing too wildly for me to make out the figures on the screen.

"Garage," she said, pulling her tank top over her head. "Now. I'll lock the door."

I scoffed, and my heart dropped into my stomach. "You're locking me in your garage?"

"You make it sound cruel. There's oxygen in there." She shimmied into her shorts and pushed me toward the door.

I paused with my hand on the doorknob while she ran toward the front hall. Maybe it was a delivery?

But then I heard a familiar voice.

Chapter 29
Adele

I dropped my hand to the doorknob, trying to take a steadying breath. Clothes? Check. Hair? Probably a mess. Body? Freaking out.

"Auntie Adele!"

I pasted on a big smile as I greeted my niece and nephew, but it dropped when I locked eyes with my brother, who was standing behind them, arms crossed and frowning.

"Are you okay?" he asked, his voice deep and rumbling.

Blinking, I racked my brain for a plausible excuse for what took me so long to answer the door. Before I could sputter out a response, Goldie pushed her way inside.

"We came to bring this back to you." She held out my hot pink Gagnon Lumber hoodie on her way past me.

I had ordered them for my team last year, because our company merch was bland and masculine. "Can I use your bathroom? I gotta pee." She didn't wait for a response before she charged through the entryway and deeper into the house.

My stomach churned, but I willed it to settle. They'd be in and out quickly. Nothing to worry about.

"You left it when you came over for dinner," Tucker explained, his hands in his pockets. He was officially a teenager now, complete with floppy hair in his face and the ever-present cell phone.

I ruffled his hair, knowing it drove him semi-crazy. "Good to see you. You haven't been by the shop in a while. I have a feller engine for you to work on."

His flat expression morphed into a gleeful grin immediately. There was nothing that kid loved more than taking apart engines. I had no doubt that when the time came, he could get into a great engineering program.

"Can I, Dad?" He looked at Henri, that grin turning hopeful.

"You can come to work with me on Thursday."

Tucker pumped his fist and followed his sister into the house.

"Why didn't you answer?" Henri asked, eyeing me, then scanning what he could see of the house behind me. "And why are you all sweaty?"

Alice hopped up the steps and threaded her arm through his.

"I was cleaning," I said, impressed with myself for coming up with an excuse off the cuff like that. "And I didn't hear the doorbell because of the music." Genius.

"I didn't hear any music when the kids were ringing your doorbell over and over again."

"Henri!" Alice chided, patting his arm. "Don't interrogate your sister."

He scrutinized me again, looking for the lie. I wasn't usually this flustered. Of course, if the kids weren't here, I'd tell him to mind his fucking business and get the hell off my lawn.

"Headphones," I said nonchalantly, hoping to move this conversation along and get them out of here.

Finn was hidden in my garage, hopefully clothed, but it didn't change the fact that he had just been eating me on the kitchen counter.

Goldie's and Tucker's voices echoed from inside. They were both crouched on the tile floor outside the kitchen, playing with He-Man. Jesus, this would never end.

"Auntie Adele," Goldie said. "Can I have a glass of water?"

I turned and scurried inside to help her, worried she'd open the garage door, and Henri and Alice followed me back toward the kitchen. Great, this was a full-blown visit now. Exactly what I needed.

"We're going out for pizza. Wanna join?" my brother asked.

I shook my head and wiped at the sweat collecting on my brow with the back of my wrist. "Thanks. Having a quiet night of cleaning."

Alice put her arm around me and gave me a squeeze. "Come with us. The kids miss you. You've been so busy lately."

God, I adored her. If anyone else was pressuring me, I'd be ready to do battle, but she was so fun and sweet and well intentioned. Henri might be a grumpy pain in my ass, but at least he was wise enough to lock her down quickly.

I smiled. "Next time, I promise. I'm exhausted. This one—I nodded in the direction of her husband—works me too hard."

He raised one eyebrow and pressed his lips together in a flat line. I made my own hours, we both knew that, but it was the best I could come up with in the moment. Shit. Flustered, I paced around my kitchen, smiling maniacally. They knew. They totally knew there was a half-naked Viking in my garage.

Henri was standing three feet from the door that would

lead straight to him too. I hoped Finn had enough sense to put all his clothes back on.

If it was only sex, it would be easier to explain. *I was in a bad place. Needed to scratch an itch.* Sure, the conversation would be uncomfortable, but it'd be worlds easier than admitting I had feelings for him.

Big, scary feelings that I was trying my best to ignore, despite how much space they'd taken up in my mind and in my heart. Sleeping with the enemy would be a huge issue in my family. But falling for him? My brothers would probably disown me. Not that I'd blame them. I'd do the same thing in their shoes.

While Henri had given Finn a chance, he was annoyingly pigheaded about me and who I dated. In high school, Ritchie LaVoie, my first boyfriend and the guy I lost my virginity to, opened his damn trap and bragged about it. He came to school with two black eyes and a dislocated shoulder the following week. I knew exactly what my brothers were capable of.

I scanned the kitchen floor, where Goldie was throwing a squeaky toy to He-Man, and my heart stopped. Balled up, right on the tile, were Finn's boxers. They had little anchors all over them. He was predictable like that. They were hanging out like they owned the place. Right there on the goddamn kitchen floor.

So far, no one had noticed, but we were only a few feet away. I must not have grabbed them in my panic to answer the door.

I tried to follow the conversation, but the boxers were screaming at me. Over and over again. How had no one else noticed? I was convinced everyone, including my eight-year-old niece, would see them and shame me forever. The floozy aunt who couldn't keep her panties on around her hot enemy.

Wood Riddance

A bead of sweat dripped down my spine, and my cheeks hurt from holding a fake smile for what felt like ages while Alice told me about Goldie's upcoming soccer season. Dammit. I needed everyone out of my house right now.

Because the boxers were like a telltale heart. No heartbeat involved, but a flashing neon sign meant to alert my guests to their presence. Every minute, they got bigger, taking up more space in the room. At this rate, they'd all trip over them on the way to the door and the jig would be up.

"Is that okay, Auntie Adele?"

I blinked, lost as to what Goldie had been asking me.

"Um."

Alice, ever the kind soul, took pity on me. "In third grade, the class does a unit on careers. Goldie wants you to come and talk to her class about your work."

"Yes," Goldie cheered, jumping up and down. "It won't be right away. But I need to lock it down. Sophie's dad is a ski instructor, and she thinks she's *so* special. My mom works at the school. I can't bring her." She planted her hands on her hips and popped a sassy little pose. "That'd be lame. And my dad has such a boring job. I want you to come to my class and show everyone I have the coolest aunt."

I couldn't help but smile. "Of course. Name the day."

Tucker laughed, tossing He-Man's toy for him. "It's months from now."

"Gotta give her time to plan something cool." Goldie looked me dead in the eyes.

Shit. Had she noticed the boxers?

"Don't be boring, okay?"

Letting out a relieved breath, I crossed my heart. "I promise."

"We should get going. Sorry to intrude," Alice said, steering her daughter back toward the door and jerking her head to signal to Tucker that it was time to head out.

I walked with them, hoping to God I was blocking their line of sight to the boxers. It was the best I could do. If I picked them up or kicked them, it would be too obvious. Fucking Finn and his underwear. I'd run half marathons and never felt this out of breath. I was clearly in the throes of some kind of underwear-induced cardiac event.

"Thanks for dropping my sweatshirt off," I chirped, herding them as quickly as I could without physically pushing them to the door.

My stomach unknotted once they'd all stepped over the threshold, and finally, I could pull in a deep breath. I followed them out and waved as they walked toward Henri's truck. My brother stopped at the edge of the driveway and glanced over his shoulder, still regarding me with suspicion, which wasn't entirely out of the ordinary. To avoid the scrutiny, I shot him a glare I knew would make him uncomfortable.

I breathed a sigh of relief when he shook his head and finally turned to open the back door for Goldie.

We were in the clear.

But then tiny paws click-clacked on the hardwood floor behind me. And lo and behold, there was He-Man, coming out to say goodbye.

With the boxers clenched between his teeth.

Alice gasped when he came into view. In response to her reaction, Henri turned from where he was getting his daughter settled. In a flash, I picked He-Man up and balled the boxers beneath my arm to keep them concealed.

I hadn't been quick enough, though, it seemed. Alice had definitely seen them, judging by the look of pure shock on her face.

"Can't wait to see you at girls' night on Thursday," she said, narrowing her eyes. "We have *so* much to talk about."

Hands shaking, I did the only thing I could think of. I shouted "bye" and then promptly slammed the door shut.

Finn was waiting for me in the kitchen, a murderous scowl firmly in place.

"I'm sorry," I said, truly feeling awful for forcing him to hide. "I panicked."

He nodded, taking the boxers out of my hand.

"Why are these wet?"

"He-Man was chewing on them."

He ran his hands through his hair, frustration rolling off him. His anger was justified, but what else was I supposed to do? Introduce him, naked, to my niece and nephew?

"I get that this wasn't the time or the place," he said, as if he was reading my mind, "but you can't shove me in a closet or a bathroom or a garage every time your family shows up. It's bound to happen again in this godforsaken tiny town, and I won't allow you to hide me forever."

His thoughts on the matter were perfectly logical. But it was still panic-inducing. My heart rate hadn't even returned to normal after my near miss with my brother, and already, he was confronting me with things I wasn't ready to work through yet. What we had was great, and I was blissfully, ridiculously happy with him. But this was still new, and I wasn't sure how I'd handle the fallout with my family.

"You can't hide from your feelings forever, Adele. We both know we've got something real here."

Tentatively stepping up to him, I flattened my hand on his chest. "I know," I said softly. "But I'm not sure what the next step is or even if I'm ready to take it."

In order for me to settle into this, we needed a fully realized plan, preferably with an exit strategy if things went south. We couldn't do this on a whim.

His nostrils flared in response to my confession, and agony swam in his eyes. Okay, that was the wrong thing to say. "Please be honest with me. Before this goes any further. Are you ever going to be ready to tell them? Because if not, I can't do this." He stepped back, putting a foot of distance between us. "I can handle the gossip, and I can take all the hatred and rumors. But I won't be hidden. Not forever."

The defeat emanating from him was breaking my heart. The last thing I wanted to do was hurt Finn. He'd been so honest with me, so vulnerable, and he'd done nothing but build me up from the moment he showed up at Gagnon Lumber.

I was already so far outside my comfort zone. What were a few more steps?

"Soon. I need time to come up with a way to approach my family. You're important to me, and I don't want you to feel hidden. I panicked today. It won't happen again."

He put one palm on the island and tipped forward, dropping a soft kiss to my lips.

"Okay," he said. "I'll give you more time."

"We need a plan," I explained, "because this could go sideways."

He cupped my cheek. "If things get bad, I'll throw you over my shoulder and make a run for it. But we're a team."

Looking into those deep blue eyes, I believed him. We *were* a team. I already depended on him more than I'd ever allowed myself to do with another person. While that should terrify me, I was proud. Lying and sneaking around was not what I wanted anymore. This was real, and I only wanted our relationship to grow.

"But I want it all, Adele. So be ready."

Chapter 30
Finn

This was the last place I wanted to be. It had taken two hours to get to the Maine State Correctional Facility, ensuring that this endeavor would eat up most of my day.

Dad was being held here until his trial. There were both state and federal charges pending, but the federal charges were being tried first.

We'd had to preregister and were given a laundry list of dos and don'ts. We wore special clothes because items like work boots and jeans were not allowed. The most exciting part of it all? Signing consent forms that gave the prison staff permission to search our persons.

All to spend a little time with dear old dad.

I'd done my best to avoid him before he went to prison. It was wild to me that I was willingly stepping foot inside one to see the bastard.

Gus had insisted on riding together. I hadn't argued because it meant more time to think about Adele. But I hadn't realized that sitting in the passenger seat would make my fingers itch to text her. I had left her house this morning to go home and shower. Of course, I made sure to use the garage and leave as early as possible to avoid being seen my any of her neighbors.

It wasn't that I wanted people up in my business, but this was a hell of a lot of work. And, for the first time since I'd left the Navy, I had a purpose other than caring for my daughter. Making Adele smile was not easy. She always made me work for it, but when she did, it made my entire day.

I wanted to walk down the street holding her hand, kiss her at town festivals, and bury all the shit between our families. Paying for the sins of the previous generation was getting old. The world had changed. Hell, we were on the verge of selling, so there was no reason to hang on to all the bad blood.

Unfortunately, the business was in absolute disarray. Owen had been digging through records, and he'd found far too much missing information and massive inconsistencies. Gus was far less upset about it, because each issue was a roadblock to selling. He was digging in his heels about a potential sale and working to convince us to give it a shot.

Jude was harder to read. Gus wanted this life. He loved logging and the woods and everything to do with Lovewell. But Jude had always seemed to be stuck.

He had big dreams, but he'd never been able to fully articulate them, so he defaulted to the easiest option. If we were as close as we once were, if the circumstances weren't quite so shitty, I'd sit him down and force him to open up. But right now, in the midst of all the strife we were dealing with day to day, there was no way he'd hear anything I had to say.

I was with Owen on this. I wanted to sell, walk away with whatever profit we could eke out of the disaster of a corporation, and then focus on starting my own business. I had connected with a couple of backcountry guides who led hikes of Katahdin, and they'd been helpful with information about tourism in the area. They'd also hooked me up with leads to follow up on. Every person I spoke to who had their toes in the water of the Maine tourism industry agreed that the area needed more bush pilots. And eventually, if I could save for a helicopter, I could take tourists up on backcountry skiing trips in the winter.

The father of one of my Navy buddies owned several ski resorts in New England and was desperate for a pilot. Tourists paid big money to be dropped off on top of mountains. Warmer winters and irregular snowfall had hit the Maine skiing industry hard, but it was starting to recover. This was the time to get my foot in and grow.

But I couldn't do that without start-up capital and a plan. So I continued to network and research the best way to handle contracts with ski resorts in the area. If I could get in with a handful of them, that'd pay the bills all winter. Then in the summer, I could focus on tourism trips.

It had been months since I'd put time into actively planning my business. After my dad's arrest, I'd mostly given up, feeling too beaten down and defeated to believe my dreams could become a reality.

But things had changed. My perspective had changed.

Adele was showing me how different my life could be, even though I couldn't leave this town.

She surprised me every day. And she was slowly drawing me out of my funk.

She asked endless questions about my ideas and had helped me draft a basic business plan. Often, we sat side by side on my couch with our laptops, working on fuel estimates and looking at seasonal tourism trends. Not only did she take my dream seriously, but she was confident that I could do it. She was confident in me.

She spoke in *when*s, not *if*s. Her faith lit a fire inside me. So did her determination. She didn't do anything halfway. She pushed herself every single day, and it inspired the hell out of me. Last week, I'd surprised her with water balloons on a particularly hot day. In typical Adele fashion, she jumped in with both feet and took our water battle seriously, hiding behind bushes and attacking me with the strategy of a four-star admiral while He-Man ran around barking at me.

We rolled around, wet and dirty, while the sun set. And then spent the night having sweaty sex with all the windows open, letting the late summer breeze flow through her house.

In two weeks' time, I'd fallen head over heels for this woman. Was it possible? A future in Lovewell? Could my dream job and dream woman *both* be within my grasp?

As we got off the endless highway and followed the grim-looking signs, Jude finally spoke up. "Did you hear about Cole?"

I shook my head, and Gus grunted from the driver's seat.

"Labrum tear. Grade four. Happened at training camp."

"Jesus."

"He's injured this hip a few times already. Needs total surgical replacement. He'll need lots of PT to walk normally."

"Awful."

I harbored plenty of resentment toward my youngest brother, but I still loved the bastard and I'd never wish an injury on him. This past season had been terrible for him. And now, at almost 29, he'd suffered what was likely a career-ending injury.

For a couple of years, things had been good. He'd been called up a few times, and he'd suited up for the Blaze. We'd all driven down to Boston to watch him. But he was never able to maintain a position in the majors.

He was inconsistent and moody, with a poor work ethic.

It was such a waste. He had immense talent. He was six-five, with a killer slapshot, every NHL coach's dream, but he couldn't get out of his own way.

As frustrated as he made me sometimes, my heart ached for him. Pampered by my dad, but largely ignored by his own mom, he'd always sort of floated through life.

For most of his life, natural talent plus my dad's money had ensured that he didn't have to try hard to get what he wanted.

Even when it came to his longtime girlfriend, Lila. She traveled with him, bent over backward to accommodate him, and was his biggest cheerleader. Yet for years, he'd barely even given her the time of day. Come to think of it, I hadn't heard anything about her in a while. Maybe she'd woken up and dumped his ass.

"He's having surgery in Boston but will probably come home for a while to recover," Jude said.

"What would he even do here? Did he ever finish his degree?" I scoffed. If my father did one thing right, it was insisting that we take our education seriously. Cole leaving U Maine and entering the NHL draft had been a major issue between them.

"I think he's a few credits short. Maybe he can work on that while he's got the time."

"Sure," Gus said. "Like that will happen without Dad's money or a hockey scholarship."

For many years, I believed he'd grow up eventually and seize the opportunities life had given him. But that was looking less and less likely these days. Yet another layer to our family dysfunction.

I closed my eyes and replaced thoughts of my fuck-up brother with those of Adele, wishing this day to be over so I could see her again.

Sadly, my daydreams were interrupted by the sight of looming gates ahead.

"We're here."

Prison was both everything and nothing like how it was portrayed on TV. Depressing, but not as intimidating as I'd anticipated. More like a really sad-looking office park surrounded by barbed wire fencing. Helpful signs guided us the whole way through the dusty parking lot and into the building that smelled like bleach. Each step of the way, we were forced to wait in a line.

There were checkpoints and cameras and metal detectors and endless forms. But eventually, we were led to a small room with an old folding table and chairs. After we'd waited about thirty minutes, tapping our feet, shifting uncomfortably, and fidgeting the whole time, my father was led in. The guard unlocked his handcuffs and then sat on a stool outside the door.

The frail man standing in front of me looked nothing like my father. He was tall, sure, but gone was the muscle and the confident posture. This man was skinny and gaunt. His hair, without its usual salon appointments, had gone completely white.

He wore a beige shirt and beige pants that hung loosely on his frame. His vibrant blue eyes, eyes we had all inherited from him, were dull, almost gray. I couldn't reconcile this man with the loud, confident man who had run around town in his Mercedes and Gucci loafers.

"Boys," he said, holding open his arms.

Gus and Jude took turns hugging him. I settled for a handshake.

Wood Riddance

"Thank you for coming to see me," he said. In place of his usual charm was thick, genuine emotion. "It's so lonely here."

I was taken aback. The man who told me my tattoos were disgraceful, the man who wore custom suits and had a collection of watches worth more than most people's homes, was nowhere to be found.

This man was humbled. This man was broken.

Gus and Jude made small talk with him. As usual, my father was most interested in Cole. His questions focused on how many of his games we had caught and if he had a chance of being called up.

My brothers exchanged subtle looks more than once. Clearly, they were not going to break the news about Cole today. He had always been Dad's favorite.

And for a long time, I resented that. But now, as an adult, I was grateful to have escaped his interest. I'd had half a chance to grow into a functional human because of it.

In fact, I had the sudden and intense urge to drive straight home and give my mom the biggest hug. The five of us would not have stood a snowflake's chance in hell of growing into decent humans if left with my dad. Our mother had always loved and supported us, while giving us firm boundaries and morals to uphold. As bad as this situation was, at least he hadn't dragged Gus or Jude down with him.

I cleared my throat, ready to get on with it. We only had forty minutes, and I didn't want to waste it. Grabbing my notebook and the No. 2 pencil that security had allowed me to take inside, I attempted to get this meeting on track.

"We're here because we have some questions," I said, grasping for control.

"About the business," Gus added. "I'm doing my best, Dad.

Daphne Elliot

We've made some big sacrifices, but I think I can get us through the worst of it.

Clenching my fists, I fought back the anger that bubbled up in my stomach. I didn't want to hate Gus, but seriously, man? We were visiting our father in prison, and he was still desperate for the bastard's approval. Still vying for the top spot on his list of favorites. And for what? He was a thirty-eight-year-old man. At some point, he'd have to live for himself rather than for Dad.

Successfully curbing the urge to snap at him, I went through the questions Owen had laid out for us.

My father's memory was shit, but he did point us to various employees to follow up with, the location of some of the records we were after, and his contact at the specialty mill in New Hampshire where he had been offloading cedar at a premium for the past few years.

I couldn't decide whether I was angry or relieved that this had been a productive conversation. He was concise and careful, and from what I could tell, he was actually trying to help us.

I'd expected him to be his usual self, ranting about his innocence and telling us what to do and how to live our lives. I envisioned him complaining about prison and trying to justify his actions. But he never once said a word about any of it. Like maybe he'd accepted his fate and understood that he would never be free again. I supposed that's what nine months in lockup could do to a guy.

And, strangest of all, he seemed happy to see us. Grateful for our visit, even. So depressing and strange. I was ready to wrap up and get out of here when Jude finally spoke.

He had sat at the end of the table, totally silent, for the entire visit. He didn't take notes or ask questions or even lift his head. He'd only stared at the gray cinderblock walls as he listened.

But here he was, finally entering the chat.

"Dad, you've got to cooperate," he said, his eyes full of tears. "Tell them something. You could get yourself out of this."

Deep down in his heart, he wanted Dad to be innocent. Wanted there to be some explanation for what he'd done. When our parents divorced, he'd taken it the hardest, and all these years later, he was still wishing they would get back together. My mom had always said Jude was the deep thinker and the deep feeler of the family, but some days, those thoughts were far too idealistic.

Dad shook his head. "No. I will not do that."

His eyes got glassy, and for a moment, I worried he would cry. I had never seen my father cry. Until this moment, I wasn't sure the man had tear ducts. He had always taken a great deal of delight in making others cry. It was one of his specialties. He'd never, in all my life, been the one doing the crying. "I can't do that, Jude," he urged. "There are others. You boys and Merry, you're all I care about."

I snorted. Sure. *Now* he cared about us.

He tilted forward and lowered his voice. "There are powerful, ruthless people out there. And I will never, ever compromise your safety. I'll rot in here forever before I let them hurt you."

"Dad, what are you saying?"

"Stick together. Take care of one another. And your mother. And Cole. Please don't punish him for my mistakes."

"We never have," I said, sitting up straight and crossing my arms over my chest.

"I know that, but you all need each other more than ever right now. I screwed up, and I took my brother down with me.

Daphne Elliot

Learn from my mistakes, boys. Take care of each other. Watch out for each other. You're all you have on this earth."

"But the business..." This from Gus.

"Sell it. Move on with your lives. Fuck the trees and fuck the bats." I had no idea what bats had to do with anything, but the conviction in his voice was surprisingly moving.

"Dad," Gus said.

He looked at his oldest son, the one he was closest to, the one who had bent over backward for him his whole life. "Son," he said. "Don't put that kind of pressure on yourself. I lost the business. I'm the one who tarnished the family legacy. I'm the one who failed my father and my grandfather and my great-grandfather. This is not your battle to fight."

"It's our legacy too."

"It doesn't have to be." He ran his hand through his thin, white hair, his face deeply lined with worry. "So many of my choices were colored by my obligations to the business, to the legacy. It's another thing that could hold you all back. Tie you down. So go live your lives. Forget about Hebert Timber. Forget about me and all this shit."

My stomach twisted into knots at the unexpected warnings. My father was the king of lectures. We couldn't hold a conversation with him without being scolded for falling short on every measure. Dad had lots of opinions about how each of us could do better. This was something else entirely. He was owning up to his actions and trying to steer us onto a better path. It was almost... fatherly?

Eventually, we said our goodbyes. Gus and Jude gave him long hugs while he apologized over and over again, wiping away tears.

When I held out my hand for a shake, he pulled me in

close. "Finn," he said, waiting for Gus and Jude to step out of the room. "I know I can count on you to keep everyone safe."

"Is Merry in danger? Mom?"

He shook his head. "No. I don't think so."

"That's not good enough, Dad," I hissed. My heart lodged in my throat, and anger once again brewed in my gut. After everything he'd put us through, he was hinting that the trouble wasn't over.

He held up a hand. "There is no reason to believe anyone is in danger. Just keep an eye out and live your lives. This goes far beyond me. There are people in Lovewell who are compromised."

"Who?" I demanded. "Give me names. Dad, we can't live like this."

He closed his eyes and took a step back. "I can't tell you. Promise me you'll stay alert and keep an eye on things. You're the practical one, the protector."

I gaped, angry at having this burden placed on my shoulders, that he wouldn't even give me a straight answer.

He grabbed me by the shoulders and pulled me into a tight hug, shocking me with his strength despite his frail appearance.

"I love you, son."

Chapter 31
Finn

I couldn't fight the grin I was sporting as Adele sat beside me in my truck and made guesses about where we were going. It had taken some planning, and I'd had to pull a few strings, but I'd planned the perfect date weekend.

My head was a strange, chaotic place at the moment. Between seeing my father, playing mediator while my brothers went rounds over what to do with the business, and stressing over the hints Dad had dropped about the safety of our family, I'd barely slept, and I was more on edge than ever.

And there was only one person who could soothe me.

My girl. Though I figured I'd better stick with *my woman.* If she knew I'd referred to her as a girl, even in my mind, she'd kick my ass into next week. And as much as I'd enjoy that, I couldn't risk ruining my romantic weekend.

"Tell me, Finn."

I shook my head. "Sorry, She-Ra. Sit back and enjoy the ride."

I'd thrown the trip together at the last minute, but every aspect was coming together perfectly.

Daphne Elliot

We cruised south down I-95, enjoying the glorious August sunshine and listening to *The Naturalist*, a Theodore Roosevelt biography I downloaded for the trip. Adele looked beautiful. She wore red sunglasses and had her hair pulled up in a ponytail that listed to one side as she reclined in the seat and listened raptly to an anecdote about the formation of the National Parks Service. She was wearing a sundress. It was the last item of clothing I expected her to even own, but holy shit, was it the sexiest thing I'd ever seen. It was blue and plaid, and it had thin straps that showed off her collarbones and shoulders. It flared out at the waist and fell to her knees. The moment she stepped out onto her porch wearing it, I wanted to crawl under that skirt and live there.

I had this goddess of a woman all to myself for the next forty-eight hours. If I was really lucky, we'd have a great time and also have a real conversation about what was going on between us and how we should proceed going forward.

Because despite declaring herself to be mine, we still hadn't defined the parameters of our relationship. And that made my chest ache. I would proudly wear any label she'd give me. But this was not a situationship. It was not casual. And it sure as hell was not friends with benefits.

But Adele was not the kind of person to be forced into a conversation. So I was taking her away to a place where we didn't have to hide a damn thing from anyone. And where, hopefully, we could figure out what our future would look like.

When we finally picked up Route 1, which hugged the entire Maine coast up to New Brunswick, she sat up a bit straighter.

"Are we going where I think we're going?" She slid her sunglasses down the bridge of her nose and raised one eyebrow at me.

I nodded. "It's not Glacier. Not yet. But I figured we should start visiting together. A new tradition."

We crossed the bridge onto Mt. Desert Island, admiring the swells of the ocean on either side of us and the vast mountains ahead. Acadia National Park was the first national park established east of the Mississippi River and one of my all-time favorite places. My mom had brought us here one summer when I was in grade school, and it was where my love affair with national parks began.

Adele practically bounced in her seat as we got closer. "I love it here so much. Can we get popovers at the Jordan Pond House?"

"Of course."

"And see the sunrise on Cadillac Mountain?"

"Definitely."

"Where are we staying?"

I gave her a wink. "Another surprise. Stay put. We're almost there."

We cruised through the picturesque town of Bar Harbor, past the park entrance, and toward the southwest tip to a tiny village called Seal Harbor.

There, I turned onto a dirt road and drove up a large wooded hill into a clearing.

"Are you shitting me?" Adele squealed as a shiny vintage Airstream came into view. The deck built into its side was strung with lights and housed two bright pink Adirondack chairs. The surrounding area was filled with colorful wildflowers that flanked the path to the forest. "This is insane." Adele threw the door open before I had the transmission shifted into park. Then she was spinning, taking in every inch of the space.

While I wrestled the keys out of the lockbox, she snapped

photos of the clearing and the Airstream and the trees surrounding us.

Once inside, she was downright giddy. "Finn," she gushed, as she took in every detail. From the white wooden cabinets to the apron sink to the blue velvet couch and gingham curtains on the windows.

While she gleefully inspected every detail, I grabbed our bags from the truck and hauled them in.

I had barely gotten them through the tiny door before she was launching herself at me, throwing her arms around my neck, and kissing me senseless.

"Thank you."

I wrapped my arms around her once I'd rid myself of our luggage, loving the way she melted into me. Closing my eyes, I breathed deeply and soaked up this moment. So often, I focused on what was missing from my life. In a perfect world, I could take this woman to far nicer places than an old Airstream, but this was the best I could do right now. Thankfully, she didn't seem to mind one bit.

She pulled back. "It's perfect. Wait. Can you even stand up straight in here?"

I shrugged.

"Oh no," she cried, spinning one way, then the other. "You're all hunched over. You can barely fit your shoulders through the door."

I grasped her upper arms to still her. "Stop stressing. I don't care if I have to sleep outside on the ground. It would be worth it just to see that look on your face."

She kissed me again and rested her head on my chest. "You knew I'd love it, then?"

I held her tight and rested my chin on the top of her head. "Yup. You love all the vintage girlie stuff. Yeah, you're a badass lady mechanic, but you have a softer side too, and you haven't done a very good job hiding it from me."

She pulled back. "Oh really? So you think you know everything I like now, huh?"

"I most certainly do. Aside from my dick, you like pretty, charming things. Like this fancy floral wallpaper and the walnut countertops." I waved a hand toward the kitchen space. "Those copper pots hanging from the ceiling too. And the wildflowers surrounding the property."

She giggled.

"This is one of your Pinterest boards come to life." I tugged on her arm and pulled her back outside.

"You've got me there," she said, following me down the steps of the deck. "How'd you find it?"

"One of my Navy buddies. He's from this area. His family bought some property, and they have been restoring Airstreams to rent to tourists. They're eco-friendly, and they're perfect for people who want to experience the outdoors in a more authentic way."

"I love it." She rose up on her tiptoes and kissed me again. Here, far away from Lovewell and all the responsibilities and expectations, she was happier, lighter.

And I was going to soak up as many of her rare smiles as I could before we headed back to reality.

Reaching into the bed of my truck, I pulled out the small cooler and the backpack I had prepared. "You good to walk for a bit in those shoes?" I asked, looking at her blue Chuck Taylors.

She nodded.

"Okay. We've gotta leave now if we wanna make it on time." I started up the path that wound behind the Airstream and headed for the tree line and shot a glance over my shoulder.

She wore a puzzled frown, and she hadn't moved from her spot beside my truck.

"Come on, She-Ra. Adventure awaits."

The walk to the secret beach was a mile, and the view was spectacular the entire way. Since returning to Lovewell, I'd had my fill of pine forests. The crisp, salty ocean air was just what I needed.

"Is this real?" she asked, looping her arm through mine.

At the edge of the clearing, we were situated on the top of a rock face with the Atlantic Ocean spread out before us. Up ahead, there was a large wooden staircase. It led down to the small beach area framed by massive boulders that kept the ocean at bay.

Adele flashed me a big smile and skipped down the steps. I stopped at the top to admire the excitement radiating from her and to pinch myself. Because she was really here with me.

A few people were scattered along the beach, but it was far from crowded. It was one of the many advantages of the hidden beach on the far side of the island—very few tourists knew of its existence. I owed Sam for telling me about this place.

Near the tree line, I spread out the blanket I'd brought and went to work setting up.

"Did you pack a picnic?" she asked, looming above me.

"Yup." I reached into the cooler. "And champagne."

"Cheesy, but I like it." She waggled her brows.

I popped the cork and poured champagne into my stainless-steel camping mug. "I told you. You're my woman now, and I'm treating you like a queen."

With wide eyes and a smile, she dropped to the blanket beside me and snuggled close.

"To National Parks," she said, taking the mug from me and bringing it to her lips.

"To the first of many adventures together," I replied when she passed the champagne to me.

We nibbled on fancy cheese and strawberries and watched as the sun began to set. The scene was peaceful, and it was made all the more beautiful by Adele's presence beside me.

Not far down the beach, an older couple was snapping photos. With my heart thumping in my chest, I pulled Adele to her feet and dragged her along the sand, hoping she wouldn't balk at my idea.

"Excuse me?" I asked, holding my phone out as we approached. "Would you mind taking a photo of us?"

The woman smiled broadly and shuffled closer to accept the device. "Oh, we'd love to."

I pulled Adele against me, positioning us so that the sunset and the ocean were directly behind us.

It felt so easy and so natural. So I let instincts take over as the woman took several photos. I picked Adele up and spun her around, then lowered her until her feet hit the sand and pulled her in for a kiss. For that second, no one else existed, only me, my girl, and the sunset.

We were wrapped up in each other, panting and grinning, when the woman approached.

"I took about a dozen." She shot me a wink.

"Thanks," I said, feeling breathless. When I finally dragged my focus from Adele's face, I noticed a handful of people nearby watching us. Not in a horrified way, but in an *aw, they're so cute* sort of way.

Here, on this secluded mountain beach, we could be us. We could live out loud. Together. There was no baggage, no history, no trauma or tragedy.

We were two people in love.

Chapter 32
Adele

The walk back to the Airstream was slow, mainly because we kept stopping to make out or admire the stars. Finn had thoughtfully packed headlamps, so we easily found our way up the trail and back to our special spot.

I was a mess of emotions. Every single minute of this day had been perfect, and I found it impossible to contain my affection for this man. I couldn't keep my hands or my lips off him. For the first time in my life, I was completely consumed by another person.

And it wasn't purely lust. That would be easy to explain, given that he walked around, day in and day out, looking the way he did. This was so much more complex. I trusted him, which was rare, and his presence soothed me. When we were together, I was less angry, more trusting. Open to all sorts of things I had never considered. Like agreeing to a full-on relationship with a man I'd considered my enemy only a month ago.

Daphne Elliot

I wanted to talk. So badly. To hash out the details and make sure he knew the depth of my feelings for him.

But I didn't know where to start.

The lights strung along the Airstream created an ethereal scene that struck me silent as we approached. Even if I'd had the words to confess the emotions that had taken over in the last few weeks, I was too in awe of the thought and effort he'd put into planning the perfect weekend. So I did the next best thing. I grabbed him and kissed the hell out of him.

He grasped my waist as he kissed me back and lifted me. In response, I wrapped my legs around his waist. I wasn't the type of woman who could be easily carried around, but Finn loved to manhandle me, and I enjoyed it way more than I should.

"I need you," I whimpered between frantic kisses.

One of his hands was already under my dress and making its way up toward my panties. I wasn't usually a dress kind of girl, but when I found it in my closet this morning, it felt right. He had made such an effort planning this spectacular weekend away. Hell, he always went out of his way to make me feel valued and important, so I wanted to make an effort for him too.

Hence the gingham sundress and very expensive lace panties.

"My God," he growled as he tromped across the open space, his fingers already stroking me over my panties. "You're already soaked." He set me on the picnic table and pushed my panties to one side.

A shiver coursed down my spine, and the heat in my core kicked up a notch. I leaned forward and kissed him again. "What can I say? Romantic gestures really get me going."

"Then I'll plan champagne picnics for you every day," he said, nipping at my earlobe and flicking my clit.

I had to grasp the edge of the table to hold myself upright as he gently eased one finger inside me. The sensation was pure ecstasy. I'd been waiting for his touch all damn day.

My initial assumptions about Finn had been dead wrong. He wasn't lazy in bed. He was alert, focused, and engaged. Much like he'd been when he was flying his plane, he was hyper-focused. This time, that focus was on my body and the noises I made instead of the sky. He tracked my responses to every one of his moves, cataloging which ones drove me absolutely wild.

He'd made a study of my body these past few weeks, teasing me in a dozen different ways until I was begging for him. Even now, he pressed the pad of his thumb to my clit with the perfect pressure, knowing exactly how I liked it.

He was in control of my body, and I was elated. As a lifelong control freak, I should have had more reservations about giving myself to him so willingly. But he had taken my trust and treated it with such reverence and care that I couldn't help but fall even deeper.

I slipped the straps of my dress off my shoulders and tugged the fabric down to free my breasts.

"No bra." He groaned, his mouth already on one tender nipple. "You are so perfect."

His constant praise and appreciation for my body went a long way to break down the walls I'd carefully built up over the years. His sincere admiration and desire burrowed deep into my heart.

"I need you inside me," I gasped.

Obediently, he scooped me up and set me on my feet on the grass beneath the awning of the Airstream.

With one hand still on my breast, he unzipped his shorts

and freed his cock. I wanted to drop to my knees and take him into my mouth, show him how much I needed him.

But he had other plans. He pushed my panties down and pointed to the steel pole above our heads.

"Hold on to that."

His demand sent desire coursing through me, and I obeyed, grasping the frame of the blue- and white-striped awning.

He hooked one arm under my knee and spread me wide as he entered me. My skirt was bunched around my waist, and my bare breasts were exposed to the cool night air as he fucked me against the Airstream, our bodies out in the open, only partially obscured by the awning.

"I love that I can fuck you standing up," he grunted, thrusting into me hard.

Dropping my head back against the stainless surface behind me, I gripped the beam, needing something to ground me. I was floating on a cloud of lust. Each thrust was the perfect balance of powerful and deep and perfect. This man somehow knew how to make every centimeter of my body ache for him.

I'd never fantasized about getting railed in a sundress under the moonlight, but I knew I'd be reliving this experience for a long time.

We kissed and licked and nipped and grabbed for one another, desperate for as much contact as possible. Heat radiated from him, soaking into me little by little with each thrust, and his scent swirled, filling my senses. This was more than sex. It was transformative. It was tearing me apart at the cellular level and piecing me back together. I was the same, yet different.

The outside world disappeared as we got lost in one

another. He was filling me up in ways I could never have imagined and certainly couldn't define. I buried my face in his neck as he took me higher and higher, clinging to him, trusting that he'd hold me after I fell apart.

And when he took me over the edge, I didn't fall apart. I shattered. My body pulsed as pleasure rolled through me and I cried out for him.

He kept going, holding me close and pushing through wave after wave of my climax. "Let go," I whispered, clenching around him again and again. Floating on a cloud of intimacy and pleasure and trust.

And he did. His steady thrusts became erratic, and he slowed his pace as my body wrung every last bit of pleasure out of him.

Dropping my leg, he wrapped his arms around me and buried his face in my neck. I collapsed against him, boneless, unable to talk or think or explain what had happened between us.

For several quiet minutes, we clung to one another, his face buried in my hair, as our heart rates slowed and reality filtered back in.

"We should do this," I said, nestling into his chest. "In Lovewell."

"What do you mean?"

"This." I sat up, the sheet falling down around my waist. "Fix up a few Airstreams and rent them to tourists. We've got land and gorgeous mountain scenery. Rivers, lakes, wildlife."

"Hmm. Maybe Clive could be good for something besides

jerky," he said, pulling me back down into the snuggle spot against his chest.

"You are not murdering the town moose." I let out a teasing huff. "If anything, we can post his antics on social media. He'd bring in the tourists. They can stay in our trailers and book aerial tours with you."

"This sounds like quite the empire you're building, She-Ra," he said.

"Yup. It makes sense. This place is incredible. Being here with you? It's like stepping into another world together." Lovewell wasn't Bar Harbor, not by a long shot, but it was charming and rural and had direct access to some of the most beautiful scenery.

"I love it here too," he said. "So you wanna buy some Airstreams? We'll have to find someone to fix them up. My brother Gus is a great carpenter."

I sat up and shot him an annoyed look. "My expertise doesn't end at machines, you know. Who do you think laid the gorgeous birch floors in my house?"

He pulled me close and nipped at my neck. "I admire your hyper-independence, but I'm starting to question why you even keep me around."

He was joking, of course, but the comment stung. Especially given my history of being dumped by guys who felt emasculated. The ability to change a tire was something I believed all women should possess. It was no big deal to me, but apparently to my ex-boyfriend Scott, it was a deal-breaker.

He flipped me over and pinned me beneath him, then went to work kissing down the column of my neck. "So it's my cock? Is that all I'm good for?"

"Not at all," I said, gasping as he bit my earlobe. "I don't need much. Just emotional support and orgasms."

"Ah, perfect. I can manage a lot of orgasms."

"Don't sell yourself short, Stretch. You're pretty good at the emotional support too. You're my personal emotional support Viking."

"It's not boyfriend or husband, but I'll take that label and wear it with pride."

Chapter 33
Finn

The next morning, we were up early to hike the Precipice Trail. Neither of us had done it before, and it was only open a few months out of the year because it was a nesting site for peregrine falcons, so we decided to tackle it together. It was the most difficult climb in the park and was a series of iron rungs, ladders, and wooden bridges that led up a massive rock face.

"Did you know that mama falcons will attack hikers during nesting season?" Adele asked over her shoulder as she pulled herself onto the next ledge.

I smiled, enjoying the view of her tiny shorts. "What a way to go. Mauled by a falcon."

She heaved herself onto the ledge and stuck her tongue out at me in response. Damn, I didn't think it possible for this woman to be any more beautiful and intriguing, but this unencumbered version of Adele had proved me wrong. Since we'd arrived, she had been completely relaxed and open. We were only a few hours from home, but the change of scenery was good for us both.

"I wonder if He-Man has destroyed Paz's house yet," I wondered out loud.

Adele turned and shot me a look. "He would never. My sweet boy is currently being spoiled rotten by Parker. She made a steak for him last night and texted me a photo of them curled up in bed watching *Housewives*."

"Where did you tell them you were going?"

"Boston. To meet a new tire supplier. They got glassy eyed when I started talking about tread depth so I figured they bought it."

We continued our scramble, stopping in a few spots for water and to take photos of the ocean crashing against the cliffs below.

"Is that," I murmured, bringing my mouth closer to Adele's ear, "Susan Stephens?"

The woman on the trail in front of us was in her early sixties. She was tall and fit, with chin-length white-blond hair, and bore a striking resemblance to Susan Stephens, chef, TV personality, and media billionaire.

Adele turned and followed my gaze. "I think so," she whispered.

Susan had a famous rags-to-riches story. As a young, single mom, she worked in a restaurant kitchen, and eventually purchased the place. She went on to publish several bestselling cookbooks and produce a line of cookware that was sold at every department store in the US. She then turned her endeavor into a multimedia empire, with magazines, TV shows and products everywhere.

My mom owned all of her cookbooks, and I had bought a set of her spatulas at Target during my last trip to Bangor with Merry.

Could that be her?

Wood Riddance

The woman on TV was always made up. This woman's face was free of all makeup, and her hair was held back by a headband, but I couldn't shake the feeling that it was really her.

The woman was surrounded by a large group of fellow hikers, some of whom seemed miserable, as she continued ahead of us. As we came up on them, the group moved to the side of the trail, which was standard hiking etiquette.

But not this woman. Nope, she remained in the middle of the trail, making it impossible for us to pass. That was how we ended up walking behind her, chatting about the trail and the park and the weather. The sound of her voice as she spoke to her companions confirmed our suspicion. It was her. Adele and I tried to play it cool as we approached the summit, hanging back a bit and doing our best to carry on a conversation while also enjoying the scenery.

Susan waited for the rest of her group to take some photos at the summit marker, and Adele and I found a spot to rest.

There were few people up here this early, but the handful that were gawked and discreetly snapped photos with their phones.

"I'm freaking out a little," Adele said, hiking one foot onto a boulder and straightening her leg to stretch out her hamstrings.

"Same. My mom would lose it."

"Mine too. She's a huge fan." Adele dropped to the rock beside me. "Alice was obsessed with her bridal magazine while she was wedding planning last year."

"Should we ask for a photo?"

"No. I don't want to be one of those people." She shook her head. "We're both sweaty and gross anyway."

"You're right. I didn't even put on deodorant this morning," I admitted.

"Finn," she huffed. "That's gross."

I shrugged. "We got up at five to climb up a rock face. I forgot."

She shimmied closer and kissed my cheek. "It's a good thing you're so handsome."

"And sweet," I said, dipping down to capture her mouth in a quick kiss.

"The sweetest. Now let's hike back down. I want pancakes."

I stood and held out a hand to help her up. It was past eight, so it wouldn't be long before the trail was crowded with tourists who didn't know how to safely navigate this type of hike.

The trail down the mountain was less dangerous, but it was long. So without any more hesitation, we headed out, scaling the large rocks at the summit.

I'd found my footing on an even patch of ground when a voice called out overhead. "Could you give me a hand?"

Squinting into the sunlight, I discovered Susan Stephens crouching above me, inching her way down the massive rock.

I held out my hand to her, and she grasped it, steading herself as she stepped down carefully.

And then she was standing directly in front of me. If I hadn't been sure of her identity before, it was obvious now.

"Thank you, sweetheart," she said. Her trademark Southern drawl was thick, and she turned on her charm. "Oh my goodness! You are a tall drink of water. How tall are you?"

If I didn't know better, I would have assumed this woman was flirting with me.

"About six foot six first thing in the morning," I replied politely.

She patted my forearm, seemingly unfazed by the sheen of sweat and dust coating it. "What's your name?"

"Finn Hebert, ma'am," I replied, "And this is my girlfriend, Adele Gagnon."

Adele gave her a tight smile, clearly starstruck.

"It's a pleasure to meet you both," she said. "Now tell me all about yourselves. We've got quite a long hike down, and my guests"—she waved at the entourage of sweating, exhausted people working their way down the boulders we'd traversed—"aren't up for the challenge of keeping up with me."

Susan Stephens was one scary woman, and she was objectively hilarious. She told us wild stories about how she brought along a cocktail shaker when she hiked Kilimanjaro so she could enjoy a decent drink at the summit. Adele and I listened as she recounted wild adventures she'd taken part in all over the world and introduced us to the folks hiking with her, which included her personal assistant, her publicist, two internationally known fashion designers, and the editor-in-chief of her travel magazine.

According to her publicist, Susan had woken them up at four a.m. for sunrise yoga, followed by this grueling hike. Apparently, as an employee, one's job requirements included jumping on her private jet for random weekend trips on demand.

She was an alpha dog. Not once did she let a person pass her on the trail, but her stories made up for it. She was damn impressive. This hike would have had most of my Navy buddies complaining, but she never slowed down.

"You're a pilot?"

"Navy," Adele cut in, elaborating for me. "And a recipient of the Flying Naval Cross."

Though I was dripping with sweat and my face was surely flushed, heat still crept up my neck. Adele was bragging about me to a real-life billionaire. I shot her a look, silently begging her to let it go, but she didn't seem deterred.

"Finn is so talented and passionate about Maine," she continued. "He's working on plans to launch a flight tourism business. That way, folks who aren't from the area can experience the wilder parts of Maine rather than settle for the usual tourist traps."

Susan's face lit up. "Authentic. I love it. I hiked Katahdin about a decade ago. That area is breathtaking."

"Finn flew me around the Katahdin summit a few weeks ago," Adele said. "In a float plane, you can land on some remote lakes and see so much wildlife. People perceive Maine to be all beaches and lobsters, but there is so much more beyond our coast."

"Take me up," Susan demanded. "I'll bring a photographer. Since I own a home here, my fans love Maine."

My stomach lurched, and I stumbled a little. Had I heard her correctly? I needed to watch my footing or I'd fall to my death down this mountain.

Susan snapped her fingers and barked, "Milo."

A skinny man in his twenties with floppy hair sprinted toward us. His sneakers were designer and clearly not made for this terrain.

"Yes, Susan?" he asked, huffing and puffing and wiping at his sweaty brow.

"Finn owns a flight tourism business."

Not quite, Susan. It was still in the planning stages, but I kept my mouth shut. I was already in over my head.

"I want him to take me up in his plane. Get my schedule."

Wood Riddance

Milo swung his backpack off one shoulder and pulled out a tablet. Deftly, he scrolled through while climbing down rocks.

"When am I free?" she asked. "Maybe fall. *Ooh*, Blythe! Get over here."

A woman in her forties wearing actual hiking boots jogged over, offering Susan a stainless-steel water bottle.

"Let's do a spread. We'll call it "Untouched Maine." She waved her hands in front of her like she could see the words written in the sky. "Wilderness, a bush plane, moose."

Blythe was nodding like a bobblehead. "Love it. So no ocean? Just rugged wilderness?"

"We could do something like "Move over Alaska, Maine is the new wild frontier.""

"Finn is a fourth-generation lumberjack and excellent at axe-throwing," Adele tossed out. "You could photograph him chopping wood." She gave me a wink.

"Brills!" Blythe exclaimed. "Instagram will lose its shit. I'm thinking fall foliage and Susan in a chunky sweater, talking about the history of the region."

"And this one"—Susan gestured to me like I was nothing more than a mannequin— "will photograph so well. Leaning against a plane with his arms crossed, maybe at sunset?"

Blythe hadn't stopped nodding, but her thumbs were flying over her phone screen as she made notes.

"And he's a war hero," Susan said.

Blythe hummed. "Even better. I'm texting the editorial team right now. We'll have an emergency meeting in an hour. Screw Morocco in fall. Those articles will be a dime a dozen. But Maine? So inspired, Susan."

I looked at Adele for confirmation that I was really hearing this. She gave me a discreet thumbs-up.

"Susan," Milo exclaimed. "I can clear three days next September."

"Ooh, that's soon," Blythe said. "But I like it. Preproduction in the spring, then get a camera crew out for stills of the area so we can capture the experience. I'll have the video crew work on content for YouTube too. You know the web team loves that."

I searched Susan's face, then Blythe's, then Milo's. These strangers were flanking us as we descended the mountain, planning out *my* future in rapid-fire fashion. My head was spinning and my heart was racing, making it impossible to keep up.

Despite the wince that struck at the words "photo shoot" and the way my stomach lurched when they mentioned me being a "war hero," I didn't stop them. Though this was worlds outside my comfort zone, it could only mean good things for me and the dream I was working to make a reality.

Beside me, Adele bumped my shoulder with hers and squeezed my hand like she could sense I was spiraling. Her touch alone brought my panic down a notch or two.

"Let's talk branding," Blythe said without looking up from her phone. These people were absolutely unconcerned that they were on a mountain, surrounded by jagged rocks. "Once I get my team on this, I'll send over contracts and other info. Give me your number."

Adele and I continued on, hand in hand, while Susan and her team buzzed around us, going on and on about their travel article. Hopefulness blossomed inside me right along with a sense of panic. Could I have a fully operational business a year from now? And could I handle the exposure that an opportunity like this would bring?

I looked over at the woman next to me, the person who told me every day that I could do this. And for the first time, I believed it.

Chapter 34
Adele

"You told Susan Stephens we were engaged," I complained. I was annoyed with him, but this surreal day had taken the wind out of my sails. He was lucky I didn't have the energy to go a few rounds.

"We will be by the time preproduction starts," he said, reclining in a chair outside the Airstream. "Plus, she offered to let us use the chapel on her compound."

"Not quite. She was half in love with you." I shook my head and pasted on a grin. "I had no idea you were catnip for billionaires. If you need to pursue that, you have my permission. She may get handsy at your photo shoot."

He glared at me, but he didn't respond to my petty comments.

In my opinion, they were justified. Susan Stephens was enamored with Finn. All the way down the mountain, she found reasons to touch him, and she asked him an endless number of questions. Not that I could blame her for shooting her shot. He was hot. And I supposed being a lady billionaire could get lonely.

Though I teased him, I didn't really mind. There was no way in hell I'd let him miss this opportunity. It was his dream to fly tourists around the wilderness of Maine, and now, thanks to a chance encounter on a hiking trail, it was happening.

So badly, I wanted to be by his side, helping him and supporting him every step of the way.

The temperature had dropped when the sun set, so we'd pulled out the s'mores supplies and started a fire in the pit near the Airstream. I was snuggled up in one of Finn's shirts, too comfortable and drowsy to muster up any real anger. Every day, a real future with him seemed more possible. And today, that possibility had jumped to probability. At least for me.

Being with him felt so natural and so right. In the past few days, we had held hands in restaurants, kissed on trails, and snuggled as we watched the sun rise.

Every aspect was organic and simple and so much easier than I had ever imagined.

But could I let it all go? The decades of dislike and competition and the loss of my father?

My brain said no. I could never give myself to Finn completely, regardless of whether I wanted to.

Not to mention the matter of my family.

My heart, on the other hand, was singing a very different tune. What was the point of all the ugliness if we couldn't move forward and embrace love and happiness?

And my vagina? That slut was not getting an invite to this debate, because we all knew where her loyalties lay.

I loved my dad, and I'd miss him every for the rest of my life. But he was an open, honest man who believed deeply in second chances. He was known around town for his generosity and kindness.

He would have loved Finn. He would have admired his

military service and his honor and his kindness. And he would have adored his sense of humor.

Most importantly, if he were here today, he would want me to be loved and cherished.

Which was exactly how Finn made me feel. What we had was very quickly beginning to resemble what my mom and dad had showed me every day of my life. That love was showing up for one another.

Beside me, Finn was reclined in his Adirondack chair. His hair was up, and his blue eyes shone in the firelight.

"Finn," I said softly. "I think I'm ready. To do this."

He grasped the armrest of my chair and slid it until it was directly next to his. "You're ready to marry me? Excellent. Maybe Susan has a justice of the peace on speed dial. We should ask her to officiate. She's got many talents."

I punched him playfully. "No. Not marriage."

"Not yet." He raised one brow and smirked.

With a roll of my eyes, I dropped my elbow to the armrest and cradled my chin in my hand. "No. But I want this. You and me. Exclusive."

Suddenly scowling, he sat up. "We've been exclusive. I'm not like the other guys you've dated, She-Ra. When I commit, I'm all in."

His words loosened the vise constricting my chest. It sounded so juvenile, but I'd learned the hard way that relationships had to be carefully defined. "Okay. How about this? If you even look at another woman, I'll cut your balls off and feed them to Clive and make you watch while you bleed out slowly in the snow."

"That's very specific." He laughed. "And dark. I gotta say, I love that you're the jealous, possessive type."

"You don't get to talk, Mr. I-had-a-nervous-breakdown-over-a-flannel-shirt-in-public."

With a low growl, he pulled me onto his lap and looped his arms around me, enveloping me with his scent. "I stand by my choices. I didn't want another man's shirt touching your precious skin." He kissed the top of my head. "You're mine. I'm glad we've established this, because I've got other plans for the night."

He bit my earlobe, and I wiggled in his lap, loving the feel of his body wrapped around mine.

"Can we take this slowly?" I asked, holding my breath. How could I even begin to explain myself to someone like him? He was open and authentic. And I had long ago closed myself behind a fortress lined with barbed wire and surrounded by a crocodile-infested moat.

"I want to work on getting there," I explained. "But telling my family will be difficult. If we're going to do this right and make it last, I need a bit more time."

He stroked my cheek. "We can face them together."

I watched the fire as we sat wrapped around one another. This perfect bubble was going to burst when we got back to Lovewell, and the thought made me sick.

"This special thing between us?" I asked. "Can we keep it this way a little longer? A week or two?"

"Of course," he murmured. "It feels impossible to keep my feelings for you a secret, but I'll do anything to make you happy."

"It's that it feels so good. And I've never had anything feel like this."

"Me neither," he admitted, running his nose along my neck and behind my ear. "It scares me too."

He was so good. So solid and so kind. How could I ever

deserve someone like him? Dammit. That thought had tears welling in my eyes. With a deep breath in, I fought them back. I didn't want to ruin this perfect night, this perfect weekend, with my tears. But they wouldn't be contained.

"Thank you." I hiccuped. "Thank you for understanding me and my anxieties. Thank you for pushing past all my walls and defense mechanisms and insecurities."

He kissed me and held my face for a moment, watching me with so much intensity and affection I swore my heart would burst from the way he made me feel. How could someone so large and intimidating be so gentle and tender?

"I'll never stop," he said. "I'll never stop fighting for you and loving you."

That was it. My heart was a goner. Was he really saying what I thought he was saying?

"Yup." He smiled, clearly reading my mind. "I love you, She-Ra. You don't have to say or do anything. But I don't play games and I don't hide my feelings. So I'm telling you now—I'm wildly, madly in love with you. I want to spend every day with you, learn every single thing about you, and spend every minute I have on this earth making you smile."

He stood, effortlessly cradling me in his arms. "Now I'm taking you to bed. Because my dream girl needs multiple orgasms and a good night's sleep."

Chapter 35
Adele

In Maine, the majority of logging took place during the winter months. The frozen ground makes cutting, hauling, and driving a lot easier. It also protects the forest undergrowth and immature trees, ensuring our ability to keep our forests healthy.

Technically, we cut all year round, but we limited those cuts to specific locations in the shoulder seasons, or specific species of trees like specialty stuff that might be in high demand.

Summers were spent repairing, surveying, and grading roads—the single most important resource we had.

And every summer, there were fights and disputes and so much bullshit I threatened to quit.

The cherry on top of the shit sundae this summer? Henri wanted me to join the upcoming meeting of the families. No, we did not belong to the mafia, but sometimes it felt like it, especially with the sheer volume of blood feuds between us.

Four families jointly owned the Golden Road, the private logging road that stretched from Lovewell all the way to

Quebec. All of our land holdings intersected the road, so the four companies came together to manage all business and any issues that pertained to the roads.

These meetings were misery. The Gagnons, the Heberts, the LeBlancs, and the Clarks tolerated each other, but things had been breaking down over the last couple of years. We'd always been in competition, but the bad blood between the Gagnons and the Heberts had now extended to everyone.

Each family's business had been impacted by Mitch Hebert, and for the last several months, the roads had been crawling with law enforcement, slowing down production and straining our tenuous allegiances further.

Nothing irked me more than bullshit politics and middle school drama. And until recently, I'd kept my distance from all of it. Henri managed these monthly meetings, with Paz's assistance. But now, my brothers were dragging me into it. And I had far more pressing issues to deal with at the moment.

Food poisoning. I'd been sick for the last few days, and I still couldn't shake the godforsaken nausea.

Last weekend, Finn and I had grilled swordfish that did not agree with me. He was a Viking, so naturally, the spoiled fish hadn't affected his iron stomach. I, on the other hand, had spent most of Sunday with my face in the toilet.

The vomiting wasn't even the worst of it. It was the nausea. The constant feeling that I was on the verge of throwing up was wearing me down. It was even more distressing than actually puking up my guts.

Finn had been lovely and sweet, holding my hair, bringing me ginger ale and crackers, and snuggling with me in front of the TV.

But my food poisoning had ruined our plan to introduce him to my family at Sunday dinner. Instead, I canceled and spent the evening on the couch. And since then, my mom had been texting me nonstop like I had contracted the bubonic plague and she was concerned that I was on the precipice of death.

Our carefully orchestrated debut as a couple had been put on hold because of some less than fresh seafood. Finn took it in stride—of course he did—but waiting only made me more nervous. Logically, I knew we could do this. We could show up, face my mom and my siblings like the adults we were, and explain that we were together.

At my mom's house, we'd have everyone there at once, and we could manage reactions. Plus, having Alice, Hazel, and Parker in attendance meant each of my brothers had a designated person to talk them down. Ultimately, my mom would love Finn. How could she not? He was a bottomless pit who would praise her cooking and clean all the dishes after.

We just had to manage the initial shock and keep the angry mob from picking up their torches and pitchforks.

Though originally I was the one who'd balked at the idea of going public, I was anxious to jump in and rip off the Band-Aid now. The initial rush of sneaking around had worn off. I was tired. So, so tired. And I hated lying to my family. We had our differences, but my brothers were important to me. Ultimately, they loved me, and once they got to know Finn and realized that he was nothing like his father, they would see how happy he made me.

Despite the vomit and the exhaustion, I *was* so much happier than I'd ever been. For years, I had yearned to find my person. A man who would embrace my Adele-ness rather than love me in spite of it. A man who pushed me to be better and who believed in me.

Sure, the family circumstances were not ideal, but after our weekend in Acadia together, it was clear that we were inevitable. This was real. Now I only needed to convince my family.

But first I had to deal with these roads.

"Adele." A gruff voice interrupted my thoughts.

Richard stood in the doorway to my office. The act of looking up from my computer screen to the man across from me was enough to send another wave of nausea through me. Swallowing back the bile threatening to escape, I checked to make sure my trash can was nearby.

Without waiting for me to invite him in, Richard strode to my desk and gave me a tight nod. Henri had recently promoted Richard. For years, he'd overseen cutting operations at our camp and managed all the inventory. But given how much we'd expanded, Henri put him in charge of managing our roads and any related issues.

Which meant that now I had to deal with Richard. He wasn't a bad person, but he wasn't a Gagnon, and that meant I couldn't yell at him like I could at my brothers.

Nope, I had to be calm and professional and explain to him why he was dead fucking wrong.

Richard was one of those older men who believed he knew everything and was adamant that the way things were done decades ago was the only way. Add a dose of good old-fashioned sexism to the mix, and it was no surprise that I did not enjoy our chats.

Richard had been my dad's right-hand man and best friend for decades. He was tall and thin, with short silver hair, and he wore round glasses and an overall air of annoyance. He was old-school in every way and had never quite come to terms with the idea that a grown-ass woman could obtain a graduate degree in engineering, let along become one of his bosses.

Wood Riddance

Nope, he preferred to speak to me like I was a little girl who couldn't possibly understand the intricacies of a grader.

Taking a deep breath, I summoned all my patience. Henri trusted him, and although I didn't exactly like the guy, he was good at his job and he was an asset to our business. So I let him make his argument as to why we needed to wait to develop Site 211 until next year and instead send our equipment up to the north side of the Golden Road, where there was even less infrastruture and a historic fire had taken out most of the trees a few decades ago.

There was no way I could spare the machinery for that, especially given the work needed at Site 211, but I listened without interrupting.

"Richard," I said when he'd finished, being sure to engage the most respectful tone I was capable of. "I'll make a note of this. Perhaps we can do some of this work during shoulder season next year. But right now, the priority is getting Site 211 fully accessible before cutting season this winter."

He stared, unblinking, while I spoke, twirling his keys around his index finger, over and over again. With each rotation, his keys would clank gently. Around and around. It was annoying and making my nausea worse.

But I persisted. I explained the limitation of the current machines and the timeline I'd put in place for road and truck repairs before the season.

And he sat there, twirling the goddamn keys like he had better things to do than speak to me. I didn't have the two spare graders lying around that his plan required, but I would have loved to throw him in front of one at that moment.

His mouth was a flat line, and he focused on something over my shoulder, as if my explanation was boring him. "I'll have to talk to Henri about this."

My eye twitched, and the tight control I had on my annoyance slipped a fraction. "Are you threatening to go above my head to my brother? Don't bother. I can tell you exactly what his response will be. My shop, my rules. My machines, my rules. And if you don't watch your tone, you'll never touch one of my trucks again."

He said nothing, only narrowed his eyes and clenched his jaw. Then he hauled himself out of the chair and stalked out of my office.

I sat back and heaved a sigh of relief once he was out of my sight. Then I reached for the trash can, just in case. What the hell was going on with me?

Pushing my chair back a couple of inches, I pulled open my desk drawers, one at a time, searching for more mints to hide my vomit breath. When I pulled open the bottom drawer to my left, the box of tampons caught my eye. The sight of them brought the nausea rushing right back, and I dove for the trash can.

No. Not possible.

Deep breaths. Deep breaths.

I adjusted my baseball cap so it sat lower on my head. I had driven all the way to Heartsborough, but now I wished I'd kept going. This town wasn't all that far from Lovewell, and it was almost as tiny. There was a chance I would be recognized here. Especially because of my height and the coveralls I should have changed out of. But I hadn't been in my right mind when I rushed out of the shop.

But I *had* done the math.

And puked some more. I was a week late. For me, that was

enough to throw up red flags. Add in the nausea and the vomiting and the constant exhaustion, and there was no denying that something was up.

So here I was, in the drugstore, buying one of every brand of pregnancy test.

My heart pounded and bile rose in my esophagus as I shuffled to the counter.

The sweet older woman behind the old-fashioned register wore glasses on a beaded chain and had a very aggressive perm. She gave me a kind smile and rang up my purchases, which also included antacids, grape soda, and hair elastics.

I tried to school my features. I went for calm and collected rather than completely unhinged, but I'd never had much of a poker face. The poor woman probably thought I was a serial killer.

"Good luck, dear," she said gently as I stepped away from the register.

I rushed outside, desperate to be alone again, and promptly retched all over the sidewalk.

He-Man snuggled against my arm on the center console the entire ride home, as if sensing how miserable I was. My mind was blank. I was so dumbstruck that it took all my mental strength to focus on driving.

At home, I considered not even bothering. Did I really want to know? Surely there was another explanation for these symptoms. Eventually, though, I pinched the bridge of my nose and tore open the first test. *Okay. Pee on stick, wait three minutes. Easy enough.*

My stomach churned as I paced the bathroom. I was on birth control. That shit was supposed to work, damn it.

And I wasn't sure how to even feel. I was thirty-three, owned a home, had a stable, healthy income and close family nearby. Pregnancy was not a tragedy. In fact, I'd always wanted a family. The timing wasn't great, but I'd always seen children in my future.

If only it were so easy. Because this thing with Finn had evolved from enemies with benefits to a complex and intense and incredible relationship. But we hadn't even gone public yet. And although what we had was feeling more and more like forever, there was no guarantee.

A baby, however, was forever. A link between us, between our families.

The alarm on my phone beeped, startling me so badly I jumped. Taking a deep breath and willing my heart to settle, I shuffled back to the counter.

Two lines. Positive.

And tears. Lots of them.

Wild sobs burst from my lungs and endless tears streamed down my face. My body shuddered so severely with each round that I dropped to the tile floor and hugged my knees to my chest.

I cried for me. Because I'd fallen for someone I might not get to keep. For Finn, because he loved being a father more than anything. And I cried for this baby, who I already loved deeply, if that was possible, because he or she would be born into this shit show.

I didn't want to have to choose between Finn and my family. Because I'd choose him and our baby every single time. And the thought of losing my brothers and my mom, after everything we'd been through over the last few years, was crippling.

And so I cried. He-Man curled up in my lap, quietly comforting me as my tears fell, dampening his fur.

This was a clusterfuck of my own creation. Maybe if I'd

been honest earlier, if I'd been brave enough to confront the truth—that I was falling in love with him—and had told my family, I wouldn't have to lose any of them.

But everything was different now. And I had to get it together for the sake of this baby. I wasn't perfect. Finn wasn't perfect. But this was happening. And I would do it right.

But I couldn't do it alone.

Chapter 36
Finn

"**T**his is the best news," I shouted, picking her up and spinning her around.

A baby? Unbelievable. When she had called me crying, my stomach had sunk and all my anxieties had rushed back. Then I'd dropped everything and rushed over, desperately worried about her.

I'd spent the past couple of weeks on pins and needles. She was working up the courage to tell her family, and I was waiting for the day I could love her publicly. The day I could tell this town and all the nasty gossips to fuck all the way off.

But now, my face hurt from smiling too widely. And I was pretty sure I'd have to get used to it. I hadn't been this happy in years, so this expression was unlikely to fade.

She punched my shoulder. "Are you out of your mind? This is a disaster!"

I pulled her close and kissed the top of her head. "Of course it's not. Babies are fucking awesome. And we made one together."

"I was on birth control," she yelled, planting her hands on my chest and pushing me away.

I flexed a bicep. "Oh, She-Ra, your birth control pills are no match for my super Viking sperm. I think we both could have predicted that."

"Maybe you should have told me you had superhuman sperm, asshole. 'By the way, Adele, we should wrap it up because my semen is impervious to pharmaceutical intervention.' The heads-up would have been nice."

I shrugged. "Sorry. I guess I was too busy making you come a million times to give you fair warning." I waggled my eyebrows. "Speaking of which. You wanna sit on my face? My baby mama seems tense. I can help with that."

"Jesus Christ, Finn. This is serious."

"Adele." I put my hands on her shoulders and dipped my head so she was forced to look at me. She was distraught, and I wanted to soothe away all her worry and assure her that everything would be okay. That this was a good thing for us. "Of course you're scared. That's natural. I'm scared too."

She bit her lip and searched my face as tears streamed down her cheeks.

Damn it. Maybe she didn't want this. Shit. I was being totally insensitive.

"Let me be clear," I added. "It's your body. I support whatever choice you want to make. But I'm here with you. We're in this together."

She buried her head in my chest and shuddered out a breath. "Thank you," she said after a few moments. She squeezed me tight around the waist and sucked in a few deep breaths, but then her body shook against mine. "I want this baby."

I released the breath I didn't know I'd been holding. I

meant what I said. I would support her choice, but in the five minutes since I learned of this child's existence, I'd already fallen desperately in love with it. And Merry. This would be amazing for her. She'd been asking for a sibling since she was old enough to talk.

I hugged Adele tighter. I already knew I was madly in love with her, but now? Now my heart was truly full. Details didn't matter. Our last names didn't matter. My father and all that shit in the past were of no consequence. This little person was our future.

So I was shocked when she pulled back, blinked up at me with red-rimmed eyes, and walked away. I followed her into the living room, where she scooped He-Man up off the couch and held him close.

"Talk to me."

There was nothing we couldn't figure out together. She was in shock, of course, but at some point, she had to let me in, let me help.

I crossed my arms. "I'll wait all day, all week, all month for you to talk to me. Eventually, you have to learn to lean on me. I know you've been let down before. But I promise, I'm here and there is nothing I won't do for you."

She paced the length of the room, burying her face in He-Man's fur, then abruptly stopped. "What are we bringing this child into, Finn? Feuds? Murder? A family that will hate it?" She choked back another sob.

I closed my eyes, praying for the strength to do this right. To say the right things. "Your brothers might be stubborn, but they could never hate an innocent child. It's time to be honest. No more sneaking around. No more secrets. We'll sit them down and tell them. We're together. We're having a baby and we're gonna get married and they'll have to deal with it."

"Who said anything about getting married?" she shouted. She set He-Man on the floor, crossed her arms over her chest, and hit me with a glare.

"I did! We're getting married, Adele. Deal with it."

"No! You can't decree it. I'm not your property."

I pinched the bridge of my nose. Dammit, I was definitely screwing this up. "Don't worry. I'll ask properly and everything."

"That's not what this is about. Don't make decisions for me. I need time to come to terms and figure out how to broach this. We can't walk into the diner, make out in front of half the town, then announce we're having a baby."

"Why not?" I fisted my hands on my hips and took a step closer to her. "Seems like the most efficient way. It'll ensure that everyone in the county is notified within minutes. Then we could get back to living our lives."

"You are impossible." She stomped a foot on the hardwood floor and tilted her head back to glare up at me. "I need to process. Make a plan. You make this all seem so simple, but it's not. What if things get ugly? You've had such a hard time in this town already."

"It's only as complicated as we make it." I flattened my palm on her stomach. "There is nothing in this world that will keep me away from you and this baby. I'm not perfect, but I'll always show up. Let them be nasty. I don't care."

Of all the shitty, disappointing things in my life, being a dad had never come remotely close to fitting in that category. Late nights, diaper blowouts, and ear infections were all part of the best job in the world.

And making a baby with this woman? This person who had turned my life upside down and made me believe that good things were possible?

Wood Riddance

My brain was spinning. I was going to be a father again. Of all the titles I had held in my life, military or civilian, Dad was the most important. It was a privilege to be Merry's dad. Already, that privilege extended to this little baby. A child I pictured having my smile and Adele's intensity. The instant she broke the news, my heart had swelled, creating space right alongside my daughter. I was already in love, and I'd known about this child's existence for minutes.

Along with that aching devotion came a desperate urge to get my business up and running. Provide for my family. Make Adele and this little munchkin proud. That sensation bordered on anxiety-inducing rather than thrilling, though.

But I had Susan Stephens's number stored in my phone, and I was going to make good use of it.

Adele dipped her head and sniffled, showing me a glimpse of the true vulnerability she so often tried to hide. "I don't want to lose them," she said into my T-shirt. "My brothers aren't perfect, but they're all I have."

"I won't force you to choose." It would kill me, but I'd let her go if that's what she needed.

"It's not even a choice. I love you, Finn. You and this baby come first."

"So you're choosing me?" I said, my heart hammering in my chest and my insecurities raring to life.

"Of course I'm choosing you. We're doing this, and you're going to be an amazing dad. You already are an amazing dad." She pulled back a little and gave me a watery smile. "I love you and I love this baby. If we have to move to an island, just us and this baby and Merry, I'm fine with that. But the thought of not sharing this joy with my family hurts so much."

She was choosing me. I let that sink in. This wasn't a choice for her. There had been no grueling consideration or weighing the benefits versus the drawbacks. She didn't want to lose them. After weeks of worrying that we'd never get past this hurdle, she was flat out saying it. No matter how her family reacted. I tipped her chin up and kissed her deeply, savoring the feel of her body sinking into me.

"She-Ra, let me make this clear," I said against her lips. "I will do anything for you. Your family can hate me forever, but I'll show up to every holiday with a smile on my face. If your brothers want to punch me, then I'll stand tall and let them. They can throw rotten eggs at me for all I care. Making you happy is all I care about. Eventually, I'll wear them all down, though, and we'll be one big, happy family."

She sobbed out a laugh. "You are absurd."

"Absurdly in love with you. My family is so splintered. I would never wish that on you. We'll make this work."

She hugged me tighter, and we stood in the middle of her living room, clinging to one another, saying nothing, letting our hearts beat together.

"But the timing," she said into my chest, squeezing me tight around the waist.

"This isn't your shop, She-Ra." I tucked my chin and took her in. "We can't set the schedule and label every tool. We're not in control. And that's okay."

In response, she glared up at me, lips pursed.

Yeah, we were going to be happy together. We were going to make this work.

This woman had taken me by surprise and knocked me on my ass in the best possible way. She was strong and determined and she'd never take it easy on me. But she had the biggest heart. Damn, she was going to be an amazing mom.

"But seriously," I teased. "Let me lick your pussy. I'll make all the stress go away." I tucked a strand of hair behind her ear.

"This is my job now," I said, dropping to my knees in front of her and pulling her shorts down. "Keeping you happy. Now let me get started already."

"Finn. You're ridiculous," she complained, but she was smiling down at me. "There's so much to think about."

Goddamn, she was gorgeous. "You're overcomplicating things. It's simple. We get married, have a bunch of babies, and live happily ever after."

Chapter 37
Adele

Happily ever after. What a concept. Childish? Sure. Naïve? Definitely. But it didn't change how much I wanted it and how, for the first time in my life, it was a real possibility.

Sure, my happily ever after didn't resemble the picture I'd envisioned when I was a kid. And, as I'd been doing since birth, I'd gone off script. I'd never been one to follow my family's playbook anyway.

Finn rolled over and pulled me close, nuzzling my hair and spreading his hand protectively across my stomach. Soaking in the warmth of his touch, I closed my eyes. This was real. It was happening.

I couldn't ignore it, especially when he was kissing my still flat belly and talking to the baby. "We love you so much," he murmured into my skin. "You and your big sister Merry are the best things to ever happen to me. I can't wait to meet you." He said some variation of the same thing every morning, despite my explaining that the baby's hearing hadn't even developed yet.

He was undeterred and so adorable. "And," he continued, "I can't wait to fly with you. Show you the sky."

This should feel uncomfortable. Too much intimacy. Too much commitment. But it felt right. I was going to be a mom, and I was in love with Finn. Easy. Simple.

But the fear and the panic still woke me every night. The bone-chilling concern that this little family we were building could be in danger was robbing me of all the joy I should feel.

Over and over, my brothers had assured me that the danger had passed. That the men responsible for all the pain our family had been through were locked up. That things would be fine. But it didn't feel that way.

I had to deal with this shit once and for all. I was a mom now. According to the app I had downloaded on my phone, the baby was the size of a blueberry, but everything had already changed for me. I wouldn't give up until I could ensure my family's safety.

Could I really shift and change on a cellular level? That remained to be seen. But I wouldn't bring a child into a world of danger and uncertainty if I could help it. Nope. I was going to finish this.

It was only seven, but I needed backup and a sounding board.

"Pregnant?"

Parker reached out and steadied herself on the doorframe.

"No one can know yet," I said, holding out a hand and gesturing for her to sit.

"How did this happen?" she asked, dropping to a chair at my kitchen table. Her eyes were wide and her mouth was ajar.

I shot her a glare.

"Okay. That was a silly question." She licked her lips. "Is it Finn's?"

"Yes," I hissed. "And keep your voice down. He's asleep upstairs."

She wrung her hands in her lap and assessed me. "You're together? For how long?" There was an edge to her questions that I did not appreciate.

Now I was annoyed. "Yes. We're together and in love." Fisting my hands at my sides, I tried to rein in my annoyance, though I was mostly unsuccessful. "Can you please watch your tone when you speak about the father of my child?"

"It's just—"

"Just nothing. I'm asking you, as my best friend, to support me right now."

She stood and padded over to me, her arms open wide. "I'm sorry. I do support you. It's only that I love you so much and I worry about you." And then she was crying on my shoulder. Parker was not a crier.

"Fucking pregnancy hormones," she cursed. "I'm a mess."

Then I was hugging her in return, and my own tears were falling.

Parker released me and stepped back. "Jesus, we're a disgrace."

"I know," I said, laughing and wiping a tear from my cheek.

"But Adele, we get to do this *together*. Our kids will be cousins and best friends." She grinned up at me. "I assume I'm here to strategize about the family?"

"No." I shook my head. "I need your help with something else."

I poured two mugs of tea and brought them to the table.

She studied me while I got situated in the chair beside her, taking my time to compose myself. I'd spent all night thinking and analyzing. I couldn't live my life looking over my shoulder.

Daphne Elliot

If I was finally getting my happily ever after, there'd be no lingering doubt, no remaining peril.

"Tell me everything you know about Henri's accident."

She blinked at me and sat back. "We can't go through this again, Adele. Especially now. We have more pressing things going on. Like, for example, informing your family that you're gestating Satan's baby. When do you plan to tell them?"

"When I feel like it," I snapped back. "And your comments aren't helping. I'm already dreading the shitty reactions I'm guaranteed to get from my brothers. I don't need yours too."

She held her hands up in surrender. "You're right. How did he take the news?"

"God, he's perfect," I said, swallowing back a fresh round of tears. "Supportive and loving and thrilled about the baby." My eyes blurred with tears despite my best efforts. So much for maintaining my composure. "He's perfect. Susan Stephens even thinks so."

"*What?* Susan Stephens? The chef lady on TV?"

I waved a hand. I'd forgotten that I hadn't told Parker about any of that. "It's just..." I sniffled. "I don't know if I'm ready for all of this. To be with him publicly. To make that commitment and to start a family. This baby will be a permanent bond between us, and I'm terrified."

"You don't want him forever?" she asked gently, stroking my hair.

"I think I might." My sniffles turned into full-blown sobs, and I buried my face in my hands. I wasn't scared about impending motherhood. I would learn as much as I could and give this child all the love it would ever need. That was guaranteed. But spending my life with Finn? Being bonded to him by this child, even if things didn't work out? That fear had settled in my bones. The sadness, the heartbreak that would come if we couldn't make this work. The fear that my family would never accept him.

For Finn, this baby was a fresh start, physical evidence of our love. But my happiness was tinged with guilt. Because I'd be grappling with what Mitch Hebert had done for the rest of my life. Could I move on someday? Could I give Finn everything he'd need from me? Could we build our own little family together?

I desperately wanted all of those things. But first, I had to get unstuck. I had to break through the fear and the paranoia that had been holding me back for almost three years.

"I need to know there is no more danger. I need to know what really happened." I tucked my chin to my chest and studied the tabletop. "And I need to forgive myself and finally stop carrying around all this guilt. We've got two Gagnon babies growing inside us right now. We can't pass all the fear and trauma on to the next generation."

Parker sat beside me with her mug to her lips, first surveying the dining space, then me, as if considering my words. Her eyes were steely, like she felt the same way. She and Paz had been kidnapped and held at gunpoint last year. If anyone was concerned that danger still lurked nearby, it was her.

After a long moment, she nodded.

"So we're doing this?" I asked. "Figuring this out and ending it all?"

"Yes. But we tell no one." She scooted forward in her chair. "Paz would shit a brick. And I want to state for the record that law enforcement is investigating this, as well as the other crimes. We have no reason to believe you or any member of your family is in danger. The Canadian drug traffickers are lying low, and there has been no recent movement."

Parker trusted the feds even less than I did, and while I appreciated her concern for me, I needed answers.

"What aren't we telling anyone about?"

I jumped in my seat and whipped around at the interruption. Finn was standing in the doorway wearing nothing but a pair of mesh shorts. His face was creased with sleep lines and his hair was down. I smiled at the sight of him. I couldn't help it. He was so damn handsome, and I loved having him here in my house. It had been a place of solitude for a long time, but he brought life to it.

Parker's eyes bulged out of her head. "We were talking about how you knocked up my best friend." Her tone was icy.

His returning smile was filled with nothing but warmth. "I know. Isn't it amazing?" He nodded. "Congrats to you too, by the way. The town is buzzing about your happy news."

Parker put her hand on her flat stomach and glared at him. "If you hurt her..."

Finn waved his hands and shuffled toward the coffee maker. "Yeah, yeah, you'll kill me, blah, blah, blah. That lecture is wasted on me." He snagged a mug from the cupboard and filled it. "I'm head over heels in love with this one and our baby. She's not getting rid of me anytime soon."

He carried his mug over to the table and dropped a kiss to the top of my head.

"And since we're plotting together, how about I make you pregnant ladies some breakfast?"

Without waiting for a response, he wandered to the fridge. He whistled while he pulled out eggs and bread and got to work.

Parker leaned forward, looking only mildly annoyed. "It's very hard to hate him when he's feeding us and looks like that."

I nodded. "Yup. I tried to hate him. I tried so hard. But he's awesome."

"I can see that." Parker nodded. "I've got your back when it's time to tell your family. Paz will lose a testicle if he does anything but fully support you. And I'll take care of the others too if their wives don't get to them first." She patted my hand. "These babies are going to be born into so much love."

We sipped our tea and watched as my man worked his magic in the kitchen. When he was finished, Finn presented our plates with a flourish. Scrambled eggs with spinach and wheat toast.

"Thank you," Parker said, mouth already full of eggs. "But I'm probably going to need a blueberry pie after this."

"Then I'll go pick one up," he said, pulling up a chair and handing me a bottle of hot sauce. I'd broken the news about my pregnancy twelve hours ago, and he was already catering to my pregnancy cravings. I doused my breakfast and brought Finn up to speed. He knew a lot of the details, but Parker and I filled in the gaps.

"So the damage to the slack adjusters is not the same?"

"Correct, but it's similar. The person who did it must have known how my dad's truck had been sabotaged and did something similar to Henri's truck." I was zooming in on photos I'd taken with my phone to point out the subtle differences. "It worked. The brakes didn't adjust as they should have and he lost control. But he jumped out in time. He ended up with serious injuries, but if he hadn't rolled out the driver's side door when he did, we would have lost him too."

Parker had raided my junk drawer for a pen and a notepad, and she was sketching out the basics of what we knew. Finn had already gone through a pot of coffee as we walked him through the evidence.

"And we're sure my dad had nothing to do with this?" he asked.

"We don't know," Parker said gently.

Over the last hour, she'd begun to warm up to him. It helped that he'd made French toast—which she slathered in butter and maple syrup—after the scrambled eggs hadn't done the trick.

"We know that Norman, a.k.a. Stinger, was working for your dad," she said. "He gave up all kinds of information. But on the day of Henri's accident, he was in Florida. The FBI has records to prove it. So the question becomes, who else was there, and who else knew about the slack adjuster damage to my dad's truck?"

"Henri had been digging through my dad's old files," I explained further. "Before he died, my dad had been acting strange. Taking home a lot of old paperwork and maps. Some of the documents were written in French. My mom said he was distracted and upset. We know now he'd discovered some of the details of the drug trafficking operation."

"Which made him a target," Finn said, burying his face in his hands.

"And we know Frank was fighting with Richard before he died," Parker said.

"What?"

My stomach lurched. No way. Richard and my dad had always been tight. He was Paz's godfather, for Christ's sake. Personally, I didn't care for the man. He was a sexist pain in the ass, but I'd never questioned his loyalty to my dad or the company. Henri trusted him. My mom trusted him. It wasn't possible.

"Sorry," Parker said, twisting her napkin in her hands. "It was something I discovered while I was investigating. Weeks before your dad died, he and Richard had a semi-public argument at the Moose."

"The Moose? Richard doesn't drink. He doesn't go out in town. He probably hasn't stepped foot in there in twenty years."

"Jim saw the whole thing. There were other witnesses too. They corroborated Jim's story. The FBI is aware, but we don't know if it's connected. Either way, it struck me as odd."

"My dad told me that there are other people in Lovewell who were involved. People we wouldn't expect," Finn added.

"Your dad?" I said, swallowing back the bile rising up in my throat.

Finn dropped his focus to the table in front of him and shifted in his chair. "My brothers and I went to visit him a few weeks ago."

It felt like all the air had been sucked out of the room. For weeks, Finn and I had been existing in this happy love bubble where we didn't discuss his dad or what he had done. Mitch Hebert was a criminal and a killer, and I wanted him as far away from me and my child as possible.

But Finn had seen him recently? And he'd kept that information from me?

"What the fuck?" I barked, tremors racking my body. "You didn't think to tell me that?"

Frowning, he shrugged. "I didn't go because I *wanted* to. Trust me. But we needed some answers regarding the business. Owen is trying to sell, but we're missing all kinds of information."

I shook my head, hoping that this was some kind of hallucination or strange pregnancy dream. "I can't believe you didn't tell me. What did he say exactly?"

Finn stood and paced to the doorway and back. "Jude was

asking him to cooperate with the feds, maybe get a deal. He said he wouldn't because there were others involved, and that if he did, we would be in danger."

My stomach dropped, and all the air left my lungs in a whoosh.

"He told me there were people in Lovewell who were involved. People we knew. And that I had to keep an eye out and protect the family."

"That motherfucker," Parker hissed.

"We're having a child!" I shouted, slamming my fist on the table. "And this child is in danger because your father's criminal accomplices are still running around out there?" I threw a hand out. "What the hell, Finn? How could you keep this from me?"

Silently, he looked from me to Parker and back again.

Parker had gone completely still, and I couldn't tell whether she was going to throw up or stab him in the eye with a fork.

"I'm terrified too, okay? Is that what you want to hear?" he asked, his voice pleading. "When he told me, I didn't want to believe him. In my mind, my dad is the big bad. He's evil and manipulative and he's always been a liar. So I didn't give his warnings a lot of thought.

"But you're right." He ran a hand down his face. "I should have told you. It was wrong of me not to. I won't keep information from you again. We're a team." He dropped into his chair and brought my hand to his lips.

"This is already hard enough," I said softly. "We can't keep secrets from each other."

He hung his head. "I'm so sorry, She-Ra. But I'll fix this."

"*We* will fix it," Parker said. "Adele, get your computer. Finn, get snacks."

"No," Finn said, sitting up straight. "Let's go to the police. Or the FBI, or whoever. If my dad was telling the truth, then poking around could make things worse. I will not let either of you put yourselves in danger. Let's work with the police, share what we know."

I slapped both palms on the table and glared at him. "I've been working with the police for years, Finn. Newsflash, they haven't done shit. The only reason your dad is behind bars is because of Parker. I met with the local police and the state police. I showed them the fucking brakes. Demanded to speak to supervisors and superior officers. Every one of them insisted it was an accident. Some even questioned my sanity."

"I'm so sorry that they wouldn't listen, She-Ra. But now they've got my dad and twelve other people in custody. Surely one will start talking. Then they'll move up the chain. Parker, help me out here." He turned to my friend, his eyes pleading. "They always want to get the big fish, right?"

Parker sighed. "Yes and no. I can reach out to my FBI contacts and dig for more information. As far as I know, not much has been done about Henri. The accident wasn't fatal, so that lowers its priority. And right now, they're overwhelmed with the complexity of the trafficking investigation."

I huffed. "That's not giving me confidence."

She shrugged. "Same. But it's the best we can do right now. While your trust in the law to get it right is sweet, Finn, it's a bit naïve. I'm not saying we go full vigilante here." She pinned me with a glare. "But I think taking a fresh look and gathering as much information as we can is a good idea."

"So what do we do?"

"This stays between us," she insisted. "I'll reach out and see what I can gather off the record. I'll go through the files again.

I've still got everything on my computer. I'll go through the personnel records from the day of Henri's accident again."

"You." She pointed at Finn. "See what you can find on your end. Other associates or friends of your dad. People connected to the business. Anyone who used to work for Hebert Timber who seems even remotely shady."

"What about me?" I asked, desperate to do something. Sitting around, growing a baby and spiraling about every possible danger did not feel like a good use of my time.

"Go back to the brakes. Study them. Study the trucks. We've got to be missing something."

After an hour of strategizing and a round of snacks, I walked Parker to the door.

She pulled me in for a tight hug and rubbed circles on my back. "I love you," she said. "And so does Finn. I was wrong to judge him. He's a good man, and he's clearly head over heels in love with you. We're going to get through all this shit and come out on the other side."

With a smile, I contemplated my amazing friend and soon to be sister. "You think so?"

She patted my cheek. "I know it. We're mamas on a mission, and no one is going to get in our way. You deserve all the good things, babe. Breaking this news will be tricky, but when you're ready to do it, I'll be by your side, ready to punch anyone who even looks at you wrong."

She gave me one last hug and headed for her car.

"Now go snuggle up with your Viking. You deserve it."

Chapter 38
Finn

It was actually happening. Meredith Aviation. Owen had helped me file the paperwork yesterday. I officially owned my own business.

On Wednesday, I'd meet with the bank to discuss my loan application.

With a small investment from Owen, my savings, and a rock-solid business plan with a contract from Susan Stephens Multimedia for a feature next fall, I was well on my way to making my dream a reality.

As soon as Adele broke the news about her pregnancy, I called Owen and filled him in on all the details. He hooked me up with a lawyer, and together, the three of us got to work on my business plan. This was happening.

Despite the recent friction between Owen and me, he was and always had been dependable. If anyone recognized my need to build something of my own, it was him. He was even coming with me to Bangor this week to meet with the bank and had offered to handle all the accounting for me.

I was searching real estate listings for a piece of property where I could build a hangar and small runway and set up my base of operations. I'd also been in contact with a few ski resorts in the area about potential helicopter contracts. Our projections showed that I was a few years away from being able to purchase a helo, but I'd get there.

I'd been out of the Navy for more than two years, and every day, I'd struggled with feeling adrift. Going through the motions while doing everything I could to be the best father I could be to Merry while simultaneously living in a town that hated my entire family.

But my life and outlook were changing. Adele had changed me. Her belief in me had helped me bust through so many silly barriers I'd created in my mind. It wasn't only the big stuff, either. She listened to my ideas and asked thoughtful questions. Her unwavering faith in my abilities as a pilot and to build my own business fueled me to keep going. With Adele, I was finally ready to turn my dreams into reality.

I was better for it. For her. More patient, more hopeful, and more grateful. And now we were having a baby. Keeping this secret from Merry was damn near killing me, but I was committed to taking every step alongside Adele. Our first step, though, had to be tackling her family. When I finally broke the news to my little girl, she would be so thrilled.

Adele might not have been ready to accept the eventuality yet, but she was going to be my wife. Like I'd done at every turn, I had to give her time and space to get used to the idea, but I'd be locking it down in the not-so-distant future. Together, we'd build a beautiful life that was completely our own. It wouldn't be easy or simple—the best things never were—but it would be amazing.

Every day, I itched to see her, desperate to fill her in on new details and strategize side by side. The whiteboard she'd surprised me with a few weeks ago was already hanging in my living room, covered with scribbled notes and ideas. That woman sure loved a whiteboard. Recently, she'd been going on about some Japanese organization technique using Post-its, which made my brain hurt. But once I had a real office, I'd give it a try. My girl ran a tight ship; I could learn a lot from her.

My fingers itched to text her, to tell her about my calls this morning. But I couldn't intrude. Today was the big adoption day. Her family had been looking forward to this for years, and although I longed to be with her, this was not the time to fill her brothers in on our relationship. This day was about Tucker and Marigold and Alice and Henri, and I refused to dampen their joy or steal an ounce of the attention they deserved.

So I did what I always did when nervous energy was threatening to bubble over. I grabbed my sneakers and went for a run.

Early October was breathtaking up here. The leaves had already turned, creating an epic autumn wonderland. I headed up the hill and began the full loop around town, crossing the river and waving to the group of old men who were fishing from the bank.

I was bursting with excitement and ideas. My brain was running at a pace my feet could only dream of. As I made my way back through town, I headed down Birch Street toward my childhood home. I figured I could refill my water bottle and see if Mom was home.

I didn't visit my mom nearly enough. Merry spent a lot of time with her, but since moving home, I'd struggled with how to kick-start our relationship. We'd never had a falling out, and there was no bad blood, but for years I hadn't put in much effort. Now, each time I thought of her, shame washed over me. I should do better. No. I would do better.

Daphne Elliot

"Finn!" she squealed when she saw me on the porch. "Get over here and hug your mother."

"Mom," I huffed, pulling in deep breaths, "I'm all sweaty."

She waved me off. She was dressed in leopard-print scrubs and her nursing clogs. "I don't have to leave for a bit. Get in here." Debbie Hebert was a tall woman with shoulder-length gray hair and a peaceful, calm demeanor. She loved astrology and crochet, and she had created an environment that allowed us to live somewhat free-range while still sheltered within her loving support. My days spent in her home were the kind most kids dreamed of.

Unlike my father, she never yelled and she rarely lectured. Instead, she let us make our mistakes, knowing we'd grow from each one. Yet she was always there to help us pick up the pieces in the aftermath.

No sooner had I sat down at the kitchen table than she was trying to cook for me. The tiny kitchen where I had inhaled so many meals as a kid and teen looked different.

"Did you get new countertops?"

She smiled widely. "Oh yes. Quartz. Backsplash too." My mother's house was within walking distance of the small downtown area. She'd bought it after she and Dad divorced, and she'd spent the last thirty years fixing the place up to her exact specifications.

"That awful laminate needed to go."

"Looks gorgeous, Mom." It truly did. The home was a small cape, with three bedrooms and a large white porch, complete with rocking chairs. The large yard had been home to hundreds of football games and dozens of Easter egg hunts over the years. The place wasn't grand by any means, but it had always felt like home.

She beamed at me. "I enjoy it—choosing things, doing the

renovations. Now that you're all grown and out of my hair, I can finally have nice things. There were some years, God... I should have bought a barn and given the five of you each a hay bale to sleep on."

She wasn't far off. With five massive boys in the house, six when Cole was around, we put a lot of wear and tear on the place. We'd all learned to patch drywall and replaced cracked tiles. They were necessary skills after arguments between brothers or roughhousing that got out of hand. And I'd need at least an extra set of hands to count all the broken windows we'd had to replace over the years.

"To what do I owe the pleasure, hmm?" she asked, raising one brow.

I gave her a soft smile, still feeling nostalgic as I scanned the room. "I missed you."

"Oh Jesus, are you okay? Is Merry okay?" Her brow was furrowed, and her mouth was turned down in a concerned frown. "Something is off, isn't it?" She put her hands on her hips and stepped closer. "Out with it."

"It's not like that, Mom. Everything is amazing, actually."

She scrutinized me, no doubt searching for the lie, and waited me out. Unlike me, my mom had no trouble being still. It had always unnerved me, and it got me talking every time. It was one of her mom ninja tricks. She'd sit still and stare at us until we spilled.

"I'm finally starting my business. Filed the papers and got insurance. Owen and I are going to the bank on Wednesday."

"Owen is coming to town?" she asked, her eyes lighting up.

"No. Sorry."

Her face instantly fell. Shit. I hated seeing her upset. Owen never visited. He was always thrilled to host us in Boston, but he hadn't been back for a few years.

"He's meeting me in Bangor."

She remained silent, though her demeanor was noticeably more subdued. So I dove into my plans and gave her a play-by-play of my chance meeting with Susan Stephens.

"I'm thrilled, sweetie." She dropped into the chair across from me. "But what aren't you telling me?" She sat back and crossed her arms, waiting.

See? Ninja skills. And she'd always had the ability to see the things I kept close to the vest. I couldn't stop myself then. It all started to spill out of me.

"I'm in love," I said softly. "She's the one."

Mom clasped her hands in front of her chest. "That's wonderful, Finn. I want to meet her."

My heart thumped hard against my ribcage. Was I really going to do this? Open up to my mom about her? "You already have, sort of. It's Adele Gagnon."

She pressed her palms to the tabletop and blinked at me, frozen in place. At a loss for how to respond to her reaction, I sat there, letting it sink in, for once forcing myself to be still.

"I'm happy for you," she said slowly. "Is this public knowledge?"

I shook my head. "Not right now, but soon. I'll bring her here and you can get to know her. She's incredible, Mom."

She patted my hand and smiled softly, but trepidation swirled in her eyes. "Then I'm thrilled for you. Do your brothers know?"

Scratching at the stubble on my cheek, I dipped my chin. "You're the only one."

She smiled and dragged her thumb and forefinger across her mouth like she was zipping her lips. "I won't tell a soul until you're ready."

"Thank you."

Wood Riddance

"Have you spoken to Cole?"

My stomach twisted at the mention of my baby brother. "No." I could have made any number of excuses as to why, but the truth was I didn't have the energy to deal with him at the moment. I didn't dislike Cole, but he and I had nothing in common. The life he lived and mine were worlds apart. He was a man-child living like a frat boy on Dad's dime while squandering all his God-given talent. I was a father and a veteran, and I was busting my ass night and day so I could start a small business.

I wished him well, I did, but that didn't mean we would ever be close.

"His career is over," my mom said, her shoulders slumping. "I offered him a room here while he gets back on his feet."

"Mom! Why?"

She pressed her lips together and narrowed her eyes at me. "He might not be my blood, but I love him like he is. And right now, he's struggling."

"He'll be fine, Mom." I waved her off. Cole had no one to blame but himself.

"Finn Hebert, I raised you better. We open our hearts and our homes to those in need. The poor boy hasn't had an easy life."

I resisted the urge to roll my eyes. It would offend my mom, and that was the last thing I wanted to do. As a kid, it had been easy to blame Cole for breaking up our family, but my mother never let us. She worked hard to cultivate relationships between all of us. Cole had hardly had a tough life. He was a spoiled brat who my dad doted on. He'd never wanted for anything material.

Yes, his mom was awful. Hence the reason he spent a lot of time at my mother's house when he was a kid. Tammi had been my dad's secretary and hadn't been interested in raising a child, especially any time Cole became an inconvenience to her ideal trophy-wife life.

Where my mom packed lunches, took care of us when we were sick, and helped us with homework, Tammi ignored Cole. He had every toy, video game, and expensive piece of sports equipment, but he'd never opened a lunchbox and found a corny note from his mother or had someone to sit down and study spelling words with. In high school, when he was a standout with a shot at a college scholarship, Tammi never even bothered going to his games.

My mom did, though. She cheered him on and supported him the whole way through.

"You forget how lucky you are," she said. "And Cole needs family."

"He can have dad. Evil fucker."

"Finn! Don't you think it's time to get past all your anger at your father? You're on the precipice of an incredible fresh start. Why drag all that baggage with you?"

Trust my mom to really hit the nail on the head.

"It's easy to say that he's evil and unredeemable. But that's not the whole story, is it? Like the rest of us, he's a multifaceted, flawed human."

"You're talking like you forgive him, Mom. What he's done is unforgivable."

She sighed and pushed her hair behind her ears. "I have not forgiven his recent actions, and maybe I never will. I'll leave that up to the justice system. But what happened between us all those years ago? I've moved beyond it."

"How? He cheated on you and humiliated you and walked out on his family." My skin prickled, and anger coursed through my veins at the thought of how terribly he'd treated her. Shit. I'd started off looking for a way to work off my anxiety, but here I was adding to it. What had started as a quick, pleasant visit had very quickly gone too deep.

"I forgave him for me. Not for him. I held on to so much anger and shame for too many years. It weighed me down. Kept me from moving forward and creating the life of my dreams. Forgiveness is for you, not for the person who wronged you. You can hate what he did. You can hate the pain he caused so many people. But I promise, if you let it go and stop carrying it with you, you'll feel so much better."

"I don't know if I can do that."

"My sweet boy. Of course you can. You have such a caring, empathetic heart. You are capable of anything you set your mind to. You are such a wonderful father, and you have the deepest sense of honor. You've always been willing to make sacrifices for the things you love. First for this country, and now for Alicia and Merry."

Her words hit me hard. What if I did let it all go? The betrayal, the hurt, the embarrassment of my dad leaving us and creating a shiny new life with Tammi and Cole. The pain his judgment and cruelty and lies caused us as kids. Was it even possible to do so?

For so long, I'd been asking Adele to move beyond my dad's actions. But maybe I had to do it first.

"You deserve to be happy."

"I'm not sure I can be happy here. There's a good chance the people here will never forget what Dad did."

"They might not." She gave me a sad smile. "But you can move beyond it. Create a wild and wonderful life filled with joy and love. If you do that? I think you'll find that your father and all his bad deeds won't matter."

Feeling heavier than I had when I left for my run, I hugged

her goodbye and started home. As I jogged the long way around town, I worked through all she'd told me, trying to make sense of it and my own feelings on the matter. By the time I hoofed it up the steps to my apartment, I knew. She was right. I'd been carrying a lot of baggage around.

Now, though, I had been given a fresh start. The possibility of building my dream business was within reach, and I was already headed toward creating a family with the love of my life.

Maybe it was time to let it all go.

Chapter 39
Adele

I was crying. In public.
A first for me. But these days, I cried all the time, so at least this was a worthy occasion.

The whole day had been so damn beautiful. I sat in the back, unsure of how to manage the emotions of this big day and wanting to hide from the scrutiny of my brothers and my mother.

They were becoming a family. Alice, Henri, Goldie, and Tucker. Two years ago, these people didn't know one another. And today? They were legally a unit, a team. Forever.

The entire family had driven to Bangor for the finalization hearing. Two years after Tucker and Goldie had been placed in Alice's care, she and Henri were now officially and irrevocably their parents. They'd become our family the instant Alice picked them up from the police station after they'd been removed from their previous foster home, but until today, there had always been some worry, some anxiety, that it wouldn't be forever.

And now it was.

Daphne Elliot

A few rows ahead of me, my mother openly sobbed as the cranky old judge rambled through the legalese. Henri, Alice, Tucker, and Goldie stood in front of the bench, dressed to the nines. Tucker looked so grown up and handsome in his blue suit. He kept fiddling with his tie, no doubt counting down the minutes until he could take it off. He had shot up overnight and was already taller than Alice.

Henri stood next to him, his arm around his shoulders, wearing a smile bigger than any I'd ever seen from my oldest brother. The closed-off, grumpy lumberjack had finally achieved the thing he'd always wanted most. A family.

Goldie's blond hair was carefully braided, and she was twisting her fingers in the hem of her puffy purple dress, looking up at Alice every minute or two for reassurance.

This dusty old courtroom, with its wood molding and rows of portraits of intimidating old men in robes, had never seen a crowd like this. My entire family, as well as Alice's sisters and parents from Massachusetts and probably half of Lovewell, were in attendance. Bernice and Louie, Becca from the salon, the Smiths from the market, most of the faculty and staff at Alice's school, and Father Renee. Everyone was here to share in this joy.

The sight of all these familiar faces made me miss Finn. I wanted him here on this big day, with his strong arm around my shoulders, holding me as I cried happy tears. The ache to have my person with me was overwhelming.

But we were all missing Dad today. Moreso than we had in quite a while. So as much as I hoped my family would eventually come to love and accept Finn, today was not the day to test them.

Mom brought a framed photo of him with her and propped it up on the seat beside her. He would have loved this whole process. He would have been the one taking endless photos, cracking jokes, and squeezing us all too tightly. He lived for these moments.

The second the judge declared them a family, the place erupted in cheers. Every person in the room was shouting and hugging and dancing. I had to wade through the crowd to get to them, and when I finally did, Henri was holding Alice while she sobbed. Goldie was spinning around in circles, and my mother was smothering Tucker with hugs.

I squeezed Henri's arm. "I'm proud of you."

He looked down at me, his cheeks tearstained. The last time I'd seen him cry was at my dad's funeral. Like me, he kept his emotions locked up tight. But he'd been evolving since he'd become a husband and father. We were all capable of growth and change.

Wrapping his arms around me, he hiccuped into my hair. "This is the best day of my life."

I patted his back and fought back my own tears. "Love you, big brother. You're the best dad ever."

"I'm only trying to live up to his standards," he said. "Dad set the bar really high."

Aw, shit. So much for keeping the tears at bay. That statement instantly brought a rush of sorrow mixed with elation crashing over me, and now I was sobbing again. Because Dad was here. His presence was so palpable that I had to fight the urge to search the room for him. Henri was right. Dad loved us with his whole heart. He had the innate ability to somehow bend the laws of space and time to make us all feel seen and supported, even while he ran a business, helped any neighbor in need, and lent his time to any cause brought to his attention.

After hundreds of photos and lots of hugs, I headed to my

car. Henri and Alice were hosting a party at their house, and the crowd was headed there.

But I needed a minute. So I sat in my car in the municipal parking lot and let the tears flow. Happy tears for the beautiful family that had been born today.

And tears for my own baby and our little family. Happiness and sadness and worry. Would my baby get this version of my family? Would they have a mother and father who were madly in love? Siblings and cousins and family dinners and summer vacations?

Or would this baby be stuck with me? Would my child be shuttled between parents who couldn't make it work because the deck was stacked against us? Would they live their life feeling like an outsider?

And then there was Finn. He was generous and thoughtful and so much more than I had ever anticipated. He continued to surprise me every day. Why couldn't I come clean and tell my family and the people of our little hometown? He deserved to be loved openly and publicly.

The memory of the joy that poured from him the moment I told him I was pregnant should have bolstered me, but instead, it only made me feel guilty. Because I wasn't sure I could give him what he wanted. He wanted everything. But I was stuck, desperate for the happily ever after that was within my grasp but unable to move toward it.

If I'd learned one thing in the difficult years since my father's death, though, it was that life was short and hard. We had to seize the good and hang on with both hands. Maybe I was stuck, but God dammit, I was determined to find a way to grab this happy ending by the balls.

Wood Riddance

The party lasted for hours and the happiness was contagious. Goldie cornered me and grilled me about my plans for career day. We still had several weeks to go, but she was not letting up. She was sure to remind me that she'd been telling the entire third grade how cool I was. I thanked her for the soul-crushing pressure, and in response, she shrugged, then scurried off in search of another piece of cake.

By the time I left Henri's house, it was past nine. Finn had texted and called a few times, but I'd typed out a quick response, telling him I was hanging out with my family. I couldn't talk to him right now. Emotions were running too high. Today had thrown me for an emotional loop that would take a bit to recover from. These pregnancy hormones were no joke. I'd gone from laughing to crying and back again in the span of minutes. My brothers were clearly freaked out by my theatrics. Parker, on the other hand, kept winking at me.

Instead of heading home, I drove straight to the shop. Once I unlocked the door, I turned on every light in the place. In the storage room, I pulled out the two massive plastic bins I'd used to store the braking mechanisms I'd recovered from each truck.

Last night, as Finn held me in bed, I'd told him about my dad's truck. How it had sat in the scrapyard for over a year before I towed it in and took it apart. After Dad died, Henri had forbidden me from working on it in some misguided attempt to protect me. But from the beginning, I had known, deep in my bones, that it wasn't an accident. The safety inspectors said driver error, but I knew better. My dad could have driven those roads blindfolded, and he could have maneuvered a loaded truck with one hand tied behind his back. Gagnon Lumber had been his life since he was a child.

Finn stroked my hair and praised me when I told him. "Of course you got the truck. That's my girl."

Once I had access to it, I spent every night going system by system, checking and inspecting every detail. When I found the slack adjuster, I knew. Of course the brakes had been tampered with. Of course it wasn't driver error.

"You are incredible," he had whispered into my hair as I fell asleep. "I'm so proud of you."

We'd come full circle. Almost. I'd started this. Now my father's killer was behind bars and an international drug trafficking operation had been shut down. Now it was time for me to end it.

Still in my dress from the ceremony, I kicked off my uncomfortable shoes and tied my hair back. I pulled together the worktables, grateful that the workspace was spotless like always. I'd left Estrella in charge so I could take the day off, and she'd crushed it. The board was already updated with tomorrow's work, and there wasn't a single tool out of place. I grabbed a couple of the industrial spotlights we used for outdoor jobs and dragged them inside.

I laid my dad's slack adjuster on one table and Henri's on the other.

Using my magnifying eyewear, I studied them over and over, examining every scratch.

Then I used my slide calipers to measure the width and depth of the scratches.

It was clear that, in both cases, a wrench had been used. I closed my eyes and visualized how one would have tampered with the equipment. When that didn't lead me to an epiphany, I grabbed a few wrenches and tried to walk through why Henri's marks were deeper on the bottom and positioned differently.

Around and around the tables I walked, studying each one

carefully and comparing them. Wrench size didn't matter. I'd already tried that test. So what was the difference here?

The direction of the striations was the most obvious variation. Could that mean...?

I picked up one of the wrenches with my left hand.

In order to loosen the slack adjuster left-handed, I'd have to hold it upside down.

Well, I'll be damned.

This would explain the depth at the bottom. If a lefty loosened it, the scratches from the wrench would look different from the ones on my dad's slack adjuster. And if it was held at this angle...

Shit. This was it.

I snatched my phone off the stainless-steel table and dialed Finn.

"Stretch. Come to the shop," I rushed out "The wrench. I think I figured it out." Without waiting for a response from him, I hung up and picked up the slack adjuster again.

Chapter 40
Finn

Adele was a goddamn genius. She had walked me through her theory, showing me how the scratch marks left on the automatic slack adjuster by a left-handed person would differ from those of someone who was right-handed.

My mind was blown. She was right. I didn't have to be a mechanic to recognize that. And even if I wasn't so obsessed with her, I still would have believed that no one else in the world could have caught these details like she did.

"Norman admitted to tampering with your dad's truck, right?"

"Yes. According to his arrest report, he's right-handed. Parker confirmed it."

I tapped the table beside the second slack adjuster. "And this was definitely a lefty."

She nodded. "Parker is going through the lists of employees she created right now. We may have to do some sleuthing of our own, but there's got to be at least one lefty on them."

She was still working through theories when I carried her upstairs to bed. It was past midnight, and she was exhausted.

"Sleep first. We'll deal with this in the morning."

"Gotta call Parker one more time."

I tucked her in. "No, She-Ra. You need rest."

"Can you stay?" she asked, grasping my wrist and looking up at me with wide eyes.

As if there was any place on earth I'd rather be.

"Of course. I already told you I'd stay forever."

She smiled, and this time she didn't roll her eyes. When I shucked my clothes and joined her, she immediately tucked herself into my chest. Moments later, her breathing evened out. So I closed my eyes and focused on quieting my mind. This, right here, was it. I would do whatever it took to keep this woman forever. And Merry and our baby. We'd be together. The idea of breaking the news to her family was daunting, and life might be a challenge for a bit, but it would all be worth it.

I lay awake for a long time, letting my mother's advice percolate. She was right, of course. For too long, I'd let distance and anger pull me away from Lovewell and my family. But no more. The future was bright and exciting, and I would no longer let my past tarnish it.

"Finn. Finn!" What felt like moments after I finally dozed off, I opened one eye and found Adele sitting over me, shaking my shoulders.

"Are you okay?" I asked, peering at the clock. It was four thirty.

"Yes. I'm fine. Richard."

Richard? "Huh?"

"Richard is left-handed. At least I think he is. A few weeks ago, he was lecturing me in my office. He was swinging his keys around with his left hand. I woke up to pee, and when I got back in bed, it popped into my head." She was wide awake and vibrating.

"That's a lot for four a.m. Come here." I opened my arms.

Without argument, she settled back into me.

Stroking her hair, I tucked her in close. "Please rest. We'll deal with all of this in the morning. Let's not jump to any conclusions yet."

She nodded, nuzzling up against me. "You're right. It could never be him. I'll call Parker in a couple of hours and see what she thinks."

Early the next morning, Adele and I headed into the office, hell-bent on digging up more details. Parker had given us a list of names. There were eleven people at camp the day of Henri's accident. Some were easily eliminated, either because we knew they were right-handed or because they were miles away operating a crane that day.

That allowed us to narrow down the suspect pool considerably. Thankfully, Ellen, the comptroller who had worked for Gagnon for thirty years, knew everything about everyone.

Her nephew Nate had been out there that day, but he was right-handed. Alex had been a baseball star in high school, so we were able to confirm he was also a righty after a quick google search.

Parker had raised our suspicions about Richard when we'd spoken this morning. She claimed that she'd never been able to fully eliminate him from her list.

Thankfully, he was in the office today. He had come in for a meeting with Henri to discuss the roads ahead of cutting season. Adele had joined them, hoping she'd witness him taking notes. Unfortunately, he hadn't even brought a notebook with him.

"I have one more idea," she said while we were in her office strategizing. "I'll have Ellen text me when he's leaving."

When the notification came through near the end of the day, Adele grabbed a tennis ball from He-Man's overflowing basket of toys and signaled for the dog and I to follow her. Obediently, I trailed as she headed toward the parking lot, her long legs eating up the pavement. He-Man trotted happily next to her, head up, tongue out, and eyes on the ball in her hand.

"Hey, Richard," she called.

In response, Richard spun, wearing a scowl on his face.

Without warning, she threw the yellow tennis ball at him, and on instinct, he reached up and caught it. With his left hand.

He-Man scurried to him, barking and protesting and demanding the man relinquish his ball. Richard glowered at the dog in return.

This guy was definitely not an animal lover.

"What do you want, Adele?" he asked. His tone wasn't rude, but he was clearly annoyed.

"When you pulled in this morning, I noticed that you have a headlight out." She pointed to the bright blue Tacoma he was standing next to. "If you drive into one of the bays, I'll swap it out for you really quick. Wouldn't want you to be unsafe on these country roads after dark."

He tilted his head and frowned at her, tossing the tennis ball in the air a few times, which only irritated He-Man more.

"It'll only take me ten minutes," she added, plastering on a smile.

"No need. I've got an appointment at Thompson's in a few days. I'll have them replace it when they change my oil."

Wood Riddance

She went stiff for a moment, but quickly let out a breath and affected a casual stance again. "You sure? Wouldn't want you to get a ticket between now and then. You know Chief Souza is a stickler. Let me fix it for you."

He pinned her with a sharp glare, his eyes practically murderous. Over a fucking headlight.

Dammit. This many really could be dangerous.

"No," Richard growled.

Feigning a calm I knew she didn't feel, Adele gave an exaggerated shrug. "Okay. thought I'd offer."

She turned around and snapped her fingers, and He-Man scampered to her.

"You forgot your ball," Richard grumbled.

She spun on her heel and watched as he tossed it at her. With his left arm.

Jackpot.

"Have a good night, Richard," she said sweetly before walking back toward the shop.

Chapter 41
Adele

"I need to talk to him." As the pieces clicked into place, I knew in my bones Richard had been involved. Not only because he was left-handed, either. The comment Parker had made about his fight with my dad had bothered me. It had also struck me as odd that he'd let his criminal nephew work off the books at our camp. In his position, he was expected to follow the letter of the law and set a good example for his subordinates. That was not the kind of behavior my father or Henri would have tolerated.

Henri and Paz may not have seen him for who he really was, but I did. And it was time for answers.

"No." Finn's voice was more firm than I'd ever heard it. "We're going to the police."

Oh, Finn. Sweet, naïve Finn. All tall and strong with his do-gooder military training. No amount of long hair and tattoos could hide his inherently good nature. He was a rule follower through and through. A man who respected the way things should be.

And while I loved those things about him, we were far past that stage.

"I've been to the cops," I explained. "You know what their response was? They mansplained brakes to me and questioned my conclusions."

His sharp intake of breath was reassuring. "Shit."

"Yes. So if I could just talk to Richard—"

Finn held a hand up. "Let's not jump to conclusions. Richard is left-handed, but we don't know that he's the one who tampered with the brakes. Wasn't he your dad's best friend?"

It was true. He had been Dad's best friend for years, and he'd worked for our family for even longer. Even now, he held a position of authority. Henri and Paz trusted him. "Yes. But things have been different since Dad died."

In my head, it was simple. I'd go over to his house and ask a few questions, and that would be it. Richard wasn't a murderer. He had probably gotten caught up in illegal activity. His nephew had been trafficking opioids across the border from Canada, after all. But surely once he understood the ramifications and how serious the issue was, he would have untangled himself from that web.

"I need to talk to him. To see what he knows," I reasoned.

But Finn wasn't buying it. His jaw was clenched as tight as his fists. Shit. My gentle giant was getting upset. He was protective. I couldn't deny I loved the security of being in his arms and in his heart, but I could handle this.

"No. Let's review the evidence and talk to Parker before taking any more steps. Maybe she can put us in touch with the FBI team. Surely there's something they can do."

"No way." I shouted, my anger taking over. "They won't do shit. Two years, Finn. I've been staring at those brakes for two years." I was shaking. Didn't he understand?

Wood Riddance

From across the kitchen, he assessed me. Those icy eyes said everything his words could not.

"I swear. I've got this feeling that he knows something. If I can get to him, he will crack." The urge to stomp my feet was overwhelming, but I held myself in check. My emotions were running wild and nausea was creeping up inside me again.

He crossed the kitchen and gently grasped me by the shoulders. "Adele, I need you to look at me and listen carefully." Ducking his head, he waited until I obeyed. His brow was furrowed and his expression was so earnest. "You can't do that. He could be dangerous. You cannot take those risks. You're pregnant, for God's sake. Please, please, can we sit with this information and work together to figure out the next steps?"

I scanned his handsome face. He was so worried and so scared. I'd truly never seen him like this.

And then it hit me.

This wasn't about me. It wasn't about him. It was about us. The two of us and our baby. He was right. We didn't know if Richard was dangerous. And while I was almost certain he wasn't, it didn't matter. It was not a call I got to make on my own. Finn and I were a team now.

I loved him and respected him. And I wouldn't put myself or our baby in danger.

"I'm sorry," I said, tears welling in my eyes and blurring my vision. "I'm so sorry."

Without a word, he pulled me into a hug, resting his chin on the top of my head.

"I'm so used to doing whatever I want. Believing that I know best all the time. But I haven't been fair to you."

Smoothing my hair, he held me and rocked me from side to side as I cried. Dammit. I did not deserve this incredible man. This generous, kind person had given me all the time and space and latitude I needed. And I repaid him by behaving like a brat. I had to do better.

"I want this," I said between sobs. "I want the real thing. Partnership. Love. Respect."

He pulled back and cupped my face. "I want that too. And we'll have it. But we've got to work together and listen to one another."

"You're right. And we can't hide anymore. I don't want to."

It was time. To come clean. To tell the world. How could this relationship grow and evolve if we continued to keep it secret? This baby was coming, and before long, I'd be showing. Our little family deserved to live out loud, truthfully and joyfully.

"I'm telling my family," I said. "As soon as possible."

He laughed softly and kissed my lips. "We're telling your family."

"Can we do it right now? I could call Parker. Have her help me round everybody—"

"It's dinnertime on a Tuesday." Finn chuckled. "Maybe wait a day or two?" he suggested, pulling me into his chest again.

"Okay fine. Tomorrow I'll call a family meeting. Once we break the news to them, we'll head straight to your mom's house and tell her."

"Whatever you want, She-Ra. But how about we take a moment to breathe first? Let's get some food in you."

I nodded. "I am feeling nauseous."

"Then you need a cheeseburger."

"With bacon," I added.

"Okay. I'll order takeout from the Moose. Bacon cheeseburger for my girl and my baby. Anything else?"

I shook my head. My stomach was already rumbling.

"Do you want to come with me to pick it up?"

"He-Man has been cooped up all day. I think I'll take him for a walk around the neighborhood while you go." I needed a few minutes to myself to settle anyway. All my frustration, fear, and grief were still simmering right below the surface. Fresh air would do me good. Finn didn't deserve to be the target of all my feelings, so I'd process on my own for a bit.

"Okay. Be careful," he said. He pecked my cheek, then grabbed his keys and phone.

Fall nights in Maine could be crisp, so I grabbed my sweatshirt, then I snagged He-Man's leash from its hook beside the garage door. He immediately jumped up on my legs and whined. Nightly walks had been our routine for a long time, but I'd been feeling so sick lately that I'd been neglecting my fur baby.

I picked him up and gave him some snuggles. "I love you. You'll always be my baby too."

Garnering all my fortitude, I set off into the cool night air, determined to recalibrate before Finn returned. I was already feeling better. After thirty-three years of relying on no one but myself, I had finally found my person. And yes, I had some growing to do, because I wanted to be as encouraging and supportive to my man as he was to me. And right now, that didn't seem like an impossibility at all.

Chapter 42
Finn

She was ready. *Damn.* We were ready. The future I'd envisioned was so close to becoming my reality. I needed to get through the meeting with the bank tomorrow, and then we'd tell our families.

After that, I'd spend the rest of my life working my ass off to deserve all the amazing gifts I'd been given.

For a while, I worried that I loved Adele in a way she may never reciprocate. That she might not be able to give me what I wanted. So I'd waited and hoped that someday we'd get there.

That day was here. She was choosing me. Choosing our baby. And she was ready to tell the world. This was the best feeling in the world. But the road ahead of us was still long.

I turned out of Adele's small neighborhood and onto the main road. The sun was just setting, the last bit of daylight a line on the horizon.

Mentally, I was running through my checklist for tomorrow's meeting. I was nervous as hell. I was a pilot, not a businessman, and I had no idea how to pitch an idea like this.

Thank God I'd have Owen there. If things went well, I'd be up and running before the baby arrived.

Heading out to pick up dinner also meant some time to work through my racing thoughts and will away the restlessness that had once again settled over me.

So I drove, tapping my fingers to the song on the radio and nodding my head the whole way.

The road to town was empty, except for a lone vehicle with a headlight out coming from the other direction. It was still light enough that I could tell it was blue or maybe black. As it passed me, a lump of dread formed in my gut.

My body immediately went on alert, and I scanned my surroundings for danger. This was what I felt like while flying missions. The world around me came into sharp focus. The skill had been ingrained in me for years. But why had the sensation hit now?

My instincts were telling me something wasn't right, but for the life of me, I couldn't figure out what.

I was sleep-deprived and stressed and needed to get it together. So I turned up the radio and continued toward the Moose.

It was only when I pulled into the parking lot ten minutes later that it hit me. The truck I'd passed was familiar. Was it Richard's? There were lots of blue trucks in northern Maine, but with a headlight out?

The headlight. Adele had mentioned it to Richard in the parking lot. Panic coursed through me, and the hair on my arms stood on end. Then my training kicked in. I took a few deep breaths and ran through what I knew.

Adele was home alone. The only destinations down that road were the few residential neighborhoods on the north side of town. Richard lived near Heartsborough, so it wasn't likely that he'd have reason to be there on a Tuesday night.

I picked my phone up from the center console and dialed Parker.

"Adele is alone, and I think I saw Richard's truck heading toward her house."

"Are you sure?"

"No. But I have this feeling. We were discussing him and debating about how he could be dangerous. We were hungry and irritable, so I left to get food, and I just didn't think..."

"How long ago?"

"Maybe fifteen minutes."

"Okay. Paz and I will head there now. We're twenty minutes out. Don't panic. It's probably nothing."

I put the truck in drive and peeled out of the parking lot. "I'm heading back now. I'll call her and see you there. Call the police. Call the FBI. Call everyone."

Once I was on the main road, I picked up speed, flying through town at three times the speed limit. Then I dialed Adele. She didn't pick up. So I tried again. And again. Nothing.

Every instinct in my body was screaming to get to her. I hoped I could make it in time.

Chapter 43
Adele

After a lap around the block and up the hill toward the park, both He-Man and I were feeling better. It was dark now, and Finn should be back any time. I had stupidly left my phone on the counter when I was putting He-Man's harness on. I hoped he got onion rings too.

The longer I thought about our discussion, the more I realized Finn was right. We needed to process and plan. Acting rashly wouldn't get me anywhere. I risked offending people and causing more strife if I did. So I'd put on my comfiest sweats and cuddle up with my Viking tonight and put it out of my mind. The next couple of days would be intense, but together, we could do it.

I patted my tummy and smiled. I'd felt every single minute of this pregnancy so far. And not only because of the nausea or exhaustion. It had changed me. The book I was reading explained how the baby's cells were already circulating in my bloodstream, and I swore I could feel it.

My world had shifted. My identity was shifting too. And although my list of worries was a mile long, I was calmer, more centered than I had been in years. I was a mom now. I could do anything.

Punching the code into the keypad outside the garage door, I stepped back and waited for the overhead door to open. As I approached the door to the kitchen, a vehicle pulled up in front of the house. Yes. Hopefully it was Finn with my cheeseburger.

Grinning and relishing the lightness in my chest, I spun, ready to call out. The truck parked on the street in front of my house wasn't Finn's, though. This one was blue, and it had only one working headlight.

The door opened, and the dome light illuminated the cab. Then Richard stepped out.

I froze as he sauntered toward me. "Richard, hey. What are you doing here?"

He remained quiet as he stepped into the garage. "Shut the door," he finally said, his tone far more firm than I'd ever heard.

"Not going to do that," I said. "Why are you here?"

He moved closer. His eyes were hard and his shoulders were tense. "We have a lot to talk about. I know what you're doing. Old files, talking to Ellen, looking at those brakes the other night."

My stomach dropped. "What I do in my shop is none of your business. Please leave."

He reached behind him and produced a handgun from where it was tucked in the waistband of his jeans. Pointing it at me, he growled. "Shut the door."

I hit the button on the wall next to me, and the door shut slowly behind him. It was dark, but my neighbors, especially Mrs. Dupont were nosy. Hopefully they'd see the strange car and call the cops.

With the gun still pointed at me, he stalked closer.

I held on to the wall for support. This was not happening.

"What are you doing? Why are you pointing a gun at me? We work together. You're my dad's best friend."

"Was. For a long time. But we hadn't been friends for years before he died, sweetheart."

Nausea roiled in my stomach so much more violently than it had over the last several days. What was he talking about?

"Your dad was a goody two-shoes who caused a lot of problems for a lot of powerful people. And when given the chance to actually make money, he refused. Righteous bastard. Not all of us are content to labor every fucking day until we die."

He had lowered the gun to his side as he spoke, thank God, so I remained silent, letting him continue his story. Shit, Finn was going to be so mad. After our whole heart-to-heart, where I promised not to confront Richard, that asshole showed up at my damn house. Jesus, what was the point of emotional growth if a psycho with a gun was going to show up anyway?

With my heart in my throat, I willed myself to remain calm and nodded. "I get it. What happened?"

"I didn't want him to die. I'd loved him like a brother for decades. But it wasn't personal." He shrugged. "It was business. Management felt it was necessary."

"*You* killed my father?"

He shook his head and huffed. "God, no. My idiot nephew did. And Hebert. That guy's the worst. Proud and greedy is a great combination. Makes for very useful idiots." He shrugged.

What struck me most was how relaxed he was. Most people would be amped up. They'd be nervous and prone to making mistakes in a tense situation like this. But he stood before me like holding his best friend's daughter at gunpoint wasn't out of the ordinary for him.

"I was supposed to be named CEO after he passed. We'd talked about it years ago. The plan in case something happened to him. You kids would still retain some rights, but I'd run the show. And unlike your dad, I would be open to more lucrative..." He paused and scratched at his cheek. "Partnerships."

"Drugs," I spat. "You're talking about drugs. I thought you were better than that, Richard."

He shook his head and laughed. "Oh, sweetheart, how little you know about life. We have to play the hands we're dealt. There's no money left in fucking trees. Too many regulations in the states. Cheap lumber from China has ruined the industry. The most valuable assets we have are the roads. Private roads that go straight to Canada."

As he talked, his voice got louder and he spoke more quickly. He waved his right arm around to emphasize his points while he held the gun steady in his left hand. I inched along the wall toward my workbench.

He-Man had picked up on the tension, and he'd gone into guardian mode. He barked and growled, lunging on his leash.

"So that's why you tried to kill Henri?" I asked.

He shrugged. "One of the reasons. I hadn't counted on him thinking quickly enough to jump out like that, let alone surviving the injuries. And unlike with your father, it was personal. That prick sidelined me when he took over as CEO."

I scoffed. "He trusted you and promoted you. How could you do this? You were a member of our family. Paz's godfather, best man at my parents wedding. Why?"

"He was getting close to learning the truth. Then Remy had to marry that meddling little bitch. Once she started sticking her nose where it doesn't belong, we had to change our plans. Making sure Hebert took the fall was easy, but you nosy Gagnons destroyed a decade of work and planning."

"I have no idea what you're talking about. I'm doing my job, living my life."

"God, you've always been such a mouthy bitch. I know exactly what you've been doing. I have access to the security cameras at the shop. Have to admit you're smart, but I figured you'd drop it after a while. Should have known you'd rather get yourself killed than let it go."

"Put the gun down," I pleaded, willing my heart not to beat right out of my chest. "We can talk about this. I have neighbors. You can't shoot me."

"Sure I can. I've got powerful allies. Including some in law enforcement. Management will protect me. And honestly, I'm tired. Shooting you is the easiest option. Sometimes it's best to keep things simple."

His mouth kicked up in a nasty grin, and he raised his gun. As I stared down the barrel, the world fell away. I became singularly focused. There was no way I was getting shot. *Protect my baby* played on a loop in my head. Slowly, subtly, I reached behind me and snagged a wrench off the wall. Then, without a second of hesitation, I threw it as hard as I could and dropped to the floor.

The axe-throwing I'd done for years came in handy at that moment. The wrench hit him in the shoulder, and the gun went off, piercing the air. The sound sent a violent tremor through my body, but the shot was wild. He-Man darted forward, yanking his leash from my hand, and ran toward Richard, teeth bared.

With my head tucked to my chin, I crawled toward the kitchen door. If I could just get inside...

Behind me, He-Man was barking more viciously than I knew he was capable of, and Richard was swearing.

I risked a peek and caught sight of my heroic pup biting at my attacker's ankles. Richard was still cursing and shaking his leg, trying to dislodge He-Man.

Daphne Elliot

My legs were shaking so badly I could barely move, but I channeled all my fortitude and pulled myself up. Luckily, my fall had knocked several things off the workbench, so I gathered them to use them as weapons. I was not going down without a fight.

Richard stomped forward, but He-Man persisted.

"Fucking dog," he said, raising the gun again.

In the next second, a deafening crash—more of a crunch, really—echoed around us, and Richard's eyes went wide. The garage door buckled, and debris scattered. I covered my head and ducked as wood and plastic rained down around me.

Where the mangled steel stood was a truck. Finn's truck. He had driven right through the door. Richard was on the ground in front of his grill. And so was the gun.

Finn hopped out of the truck and launched himself at Richard.

Richard lunged for the gun before Finn could tackle him. My heart stopped for an instant, and then I let out a scream of warning. But before he could get it, He-Man was on him again. This time, he sank his teeth into Richard's hand.

Overtaken with the urge to protect not only my baby, but the man I loved, I ran toward them, ready to pummel him.

"Adele, get back," Finn yelled, straddling Richard and grasping him by the front of his shirt.

Ignoring him, I stayed on course and snatched the gun off the cement floor.

Richard was fighting back, but he was no match for my man, who had pinned him to the ground and unleashed on him. Finn landed one punch after another to the asshole's face.

With the gun in one hand, I hovered nearby, my entire body shaking.

Over the ringing in my ears and the pounding of my heart, I

could just make out the sound of voices outside the mess that had once been my garage door.

"You motherfucker," Parker yelled, running toward the garage.

Paz's Beemer was parked haphazardly in the street.

My best friend was wearing pajama pants and a Taylor Swift T-shirt. The getup was in total juxtaposition to the gear she was equipped with. In one hand, she held a handgun, and in the other was a pair of handcuffs.

"Jesus, Finn. The guy will have no face left," she said. "I brought cuffs."

At her insistence, Finn rolled Richard over, then Parker knelt on his back.

"You're not a cop," he spat. His cheek was pressed to the ground, and his nose and hand were bleeding.

"It's still fun to cuff you, asshole. I knew it," she growled. "I knew it."

Paz hopped over the debris scattered around Finn's truck, surveying the scene. I was sobbing and holding a gun, Richard was bleeding and in handcuffs, Parker was gloating, and Finn's truck had driven through my garage door.

"Why am I the only one who has no idea what is going on?"

Parker looked up at him. "Oh, sweetie. I'll explain later. Go to the street and direct the cops, please. They're on their way."

"I told you not to jump out of a moving car, Parker." My brother shot her his signature glower. "You can't do that shit now that you're pregnant." He kicked a large chunk of steel out of his way and picked up He-Man, who was wagging his tail at him, happy as could be now that our aggressor had been detained.

"Stop being so bossy. I was trying to save your sister's life," she snapped. "Though it looks like Finn gets credit for that. Well done."

Without a word, Finn got up off the floor, stalked over to me, and took the gun out of my hand. He took the magazine out and emptied the chamber, then he set the weapon on the workbench next to me.

With tears in his eyes, he grabbed my face and kissed me hard. It was hungry and messy and exhilarating.

Then he dropped to his knees, pressed his head to my stomach and hugged me while I continued to cry.

"Anyone want to fill me in on what's going on?" Paz asked, though the words were more of a demand.

But his rant was interrupted by sirens. *Finally.*

Chapter 44
Finn

"Can you all stop shouting now?" I gritted out. "We're exhausted."

We were surrounded by a sea of shocked faces.

After the police had taken Richard away and interviewed Adele and Parker and me, her family descended on the house. It was after ten, but the whole gang was here, shouting and asking questions. He-Man had already escaped. He was hiding under the bed, and at the moment, I wished I could join him.

Adele, always happy to take charge, whistled loudly, and hollered, "Shut up or I'm kicking you out of my house."

The room instantly fell into silence.

"Sit down," she said to Henri and Paz.

They were standing on either side of her with their arms crossed like sentries. Loraine was hovering and fussing.

"You too, Mom."

"Seriously," Parker said, pushing Paz into a floral-patterned armchair. She dropped into his lap, using her body to confine him.

"Can someone please explain what the hell happened

tonight?" Henri asked. "All I know is that Richard tried to kill my sister and Finn drove through the garage."

"Finn saved my life," Adele clarified.

"But why was he even here?" Remy shouted. He was sitting on the edge of a couch cushion, crushing a pillow between his hands. "What's going on?"

Adele let out a huge sigh and regarded me for a long moment. In response, I reached out and took her hand, giving her a reassuring smile.

"Finn and I are together," Adele said, lifting her chin and pulling her shoulders back. "We're in love, and we're not interested in your opinions on the matter."

"What the hell is going on here?"

"Adele, are you serious?"

"*Him?*"

"*My sister?*"

"Stop!" Adele shouted. "I'm not in the mood to tolerate toxic masculine aggression right now. I make my own choices. I live my life. And I sure as shit don't meddle in your love lives." She was standing tall, despite the toll this day had taken.

Sliding in behind her, I looped my arms around her middle, wishing I could make this easier on her. Wishing her family didn't hate me.

Her brothers had gotten more subdued, but there was still quite a bit of grumbling going on around us.

"And," she added, "I'm pregnant."

The house fell into utter silence then. Paz's eyes were blazing, and he was practically baring his teeth. Remy looked like he was half a second from hopping up and bolting. Henri wore a disappointed frown. None of their reactions were anything close to the kind my girl deserved in a monumental moment like this.

"A baby!" Loraine cried. She hopped up from where she'd finally perched on one of the couches and threw her arms around us both. Okay, it looked like maybe Mama Gagnon was a fan now. She grabbed my face and kissed my cheek. "This is the *best* news," she gushed. *"Two* grand babies."

She pulled both of us in for another hug, instantly making me feel a tiny bit welcome. She smelled like vanilla and had big mom energy. Yeah, she and my mother would be instant friends.

Adele pulled back and swiped her fingers under her eyes. "Thanks, Mom."

Parker, who had blood smeared on her T-shirt, probably from Richard, joined in on the hug, not the least bit bothered by the state of her clothing. In fact, she wore a giant smile, as if she were pleased at how everything had gone down. Once a cop, always a cop, I guessed.

And then I was faced with the firing squad of her three brothers.

Squaring my shoulders, I looked at Henri, then Paz, then Remy, refusing to cow to them. "If you guys wanna punch me, go for it. I'll give you each one free shot."

Paz grumbled, and Parker elbowed him hard.

"But I will not allow you to put your anger and aggression on Adele or our child," I said. "Your sister has been through enough. She's been working nonstop to keep you all safe. So instead of criticizing and questioning her choices, how about you thank her and move on with your damn lives?"

Henri took a step forward. "When did this start?"

"How did this start?" Paz added.

"None of your business," Adele snapped. "Is it any wonder I keep secrets? Look at how you Neanderthals react. I was held at gunpoint by the man who tried to murder Henri, yet you're all hung up on the fact that I got knocked up by a Hebert."

Loraine put her arm around Adele. "She's right. Shame on you all."

Remy at least had the good sense to hang his head. Henri and Paz looked angry.

"I'm sorry," Remy said, looking at me head-on. "Finn saved Hazel and me last year," he reminded his family, looking from one brother to the other. "He's a good man." He stood and extended his hand.

I took it.

"Thank you for everything you've done," he murmured. "Welcome to the family. My sister's a handful, but it seems like you're up for the challenge."

Hazel hopped up too, shooting him an annoyed look. Then she pushed herself up on her tiptoes to give me a hug. She moved on to Adele next. "I'm thrilled for you," she said, pushing her glasses up. "You are going to be such a great mom."

Tears welled in Adele's eyes again. Without a word, she nodded her thanks.

Henri, looking a little contrite, opened his arms and pulled me in. "Thank you for saving my sister. And my brother. Damn." He shook his head. "I appreciate all you've done for our family. I need a minute to get used to this, but that's on me. My wife will probably be here tomorrow with food and presents for the baby. Prepare yourselves."

Beside me, Adele gave up wiping away her tears.

Henri stepped close and wrapped his arms around her. "I love you, sis. And if you're happy, then we're all thrilled. You've been through a lot. We'll get out of here and let you rest."

He nodded toward the door, and Hazel and Remy murmured their goodbyes and filed out.

"Mom, I'll drive you home."

"We'll celebrate on Sunday," Loraine said, patting my cheek. "Please bring your daughter too. She's family now. Get my number from Adele so you can text me a list of her favorite foods. I'll get extra ice cream."

Henri offered her his arm and escorted her to the door. And then there was Paz.

"You knew about this," he said to Parker.

Looking not the least bit sheepish, she shrugged. "They needed help tracking down the person who tampered with Henri's brakes."

"Parker," he fumed. "We talked about this. You cannot put yourself in danger. You're pregnant."

"There was no danger. Adele and Finn did the work. I only got to slap the cuffs on. Stop overreacting."

"Overreacting? Tonight, my sister was shot at and my pregnant girlfriend jumped out of a moving car. Pretty sure I have every right to be furious."

She held up a hand. "You were rolling to a stop. Let's not exaggerate."

"After you *jumped out of a moving car*, you all but tackled a bleeding criminal."

She patted his cheek. "I love you too. Now go apologize to your sister and her baby daddy for acting like an asshole."

He leaned over and kissed her, then he stood.

"I owe you both an apology," he said. "I'm working on managing my anxiety, but sometimes I shut down. I'm truly happy for you both." He held out a hand, and when I shook it, he squeezed it and frowned at me. "Promise me you'll take care of her?"

I pulled Adele close and kissed the top of her head. "It would be my honor."

"I am perfectly capable of taking care of myself!" Adele protested.

Parker chuckled. "Sweetie, let them have their stoic man moment." With that piece of advice, she grabbed Paz's arm. "We'll see ourselves out. You two look beat."

As soon as the door closed, He-Man ran downstairs, and Adele scooped him up.

"You were so brave today, buddy. We're so proud of you."

Feeling brave, I scratched the mutt's ear. "You did good. But," I said, steering Adele by the shoulders toward the stairs, "it's been a long day. My future wife needs rest."

With a huff, she whipped around and shot me a glare. "We're not engaged."

"Yet," I said, gently smacking her ass. "We're not engaged yet."

Epilogue
3 weeks later

Adele

"Are you ready to see your baby?" the ultrasound tech asked. She was a middle-aged woman with a no-nonsense ponytail and funky glasses who had carefully and patiently answered every one of my questions. I already trusted her.

And I was more than ready. We'd been here for over an hour already. Every appointment thus far had dragged on. If they were going to continue on this way through my entire pregnancy, then we were going to have a problem. Urine sample, blood draws, exams, talking and talking and talking. Couldn't we just skip to the good part?

"Finally," Merry squealed. She had insisted on skipping school today to accompany us to meet her new sibling. She'd been a trooper, reading a graphic novel while we did all the boring stuff.

My heart was in my throat as the tech squirted the goo onto my skin. We had been waiting for what felt like forever to see this baby. The early days of the pregnancy had been challenging, to say the least. The surprise of it in the first place, then the morning sickness and, of course, the stress of almost being killed. But we had made it to the second trimester. In this moment, I felt completely present. It was time.

"Okay, we're going to take some measurements, check growth, and get you an updated due date. Sound good?" she asked, moving the wand around my belly.

I squeezed Finn's hand and peeked up at him. He was leaning toward the screen, one hand holding mine, his other arm wrapped around Merry's shoulders.

"Yes," he said, wearing a grin. He had literally been all smiles since the minute we pulled into the parking lot. Every day, I was amazed and impressed by how he refused to let anxiety run his life. He somehow managed to balance compartmentalizing with processing things on his own and also through talking them out. I could learn a lot from him, and I absolutely planned to.

He kept his promises and went out of his way to talk through disagreements. Best of all, he insisted on pampering me any chance he got.

"Okay. Here we are," the tech said, pulling my attention back to the screen.

There, in black and white, was our little peanut. I could see the head and the legs. "Are those tiny feet?"

"Yes," she said, clicking the mouse and dragging it across the screen to take measurements.

"See the fingers? And this flutter here? That's the heartbeat."

Wood Riddance

"Hello," I said softly, already sniffing back tears. This kid had turned me into a freaking garden hose. All I did was cry. I had gotten up to pee last night, and when I came back to bed, I found He-Man snuggling with Finn. I'd bawled so hard I woke Finn up, and he spent a good ten minutes soothing me and murmuring the sweetest words until I dozed back off. God, I was a hormonal mess.

This, though? This was on another level. I was watching our child's heart beat. Our baby. The little person growing inside my body. Above me, Finn was watching the screen intently. He, too, was losing a battle with his emotions. One single tear tracked down his cheek as he smiled at me and squeezed my hand tighter.

"We did this, She-Ra." He angled over me and kissed my forehead. "This is our baby."

Twenty minutes later, we made our way back to the parking lot with a whole strip of photos and matching goofy grins.

That was insane.

"I can't get over how adorable its little feet are," Merry said, carefully studying the photos the tech had kindly printed for us. "And the head is so giant."

Finn draped an arm over my shoulder. "Thank you," he said, pulling me close and ruffling Merry's hair. "This was the most perfect day."

"And she said the measurements are perfect," Merry continued, skipping toward the truck. "Our baby is perfect," she singsonged. "I can't wait to hold it and dress it and play with it."

"Of course it's measuring strong. This is our kid we're talking about. He or she is gonna be massive." Finn patted my belly. "This kid could set records."

"No thank you." I huffed a laugh. "I'd very much prefer to push out a normal-size baby rather than a watermelon."

He laughed as he opened the passenger door for me. "You're cute. We both know this kid will come out the size of a three-year-old."

I rolled my eyes and climbed in.

"Let's head home. I'm going to feed you, then I'll take Merry back to my place so we can pack up a few more boxes."

Finn was in the process of moving into my house, and we were already working on plans for a small addition to make more room for Merry and the baby. Life was complete chaos, but that wasn't anything new. All I could do was breathe through it and enjoy the experience of growing our family.

It had all happened so fast. A few short months ago, he'd been my sworn enemy. But I knew better now. This was destiny. Falling in love with Finn helped me work through the trauma of the loss of my dad. I'd miss him forever, especially on days like this. But he was watching over me and loving every second of my messy, beautiful life.

And I knew he'd approve of Finn. My dad had taught me never to settle. To chase my dreams and never dull my shine. And somehow, I'd found the man that challenged me, celebrated me, and made every day even better than the last.

Bonus Epilogue

Want more Finn & Adele?
SCAN HERE to read the Bonus Epilogue
Warning: it will make you laugh, cry and swoon!

Author's Note

Thank you so much for reading Wood Riddance! I am so excited to finally bring this book to you. Adele and Finn have been kicking around in my brain for almost a year, and I have been randomly writing scenes in the notes app on my phone, waiting for the right time to tell their story.

I love an angry heroine. I love a woman who owns her complicated emotions and isn't trying to please everyone all the time. And I had such a blast writing Adele. She's mad, she's frustrated, and she's not taking anyone's shit.

And I knew that she needed someone special. Not just someone to soften her, but someone who loved all the parts of her, even the sharp, pointy edges. I didn't want her to end up with some guy who loved her *despite* her Adele-ness, but someone who loved her *because* of it. And that man would need to be super secure, super confident, and super evolved.

Like a 6'6" Viking lumberjack pilot.

Finn comes from a big, messy, complex family. But he knows who he is and what he wants. And underneath the long

Author's Note

hair and tats is a man with a big squishy heart who enjoys Taylor Swift singalongs with his tween daughter.

I had so much fun watching YouTube videos about flying bush planes and learning all about how to land an aircraft in the woods. A few years ago, my husband and I took a small plane through the mountains of Northern Maine, and it was both terrifying and exhilarating. There is so much that is not accessible by road. Getting up in the air felt like visiting an entirely new place. The pilot (who was in his 80s and wore a jaunty flight suit), swooped down low over a massive lake, and we saw dozens of moose and a few bears just hanging out. It remains one of my most cherished Maine memories.

In addition to being my longest book, it also has the most autobiographical details. My husband and I bonded over a love of Theodore Roosevelt, and I did ask him to buy me a vintage Airstream instead of an engagement ring. I've also spent a lot of time in Acadia National Park and done that hike several times. One time, my husband and I even met a famous person! Give me a few glasses of wine, and I'll tell you the full story sometime.

Thank you so much for reading and loving this series. Don't worry. You will get even more Lumberjacks in 2024. We're not leaving Lovewell yet. There's still a lot of wood chopping, blueberry pies, and Clive sightings in your future.

Love you all so much!

xoxo

Daphne

Acknowledgments

Thank you for taking this trip to Lovewell with me! This book would not have been possible without the help of so many talented and dedicated people. Every book starts off feeling impossible, and I'm only able to get it over the finish line with the help of some amazing people.

This book would not exist without Erica Connors Walsh. Thank you for being my friend, my cheerleader, and the best PA ever. From cover design to finding photos and editing blurbs, you are truly in my corner every single day. We have cried and laughed and yelled together over the past two years, and I am a better person and writer because of you.

Amarilys, you are the kindest, most positive person I know. I cherish your friendship and feel so lucky to have you on my team. Thank you for believing in me.

To the incomparable Jenni Bara, you are so talented, humble, and kind. Every book I write is better because of your ideas and energy. Thank you for being a true friend and for teaching me to just roll with things.

Brittanée Nicole, you are one in a million. Thank you for finding me on Instagram two years ago and putting up with me since. You are brilliant and creative, and I love your beautiful face.

Swati M.H., you are the best thought partner and friend.

Thank you for talking me off the ledge and helping me figure my shit out on a daily basis.

To my hype team, thank you from the bottom of my heart for loving these books and this crazy world I've created. Most days, I pinch myself that I'm surrounded by such an amazing group of positive, kicks people. Special shout out to Amarilys, Jen, and Sara, who make TikTok a little less infuriating for me every day.

Beth, thank you for your thorough editing. I am amazed by your patience, professionalism, and kindness. You've worked through this series with me, tolerating my late add ons and last-minute changes. Your careful work has helped bring these characters to life, and I am truly in your debt.

Jeanne, thank you for the gorgeous photos. Taking photos of shirtless men is a hard job, and I'm grateful you do it.

Ryan and Anna, thank you for the amazing cover photo. You are beautiful people, inside and out. I can feel your love for one another through the camera lens, and I am honored to have you on the cover of my book.

Thank you to my mother, who always pushed me to do my best and believed in me even when I did not. I am the kind of person who decides to write books in my nonexistent free time because of you.

To Claire, my IRL friend and confidant. Your love and support mean so much to me. A greater power brought us together, and I am thankful every day for your humor, wit, and heart.

Thank you to my family for being hilarious and loving and silly. To my children, G & T, you push me and challenge me and surprise me every day. Thank you for never going easy on me.

And finally, thank you to my patient and devastatingly handsome husband. Thank you for the Lumbersnack inspiration and endless support. You are my original Alpha Roll.

Also by Daphne Elliot

LOVEWELL

The Lovewell Lumberjacks Series

Wood You Be Mine?

Wood You Marry Me?

Wood You Rather

Wood Riddance

HAVENPORT

The Quinn Brothers Series

Trusting You

Finding You

Keeping You

The Rossi Family Series

Resisting You

Holding You

Embracing You

Novellas

Rediscovering Us

Dad Bod Bartender

A Touch of Wrath

About the Author

In High School, Daphne Elliot was voted "most likely to become a romance novelist." After spending the last decade as a corporate lawyer, she has finally embraced her destiny. Her steamy novels are filled with flirty banter, sexy hijinks, and lots and lots of heart.

Daphne is a coffee-drinking, hot-sauce loving introvert who spends her free time gardening and practicing yoga. She lives in Massachusetts with her husband, two kids, two dogs, and twelve backyard chickens.

Where to find Daphne:

daphneelliot.com
daphneelliotauthor@gmail.com

Stay in touch with Daphne:
Subscribe to Daphne's Newsletter
Join Daphne's Reader Group
Follow Daphne on TikTok
Like Daphne on Facebook
Follow Daphne on Instagram
Hang with Daphne on GoodReads
Follow Daphne on Amazon

Made in the USA
Middletown, DE
12 November 2023

42322012R00245